My aunt was at the stove, cleaning up. Caroline was already in bed. There were two men, with stockings pulled over their heads, both carrying guns. I felt sick inside.

One of the men said harshly, "What did you do with that nugget, boy?"

I gulped, "I left it in the pie shack."

"It ain't there."

My throat felt as though someone had hold of it with powerful fingers.

"There's ways to make you talk." The voice was dangerous. "So don't be too smart." He glanced around and saw Caroline staring at him from her bunk, and started toward her. My aunt ran forward, swinging a skillet. He gave her a slap that knocked her over one of the chairs. I jumped up, but the other man caught my shoulder and pushed me down.

The first man pulled Caroline from the bunk. "Don't make me hurt the little girl."

"Let her alone!" I yelled. I started for the door. "I'll show you where it is."

His partner laughed, but the sound was chilling. He turned to my aunt, still on the floor. "Lady, if you ever want to see this boy alive again you'll stay right here, and you won't talk to anyone. Understand? Anyone!"

GOLD IN CALIFORNIA
Todhunter Ballard

CHARTER BOOKS, NEW YORK

For A, B, and C Meyer
Whose interest, help and
understanding made this
book possible and a
pleasure to write

GOLD IN CALIFORNIA

A Charter Book/published by arrangement with
Doubleday & Co., Inc.

PRINTING HISTORY
Doubleday edition published 1965
Previously published by Ace Books
Charter edition / July 1986

ISBN: 0-441-29744-7

Charter Books are published by The Berkley Publishing Group,
200 Madison Avenue, New York, New York 10016.
PRINTED IN THE UNITED STATES OF AMERICA

CHAPTER ONE

IN AFTER YEARS my Aunt Emeline maintained a strong view that my uncle had been more a prospector than he had a newspaperman. Looking back I am forced to agree with her. This is the reason I saw as much of the mother lode country as I did.

No matter how well his paper was doing he never hesitated to pick up his press, his fonts of type, and move on to the new diggings when a fresh strike was reported.

Yet he never considered himself to be a miner. He saw his role as chronicler of other men's efforts and adventures, the true reporter recording events as they happened in an objective and unemotional manner.

From almost my first memory he drummed into me thoroughly that any newspaper's function was to present both sides of each and every story and let the readers form their own opinions. This, of course, is the basic tenet of journalism. Unfortunately, newspapers too are subject to human frailities. Reporters and printers hold their own convictions, their own viewpoints, and draw their own conclusions.

I was a printer's devil before I went to school, and the print shop on South Main in Wilmington, Ohio was far nearer my home than was the big three-story yellow brick house which my uncle had built on an acre of ground where Main Ys into Rombach Avenue.

5

In 1848 Wilmington was a town of nearly three thousand inhabitants, the seat of a county already waxing prosperous on the production of corn and hogs.

It had been settled in the early 1800s by emigrants who came over the wilderness road with Daniel Boone on his second westward migration. These settlers, mostly of English or Scotch-Irish stock, had left Virginia and the Carolinas after the Revolution, pausing in Tennessee and Kentucky, then gradually working their way north until they crossed the river.

It had not been easy, clearing the rich bottom lands of forest and swamp, building their cabins and driving out the Indians. Only people of independent mind, of firm character and dedicated conviction would have accomplished it.

In crossing the mountains they had put behind them those lingering ties which bound the coastal states to European thinking and values. The new heartland established a culture and a political climate uniquely American and intended to be permanent, both personally and geographically.

I was not aware of this heritage at ten. To me there was very little real outside the confines of the dusty streets which were the fabric of the town. The world I heard of in school might be there, but it had no part in my life.

I knew that my Uncle Ben went to Cincinnati twice a year. I knew that Columbus was the capital of the state and I knew that other cities existed, for we got exchanges and correspondence from them at the *Clarion*. But my own traveling had been limited to one trip to Washington Courthouse, twenty-two miles away, and it had taken us the better part of the day to make the journey even in the new carriage.

The occasion was my Uncle Herbert's funeral. I had never really known Herbert nor his six noisy and obstreperous children. It was a hot and depressing experience, my first funeral, and I have never forgotten it.

I had been less than a year old when my own parents died of the typhoid, and my aunt and uncle had raised me. They with my cousin Caroline, who was three years younger than I and on whom I looked as a necessary nuisance, were in my mind my whole family, and though these semi-strangers in Washington Courthouse might be blood kin I had no interest in them.

I had no interest in my homeland's history, or in much of anything beyond fishing and swimming in Tod's Fork in the

6

summers, setting muskrat and skunk traps and hunting squirrels through the late fall sunshine.

My days were full and I felt no need to look farther ahead than the next morning nor farther afield than Two Mile bridge on the south and the limestone quarry a mile north on the New Vienna road until a certain Thursday after school.

I arrived at the print shop as I always did on Thursdays to help with the mailing of the paper. The fresh edition of the *Clarion* was piled on the composing stone. I came bursting into the shop, slinging my schoolbooks into the far corner, and stopped to look over the issue.

The makeup of page one caught my attention at once. Usually the front page was profitably filled with advertisements, but today they were all missing and young as I was I had the horrifying feeling that they must have been canceled and that we were in financial difficulties.

Then I saw the headline extending the full width of the sheet. There was no type in the shop big enough, and I knew that the letters were hand cut from blocks of wood.

GOLD
DISCOVERED IN CALIFORNIA
AT SUTTERS MILL

The rest of the page was devoted to a letter forwarded by our correspondent in Cincinnati, telling how a man named Marshall had picked up small lumps of gold from the sand in the bottom of a mill race which he was constructing for Captain Sutter on the banks of the American River

Old Ike Summerholdt was leaning against the press, watching me, sucking noisily on his stubby pipe. I looked around.

"Where's California?"

He made a sweeping gesture with the pipe stem toward the west wall of the shop.

"Out yonder."

"Far?"

"A good piece."

Ike was a tramp printer. He had worked all over the country and he was one of the best story tellers you could ask for. I didn't believe everything he said, but I respected him, even if my Aunt Emeline didn't. She did not hold with his drinking, for he spent both his money and his spare time in the cheap saloons in Shattagee, our shanty town, but Caroline and I loved him.

"You ever been there?"

Ike had difficulty answering that one. He seldom admitted that there was any place he had not been. It galled him to know that a spot existed on a map that he had not seen, but he shook his head. He was a blocky, middle-aged man with a bald head customarily streaked by a black smudge of ink.

"Why not? You been every place else."

That wasn't quite true, but he had fought with Jackson at the Battle of New Orleans, had been in Texas and even to Santa Fe. He thought it over for a full minute. Old Ike told stories but he always took his own time in the telling. For that matter he never did anything in a hurry.

"I don't rightly know." He said it in a mild surprise. "Maybe I'll go. Yes. I think maybe I will."

He was interrupted as Uncle Ben and Aunt Emeline bustled through the front door.

My uncle seemed quite old to me. He was nearly thirty-one, and my aunt was only three years younger.

It was my aunt who got things done. My uncle could spend hours with one foot braced up on a watering trough, discussing the slavery question and the Mexican War with any of the townsmen who had the time. Being a popular man, this was pretty frequent.

But not Aunt Emeline. I hardly remember her when she was not in motion, always flying at some chore, and pushing those around her. Her constant activity did not prevent her putting on weight and she was plumping out generously, but it was becoming and with her soft, milk-white flesh added to her considerable femininity.

"Come on, Austin," were her first words, "you haven't even got the wrappers or the glue pot out."

I was too eager with my news to obey at once. "Ike's going to California to get rich picking up gold."

"Stuff and nonsense." She put aside her shawl and bonnet and rolled her sleeves above her round forearms.

"But he is. He just said so."

She swung energetically to Ike. "What pipe dream are you putting into the boy's head now?"

Ike was on the defensive. As he had explained to me time and again, he didn't understand women. They made no living sense.

"I ain't putting nothing into his head, ma'am." He always

8

addressed my aunt respectfully, no matter what he thought of her position. "I was just saying maybe I'd mosey out and have a look-see."

She sniffed. As if she had in some hidden way won the argument she turned to the business of mailing out the paper.

I doubt that a single edition of the *Clarion* ever created as much interest as did our issue announcing the discovery of gold. There is a magic in the word. From time immemorial gold has been the widely coveted medium of exchange, and the idea that you could simply pick it up or dig it up out of the ground was as tantalizing as any dream ever indulged in by man.

Had the story lapsed with that issue the people of Wilmington and of the world might have settled back into their ordered existences, but in the middle of September the New York *Herald* gave publicity to letters from Thomas O. Larkin confirming to President Polk the finding of the metal in the new lands of California.

These letters were official and created another stir when my uncle reprinted portions of them in the *Clarion*. Then the Baltimore *Sun* and the New York *Journal of Commerce* recognized the news. The *Journal's* story caused a sensation. It read in part:

At present the people are running over the country, picking it out of the ground. Those who employ the wild Indians to hunt for them make the most. The Indians know nothing of its value and wonder what the pale faces want with it . . . They give an ounce of it for the same weight in coined silver, a thimbleful of glass beads . . .

. . . I know of ten men who worked ten days in company, employed no Indians and made fifteen hundred dollars each . . .

John Blummer strode into the office that evening, clutching his copy of the *Clarion*, with the pronouncement that he was departing that night for New York to take ship to California. He was the first to leave our part of Ohio.

Autumn chilled into winter. Snow covered the streets and the stark branches of the old maples. The seven fireplaces in the brick house fought the cold. And then in December the news was flashed that a Lieutenant Loeser had reached Washington with dispatches from Colonel Richard Mason, the acting governor, together with samples of California gold.

9

Loeser reported that there were already over four thousand men employed in the gold fields, that all other business in California had ceased as men stole away to the mines.

I could tell by Ike's face as he read that his feet were indeed itching. I was surprised that he had not taken off long before. Perhaps my uncle had something to do with his reluctance for Ike, while believing that Uncle Ben was the greatest writer alive, had a very poor opinion of Ben's ability to keep the old Washington press in operation. As he told me, he had stayed longer on this job than on any he had ever had, but the signs of bolting were beginning to build up.

"When you get to California, send me a nugget, please," I said.

He looked at me over the paper. "What brought that up?"

"Your face."

He considered me a long time. "You know, Austin, you're sharp. There ain't much you miss, I'll say that, and maybe it will get you in trouble sometime. A kid shouldn't be too all fired sharp."

As he talked a great idea flooded me.

"Take me with you."

"Take you?" He sat up straight, dropping the paper to his lap. "Now look you, youngun. That ain't no trip for a boy, no siree it ain't. It's hardly a fittin' experience for a grown man. There's wild Indians and buffalo and grizzly bears . . ."

The idea sounded better with his every word. I hid my grin.

"I'm not afraid."

"No sir, I don't reckon you are. But then, there's your aunt." He gave me a sly smile. "She'd skin me alive and lift my scalp lock if she caught me taking you to a far-off place."

I had a picture of Aunt Emeline chasing us. "She'd never catch us."

"Yes sir, she would. I got a lot of faith in that woman. There ain't nothing can stop a determined female. Not one solitary single thing."

He was wrong in that, for my Aunt Emeline certainly did not want any of us to go to California.

CHAPTER TWO

THE FIRST meeting was held in our house in January.

I don't remember who called it, and neither Caroline nor I were invited. But there was a floor register in the big upstairs sitting room, directly over the downstairs parlor, and it served us well as a listening post.

George Muller took charge. George was the type who always took charge. He ran the school board, he was superintendent of the Sunday school, and he arranged the meetings of the Lyceum. He was short and stout, crowned with a thick reddish fringe of hair around a bald spot. Since he stood directly beneath the register through which I was peering it was an almost overpowering temptation to drop one of my cherished red clay marbles at the gleaming target.

But I was far too interested in the proceedings in the room below to chance revealing my presence. Over twenty men were there: the mayor, the members of the town council, the sheriff, and my aunt's two brothers Rebel and Ephraim Ward, who owned the Central Bank.

There were no women. While the female portion of the population exercised a kind of negative control over our society they were seldom admitted openly into business discussions.

And it soon became evident that this was a business discussion, for what George Muller was suggesting was that the town form a company for the purpose of sending ten men to the glittering gold fields.

As usual he had armed himself with facts and figures, though I had no way of knowing whether or not they were in any degree accurate. But even so they impressed me. I had spent much time in the print shop listening to the wide variety of topics under discussion by my uncle and his friends, and it had stimulated a native curiosity into a burning urge to know exactly and all that was going on about me.

George Muller's face was growing redder as he talked. "There isn't any time to lose," he insisted. "Thousands of people are already on their way from the east coast. According to the New York *Herald,* itinerants are coming from South America, China, Australia, and the Philippine Islands. This is wrong. Our government should bar them. If there is gold it should be held for citizens of the United States."

He paused. There were cheers and much excited speculation. I was ready to leave at once. With Ike teetering on the verge I hoped that some of his instinct would rub off on my uncle, for in the past months I had not been able to get a glimmering of his personal reaction. I glanced toward where he was seated with Ike standing behind his chair. Both of their faces were expressionless and neither joined the conversation.

When the noise subsided somewhat George held up his hand. "I have here a copy of the Cincinnati *Atlas.*" He took a folded copy of the paper from his hip pocket, rearranged the tails of his frock coat, and read:

"A company of gold diggers has been formed in this part of the country. This gold fever is destined before twelve months have passed to relapse into a chill. Multitudes of people will be sent to the mines from Mexico and South America before our people can arrive, with the result that most of the cream of the gold will be skimmed off, while with no agriculture and exorbitant prices, numbers of these adventurers will suffer . . ."

He folded the paper and angrily returned it to the pocket. Ephraim Ward, a cautious man, nodded approval.

"That's the first sensible idea I've heard. I think it's time this country forgets about free gold and settles down to business."

"You're so wrong." George Muller's voice came up to a thunderous peak. He was in a panic of greedy frustration. "I only read that to show that we as citizens must act and act quickly, to protect the rights of the native-born Americans against this influx of foreigners. It is not only that we should by right have the gold which is found on land owned by our government, but you all remember, only a few short years ago we feared that England or France or both might seize California and block our way to the Pacific."

Murmured comments interrupted him, but George was not to be denied.

". . . So it is my suggestion that we select a committee of ten, that we pool all our resources and send them overland as soon as the weather is fit for travel. They are to be the pioneers, to find the mines, and then the rest of the company can follow at its leisure. For this reason I've asked Ike Summerholdt to come here tonight. As many of you know, Ike has made the trip to Sante Fe and therefore is familiar with travel across the plains and what we will need to take. Stand up, Ike, and tell us what you think."

I didn't get to hear what Ike thought that night for a board creaked behind me and I turned. Aunt Emeline was standing in the doorway of the room, a lighted lamp in her hand. She wore a long striped flannel nightgown and her hair was covered by a ruffled nightcap. I knew that she was angry, the rigid way she stood, and bounced to my feet.

"Austin, go to bed."

I hurried past her and scurried into my room. Behind me I heard her scolding Caroline and heard my cousin start to cry. I burrowed down in the feather bed and tried to go to sleep, but all I could do was lie there and think about California.

Next morning's breakfast was a silent meal. At this season we ate at the round kitchen table since it was too difficult to heat the dining room during the extreme cold weather, and usually it was a warm and friendly time with my uncle full of bubbling spirit, commenting on the happenings of the day before. But this morning he hardly lifted his eyes from his plate of sausages and eggs when I came into the room.

I sat down silently, pouring the thick sweet cream over my bowl of smoking oatmeal, and was half through with it by the time my uncle finished and thrust back his chair. I was still engrossed with the gold mines or I would not have spoken.

"Is George Muller going to California?"

My uncle's head came up then but he still did not speak. It was my Aunt Emeline who answered from her place beside the black wood stove.

"Of course not . . . a married man with three children . . ."

"But he said last night . . ." I got that far before I realized my mistake. It was very unwise to remind my aunt that I had been listening at the register.

She came away from the stove and stood at the table over me, bringing the rich odors of baking bread and frying meat with her as a soft, hot cloud. But there was a sting to her voice.

13

"Austin Garner, if I ever again catch you eavesdropping I'll take the buggy whip to you."

"But I wanted to know . . . I didn't mean . . ."

"You know better. You're more than old enough to know the difference between right and wrong."

"Let the boy alone."

It startled me as much as it did my aunt. I had very seldom heard my uncle use that tone to anyone, least of all to her. If they quarreled between themselves it was never in public. Caroline sat across the table from me, looking like a doll with her chubby face and dark hair. Her snapping black eyes grew blacker as they rounded in her amazement.

"Ben"—it was my aunt—"don't you dare speak to me in that . . ."

"Leave the room, both you kids."

There was no denying the order. Ben Garner was a man slow to anger, but once his dander was roused he was not one to brook argument.

Caroline and I slid to our feet and made for the dining room door. As it closed behind us we heard their angry voices but could not distinguish the words, for even under stress my aunt and uncle held themselves in tight control.

Caroline, usually as independent as a full-grown cat, caught the edge of my jacket and hung on as if afraid that I would run away and leave her to face the crisis alone.

"You suppose he'll hit her?"

I said no, although I wasn't too sure myself, for I had seen the way his eyes changed. "Grownups don't hit women."

"You're silly," said Caroline. "Joe Stoop's a grownup."

The Stoops lived down below Main on the edge of Shattagee, in an unpainted board-and-batten shack. Mountain trash, they had drifted up from the hills which flanked the river in Brown County. There were seven children, most of them younger than Caroline. I wasn't supposed to play with them, but Sandy, the oldest, sat behind me in school.

I guess I hated her as nearly as I hated any kid. She was a couple of years older than I and she was in my class. Not that she wasn't smart, but I don't think she'd ever been inside of a schoolhouse until they came to Wilmington. She was always pestering me, pulling my hair, stealing my books, putting tacks on my seat, or grabbing part of my lunch. It had gotten so I didn't want to go out into the play yard at recess, and the other boys kidded me about her.

Joe did odd jobs around town. He had two spavined

horses and a broken-down wagon that he used to haul rubbish.

Caroline went on with her woman's logic. "Joe hits Myrtle every Saturday night. That's what they say."

"He gets drunk." There were few secrets in our small town. "But they're trash. Uncle Ben's not like that."

"Course not." Caroline was impatient. "But Joe's a grown-up and he hits Myrtle . . ." Then having made her point she ran upstairs to get her schoolbooks.

I got my stocking cap from the newel post and ducked out into the cold. I stopped in front of the Muller house as Dave and Tommy came out. They were twins, about two years older than I but small for their age.

I waited for them at the foot of their brick walk. It slanted down to street level at a shallow angle and was covered with a thin film of smooth ice. They slid down to join me and I said,

"Your paw's going to California."

"Maybe." Tommy was laconic. He was a quiet kid, never saying much, never enthusiastic. "Maw don't want him to go."

"But he's going." I felt a vague disappointment. To know someone who was really going . . . Old Ike said he was going of course, but he had not yet made a move.

"Sure," said Dave, "and I'm going with him. Question is, the best way to go."

I said, "How many ways are there?"

"Eight," he said promptly. "Pa's got a history of Oregon and California by a guy named Hastings. Here." He laid down his armload of books and undid the strap and found the right volume, putting it into my hands. "You can read it before recess."

I opened the book. It had been published in Cincinnati a few weeks before.

"Your pa know you've got it?"

"No, but he won't have time to look at it before tonight. I'll have it back by then."

I tucked it under my own strap and we went on to school. The snow was banked against one wall of the two-room building, but inside the stove in the corner gave out a shimmering heat.

During the study hour while the first four grades had the teacher's attention I opened the Hastings book under cover of my geography, and read about the eight possible routes

15

listed. Six of them crossed the plains and the mountains beyond, using various mountain passes. The seventh went by way of New Orleans, Vera Cruz, the city of Mexico, and Mazatlán.

The last route was by sea around Cape Horn.

A shadow fell over my desk and I looked up to find Miles Fendler, the teacher, standing at my elbow.

He was a slight man in his early twenties, his pale face intent and solemn behind steel-rimmed spectacles. He reminded me of an owl because his nearsighted eyes seemed too big for the rest of him.

I tried to hide the volume but he was too quick for me. His thin hand snaked out and pulled it from my grasp. There were some forty kids watching, for Fendler taught all eight lower grades. The upstairs room was occupied by the high school.

"What are you reading, Austin?"

"Geography."

He glanced down at the book he held, seeing its title.

"Hmmm."

He was new that year, and he was a foreigner, having come from somewhere in New York state. His ways were strange to us and none of us liked him very well.

"There is some truth in what you say. Do you know how far it is to California?"

I didn't. I looked around. Everyone in the class was listening, and there were no snickers.

"Nearly three thousand miles. And we have no real knowledge that there is very much gold there."

He had said the wrong thing. Every kid in the class began to talk at once. Each of them had heard a different story about the fabulous mines. The price of gold on the world market was going down because there was so much of the stuff: the Chinese were organizing an army to invade the coast: the Russians were moving down from the north: the Mexicans were preparing to reinvade the territory.

The only way he succeeded in silencing the argument was by dismissing school.

CHAPTER THREE

UNTIL THE DISCOVERY of gold ours had been an ordered household and the town in which we lived a quiet, regulated, unhurried community. I don't recall that there had even been many political differences, since almost everyone was anti-slavery and most favored the Mexican War.

But it seemed that an unseen force erupted from the center of the earth, changing men and women overnight from their contented daily norm to a fevered restlessness.

Several of the young unmarried men took off for the East seeking ships to take them to the gold fields, but for the most part the town's imagination was caught up in George Muller's gold company.

Our shop printed up the stock certificates. I came in to find Old Ike running them off carefully from the plates he had laboriously carved. They weren't fancy, just sheets of stiff, coated paper printed with black ink. They showed a miner with a pick on his shoulder, and the fine print stated that in return for ten dollars the holder was granted a one thousandth interest in the gold discovered by the Clinton Mining Company.

The company had been organized the week before, with my uncle as president and George Muller manager. Their purpose was to raise ten thousand dollars, the sum to be used to outfit a party of ten volunteers who would be sent westward to the gold country.

These ten were to keep one half of the gold they found. The other half was to be shipped east and divided among the investors. It was also understood that any investor who chose, after the company was established, would be free to go west himself and take his place in the diggings.

To cinch his argument George Muller had built a mining machine. He had gotten the idea from his uncle who had done some mining in Georgia. It was an ingenious affair with a screen to take out the larger rocks, and a tray beneath it, mounted on leather straps, which was moved back and forth in a small tank of water by means of an eccentric and a hand crank.

He shut off the press and slowly filled his pipe.

"What do you think of them, Austin?" He indicated the pile of still damp stock certificates with a wave of the pipe stem.

"They're right pretty," I said.

"Um."

"Don't you think so? You made the plates."

"Best I could do with what I had. Still, I don't cotton much to the idea."

"What's wrong with it?"

He took time to light the pipe. "Well, several things. First off, who are the ten men they're going to send?"

I hadn't heard. After that first meeting at our house the group had gathered at George Muller's, and neither Dave nor Tommy had been able to listen in.

"Second, how they going to make certain them fellows will send back that half of the gold?"

I didn't know that either.

"Third, how they going to get there?"

I had the answer to that one. I mentioned the eight routes across the country, naming the mountain passes.

Ike grunted. "I went out to Santa Fe in thirty-one and it was a rough trip, and the men I was with knew what they was doing. There ain't no one in this town who does. And the trail north of that, the one the folks for Oregon have been using, is a lot worse from all I hear."

"Then you aren't going?"

He grunted again. "Oh, I'll probably go, when I have a mind. But then I never did have much sense nohow."

I heard my aunt saying almost the same thing that night at dinner. Relations between her and my uncle had become more strained each day as the agitation for the trek increased.

"I simply cannot understand you," she said as she placed the boiled dinner on the table. "Here you have about the best house in town. And the county newspaper. You are looked up to and respected, and why you should lend your name to anything as wild as this scheme of George Muller's is beyond me."

Uncle Ben was spreading freshly churned butter on a thick slice of new bread. He laid the knife and the bread down on the red-checked tablecloth.

"Please, let's not discuss it in front of the children."

18

"They're going to know soon enough. I was talking to Rebel and Ephraim this afternoon. They are very concerned."

My uncle said dryly, "Your brothers live in a state of constant concern. They are a little conservative, don't you think?"

"If you call showing good sound sense being conservative, they certainly are. As they point out it was rather absurd for us to take California in the first place, and perfectly idiotic to think that people will want to stay in that Godforsaken land once they have dug up all the gold."

My uncle picked up his bread slowly. He spoke mildly but I was not deceived, he always spoke mildly when he was making a telling point.

"I seem to remember that your grandfather came out to Virginia with the shirt on his back and no baggage."

Aunt Emeline flushed. "What's that to do with it?"

"And your father came over the mountains, settled first in Kentucky and then moved on up here."

"So?"

"If your grandfather had stayed in England where would you be? If your father had stuck there in Virginia where he owned not one acre of ground what would you and your brothers have now?"

"But they didn't."

"So"—Uncle Ben leaned forward—"let's not let the spirit of adventure die in two generations. There's a lot of interesting land between here and California, but before Austin dies most of it will be filled up."

"Now I know you are insane. And about this gold company: Who are the ten men you intend to send?"

"We haven't chosen them yet."

"And what makes you think that if they find any gold at all they will ship it three thousand miles back here?"

He looked up at her then and I saw a look on his face that I had never seen there before, a tight strain.

"We've taken care of that. It was decided this afternoon. George and I are going with them."

Goose pimples raised the hair on my arms, but before I could let out a whoop the sudden chill silence of the room stabbed me. Then came Aunt Emeline's long, ragged gasp.

"Ben Garner. You don't mean it."

She sat in a state of shock, unable to find the words she needed, the words which were trying to thrust out of her.

"You would go away and leave me?"

He looked at her, harried. "I am not leaving you. I'll send for you and the children as soon as we get established, as soon as I find a proper place for you to live."

She rose and left the table and the room. Later I heard her crying in the darkness of her bedroom. Caroline heard it too. Caroline came and crawled into bed with me. Her nightgown crept up to her skinny knees and her feet were like lumps of ice as she pressed them against mine.

"Austin, I'm scared."

I was scared too, but I couldn't admit it to a seven-year-old girl.

"What are you scared of, sissy?"

I knew, although I did not know the proper words at the time. She was scared for her security, of the crumbling of the family structure which had made us immune to the doubts and fears that harassed some of the kids we knew.

My uncle had gone downtown, and when he came back I heard his feet on the uncarpeted stairs. Caroline had gone to sleep in my arms. I could feel the bones of her thin body through the flannel gown. I knew that she was not supposed to be in bed with me. My aunt had not let us sleep in the same bed for the last three years, but I didn't want to make any noise.

My uncle's steps were uncertain and he bumped into the doorjamb as he turned into the main bedroom. I heard the scratch of the match and saw the quick light reflected in the hall, and heard my aunt's horrified voice.

"You've been drinking."

I couldn't make out the mumbled answer at first, then he said,

"It's enough to make a man want to drink, Emeline, when his wife sets herself against him."

"Ben."

"It's something I've got to do, Emmy." His voice broke and I knew that he was crying, and that was as great a shock to me as anything else. "You've got to understand, Emmy. I waan't meant to just sit here all my life and write how many hogs Silas Appleby raised, or how Mrs. Sommers won the prize at the church supper."

"Ben Garner."

"Please understand. I'm thirty-one, Emmy, and I've never been anywhere or seen anything."

"Let's talk about it in the morning."

"No. I've got to talk about it now."

"I've never seen you drunk before. What will I tell the ladies at the . . ."

"To hell with the temperance women."

Silence.

"I sold the paper. Sold it to Malcolm Reed."

"You didn't."

"I did. We went to Fellow's saloon and sealed the bargain. He's going to take over the first of February."

She began to cry again. I heard him trying to sooth her. Then he blew out the light and I heard him try to comfort her, but the sobs continued until I went to sleep.

In the morning Aunt Emeline was unusually silent, but by then I hardly noticed. I couldn't wait to get to school and spread the news. My uncle Ben was going to California and so was I, as soon as he found us a home there.

By the time the bell rang I had the whole place in an uproar. Dave and Tommy Muller resented the attention I was getting, claiming rightly that their father had originated the idea of sending a company of men West, but nobody really listened to them.

After school I raced to the print shop, expecting to find Old Ike as excited as I was. Instead he looked as if the press had just fallen apart.

"What's the matter with you?"

He rubbed the side of his head with an ink-stained hand, leaving black streaks across his ear.

"Your uncle shouldn't have done it."

"Say he was going to California?"

"No. Sold his paper. Some of the men who pledged money to the gold company are already backing out."

I stared at him, stunned. "But why?"

"Your aunt's brothers. They've been busying around town all day, talking to one man after another. They're calling it a golden bubble, hollering that it's going to bust."

"But what for?"

Ike looked both ways to make sure he wasn't overheard.

"Your aunt," he said, "she doesn't want your uncle to go."

"I know that, but . . ."

"So she's got her brothers doing everything they can to stop him."

"Nobody listened to them before."

"They wasn't really fighting it then, just being cautious. But they're the bankers. They got a mortgage on about half the houses in this town, and most of the businessmen owe

21

them money. And when you owe a man money you'd maybe better heed him."

This was a new idea to me, the power of money.

I said, "That's a mean trick."

"Don't you ever tell your uncle," he warned.

"Why not, if it's a mean trick?"

"You ain't old enough to understand," he said. "Women got their own method of doing things, their own way of figuring what's right and wrong. Ain't one woman in a thousand thinks her husband has got real good sense. They connive to catch a man and once they got him they ain't satisfied with the way he is. They can't leave him the way the good Lord made him, they got to plump for an alteration job."

"Is that the reason you didn't get married?"

He hesitated for a long moment. "I was married," he said. He'd never mentioned it before. I said, "What happened to her?"

"I don't rightly know."

I didn't understand. "How come?"

He scratched his nose thoughtfully as if he couldn't make up his mind if he was wise in telling me.

"She was a French gal, down in New Orleans when I was down there with Andy Jackson. I wasn't much more than a button and she wasn't as old as me. Anyhow, we up and got married and after the fighting stopped I wanted to bring her North, only she wouldn't come."

"So you came without her?"

"Well, not right away. She was as cute as a bug's ear and it was kind of fun having her around. I stayed maybe six months. Her pa was dead and she and her maw had an old house with balconies and such, right at the edge of the Quarter. They tried to dress me up and make me a gentleman, only I couldn't take it. I lit out one night and never went back."

I didn't say anything. I knew by the look on his face that he wasn't thinking of me, that he was thinking back nearly forty years.

I didn't tell my uncle what the Wards were doing, but it wasn't surprising that he found out. Very little goes on in a town the size of ours that most people don't know about shortly.

It happened three nights later. I'd been out milking the ccw and feeding old Jimmy, our carriage horse. It had been a warm day and the snow had nearly vanished. I went through the back porch and into the summer kitchen. In winter my aunt used this for a cold room, since there was no heat, and the milk crocks were lined up before the tin bathtub which we used only during the summer months.

I had begun to fill the crocks from the bucket of warm milk that steamed lightly in the chill air. I heard them come into the kitchen from the dining room. Caroline was spending the night with one of her friends and I suppose they thought I was still in the barn.

"Why did you do it to me?" It was the first thing I heard my uncle say. "How could you do such a thing behind my back?"

My aunt's tone was too low to hear but I realized that something terrible was the matter. Uncle Ben sounded like a small child, not angry but hurt, puzzled, completely unbelieving and bewildered.

"Everyone in town is laughing at me."

"Ben"—I now had no difficulty in hearing her—"you are acting like a fool."

"Sure," he said bitterly. "Your two brothers have gone from one end of the county to the other telling everyone that I am a fool. So why shouldn't I act like one? Tell me why?"

"You'll thank them and me once you've had time to think it over."

"I'm not going to have time."

"What do you mean by that?"

"I'm going to California. I said I would and I am going."

"You can't go. Why, everyone has deserted that crazy company, everyone but George Muller."

"That makes no difference. I am going." I heard him cross the kitchen and pull open the back door.

"Ben, if you leave this house . . ."

She did not say what would happen. She didn't have the chance, for he slammed the door and I heard his boots as he stamped away.

He didn't come home until late. My Aunt Emeline fed me in stony silence. I don't know whether or not she knew that I had overheard them. I ate rapidly and then ducked up the back stairs to my room. For a long time I heard her moving around in the kitchen below me, and then the house grew still.

CHAPTER FOUR

To say that Emeline Garner was a determined woman would be a timid understatement. She was the youngest of Archer Ward's three children. There were all kinds of stories about old Arch Ward. Some said he had been a saloon-keeper in Cincinnati, some that earlier he had been a black-birder in New Orleans, forced to flee the city for running slaves long after their importation had been forbidden.

Whatever the truth of the rumors, he was a character in his own right. I remember him only vaguely. He died when I was six. A banty rooster of a man, I can barely recall him driving his team of high-stepping matched horses down Main Street, returning from a visit to one of his farms.

At that period there were very few rich people in our part of the country, and the dividing line between country folk and townspeople was not sharply drawn. Most of the residents of Wilmington had either been raised upon the land or had close relatives still engaged in farming, and were so intermarried that the idea of any one family being better than another was ridiculous.

But the Wards were not native to the county. Old Arch and his wife had appeared some fifteen years before with their children and seemingly endless money. They had started the bank and bought up or foreclosed on a great deal of land, until they undoubtedly owned more farms than anyone else. And they had started the *Clarion*.

On the other hand, the Garners were farm raised and my uncle Herbert had lived his full life on the family acres just outside Washington Courthouse.

But Uncle Ben had come to town. He had been employed on the *Clarion*, had met my aunt and married her against the Wards' will. Then at old Arch's death he had bought out his brothers-in-law.

I knew, but was not acutely aware of all this until I heard the family conference which took place on Saturday afternoon two days after Uncle Ben had told my aunt that he was going to California alone.

They sat in the parlor, four thoroughly angry people, sat in the stiff red-velvet-backed chairs which had come all the way from New York City. I deliberately listened, for my curiosity could not contain any further mystery.

Rebel Ward, as eldest and therefore head of the family, had the floor. He was small, intense, and looked not unlike Arch, but where his father had always been the dandy, Rebel was as dry as alum, his nutcracker face pinched and his clothes dark and somber.

"Benjamin," he said, using the tone that Aunt Emeline sometimes employed in reproving me, "since I have known you, you have done many things the wisdom of which I have questioned. But this is the most headstrong and foolhardy idiocy you have ever attempted."

My uncle stood up slowly. He was not a large man but he seemed to tower above Rebel. "That's enough."

"Is it?" said Rebel Ward. His voice was so cold that the hairs at the back of my neck prickled. I don't know what I was afraid of, but I was suddenly terribly afraid. The man below me wasn't a man at all, he was a machine.

I knew my uncle to be warmhearted, generous, and out-giving. No one ever came to Ben Garner without receiving help. I was afraid that Rebel Ward, the icy-banker, would destroy him. I lay there on my belly in the middle of the upstairs living room, peering down at the grownups. Caroline was out somewhere playing, and I was thankful that she was not with me to hear.

Rebel's voice never changed its intonation. He continued, matter of fact as a grocer quoting the price of butter.

"First, you have been dishonest. The money you used to buy out the *Clarion* was the money my sister received from our father's estate. Yet now you feel at liberty to sell the paper without so much as consulting her."

My uncle turned to my aunt. "Is this the way you feel?"

Her eyes were on the rug at her feet and she did not lift them.

"All right," he said. "The money is in the bank. I'll leave tomorrow without it."

Rebel managed to look further annoyed. His brother Ephraim shifted his shoes and cleared his throat, but a sharp glance from Rebel silenced him.

"That isn't the whole story," Rebel said. "This is a small town, Ben, and you know what gossip is."

"I should," my uncle said, "you've started enough about me in the last few days."

Rebel lifted his eyebrows, raising himself above this charge. "You cannot simply walk away and leave my sister. There are appearances to maintain."

There was pain behind my uncle's eyes. "I am not walking away and leaving your sister. I have asked my wife to accompany me. As for appearances, Rebel, there is something more important, which you probably do not comprehend. It is necessary for every human being to find his own place in this world, to follow his own destiny if he wants to sleep well at night.

"It doesn't matter what you think of me. I know that your family has always considered itself better than its neighbors, and you've believed that Emeline married beneath her, which she probably did. I've met mighty few men good enough for her. I only wish that she could see my viewpoint."

He broke off to smile tiredly at his wife. This time she raised her head to look at him, but she did not return his smile.

Rebel snorted. "So this is your last word?"

"My last word," Uncle Ben told him. "I feel very strongly about this, Rebel. If I am not my own man I do not count for much."

"Get your things, Em. There's no sense in him." Rebel's tone hadn't altered in the least. "If you're going to leave him it's better that you do so now, so the town will realize that the move is yours."

Aunt Emeline stood up abruptly, and her voice was surprisingly strong. "But I'm not leaving him, Rebel."

"Not leaving him? He's leaving you. Do you want everyone . . ."

Rebel sighed and settled back to pursue the argument, but Uncle Ben's face was suddenly relaxed. He looked straight up, straight through the register and gave me a long wink.

I waited only until he looked away. There was a lot of noise in the room below. I could still hear them as I sneaked down the back stairs, crossed the kitchen and slipped out through the rear door.

I knew that Old Ike would be at the shop. He was cleaning up for the new owner, who was to take possession on Monday. I found him packing the type cases, for my uncle had sold neither them nor the press. These he planned to take West with him.

I burst in as if the devils were after me, stammering out my news, my words tripping over one another.

"We're going to California. We're all of us going to California."

Old Ike dropped the case he had been handling. The type scattered across the floor in a hopeless jumble. He looked down at it, shrugged, then turned reproachfully to me.

"Look what you made me do with your nonsense."

"It's not nonsense," I told him. "We're going, Aunt Emeline and Uncle Ben and me, and Caroline. Aunt Emeline just said so."

"Whoa down," Ike interrupted. "Now, just what happened?"

I repeated it, word for word as nearly as I could. Ike had gotten down on his knees and resignedly begun to gather up handfuls of type and dump it into the case. It would take days to sort it. In fact it took weeks.

"So Rebel Ward finally went too far."

"He didn't go anyplace. He's still at the house."

"People can be pushed just so far, Austin. Remember that. Then they fight back, even if they don't want to."

"What do you mean?"

He sat back on his heels to light his pipe. "I been watching the Wards ever since I come here. They're the same kind as my maw-in-law down in New Orleans. They got ideas they're some different from other folks, like their crap don't stink.

"And your aunt, she was the youngest and the only girl. Her pa babied her and bullied her, and then her brothers babied and bullied her, all trying to make her see things like they see them."

I didn't say anything.

"But she stood up to them once, to marry your uncle, and Rebel shoulda known that if the chips was down she'd stand with her husband, if for no other reason than she can't allow she made a mistake marrying him in the first place."

"Anyway," I said, "it doesn't matter. We're going to California."

"Yes," said Ike. "It does look like we are." And this was the first indication I had that he was accompanying us.

We made quite a stir leaving. It was better than the Fourth of July parade except that they didn't shoot off any cannon or blow up a keg of black powder. It was the last week in March before we pulled out, and the time until then was the most hectic I can remember.

My uncle, a meticulous man, spent the weeks making arrangements. He sold the house to Ephraim, who, when Rebel failed to dissuade their sister, turned in sheepishly to help. He got two wagons. Uncle Ben would drive one, Old Ike the other.

One wagon would carry the press, the fonts of type, stock enough to bring out the first five issues of the new paper we planned to start and whatever Aunt Emeline elected to take in the way of equipage and clothing. The other wagon would haul the supplies, and my uncle laid in two barrels of flour, one of meal, one of beans and, it seemed to me, enough ham, bacon, and hard biscuit to feed every emigrant clear to California.

On Ike's advice the wagons would be drawn by cattle. "They ain't fast," he said, "but the Indians won't steal them like they will horses, they ain't as temperamental as mules, and they chew while they're traveling."

Uncle Ben was acting younger, more like my older brother than a sober grownup, but he didn't let his eagerness hurry him into any carelessness. He did a thorough job, down to hammer and nails and leather for repairs to the wagons on the road.

Night after night Old Ike was at the house, and Aunt Emeline and I joined the planning councils around the kitchen table. Every detail, every contingency, was haggled over until I felt that I could, unaided, lead a wagon train all the way to the gold fields.

But Aunt Emeline's role was the hardest. Even though she had the generous advice of the ladies of the town, there was not among them any who personally had made such a trip. Yet out of the rumors, out of the memories of the old grandmothers who had crossed the eastern mountains in an earlier trek, and out of her own common sense a pattern began to evolve.

I was conscious of her roaming the house, stopping, thoughtfully regarding the walnut grandfather clock in the lower hall or handling the slim china candlesticks that sat on the huge cherry sideboard in the unheated dining room. She had linens and dishes which had been brought over from England by her great-grandmother, and our furniture was as fine as any in that part of Ohio.

She could take with her what one wagon would carry, after the press and type and paper were loaded.

Uncle Ben's gaiety was not reflected in my aunt. She

picked and chose, discarded, repicked, culled. And on the last day when we were doing the final loading, she was forced by lack of space to leave half of her short list for the use of her brother's wife. This galled her. She had never cared for her sister-in-law and would, I am certain, rather have thrown it into the street.

Weighing in her hands the bundle of table damasks and bed linens against the sack of seed potatoes, garden seed and grape slips, she looked at her husband. He came to her away from the wagon he was packing, and pointed to the sack.

"You got a rose or two in there?"

Her chin went up and she nodded sharply. He grinned, touching her cheek with his fingers.

"Take the sack. We'll sleep in blankets."

She offered no complaint. Once she had told Rebel that she was going she made no further obstruction, but went about her task with forthright logic. But as we pulled out for Cincinnati, heading for the riverboat that would carry us to St. Louis and then up the Missouri to Wayne City, I thought she was going to break down.

We did not get so early a start as we had planned. There were last-minute chores to do and a hundred goodbyes to say, and then we were escorted to the southwest edge of town by half the population in a holiday mood.

My uncle's first intent had been to drive overland, picking up the extension of the National Road at Richmond and following that to St. Louis. But Old Ike pointed out that at this time of the year the roads would be extremely bad, the frost was beginning to come out of the ground. If we struck a spell of warm weather we would find ourselves in axle-deep mud and our cattle would be worn out before the real part of the journey commenced.

We were drawn up in a line before the house, Ike's wagon in the lead, Uncle Ben's next and the carriage with two young horses at the rear. I sat in the carriage seat, holding the reins. I had never felt so important. I wore a pair of heavy wool britches tucked into the tops of my boots, a shirt of wool flannel, a sweater, and a leather coat that Ike had made for me.

It was a cold day, the sun yellow and distant, trying to fight its way through snow clouds. A crowd was gathered around the wagons and Aunt Emeline's relatives stood on the porch, her two brothers, their wives and children.

My aunt came through the door looking very straight, very

dignified. She had Caroline by the hand. She paused as her brothers kissed her cheeks, then turned to her sisters-in-law. Both were crying. She kissed them perfunctorily, then came slowly down the steps.

My uncle appeared behind her, carrying her hand valise. He put it into the carriage boot and helped her into the seat at my side. Between her feet he set the oak bucket containing the rhubarb root planted in its own soil and solemnly placed in her lap the stem-glass applesauce dish that had been as much a part of our table as the legs that supported it. Then he swung Caroline into the rear seat and tucked the robe around her skinny knees.

Finally he turned, raising a hand to the Wards who had followed him across the lawn, moved on to his wagon and vaulted up into place. Somehow his voice sounded a little tight.

"Let 'er go, Ike."

Ike nudged the oxen into motion.

Theirs was a slow, lumbering, rolling step which never varied except when they smelled water after a hard drive across the blistering desert. It was a pace which seemed endless, to get nowhere.

I looked at my aunt as Uncle Ben's wagon moved and I chirruped my horses out. This was the great moment. The crowd along the street set up a cheer as if we were an army marching off to battle for the republic. I had never been so excited, but one look at Aunt Emeline sobered me. She was not looking back at the house which had been her home. She was not looking forward, not looking at anything. Her plump face was washed of expression, dead. Her eyes were tightly closed and her lower lip was caught between her teeth.

For her this was no beginning of high adventure. This was the end of the world as she knew it, the end to comfort and stability and security.

Vaguely, I sensed her courage. To a man a home was a place to live, a place of retreat for rest and solitude. For a woman it was her full existence. My aunt was leaving her life, as her great-grandmother had left England, as her mother had left Virginia. She would never find another home which was much more than temporary.

30

CHAPTER FIVE

WAYNE CITY WAS a sprawl of earth-chinked log buildings half lost in the mud flats of the Missouri river bank. It was dripping under the heavy drizzle as the *Ohio Belle* nosed her blunt bow in to the shore on the raw April day and we began to debark.

The trip down the Ohio and then into the Missouri had been one long picnic to me. Cincinnati was the first city I had ever seen. I was enthralled with its steep cobbled streets sloping down to the water, its horse cars, its warehouses along the wharfs, the stock yards filled with sleek cattle from the feeding pens of the counties to the north. I had never dreamed such a metropolis existed.

It had taken us six days to drive the fifty miles to the river, stopping at night at the inns along the road. We had had the thaw predicted by Ike.

In Cincinnati we stayed at the Raymond Inn, where Caroline and I slept in trundle beds in my aunt and uncle's room, and Old Ike found lodging in the barn. My uncle tried to get him a room, but he preferred not to leave the wagons. Ike, I was to learn, had small faith in the honesty of his fellow men.

If we had thought there was gold fever in Wilmington it was nothing to what we found in Cincinnati. The word California was on every lip and the town agog with outfitting men, all headed for the new El Dorado.

Some were going downriver to New Orleans to ship out from there for Panama or around the Horn, but most were headed for the Indian frontier and the long drive across the plains.

Every boat on the vast river system had been diverted to carrying emigrants and their belongings to the western ports, and goods which usually moved regularly upon the streams were stacking up on the docks while the shipowners reaped the unexpected golden harvest.

We might have had to spend days, even weeks, waiting for transportation, but my uncle had letters from Rebel Ward

31

to the owners of the River Line, and within twenty-four hours we were aboard.

Early the third morning the hawsers were thrown off and the sidewheeler turned downstream toward Louisville, Cairo, and then up to St. Louis. The boat was jammed with gold seekers. The cattle were penned on the lower deck and the wagons ranged so closely together that there was no room to move between them.

I don't know how many people were on the *Ohio Belle*, but they overflowed the cabin space, slept on the decks and lay wrapped in their blankets on the floor of the grand salon, men and women alike. Because of my uncle's letters we were fortunate and had a cabin, but it was very tiny, one bunk in which my aunt and Caroline slept and one above it which I shared with Uncle Ben. The bunk was hard and I felt shut in, stifled, crowded against the low ceiling. Still, it was next to the last real bed I was to know for over two months.

My aunt had cautioned Caroline and me not to speak to strangers in the city, but once on the boat I felt relieved of that obstacle to acquiring knowledge. I met Edmond Jones the second morning out, when I was standing at the rail with my cousin hanging grimly to my belt watching the buildings of Louisville as we slid past.

Somebody shoved me. I turned to find two kids trying to worm their way in to the boat side. There was very little room and although they were bigger than I, I shouldered them back.

"We were here first."

"Go on, get!" One of them seized my arm and tried to pull me away.

I grabbed the rail with both hands, holding on for dear life. Caroline started to cry. Most of the people around us paid no attention, but a slight, dark-haired man reached out. He fastened his fingers neatly in the collars of my attackers and yanked.

"Go away." He said it mildly, almost as an afterthought, as if his mind was occupied somewhere else.

They twisted in his grasp. They were about thirteen, of a size, nearly as heavy as he was.

"Go to hell."

He didn't seem to move but suddenly their heads cracked together with a popping sound. The grip they had had on me relaxed and he pushed them off through the crowd without anyone around us really knowing what had happened.

32

Then he smiled at me. There was a warmth, a feeling of laughter in the smile as if we were equals and old friends enjoying a joke together.

Caroline had stopped crying out of sheer surprise. I said, "Thanks." My arm still hurt where the kid's fingers had bitten into it. He nodded, still smiling.

"I'm Edmond Jones."

"I'm Austin Garner."

"And I judge you are on your way to California to get rich?"

"That's right."

He extended a hand. It was long, tapering, a little soft, a little like a woman's.

"Then we'll probably see a lot of each other."

I took the hand. It made me feel grown up, shaking hands with Edmond Jones.

"We're from Wilmington," I told him. "Where you from?"

"Lexington."

"Kentucky?"

He bobbed his head. He wore a black hat with a soft wide brim, a black suit, the coat rather long, and the whitest, fanciest shirt I'd ever seen.

Old Ike said he looked like a riverboat gambler. I introduced them that afternoon. Ike was sitting on the seat of the carriage. It was wedged in between our two wagons and Ike refused to stir more than a few feet from his perch.

"Bunch of thieves and pickpockets," he warned me. "Never saw a ragtailed crowd like this that wasn't filled with cheats."

"Edmond's no gambler," I said. "His pa owns a big farm down by Lexington. He's got a servant with him, a black man."

"You don't say."

"And he wears a pistol and he carries a knife. I saw it."

Ike nodded slowly. "I might have known. Soft-handed gentry, that's what he is. Young sprig, probably the bad one, always in trouble, so the family ships him West to get shut of him."

"I like him. He's my friend."

It started a rivalry. Ike had always considered himself my mentor, and during the river trip I spent a lot of time listening to Edmond Jones. I never heard anyone call him Ed. He was friendly with everybody, there was nothing standoffish about him, yet there was some quality that kept men from being too familiar.

33

I saw little of Uncle Ben on the boat and less of Aunt Emeline. The strange motion distressed her and she stayed close to the cabin. Old Ike fed Caroline and me, and after the first night I slept beside him on the deck rolled in a blanket.

For the most part the weather was warm and clear, but after we left St. Louis and started up the Missouri it turned cold and raw and rainy. By the time the *Ohio Belle* pulled to the bank at Wayne City I was thoroughly glad to say goodbye to the riverboat and the smelly press of people who swarmed her decks.

It was six hours before my uncle and Ike got the wagons, the carriage, and the cattle unloaded, before we started toward the town of Independence, three miles distant, which Ike said was the official jumping-off point.

From there it was twenty-two miles to the edge of Indian Territory, but there was little in between, just empty land and the muddy, crowded roadway.

Independence itself was a pretty town set in rolling country now freshening with the coming spring. The town square held a courthouse with a fence around it and oak trees shading the grounds. The business edifices mostly faced the square. It was impossible to tell how big the town normally was, for it was swollen with people preparing to set off West. The place was crackling with business, for many of the emigrants had arrived there with insufficient supplies and equipment.

Thanks to Old Ike's experience on the Santa Fe trail and my uncle's attention to detail, we had brought with us most of what we needed. Therefore we stayed only overnight, and again Uncle Ben found us a room. It was indeed the jumping-off place, the last town, the last white-painted picket fence, the last orderliness of the eastern society.

Beyond Independence was the campground of Elm Grove, where the wagons gathered into trains before filing up the Kansas River on the long haul toward distant Fort Laramie. The way was well marked. This ground had been used for a long time now by the Santa Fe traders and those seeking the new lands of Oregon.

There was plenty of grass. The cattle were fat and fresh and stepped out as if they too were anxious to reach the nearest gold field. The road although wet in places was fairly passable and we made good time.

My aunt looked wan for a full day after we left the boat, but after the noon break out of Independence she seemed to feel better and I gave her the carriage reins. She even gave me a small smile as I jumped down to join Ike.

We moved slowly, the oxen on the long line of wagons ahead of us setting our pace, and we made our first camp that night five miles short of Elm Grove.

We were not alone. Old Ike built a cooking fire and as Aunt Emeline initiated herself into the new methods of getting our supper we men set up the camp. The cattle were unhitched and set to graze, the horses hobbled, the tent which my uncle had brought for my aunt and Caroline was erected. Already the shadows were long and it would soon be dark. In the gathering gloom I saw at least a hundred other campfires, and as I sat down on the ground to my supper of boiled ham, beans, and dried fruit with pilot bread I saw the silhouette of a big man cross toward us from the neighboring wagon.

He stood better than six feet four and in the fire glow his copper-gold whiskers were as wild as a briar patch. He wore a light vest over a heavy red shirt and although the wind had turned chill with the coming of dusk he seemed impervious to the cold. He came into our circle and doffed his broken hat and looked at each of us carefully. He was an arresting figure, his size, the lean, quick way he carried himself, the mild manner which still held no hint of subservience.

"I'm Samson Dohne," he said, his voice matching his bulk. "From Horse Cave, down Kentucky way."

My uncle introduced us and Samson shook hands solemnly all around. As his and Ike's fingers touched I could tell that they took to each other on first sight. Then Samson squatted down beside Ike and accepted the cup of coffee Aunt Emeline silently proffered.

"Heading for California or Oregon?"

Uncle Ben said California. Samson nodded his big head. His hair was a copper yellow and looked as if it had never been cut.

"Aim to get on the road early," he said. "Man back in Independence says I should be moving by the first of May."

"That's what I figure," my uncle said. "Word is there's twenty thousand people waiting at the line. Means a lot of cattle and horses and mules will be eating the grass. You with a wagon train?"

"Not yet," said Samson. "No one from my part of the country's going as I know of. Figured I'd tie up with some outfit at the Grove."

My uncle glanced at Ike for an opinion. Ike spat studiously into the fire.

"People you tie up with is some important," he said. "You're going to be with them day after day for quite a spell, and if they bother you it makes for trouble."

Samson said, "Yup."

"Maybe you'd like to string along with us?"

"Well now," said the big man, "that's a right interesting idea. Sure you wouldn't mind?"

After he had gone back to his own camp and Aunt Emeline and Caroline had retired to the tent, Uncle Ben and Ike sat talking beside the embers. I always liked to listen while they talked this way, in half sentences as if each read the other's mind.

"Good man," said Ike. "Raised in the hills. Knows how to handle a rifle."

Uncle Ben let a little silence go by. "And open minded, from the way he talks. Afraid of mountain-bred people sometimes. Too clannish."

"Clannishness a good thing." Ike was reloading his pipe. "When it's used right, Ben. Moving into tough country. We'll see plenty of fools on the way. Might be good, have this Dohne along. Man you can tie to when the going goes rough."

I went to sleep beside the fire, still hearing the murmur of their voices mingled with the soft night sounds. It gave me a feeling of comfort that the yellow-haired giant would be with us.

My uncle had belated reservations when in the morning light he had a look at Samson's outfit. Everything Dohne owned, he said, was packed into a worn buckboard, and the mud wagon was not overly full. Neither were the two mules that drew it. It was a sorry-looking rig, but not so sorry as some we saw before the day was out.

There was a multitude camped along the line which separated Missouri from the country to the west, the area designated by the government as Indian Territory. We pulled into Elm Grove, seeing wagons as far as the eye could reach, hearing a great hubbub.

The whole frontier seemed to be in utter chaos, and Old Ike, coming back from his wagon to help Aunt Emeline to the ground, shook his head.

"Beats all," he said. "Ain't much like it was in thirty-one, that I can tell you."

He kept muttering disgustedly as we set up the camp. We

pulled the two wagons into a sandy spot beside a tiny creek and stretched the carriage and Samson's buckboard across one end. This was Ike's decision. He said that once on the trail the wagons were used as an enclosure to guard the camp and protect the stock.

Samson got an ax from his wagon and went along the creek looking for dry wood. There wasn't much, for it had been pretty well picked over, but he came back finally with an armload and stacked it neatly beside the small fire Ike had built for Aunt Emeline to start water heating.

She was in a fret because we had been on the road long past the weekly wash day and were all as dirty as pigs, and first thing had made Uncle Ben dig out the wooden washtub she had insisted was essential equipment. She had gathered up everything she could lay her hands on to wash.

Samson put down his ax, fetched more water, then rolled up his red shirt sleeves and thrust his heavy arms into the steaming tub.

Aunt Emeline gasped. "Mr. Dohne, a man isn't supposed to wash clothes . . ."

Samson looked at her in utter amazement. He had shaved off his beard that morning and his exposed face was white and long, angular and bony. He looked so much younger that I asked him outright. He said he was nineteen.

"Shucks, ma'am"—he was embarrassed—"ain't nothing, me doing a wash. My maw was sickly mostly. Wasn't nothing for me to do the house chores. Wasn't nobody else."

Aunt Emeline straightened to look at him fully. "What's your mother doing now that you've left her?"

"She up and died. Christmastime it was, so right then I start to get ready to go somewhere. Then this man he stops at the store one night, and he's telling all about the gold lying out on top of the hills in California, so I ask the schoolteacher where this California is, and here I am."

She was studying him. The night before she hadn't been much taken with him, but I could see her now changing her mind.

"And your father?"

"Ah, Paw took up with another woman right after Maw died. I guess he likely took up with her some before, if the truth was known. Me and her didn't get along. She never washed." He said this last as if it explained his whole emotion.

My aunt's cheekbones colored. She glanced around, saw Caroline and me listening and said quickly:

"You two go down and play along the creek. But Austin, don't get lost and be sure you're both back for supper."

I had already planned to explore the camp, and I didn't welcome the idea of being tagged by my cousin, but now there was no way of avoiding it.

We worked slowly along the creek bank. It was like the camp meeting grounds during a revival with even more excitement. People, wagons, animals were everywhere. There must have been two hundred children but I towed Caroline along with me from one to another of the milling groups of men, wanting to hear what they were talking about so earnestly. I found they were forming the wagon trains, companies gathering to elect their captains and draw up the by-laws which would govern the members of each train during the long trip.

And then I heard a voice I knew. There was no mistaking George Muller's resonant tones although I had not known that he had left Wilmington.

I pushed through the men who surrounded George and found him standing on a stump. He looked much the same as he had the night he had stood in our parlor, except that he had changed the frock coat for traveling clothes, and he was saying exactly the same things.

"It is the duty of every man, woman, and child to get to California as soon as he can. Only by settling up the ground and covering the gold fields can we be certain of holding that which belongs to us in the face of a foreign invasion."

George belonged to the Know-Nothing party, that organization of native-born Americans who did not hold with the stream of immigrants pouring into the country from Ireland, Germany, and elsewhere. Evidently the crowd agreed with him, for there were cheers when he finished.

Caroline and I had squirmed into the front of the group. George looked down, saw us, and let out a yell. He jumped from his stump and caught my shoulder, shaking me.

"Austin, boy. Where's your uncle?"

"Back yonder." I jerked my thumb in the direction of our camp.

"I've been looking all over for him. We got a train formed and I want him and Ike with us." He turned around. "Boys, this is the nephew of the man I was telling you about. Now we can get started."

He held my arm tightly. "Show me where Ben is at."

I led him back up along the creek. If it hadn't been for that trickle of water I couldn't have found the way.

"Where's Dave and Tommy?"

"Back in Wilmington."

I was disappointed. Seeing him I had assumed that the whole Muller family had started West.

"I'm going to send for them later," he said. "I couldn't wait to clean things up there. Abigail will sell the place and get things arranged, then they'll probably come out by sea."

My uncle Ben was very glad to see George Muller. Old Ike didn't share his enthusiasm. He didn't say much, but I had heard him call George a windbag before we had left home. I hadn't thought about it myself. George was a lawyer and I just supposed lawyers were expected to talk a lot.

"You just got here in time." George pumped Uncle Ben's hand. "We've got the company all organized, a fine bunch of men, the finest. You'll like them all."

My aunt was cooking the noon dinner. Samson had built her a stove out of rocks and he was standing by, helping. I could tell that he liked her very much. He spent all of his time hanging around, guessing what she would want next and getting it for her before she could ask.

She had nodded as we came up but had not left her frying meat. Now though she straightened, brushing a loose lock of hair back from her forehead. Her face was flushed with the heat from the fire and I was suddenly conscious that she looked pretty. It was the first time I had been really aware of what she looked like.

"All men? No women?"

"Twelve." George beamed. "Twelve women and thirty-one kids."

Ike made a noise deep in his throat. I couldn't tell whether it was a cough or not. I saw relief come into my aunt's eyes as if she had been afraid she had been setting out across the country, a lone woman in a male company. She bowed her head again then over the smoking skillet.

Ike said, "You got any mountain men along, anyone who's been over the trail?"

George turned to him, shaking his head and smiling. "The trail's well marked. We won't need any guide."

Ike shrugged. "Who's the captain?"

George laughed heartily. "You don't have to worry on that score, Ike. I am."

CHAPTER SIX

WE DID NOT start the next morning as Ike and Uncle Ben had planned. A hundred things delayed us. We started the day after, but in the meantime several things happened which altered the picture for us.

First off, when George Muller had gone back to his own camp, Ike motioned to my uncle and they walked down along the creek. I trailed after them unnoticed.

"I don't like it," said Ike when they were out of hearing of the fire. "Muller's a blowhard and we both know it."

If my uncle had a weakness it was his inability to see the shortcomings of his friends. Aunt Emeline always said that if we had one half of the money Ben had loaned out and never got back we'd be millionaires. He shook his head now.

"I've known George for years, Ike, and I never had any real trouble with him."

"Sure," Ike growled. "Back in Ohio it didn't matter that he was all the time making damn-fool mistakes. But here it's different. You don't make a mistake more than once. I'd feel a lot better if we had some experienced men in the crowd."

"At least he's an organizer." Ben was not worried. "And we have you along."

Ike looked at him, turned and walked away. My uncle sighed. Then he discovered me and smiled.

"The main trouble of the world, Austin. Everyone looks on the dark side."

I was puzzled. "Yes sir."

He put an arm about my shoulder. That surprised me. My uncle was not one to display affection, especially so publicly.

"I wonder if you're old enough to appreciate what is happening here. I hope maybe you are, for this is an historic occasion."

I waited for his explanation.

"People mainly have little vision. When the government set up that country out there as Indian land the men back in

Washington firmly believed that the United States would never grow any bigger than it was. Now the whole population is shifting westward. I'll wager that within your lifetime you'll see California as a state."

"Slave or free?"

We both turned at the sound of the strange voice. Edmond Jones was standing near, smiling at us. I slipped out of my uncle's grasp and ran to him.

"You haven't gone yet?"

"It's really obvious, isn't it, since I'm still here?" he said. "You should never ask the obvious, boy."

I flushed and was embarrassed until Edmond winked at my uncle.

Uncle Ben was considering him carefully. I don't think he ever got to really understand Edmond. I don't think many people did.

"You were serious about your question?"

"What question? Oh, as to whether California would come into the Union as a slave state or a free one? The answer is no."

"You weren't serious?" My uncle was disappointed to lose this chance for a discussion.

"Politics has small interest for me, Mr. Garner."

I wasn't interested in politics either. "What wagon train are you going with?"

Edmond looked down at me. "Why, I haven't decided yet."

"Then come with us."

He glanced at my uncle, who said hesitantly:

"Now, Austin, it isn't your place to ask, nor for that matter, mine. George Muller is captain, and . . ."

"Thank you very much," Edmond said. "I'll be glad to join you."

My uncle was disconcerted. "Well, sir, I'd be very glad to have you, but . . ."

"That's all right," said Edmond. "Of course."

He walked off and I felt a sharp pang of loss. But his wagon was in line when we started off next day.

It was very cold and my uncle had routed us out before daylight, but what with one delay and another it was nearly noon before George Muller gave the word and the wagons began to roll.

It was a big train. Too big, Ike complained. "You shouldn't have more than twenty wagons in any train," he said. "That's

41

enough animals to eat the grass, enough people to burn the wood."

Uncle Ben paid him no attention and Ike stomped off to his wagon. We waited for our assigned places as different units moved out in front of us. Other trains were forming at the same time and there was a good deal of confusion. I'd been looking for Edmond Jones all morning and had about decided that he wasn't coming when I suddenly saw him working through the press.

He was riding a big black horse, the most beautiful I'd ever seen. At first I thought that was all the gear he had, then I realized there was a wagon following him, a wagon driven by a Negro.

I jumped out of the carriage and ran to meet him. "Edmond, Edmond, I thought you weren't coming."

"I promised I would." He sounded surprised, as if it had not occurred to him that anyone wuuld doubt his promise. "I got a little tied up. Man came around hunting your uncle. I had to wait until he went and got his folks."

"A man? Who?"

"Back there."

I turned to look, and stood horrified. Following Edmond's wagon came a sorry outfit. There was no difficulty in recognizing it. There could not be two such rattletrap vehicles in existence. Joe and Myrtle Stoop sat on the seat with Sandy between them.

He had rigged bows on the wagon and fixed a piece of patched canvas over them. I guessed that the younger children were under this cover.

Sandy spotted me and waved, crawled over her father and leaped to the ground. She wore a gingham dress and from the way it hung I guessed there was not much underneath it. The dress had been washed until it was colorless and no life left in the cloth. She came racing to where I stood. I would have liked to run away from her, but there was no place to run.

"Hi, Austin."

I said, "Hi," putting no enthusiasm into it.

"Surprised?"

I admitted that I was.

"Pa just decided to come, so we hitched up and here we are."

I was looking at the Stoop wagon. Joe had handed the lines to Myrtle and clambered to the ground. He wore a blue shirt and new butternut pants and his suspenders were a fireman red. He was more dressed up than I had ever seen him. He had even shaved. He walked past us without a word and on to Uncle Ben's side.

"Howdy, Ben."

My uncle was never consciously rude to anyone. He nodded. "Hello, Joe. Headed for California?"

"That's right. Been looking for you. Figured being from the same town we could go together."

I missed what else was said for Sandy grabbed my arm and was trying to wrestle me from my feet. I jerked free.

"Let go. Go on, get away from me."

"Austin." It was my aunt, calling from the carriage. "Come here at once."

I went thankfully. I climbed back up into my place. Aunt Emeline said in a low voice,

"What are those people doing here?"

"Going to California, same as we are."

"I know, but what does Joe Stoop want with Ben?"

"He wants to join our train."

"Join our train . . . ? Ben won't let him do that. I don't want that woman around."

She started to get out of the carriage, but just as she moved a horseman appeared, yelling for my uncle to gee up. Joe Stoop stepped away from the wagon. My uncle cracked his whip and the oxen lurched into motion and we were on our way.

I looked around us. Aunt Emeline was driving the carriage. Old Ike's wagon lumbered along on our right. Uncle Ben was on our left and beyond him the Negro pulled Edmond Jones' wagon into line.

The train went four abreast, some ten to fifteen feet separating us. It was very impressive. In the next wave Samson Dohne was behind the carriage and Joe Stoop trailed Uncle Ben. Three of the kids were out, walking beside the old horse. My aunt glanced around and I saw her lips tighten in a straight line and knew that there was going to be trouble.

We made only five miles that day because of the late start. The road we traveled, if it could be called a road, was already heavily rutted by the trains that had gone before us, and the wagons did not pull into a circle that night as Old Ike had told me they would. The cattle and horses were allowed to graze and a necklace of fire sprang up as the company went about getting the evening meal.

Samson Dohne had definitely attached himself to our party. He brought the wood and built the fire and danced a helpful attendance to Aunt Emeline.

My uncle and Ike brought the stock in just before dark, tethering them to the wheels of the wagons. Edmond Jones was some twenty feet down the creek from us and beyond him were the Stoops. I could hear the kids as they played in and out of the heavy brush along the creek.

I saw Joe Stoop come up through the willows to where Uncle Ben stood with Ike. I followed, curious to know what he wanted, and was within earshot in time to hear him say:

"Would you have a spare piece of rope, Ben? One of our straps broke today."

My uncle hesitated and I could see by his expression that he was not happy. I knew why, because my aunt had informed him that afternoon that unless the Stoops left the train she intended to, even if she and Caroline had to turn back alone.

He sighed. "Joe," he said, "how well are you equipped for this trip?"

Joe Stoop's slack face showed his surprise. "Equipped? You mean food and things?"

"That's exactly what I mean. You've got a lot of children, that wagon of yours isn't very good and your horses have seen their best days. It's a tough country we're heading into."

"I reckon it is." Joe did not sound concerned. "But we'll get by, Myrtle and me. We're kind of used to thin living, as it were."

"I know," said Uncle Ben, and I could tell that he was liking what he had to say less and less. "This is a free country, Joe, and no man has the right to tell another where he can go or what he can do. But there is more to consider here. When people are traveling together in a wagon train they are naturally dependent on one another. It is only fair that everyone start with the proper equipment so that he does not become a burden on the others. For your own sake and for the good of your children, don't you think you should turn back before you get too far from Independence?"

Joe Stoop looked at him for a long moment, then he drew himself up straighter than I had ever seen him.

"All right, Ben. I won't be troubling you again. I find I don't need that rope after all."

He turned away and walked back toward his wagon. My uncle shook his head, and said to Ike, "I didn't mean to hurt his feelings, but what do you do? He can't cross the country in that rig. It's utterly absurd for him to try, and it's unfair to the rest of the company for us to be saddled with him."

Ike blew his smoke out softly. "I wouldn't worry too much about that."

"What do you mean?"

Ike shrugged. "People like the Stoops have a way of surviving. They may not have the good horses and wagons, but like he says, they're used to doing without. And they aren't soft. I'd rather have Joe Stoop with me in the mountains than George Muller. He knows how to fix things with damn little, he knows how to travel on a flat belly, and he can come nearer to living off the country than any man in the train with the possible exception of Samson Dohne."

"He can't go on with us," Ben said it firmly.

"He'll go. You can't stop him."

"Not in this train," said Uncle Ben. "I'll speak to George about it."

Old Ike shook his head. "Don't do it, Ben. You'll regret it sooner or later. Don't mix in women's quarrels."

My uncle flushed, then without another word he went in search of George Muller.

We found him talking to Grover Peyton. Peyton was from the State of Maine. He had been a merchant in Augusta and he had loaded all of his goods into two wagons, one of which he drove. The other was driven by Lysander Cox.

I didn't know either of the men very well, they were both close mouthed, but I had gotten acquainted with Peyton's daughter Lisbeth. She was at the fire stirring an iron pot, with Lysander hulking by her. He was a big man, fair haired and blue eyes, a deliberate man, solid and without humor.

Uncle Ben motioned to George, said, "See you a minute?" and led our captain away from the Peyton wagon. I trailed behind them, close enough to hear my uncle say,

"But the Stoops haven't got the equipment for the trip."

George looked at him suspiciously. "Is this you talking, Ben, or is it Emeline?"

My uncle fumbled for an answer.

"Look," Muller said, "I don't like Stoop any better than you do, but I got trapped into saying he could go and I ain't going to look like a fool, changing my mind. A captain's got to act steady."

"But George . . ."

Muller shrugged and walked away and after a moment

my uncle left. I hesitated, then went back to the Peyton fire.

Lisbeth saw me and smiled. "Evening, Austin."

I said, "Evening." To my mind she was about the prettiest thing in the world. I spoke to Lysander, but he only grunted. I didn't like him very well. He was too bullheaded and surly and I tried to ignore him.

"Still excited about going to California?" the girl said.

I nodded. "It's great."

Lysander grunted again. "Wait until we get to the desert."

His manner annoyed me. "You sound like you don't want to go. Why'd you come if you don't like it?"

I saw him glance at Lisbeth and suddenly realized that he had come only because of her. An empty feeling went through me. I'd been in love from the first time I'd seen her, back at Elm Grove, and now I found myself jealous of Lysander Cox.

I didn't know what to say. I wanted to get away from there as fast as I could, and I didn't know how. Edmond Jones saved me. He had come up through the trees behind me without my knowing that he was there until he spoke.

"Hi, Austin. Where's your uncle?"

I turned around, thankful for his presence. "He went down the creek with George Muller. I'll show you."

He raised a hand to halt me as I bolted off. "Aren't you going to introduce me to your friends?" But he wasn't looking at me. He was looking at Lisbeth.

I decided that I could share her with Edmond, though never with Lysander, and nodded.

"This is Edmond Jones. He's from Kentucky. This is Lisbeth Peyton and her father."

Peyton had been sitting cross kneed on the wagon tongue a few feet away. He rose and came to shake hands.

"And this is Lysander Cox. They're all from the State of Maine."

Cox did not offer his hand but Lisbeth did, and it seemed to me that Edmond held her fingers a minute longer than was necessary. I was about to interrupt when he said:

"Do you by any chance play the piano?"

Her eyes widened, then she started to laugh. "What an absurd question. And why do you ask? There isn't a piano within miles of here."

"Oh, but you're wrong," he told her in his soft voice. "Donny Scranton, who is camped just above you, has a piano in his wagon."

46

Her eyes danced. "I wish I could see it."

"Nothing easier," he said. "Donny is right proud of that piano, believe me. Come along."

She hesitated for a moment, then glanced at her father. "Watch the stew, will you?"

Edmond took her arm with as much grace as if he were escorting her across a cotillion floor and turned up the creek. For a moment Lysander stared after them darkly, then he followed. I followed Lysander. Apparently Edmond was not in much of a hurry to see Uncle Ben.

Donny Scranton was about Edmond's age, taller and some twenty pounds heavier. He was eating when we got there but he put aside his plate and stood up as soon as he saw Lisbeth.

"Well, hello."

Edmond said, "I was telling Miss Peyton about your piano and she expressed a desire to see it, if you don't mind."

"Pleasure." Donny Scranton beamed.

"This is Lisbeth Peyton. That's Lysander Cox, and Austin Garner lurking in the background."

Donny Scranton waved his hand at us, but his full attention was centered on the girl.

"You play, Miss Peyton?"

She shook her curls. "I truly wish I could."

His face fell. "Gosh, I was hoping you could . . ."

"Would you play it for us?"

"Shucks, I can't play."

She showed her amazement. "You don't play? Then why in the world are you dragging a piano all the way to California?"

He got red under the heavy tan of his fair skin. "Well, ma'am, I'll admit maybe it sounds a mite crazy, but from the time I was real little I decided that the girl I get married to would play the piano. I decided to save my money, and I bought it, and when I decided to head for the gold fields I just couldn't bring myself to leave it behind."

"And your girl, is she coming out to California?"

"There ain't no girl, ma'am. I never yet found the one I'm looking for. That's the reason I hoped you could play. I thought when I seen you you might be her."

I heard Lysander growl, a low sound like the warning of a dog. Edmond looked secretly amused. Lisbeth colored again, but she managed to laugh.

"I'm afraid I don't qualify. Now, may we see the piano?"

He turned eagerly to the wagon, loosening the canvas and stripping it back from the bows. The piano was wrapped lovingly in more canvas. He climbed to the wagon bed and unswathed the bulky instrument.

It sat, gleaming and enticing, surrounded by his boxes of food and clothing and tools.

"Ain't she a dandy?" He opened the keyboard and ran his fingers over the ivory keys. "Listen to her sing."

Lisbeth's eyes sparkled. Edmond was grinning approval. Only Lysander refused to be moved. "Wait 'til you get to the desert," he said, and walked away.

Donny Scranton stared after him in surprise. "What's wrong with him?"

"Nothing," said Lisbeth. "He doesn't mean to be rude. It's just his way."

"He'd better find a different way with me," Scranton threatened, but after a glance at his piano his eagerness returned. "She's a Wornum cottage type with a crank action. She was made in 1829. She's vertically strung, and the man who sold her to me said she's the best instrument the company ever made."

Lisbeth and I were duly impressed. I hadn't seen many pianos. There was one at the Lodge Hall, but most of the houses I knew had parlor organs. Lisbeth swung to Edmond, lifting her eyes.

"Help me up, please."

He stooped, caught her around her knees and hoisted her within reach of Donny's outstretched arms. Donny lifted her over the tail gate and she clambered through the boxes to the piano, putting out a hand.

"May I?"

"Welcome to," he said, and with one finger she ran the scales. Donny watched her with a soft glance, and sighed. "Gee, I wish someone could play her."

"I can," said Edmond Jones.

"You mean it? Well, come on up and do it."

"I will if Lisbeth will sing."

She flushed prettily. "I don't sing well."

"I'll bet you do." Edmond climbed lightly into the wagon. "What do you want?"

She thought for a moment. "Do you know that trail song, 'Sweet Betsey from Pike'?"

"Sing it," he said. "I'll follow you."

She began to sing. Her voice was not strong but it had a pleasing, lilting quality.

> "Oh, have you heard tell of Sweet Betsey from Pike,
> Who crossed the wide prairie with her husband Ike? . . ."

Edmond picked up the melody, faking it. When she finished he made her sing it again, and his accompaniment was sure and light. People began to gather around the wagon. Donny sat on a box, kicking his foot to the time and grinning like a kid. Other voices joined in. The song changed to another and another until Lisbeth called a halt, protesting that she had to get back and give her father his supper.

Edmond jumped to the ground and lifted her down. They called their thanks up to Donny, both of them laughing. The girl turned her shining face to Edmond Jones.

"Oh, I'd love to be able to play like that."

"I'd teach you," he said, "but then you'd qualify as Donny's dream wife."

"I could do worse."

"You can do better," he told her in a voice I barely heard. "I've decided to marry you myself."

CHAPTER SEVEN

IN THE MORNING I watched the Stoops swing their wagon into the end of the line as the train began to move out. My aunt watched too, and the corners of her mouth tucked in, but she had no chance to question my uncle until the noon break. Then she said in a dangerous tone:

"Didn't you tell George Muller to get rid of those people?"

He nodded.

"They're still with us."

"George wouldn't send them back. He said he'd promised them they could go, and he won't reverse himself."

My aunt's chin set squarely. "If you won't make him see reason, I will. I'll talk to him."

"You will not." My uncle's jaw was as rigid as hers. "You will keep out of this."

49

There was a long strained silence, then she turned and discovered me, listening, and walked away around the wagon.

I didn't know what would happen. Nothing did, although my aunt hardly spoke to my uncle during the next three days. The more I thought about it the more certain I was that I did not understand grownups.

But I forgot their argument, for there was fresh trouble brewing in the train. We had reached the Kansas River and were waiting for the Frenchman who ran the ferry to take us across.

The ferry is about a hundred and thirty miles west of the Missouri and we had had few difficulties this far, rolling over a good road across the alluvial plain. My uncle was talking to Ike when I joined them and I heard him say: "I guess it was bound to happen."

"What was bound to happen?" Ike was examining the right front wheel of his wagon.

"Trouble over Jones' nigger. They shouldn't have come with this train."

I was shocked. "But Bob isn't causing any trouble."

"No," my uncle agreed, "but most of these people are from the free states and don't hold with slavery. They are liable to turn the black man loose, and your friend Edmond carries a pistol."

"Bob's not a slave," I said. "He's got papers. He's free."

I heard Ike chuckle. My uncle looked at me in surprise.

"How do you know this?"

"Bob told me. He's my friend."

"You beat me, Austin." My uncle laughed. "You have a way of knowing everything that's going on. Anyway, George has called a meeting for tonight to discuss the situation."

I couldn't see that there was anything to discuss, but we had the meeting. It was late when we finally all got across the river and set up camp, so it was full dark before the men gathered around the blazing fire.

Most of them knew what the meeting was about, but apparently Edmond had no warning as he paused beside us at the edge of the crowd. George was standing on the tailgate of a wagon, and he was uncomfortable as he began to speak.

"Any time," he said, "that a group of people travel together there is bound to be some friction. Men seldom agree with all their fellows as to politics, religion, or manners. Most of this company here comes from our free states . . ."

I saw Edmond start, but he did not change expression as George blundered on. "Most of us don't hold with slavery, and yet one of our number has chosen to bring a slave along . . ."

Uncle Ben took a breath, getting ready to speak, but Edmond stopped him, putting a hand on his arm.

". . . Now I'm not attacking Mr. Jones or his rights to his beliefs, but a lot of our members are concerned. So to avoid trouble I suggest that we have a vote, and if the vote goes against Edmond Jones he take his wagon and his slave and join another outfit."

There were mutters from the crowd, of indignation and of approval to the action. Then Edmond said evenly:

"Before the vote is taken, gentlemen, may I ask that the comments of one man be heard?"

"Go ahead," said George expansively. "Speak out."

"I'm not the man. Bob is." Edmond turned to the Negro directly behind him. "Go on up there, Bob, and answer their questions."

Bob shifted uneasily from one big foot to the other. He was a tall man, a full six feet, middle aged, with a bare dome-like head that looked like a chocolate drop.

"I don't want to cause no trouble, Mr. Edmond."

"There won't be any trouble," said Edmond Jones. He spoke quietly, but everyone who heard him recognized the warning.

George Muller moved aside now, making way for the Negro as Bob climbed to the exposed position.

"What is it you want me to say?" He looked over the heads at Edmond Jones.

"Just answer any questions they want to ask you. Who wants to ask the first question?"

Grover Peyton did. I should have guessed that he was one of those who had stirred up the fuss. I knew that he looked with no favor on the piano lessons Edmond had been giving Lisbeth.

"Did you want to go to California?"

"What would I be doing here if I didn't want to come?"

"Slaves don't have a choice."

"I'm a free man." Bob said it proudly. "Mr. Edmond's father gave me my papers twenty year ago."

The shifting of surprise went through the crowd.

"I don't believe it," Lysander Cox called out. "The black man's afraid of his master. He's lying."

51

Edmond Jones spoke softly. "I'd be careful there, Mr. Cox. I've seen Bob fight. He can be dangerous when he's roused. The papers are in my wagon, if you'd care to see them."

Peyton was still not satisfied. "If you're free why did you stay with the Joneses?"

The Negro looked squarely at him. "Where else would I go? That's my home. I was raised up there. All my friends, they live on the farm. Why wouldn't I stay?"

The answer by its very simplicity seemed to baffle Peyton. "Well, if you like it so much there, why did you come on this journey?"

"Mr. Edmond, he come. I come with him. I go wherever he goes."

"Then you aren't free after all."

The Negro seemed puzzled now. "Sure I'm free. I didn't have to come, only I wouldn't be happy if I didn't."

My uncle Ben started to laugh. He was joined by others and soon everybody chimed in. Bob climbed down sheepishly and came over to us.

"What'd I say so funny?" He was speaking to Edmond.

"They're not laughing at you," Edmond told him. "I think maybe they're laughing at themselves."

Bob shook his head. "I don't get it, Mr. Austin. I don't rightly understand."

I didn't either, but my uncle did. "Nobody ever feels more foolish than the man who tries to right an injustice only to learn that no real injustice exists."

I had made a discovery. I was standing close to Edmond and touched his arm. "Grover Peyton don't like you."

He smiled. "That is a family disharmony which I'll try to change."

"He doesn't like you teaching Lisbeth to play the piano."

"Music hath charms to soothe the savage . . ."

It was not what I'd expected Edmond to say, but by that time I'd learned that he seldom said or did the expected. Twice I'd seen him put men in their places, quietly and without commotion, yet here he simply was shrugging off my warning of impending trouble.

I started to go with Bob to find out what he thought about the meeting, but Sandy came up from the river where she'd been wading with two of her younger brothers. She stopped me.

"What were they talking about, Austin?" she asked.

52

I'd been keeping well out of Sandy's way. Although Aunt Emeline had not mentioned the Stoops since my uncle told her to stay out of it I did not intend to risk her wrath by playing with any of them.

Nor had I needed their company. Our carriage had broken a wheel which could not be repaired and we had abandoned it, so that Caroline and Aunt Emeline now rode in my uncle's wagon. I had inherited one of the carriage horses and rode proudly with the men.

I explained what had happened as shortly as I could. She listened, her pixy face very grave.

"Why do they want to pick on Bob? Why are people so mean to people?"

For that I had no answer.

"Why doesn't your aunt want you to play with me?"

I hadn't realized that she knew, and for some reason I did not want to hurt her feelings by admitting the truth.

"It isn't that."

"Then what is it?"

"It's just . . . you pester me."

"You're a liar," she said. "Your aunt tried to run us clear out of the train. I heard George Muller telling Pa. You don't think we're good enough to associate with."

"Sure I do."

"Then let's go down around the bend and go swimming."

The night was hot and I was tempted, but I didn't dare. I shook my head and escaped back to the wagon. It was bright moonlight, and Aunt Emeline sent me off to collect wood.

Wood was hard to find, since a lot of other travelers had used the ferry before we got there, and had stripped the banks of most of the usable deadfall. I wandered down the stream, past the bend, a good quarter of a mile below the camp. The water looked so cool and inviting that I finally stripped off my clothes and jumped in.

My head went under, although when I stood up the water reached only to my armpits. I dived and swam along the sandy bottom for as long as my breath lasted.

When I surfaced Sandy was standing on the bank above me. She had peeled off her dress and her brown skin glowed in the moonlight.

"You're real mean." She sounded angry. "Running away like that when you knew I wanted a swim too." Then she made a shallow dive, coming up like a playful otter at my

53

side, reaching for me, grabbing my hair and pulling me under.

I came up sputtering. "What'd you do that for?" I jumped for her, intending to drive her down, but she was too quick for me and darted back with a flashing overhand stroke.

I never would have caught her unless she had let me, but I finally grabbed her shoulders and pushed her under. It was her turn to come up choking.

"Quit trying to drown me," she coughed. "You hate me."

"You ducked me first, and I don't hate you. I like you all right." I said it without thinking, but then I realized that I did like her, a lot.

She pushed the wet mop of hair back so she could see and laughed. "Will you go swimming next time I ask you?"

"I guess so."

I don't know what else I might have said, for suddenly I saw the Indian. He stepped out of the bushes like a silent shadow. I had seen a number of Kaws along the way and knew them for a bunch of dirty beggars, but this one looked different. He was taller and better dressed, and he stood on the bank staring down at us impassively. My first impulse was to run but I was too paralyzed to move. I just stared back at him. Sandy had seen him too and was retreating into deeper water, and as we watched he stooped and methodically gathered up our clothes.

Sandy gasped, then yelled angrily, "Put those down."

He paid no attention, bundling the garments under his arm, turning, vanishing into the brush.

I thrashed ashore and sat down in dismay. I had a picture of myself explaining what had happened to Aunt Emeline. Then Sandy came out of the water uncertainly.

"What do we do now?"

I had no idea. Then another sound made me freeze and I turned to see Black Bob coming through the thicket.

"Why, Mister Austin . . ."

My tongue tangled itself up as I tried to tell him about our predicament, but I managed to make him understand.

He didn't laugh. He began solemnly to ponder the problem, then he unbottoned his shirt and pulled it off, exposing his red undersuit.

"Here, little missy," he said, tossing the shirt to her. "You put this on."

Sandy caught the garment before it fell on the wet sand, and slid into it. The tails came below her knobby knees and

54

it was twice as wide across the shoulders as it needed to be, but it did effectively cover her.

Bob was considering me as Sandy buttoned the shirt and rolled the dangling sleeves. He wore a large red bandanna around his neck. Once he had explained that it was to keep off the mosquitoes which pestered him unmercifully. He removed it, spread it out thoughtfully, stepped down on the sand to my side and draped the bandanna around my hips like a loin cloth. Then he stood back to survey his handiwork, and his white teeth showed in his pleased smile.

"Stick a feather in your hair and give you a bow and you'd make a fine brave. You sure for certain would."

Sandy chortled. She could never resist laughter for long. But I did not think it funny.

"Aunt Emeline isn't going to like it. Those was my best pants."

"Shore enough." Bob shook his head. "We ain't out of the woods yet, no sir. We better go up to our camp and let Mr. Edmond figure out from there."

He turned and led the way. Fortunately Edmond Jones' camp was the first we would reach. His wagon was drawn up and all the equipment arranged with neat efficiency. Lines were strung between trees and the things that had gotten wet in the crossing of the river were hung to dry. My aunt had learned to keep a decent camp, but in none of the units had I felt the sense of settled permanence that Edmond and Bob managed to impart to their overnight set-ups.

Bob motioned for us to wait in the bushes and went ahead, scouting to see that we would not be observed, then he came slipping back, with all the stealth of a professional conspirator.

"Nobody 'round. You kids duck up and scramble into the wagon. I go find Mr. Edmond. Chances are he's playin' that doggone piano with that Peyton gal."

"You don't like Lisbeth." I was dismayed by his tone.

He thought it over deliberately. Bob could be as deliberate in his pronouncements as Old Ike was.

"Well, Mr. Austin, it ain't that I don't like her really. She's nice and gentle and she acts like a lady should, sometimes. But Mr. Edmond, he's right special. I ain't seen any female yet that's good enough for him. You git along now, before somebody comes pokin' around after you."

We scooted for the wagon and crawled under its sheltering canvas where an oil lamp burned dimly. I had been in there before, and knew the fine clothes Edmond had in his bell-topped trunk, its lid turned back now to let the air sweeten the cloth and prevent its molding. And I had looked covetously upon his wonderful collection of guns. But Sandy had never seen them.

"My, he must be rich," she said breathlessly.

"He is," I told her. I could not resist bragging a little, although the only information I had came from Bob's talking about the big farm south of Lexington. "He's real rich. His father owns half of Kentucky, and they raise the finest horses in the world."

"Why's a man like him want to drag clear across to California after gold if he's already got so much?"

It was a point that had not come to my mind, and I had no chance to worry about it then, for a small voice outside was calling Sandy's name. It was her brother Joe. He was a year younger than I and I had always considered him beneath my interest.

"Here I am," Sandy yelled automatically, and then it was too late.

I peered out to see Joe staring around him in bewilderment.

"Where? You come out. Maw wants you."

I said, "Shush," but Sandy pushed me aside.

"It's all right. Over here, Joe, in the wagon."

Joe came over, his thin, freckled face twisted in concern. "You'll catch hell if Mr. Jones finds you in there."

"No we won't." Sandy held the canvas back so that her brother could wriggle in. "Bob told us to hide in here."

Joe's head came through the opening. "Why you hiding?"

Sandy told him quickly and Joe began to laugh, earning my indignation.

"Bare assed," he chortled, more to himself than to us. "Bare assed with him. Wait until Paw finds out. He'll tan your backside good."

"He ain't going to find out," said Sandy. "You sneak over to our place and bring me my other dress. You hear?"

"Maw said to bring you."

"Tell her I found a rabbit hole and set a snare. Tell her I can't come just yet."

Joe looked dubious, but Sandy shoved him out of the wagon.

"You hurry now."

He took off then as fast as his skinny legs could carry

him. I sat by the crack in the canvas, one eye against it. Edmond Jones had chosen a site a hundred or so yards from his nearest neighbor. I had noticed all during the trip that he managed to achieve a degree of privacy whenever possible.

I could hear noise from the clustered camp above, and I was beginning to get chilly in my abbreviated costume. I expected every moment to see someone coming after me, but when I finally heard the rustling through the bushes it was Bob returning.

"You find Mr. Edmond?" I called as he approached.

He nodded.

"And he didn't come?" I knew a new despair. I had great faith in Edmond Jones.

"He take care of it. He said he get you some clothes from your wagon."

"How's he going to do that?"

"You leave it to Mr. Edmond. He'll find a way. He always does."

With that I had to be content. Bob stayed outside and built up his supper fire, and Sandy and I waited in nervous silence. Suddenly I let out a gasp of horror. Myrtle Stoop had parted the bushes and come through, a limp dress hanging over her well-formed arm.

Sandy had been looking through one of Edmond's books. Her head came up sharply.

"What's the matter?"

"Here comes your maw. She's got your dress, so she knows."

Sandy sat very still. She didn't say anything, but her face turned pale under her even tan. I looked back outside. Myrtle paused beside the fire and nodded to Bob, then I heard her say, "My girl around?"

He didn't hesitate and he did not lie. "In the wagon, ma'am."

Myrtle looked up. "Sandy, come out of there."

Sandy crawled meekly over the tailgate, looking very small, almost shrunken in the folds of Bob's shirt. Her mother didn't say a word. She merely tossed her the dress. Sandy caught it. She hesitated for a moment, then ducked into the brush, to reappear a minute later wearing the dress and holding Bob's shirt. Silently her bare feet brought her forward and she extended the shirt to its owner.

"Thanks."

"You're welcome, missy."

Myrtle looked at Sandy, then at Bob.

"That was a nice thing you did," she told him. "I ain't likely to forget."

She took Sandy's hand in hers and they moved away up stream. I poked my head out.

"You suppose she'll get a licking?"

Bob thought about it. "No, sir, I don't think so. That's a real smart woman. Yes sir, a real smart woman."

I was surprised. I had never heard anyone refer to Myrtle Stoop as smart. I crawled out and went over to sit close to the fire, shivering and wondering if I would be let off as easy as Sandy.

It was ten minutes later when Edmond appeared, carrying a pair of my pants and a shirt. He handed them to me without comment and I hurried to put them on, asking, "What did my aunt say?"

"She doesn't know anything about it. Ike got them for you."

"Thanks. Thanks a lot."

"Austin."

"Yes, sir?"

"The next time you go for a swim make sure there aren't any Indians around."

He turned and walked off, and behind me I heard Bob at last give way to soft, quiet laughter.

CHAPTER EIGHT

NEXT MORNING we reached the Methodist mission school, ten miles ahead, where the women insisted on stopping. It wasn't hard convincing the men, for after the days of unaccustomed moving it was good to look at solid buildings again. They had more than four hundred Indian pupils, and the place seemed prosperous.

There was talk that we should make the noon camp there, but it was too early and we moved on, making about thirty miles that day.

The rolling country was beginning to rise a little and we

crossed one row of low hills after another. But the road continued good and there was plenty of grass, though we had to go a mile off the trail for it so that the animals might eat. Along a small stream we even found wild peas tangled near the bank, and while the men arranged the wagons in the grove of large old cottonwood trees the woman and younger children picked messes of the peas for supper.

I had stayed close to Edmond Jones all day, keeping away from Aunt Emeline in case she had any inkling about my lost pants. I helped him make his camp, then he took his shotgun and waved me with him. We went out across the prairie in search of birds.

He shot a dozen and we got back to camp well before dark, to find everything secured and the supper fires burning brightly. We rode to our fire and Edmond presented the birds to my aunt, then went to tell Black Bob to dress them. Then he wandered over to Donny Scranton's wagon, stripped the cover from the bows and sat down at the piano.

He played half a dozen pieces while the birds roasted on their spits, and after we had eaten, half the wagon train gathered about the Scranton camp and Edmond played some more. It was a soft night and there was a restlessness among us as if the sight of the mission buildings had reminded everyone of their homes, so far behind.

The next thing we knew, Samson Dohne appeared with his old banjo. Then Joe Stoop, who had kept very much to himself since my uncle had tried to get him to turn back, came hesitantly forward carrying a battered fiddle. He squatted down beside the wagon's high wheel and began to play softly.

Edmond Jones stopped and looked down to where Lisbeth Peyton stood between her father and Lysander Cox. He smiled and beckoned to her.

"Come on up here and sing for us."

She shook her head, embarrassed, and wouldn't go.

"I will."

It was Sandy, hanging back under one of the big trees.

Edmond turned, nodding. "All right, Sandy, come on."

I heard my aunt mutter something under her breath about forwardness. She was sitting on the ground between Caroline and me, holding Caroline's head in her lap. I glanced at her. In the deepening evening light it seemed to me that she had lost weight and looked very tired.

Sandy was clambering up into the wagon, squirming in between the boxes to the piano.

"What do you want to sing?" Edmond asked.

"She sings 'Oh! Susanna' real pretty." It was Joe Stoop, calling up the wheel.

Edmond nodded, struck the chord, Samson and Joe came in with him, and the girl lifted her head and opened her mouth.

I'd never heard her sing before, and was ready to laugh at her. Instead of the squeak I expected, her singing voice was deeper than her speaking pitch, as if the words originated down in her throat, and there was more volume than you would think could come from anyone her size.

The chatter of the company hushed as people began to listen. She sang verse after verse, and one after another other voices joined the chorus.

She sang two more songs, and in the hush after she had finished Lisbeth Peyton said, "That was lovely, Sandy. Very lovely."

Sandy stepped over the wagon's rim to the wheel and dropped beside her father, her bare legs flashing gawkily in the firelight. Her face was flushed and her eyes bright, and I knew that she was pleased.

Old Ike had advanced toward the center of the circle, and now looked up to Edmond. "Play us a square, boys. Come on, folks, choose your partners."

Ike was a noted caller and had been much in demand at the monthly dances back home.

There was a whoop from the crowd, a bustle as people moved to clear a space of the soft ground, Joe Stoop's fiddle rose to a high-swinging tune, Samson's banjo picked it up, and Edmond filled it out with the piano.

Uncle Ben left George Muller, with whom he'd been talking, hurdled the wagon tongue, kicked his heels together and waltzed over to where we sat.

"Come on, Emeline, let's show 'em."

"Oh you, Ben. I couldn't. Way out doors here . . ."

"Sure you can. You're the best dancer in Clinton County and you know it."

Her face tinted with a pretty color and she looked more alive than I had seen her since the start of the trip. She let him draw her to her feet and they joined one of the forming squares. In a couple of minutes the firelit glade was swirling with swinging skirts and bobbing figures and the open night was pushed back by laughter.

Caroline had gone to sleep, curled up on the ground at my side. I got to my feet and started around to where Black Bob was watching the dancers from the edge of the circle. The crowd had grown. Another wagon train was camped just above us, and some of those travelers joined us, attracted by the music.

Sandy appeared from nowhere, followed by her brother Joe and one of her younger sisters. She was grinning.

"You like my singing?"

I nodded shortly, embarrassed. We hadn't spoken since the swimming catastrophe.

"It's all right."

"It's good," said Sandy with ready conviction. "Lisbeth Peyton said she never heard anyone sing better."

I was impressed. Lisbeth Peyton was about the smartest person around, in my estimation, with the possible exception of Edmond Jones.

"She said that?" I sounded as if I didn't believe it.

"She sure did, didn't she, Joe?"

Joe was not much interested. He had discovered a frog behind a rock that thrust up out of the heavy turf, and was jumping after it, pouncing on it like a big frog himself. I decided to accept the quote as true.

"Where'd you learn to sing like that?"

"Paw taught me. Paw used to be the best fiddler in Brown County, before we moved up to Wilmington."

The idea of Joe Stoop being the best anything was more than I could fully believe. I ducked away from them and pushed through the swaying circle to watch the dancers.

Ike was in his element, up on the tailgate, his bull voice in the singsong chant directing the kaleidoscopic patterns of the interweaving figures. He finished with a flourish, a grand march, which the leaders turned into a serpentine in and out among the trees.

Then George Muller leaped into the wagon, never able to resist the opportunity for a speech.

"This has been fine, folks, fine." He waved his arms expansively. "But we roll out at daylight. We been lucky so far, mighty lucky. We've come near two hundred miles in two weeks and we ain't had any trouble you could speak of. Here's to California."

He gave a couple of hoorays, everybody yelled and Edmond played a loud, fast "Oh! Susanna."

I think it was the happiest night of the whole trip. I guess my aunt and uncle thought so too. I heard them talking, even heard Aunt Emeline laugh, in the tent long after they had blown out the lantern.

The next day we made twenty-five miles, up another river, the Big Blue, and stayed the night on the near side to allow plenty of time in its crossing.

The Big Blue wasn't as big as the Kansas, but it must have been a hundred and fifty feet wide and so deep that we had to tie logs to the sides of the wagons and float them across.

Three or four hundred people lined the bank. Some of them had been there for days, rigging improvised ferries, figuring different ways to cross, and one man told my uncle that four people had drowned in the preceding week.

I went with Uncle Ben and Ike and a group, visiting down the river, sizing up what others were doing about the problem.

Then in the morning we ferried over four wagons at a time, with half a dozen men on saddle horses swimming beside them and the woman and children riding inside. As he had at the Kansas, Edmond Jones took quiet charge. No one elected him, but no one questioned his orders.

George Muller didn't notice. He was everywhere, shouting directions that no one heeded, generally getting in the way.

The crossing was made by lot, each wagon driver drawing a numbered slip from George Muller's hat. Uncle Ben drew number one.

Ike took Caroline with him. Two thick cottonwood logs were roped to the wagon's sides and the oxen were urged down the sharp bank, the wagon tilting and slipping, until all were in the swiftly moving water. Edmond, Samson Dohne, Lysander Cox, and three other men swam their horses beside it on the upstream side, with ropes strung from it to their saddle horns to keep it from drifting down the river.

My Aunt Emeline objected, but I begged so hard that Uncle Ben let me ride Prince across. The horse didn't like the water and it took some pummeling with my bare heels against his sides before he made a surging plunge. It almost threw me from the saddle, and I clung there desperately as he lunged out, swimming strongly for the opposite shore.

He made it far ahead of the wagons, struggling up the slick clay bank to stand trembling at its rim. For myself, though I didn't let anyone know it, I was glad enough to drop from the saddle and lead him out of the way.

Thanks to Edmond's precautions we crossed without the loss of a single wagon, though the goods in several got wet and Uncle Ben was forced to discard a bundle of his precious newsprint. The only near tragedy was the Stoops' wagon. The horses, poor at the beginning of the trek, now showed signs of near exhaustion. One of them simply ceased to struggle when it reached midstream. Myrtle and the kids were all in the wagon, but Joe had borrowed a horse and was towing with a rope.

It was Black Bob who saved the situation. His wagon was safely across and he had mounted one of the horses and come back into the water to help. When the Stoops' horse stopped swimming and began to sink, Bob rode alongside. With one hand he caught the bridle and by sheer strength held the creature's head above the current while the other riders tightened their ropes and dragged the light wagon to safety.

I saw the small, scared faces as the kids tumbled out, and Joe rode up, jumping off his borrowed horse and lifting Myrtle to the solid ground. She must have weighed near twice what he did but he hefted her down as if she were a feather.

"You safe, honey?" He looked worried.

"You big lug, of course I'm safe."

She kissed him then right in front of everybody. I heard my aunt sniff, but somehow I thought it was kind of nice.

It took most of the afternoon to build up fires and dry things out and rest the animals, so we did not move on up the Little Blue until the next day.

By this time the train was, as Ike put it, well shook out. Everybody knew his place in line and if a wagon broke down it automatically pulled out of the track so the others could pass. But the days of steady travel had taken their toll of our animals, and the trail was now littered with things that others before us had fondly brought from home. It was like some strange store, with everything from feather beds to cut-glass pitchers and portraits of long dead ancestors strung out on display.

It was a temptation to forage and pick up some of the choice treasures, but Aunt Emeline forbade either Caroline or me from touching anything. It was, she said, like robbing a grave. Ike concurred with her, but his reason was that we had no room for any more truck. But the Stoops had no such compunctions, and their wagon blossomed out in much equipment that it had not originally boasted.

Our own entourage had been lucky. Aside from the bundle of paper drenched in the river, and what we had eaten, our wagons still carried everything with which we had left Ohio. True, the carriage was gone, but it had not been practical from the first, and Aunt Emeline seemed resigned to making the rest of the journey on the high, springless wagon seat.

The Little Blue we did not have to cross, but followed along it and made an early camp on its bank. I wandered down to Edmond's wagon to find Bob fastening a hook and fishline to a willow pole he had freshly cut. He set me to catching grasshoppers, and between us we hooked a good mess of fish before dark. Sandy and her brother Joe were fishing below us, and although I did not go near them I judged from their shouts that their string was even bigger than ours.

We followed the Little Blue for days, northwestward, almost to Fort Kearny on the great Platte River. I had been hearing about this river ever since we entered Indian Territory, and I was further excited at the prospect of seeing a fort and real soldiers, stationed there to awe the Indians.

The place was a disappointment. There was no fortification and the garrison was made up of portions of three companies, only one of which was mounted. Their buildings were only raw chunks of sod, cut in the shape of bricks and laid up in thick walls, and the roofs were framed with poles, also covered with sod.

But it was the first civilization we had encountered since the Methodist mission, and my aunt discovered a vegetable garden behind the earth buildings and bargained a sergeant out of some fresh turnips and onions. That night we had a stew that was a welcome change from the wild or dried vegetables and salt meat which had been our main fare, for we had not always been rewarded in fishing or hunting.

Beyond the fort it was only a short distance to the Platte, and the river fully satisfied all of my imaginings. It varied from a quarter of a mile to over a mile in breadth and was truly the highway to the west. It was followed by the early explorers, by the Mormons in their search for a new home, by the emigrants to Oregon and finally by the California gold seekers. It furnished water and grass and easy passage for nearly seven hundred miles of the wearying journey.

Some of the trains elected to cross over here and take the road of the Mormons along the north bank, but at the fort we heard rumors that there was quicksand at the river. George Muller wanted to chance it, but Edmond Jones talked him into remaining on the south side.

Thus far we had found wood aplenty, although we sometimes had to go several miles off the trail for it and for good grass. But along the Platte all we had to burn was the dried buffalo chips dropped by the shaggy animals in their migrations.

Now we followed the river until it seemed to me that I had always lived on it, clear to the junction of the South Fork with the main stream, then had to turn along the lower branch, which swung farther and farther away from our general direction, searching for a fording place.

All the way from Fort Kearny we had glimpses of the trail north of the wide waterway, seeing the solid line of wagons which had started from the upper Missouri ports, and those who had crossed over, but when we turned south the only travelers we saw were on our bank. The place we finally chose to ford was a hundred and twenty-five miles or more from the fort.

Thus far we had made good time, with no trouble and none of the harrowing experiences we had been warned awaited us. Along the South Fork though we came upon more and more emigrants stranded by a sickness. In spots the way was lined with tents. We began to stagger our campgrounds to avoid the contagion, and managed to do so for several days. But the morning finally came, fraught with worry. Aunt Emeline could not leave her tent.

It was hot and humid along the bank even though the sun was barely up. I saw Uncle Ben talking to Old Ike, then Ike came over to where I was trying to get the small pile of dried dung to burn. His face looked serious.

Without preamble he told me, "Your aunt's poorly."

Caroline and I stared at him in silent apprehension.

"What's the matter with her?"

Ike shook his head. "The sickness, I guess. Ben's gone to try and find a doctor."

There were a dozen trains camped within a radius of a square mile, and half an hour later my uncle came back with a very tall man who carried a small bag.

Without so much as looking at me, they disappeared into the tent. I started after them but Ike called me back. All I could hear of the mysterious conference inside was the low murmur of the men's voices. Ike cooked our breakfast, making no attempt to hide his concern, but I wasn't hungry. Somehow, without my aunt bustling competently about the fire, things were not the same.

Samson wandered over with deliberate casualness, and he and Ike talked in tones too hushed for me to hear, then he turned and stalked off. My misgivings increased. A few minutes later Samson came back with Edmond Jones and Donny Scranton and they stood around the fire, drinking the steaming coffee that Ike poured from the blackened pot, not speaking, just kind of waiting.

George Muller rode up on his gray horse. He saw the group beside our fire and pulled over importantly.

"Come on, come on, let's get harnessed up."

He rode around each morning, making certain that all the wagons were ready to take the trail.

"Emeline Garner is ill," Edmond said.

George frowned down at him. "Ill? What's the matter with her?"

"We don't know yet. Ben found a doctor. He's with her now."

"Cholera."

It was a dread word. We had been hearing whispers of it from other trains, and Ike had told me that at least half a dozen people had already died of it.

I felt a cold fear in spite of the muggy heat. It was Aunt Emeline who took care of us all when we got sick, but as long as I could remember she had never spent one day in bed.

The tent flap was pushed back and my uncle followed the doctor out. I never did know his name, for I never saw him again. He was like so many others we met casually on the trail, who then traveled out of our lives.

George Muller said at once, "What is it, cholera?"

The doctor lifted his bony shoulders. "It may be. I'm not sure. It's the same sickness most of these poor people have. It may be cholera or it may be caused by bad diet, bad water, and the general unsanitary conditions." He sounded very disapproving.

George Muller looked stricken. "You mean she's too sick to travel?"

The doctor looked at him wearily. "Some people have

chanced it. I do not know how they have fared. But Mrs. Garner is a very ill woman."

Uncle Ben's face was gray and drawn. "We'll stay here, George. We'll give her every chance."

George Muller cleared his throat and it was obvious that he was horribly embarrassed.

"Ben," he said, "I don't know what to say. You know the rule. You helped make it yourself."

My uncle bowed his head.

Samson Dohne bridled. "What rule you talking about?" Samson had not liked George Muller very much and took no pains at concealing it.

"If someone can't keep up, they drop out of the train."

Samson was unbelieving. "You mean you'd just pull out and leave Ben all by himself, with two kids and his wife down like this?"

"He has Ike," George insisted. "Maybe she'll be better tomorrow. Maybe they can catch up."

I noticed that he was sweating. He pulled a red handkerchief from his hip pocket and mopped his forehead.

"I didn't make the rule alone." He was on the defensive. "And there's all these other people to think about. Maybe Ben can join another train when his woman can move."

Samson straightened around, facing him squarely, and I thought for a moment that he was about to drag the captain out of his saddle.

"You're a blowhard, Muller, and a coward," he said. "Go on with you and your train. I wouldn't stay with you now if you offered to carry me to California on a feather bed."

Edmond Jones cut in with his quiet voice, probably staving off a physical clash.

"Why don't you call a meeting, George, and see what the rest think. Those who want to go on can go with you. Those who choose to stay can stay."

George looked at him in grateful relief. He did not like the idea of splitting the train, but a vote would take the onus of leaving Ben Garner from his shoulders.

Around us the members were already harnessing their cattle, getting ready to start. George rode among them and soon they congregated around his wagon. He was self-conscious and uncomfortable as he mounted to his seat and faced them. My uncle did not come to the meeting, remaining close to my aunt, whom I could hear through the tent canvas, groaning weakly. But I slipped forward, following Edmond and Samson.

George waved his hands for silence and raised his voice.

"Emeline Garner is down sick. We're afraid she has the cholera."

The crowd reacted at the terrifying word and George went on hurriedly.

"We all hope the best for her, but we don't want cholera spread among the rest of us. We got to leave her here. It's in the company rules that we made up at the Grove, that if anyone had to stop because of accident or sickness, the train should go on."

"Hold up a minute." It was Samson. "That rule don't apply to women. Anybody who goes off and leaves a sick woman in this wilderness is a low-down coward."

George's face turned very red and he leaned forward angrily. "I don't have to take talk like that from anyone, certainly not from some ignorant hillbilly."

Samson had been carrying his rifle in the crook of his arms. He seldom moved very far from it. He swung it around now, his thin face looking more gaunt than ever, and his eyes seemed to pale.

Edmond grabbed him quickly. He was not as strong as Samson, but he took him by surprise and jerked the gun from his hands.

Samson spun on him, furious. "Gimme that gun, Jones."

Edmond trained the rifle on Samson, watching George over Samson's head. He said levelly, "It will not do Emeline one ounce of good for you to shoot Muller. Let them go. I don't believe we really need them."

He turned as if the matter were settled and walked away. Samson was still boiling, and started for George, but I wrapped my arms around his middle.

"Please don't." I was scared and my voice cracked. "We got lots of trouble. It ain't going to help, you fighting. Come on away."

He stopped, looking down at me. His face did not relax, but after a minute he patted the top of my head and turned. I led him, still grumbling, to where Edmond and Ike were talking to Lisbeth Peyton. I thought maybe Lisbeth could calm him down.

Grover Peyton and Lysander Cox came up just as we did, and Lisbeth turned to her father.

"Mrs. Garner is very sick."

The New Englander said sourly, "George Muller just told us. Cholera. Let's get moving."

"Moving?" Lisbeth gasped. "You don't think I'm going to leave that poor woman here with no one but men to care for her?"

"Yup." Her father nodded. "That's exactly what you're going to do. We've got a long way to go, and the worst is still ahead. We can't afford to lose a day."

"You go right ahead," she said. "For myself, I am staying right here until Emeline is able to travel."

"No you're not, daughter." Peyton was not a large man, but he could be forceful when he chose. "She'll likely die. Most of them do." He said it as indifferently as he might have remarked on the weather.

I stared at him, stabbed by the thought. I think I hated him from that moment. It is not a feeling that I ever lost. The idea of anyone saying Aunt Emeline would die, and not even caring, hit the pit of my stomach like ice.

Lisbeth flushed and put her hand across my shoulders, drawing me to her. Samson let out a roar, but Lisbeth turned on him sharply.

"You be still, Samson. I will handle this." She swung again to her father, and her tone was level and determined. "If such a tragedy should happen, Caroline and Austin would need me. You leave if you want to, but frankly I'll feel safer in a company with Ike Summerholdt and Ben Garner and Samson Dohne than with that pompous George Muller and his Know-Nothing crew."

I noticed that she didn't mention Edmond Jones, but I saw Lysander Cox looking in his direction, and I knew suddenly that he would never go off and leave the girl with him.

She flounced around and strode toward their wagons, where the teams were already in yoke. Lysander shook his head and growled something to Mr. Peyton, then the two men went after Lisbeth and began unhitching the cattle. I turned back to Samson and Edmond.

"I'm sure glad Lisbeth is staying, but I wish her father and Lysander would go on. I don't think they will though, with you here."

Edmond winked at me as if he understood what I meant, then looked up as Donny Scranton moved toward us with a small, lopsided grin.

"Since you're the only one who can keep the piano in tune I'd better stay with you."

Edmond nodded solemnly. "Glad to have you."

The men separated then, heading for their own camps. I waited there, watching George Muller's wagon haul out, watching as one after another team fell into its place. It was a strange feeling, seeing the long train draw away and leave us alone in the middle of the vast, empty prairie.

Joe Stoops' wagon was, as usual, the last in line. Joe had not been at the meeting. I recalled this as the miserable rig came up. He had been at the far end of the campground and as often happened, no one had bothered to tell him. He followed the slow procession, his ill-matched team already struggling although the day's journey had but begun.

He saw me standing forlornly beside the passing outfits, looked over and saw that our tent had not been struck nor our cattle yoked. He pulled up. He and Myrtle sat on the high seat, the children following afoot with Sandy bringing up the stragglers like a goose girl, a hundred yards behind.

"Trouble, Austin?"

"Aunt Emeline's real sick. We think she's got the cholera."

Joe's face puckered up as if he were in pain. He looked off at the wagons pulling away from him.

"They all leaving you?"

"Donny and Edmond and Samson and the Peytons are staying here."

Myrtle leaned back, peering at me over Joe's shoulder. "Who's taking care of your aunt?"

"Well, Uncle Ben is, and Ike is heating water and Samson is getting wood and Black Bob is hunting herbs to make her some tea, and I just saw Lisbeth go in the tent."

Myrtle rose, stepped out on the wagon wheel and despite her full-blown weight, dropped to the ground.

"Stoop, pick us a place to camp and get the team unhitched. Don't get too close, no need exposing the kids more than necessary. Then find out from Ben what you can do to help."

She started toward the tent, arriving before it just as Uncle Ben came out. He stopped in surprise at sight of her, then flushed in embarrassment.

"I thought you were already on the road."

"Nobody told us about Mrs. Garner." Myrtle shook her head. "We'll stick around with you."

"That's right nice." Uncle Ben gave her a harried smile. "But really . . . we'll get along all right. Jones' Bob seems to

70

know something about medicine. Edmond says he used to take care of the Negroes down on the farm."

"Bob's a man. Your wife needs a woman."

"Lisbeth Peyton's here . . ."

Myrtle ducked her head. "Lisbeth's a nice girl, but she hasn't brought seven kids alive through every misery in the book." She almost pushed him out of the way and disappeared into the tent.

Uncle Ben hesitated, then came over to the wagon slowly. "This is good of you, Joe, after the way I acted."

"Shucks," said Joe Stoop, "what are neighbors for?" He clucked the thin horses into movement and drove them down the emptied camping ground.

CHAPTER NINE

A COUNCIL of war grouped around our fire. Lisbeth Peyton was in the tent, sitting with my aunt. The other adults of the shrunken wagon train argued the problems of the sickness. Myrtle Stoop, after a visit of inspection, had come out to assume full charge, and no one had challenged her, not even Lysander Cox.

"I've never seen the cholera before, but the diarrhea, I can stop that. Ben, what did the doctor say?"

I had never seen Uncle Ben so helpless before. It was as if his last anchor in this world had pulled loose. Until that moment I had not comprehended how much he leaned on Aunt Emeline. Now he was instinctively leaning on Myrtle Stoop.

"He said give her gruel and opium. He gave me some powder."

Myrtle nodded briskly. "Peyton's got barley in his wagon. The gruel will coat her gut. She oughta have boiled milk to bind her up, and I've got turpentine for a stupe."

Curiosity goaded me and I asked, "What's opium?" although I knew better than to interrupt the grownups in serious conversation.

Everyone looked at me, no one willing to answer, then Edmond Jones said,

71

"A narcotic, useful when handled with respect. It soothes the griping."

It seemed to me a formidable array of medicines, and even Black Bob, brewing his tea of mint leaves and herbs from the swampy river bottom, relinquished his post as prior adviser.

Edmond looked at Myrtle. "And what do you want us to do?"

"First, get me some milk."

The men looked at each other, as helpless as Uncle Ben. Then Bob said:

"There's a train camped downriver a mile that's got a couple of cows. I saw them when I was out hunting last night."

Edmond Jones had been leaning against a tree. He straightened.

"Show me where they are."

Samson rose from where he squatted on the ground.

"I'll go with you."

Edmond didn't even nod. He was already walking toward his horse. I hesitated. I wanted to go, and I wanted to be around to see what happened. But Myrtle decided me, having discovered me when I spoke.

"Austin, you get away from here. I don't want either you or Caroline within a hundred feet of this tent. You go on down and play with my kids."

Obediently I took Caroline by the hand and towed her off to where Joe Stoop and the children were setting up their new camp. Then I got Prince and rode after the men on their errand. They paid no attention as I came up. I don't think they were really aware that I was tagging behind them. Bob was out front, leading the way, and Samson and Edmond followed side by side.

They were silent for quite a while, then Samson grunted.

"She can't die, Edmond. She just can't. Not her."

Edmond glanced toward him, then nodded. "If anything or anybody can bring her through, my money's on Myrtle Stoop."

Sampson was troubled. "I heard some talk about that woman back before the train split up."

"You will hear talk about many people." Edmond's tone was a trifle sharp. "One of the great weaknesses of the human race is our tendency to sit in judgment of our fellows. Whatever failings Myrtle Stoop has, she has the virtue of competence to meet whatever situation she finds herself in

72

and to cope with it in one way or another. Believe me, I would rather have her taking care of Emeline Garner than anyone else in the full train."

Samson breathed deeply, as if he found strength in Edmond's words, and they rode on in resumed silence, each engrossed in his own thoughts.

The train we sought was ready to pull out as we reached it. It was a big one, over fifty wagons, coming from someplace in Indiana. Bob hung back on its fringe and I followed Samson and Edmond in, hearing Samson ask of the first family we came to where he would find the captain.

The captain turned out to be a very thin, very tall man, bearded like a pirate. His name was Kern and he listened to Samson's story with quick sympathy.

"Sure sorry to hear about the woman being sick, and sure would like to help you out, but I got nothing to do with them two blamed cows. Caused us nothing but trouble the full trip."

Edmond Jones said, "Who owns them?"

"Man named Petrie. And it's only fair to warn you he wouldn't sell either of them for a hundred dollars . . . No sir. He says he's going to raise a big herd from them once he gets to California."

"Where is he?"

"Over yonder." Kern pointed to the far side of the camp. "You can't mistake his outfit, he'll have the critters roped to the back of his wagon."

Edmond touched his broad hat in thanks and turned through the bustling train to where a short fat man and a half-grown boy were finishing yoking their oxen. The cows were black and white and looked hollow, gaunted by their long walk.

Edmond stepped down from his horse, tossing the reins to Samson. Petrie did not even look around as he finished fastening the trace chains. The boy had lifted his head to stare at us in curiosity and a woman's voice came shrilly from the interior of the wagon.

"Elmer, get moving there."

Dully the boy returned to his task.

Edmond said, "Good morning."

Petrie grunted.

"My name is Jones, from a train up the river. We have a sick woman on our hands."

Petrie showed no interest. "Everybody's sick. Man died in this camp last night."

Edmond's manner remained quiet. "This woman needs milk, and I see you have two cows."

"No milk." Petrie shook his head. "Milked them 'fore daylight. Sold it all. Get a dollar a quart."

I stared at him, figuring he was a liar. I'd never heard of milk costing more than ten cents a gallon in my life. Still Edmond held his patience.

"I'd like to buy one of the animals."

Petrie straightened quickly. He wasn't more than five feet and looked to be nearly as wide as he was high. He gave Edmond an insolent laugh.

"You ain't got enough money, mister."

For answer Edmond reached into the pocket of his tight trousers and produced five gold pieces, which he clinked invitingly in his hand.

"One hundred dollars."

"Nope. Critter will bring me double that afore we git where we're goin'. Then I use her to start my herd."

"If she survives," Edmond said evenly. "You've got a lot of dry country to cross before you hit the Sierras, and then a lot of rough country. A hundred and twenty. There are herds of cows in California. The Mexicans have been raising them by the thousands there for years, and you can buy one for the price of the hide."

The woman had crawled out of the canvas and stood in front of the seat, listening. She appeared nearly six feet tall and as if she had never had a decent meal.

Samson was gaping at Edmond, horror written clearly across his large face. I don't suppose he had ever seen a hundred dollars in cash. Certainly I had not. Even as prosperous as the country around Wilmington was there had never been much cash. A good third of the subscriptions to the *Clarion* had always been paid for in produce, eggs, and freshly butchered meat.

Samson growled, "You're offering too much."

Edmond either did not hear him or pretended that he did not.

"A hundred and twenty, my friend." He dipped into his pocket and came up with another gold piece. "Wouldn't you rather have a hundred and twenty dollars than a dead cow stretched out beside the Humboldt?"

74

Petrie licked his fat lips, but his voice was the voice of a man so stubborn that no reason would alter his thinking.

"No."

Samson urged his horse a step forward. In a quick gesture he leaned down and caught the front of Petrie's dirty shirt. Before the startled man could move he was lifted clear of the ground and Samson was shaking him, gently, like a rag doll.

"You better listen, little man, 'cause we're going to take that old cow anyhow."

The boy beyond the wagon made a convulsive crouch. Edmond caught the action from the tail of his eye.

"Don't try, sonny."

Edmond's coattail was casually swept back and I saw that he was wearing the single-action Colts that I so much admired. The boy stiffened.

"Put him down, Samson," Edmond said easily.

Samson opened his huge fingers and let the man drop. Petrie fell perhaps a foot, landing on his feet with a force that jarred him. He was sputtering with indignant rage.

"I'll get you for this. No stinkin' thieves is going to walk off with my property."

"We are not thieves." Edmond Jones' voice had tightened a notch. "And you will not do any getting, for the simple reason that you are a coward and have no desire to be hurt. Nor are we going to take your cow without proper payment. I will make one last offer. One hundred and forty dollars."

"Take it." It was the woman, still on the high wagon. "Take it, you crazy fool. That cow only cost you fifteen."

Petrie's head swiveled up to look at her and his lips started to form another *no*, but Edmond was too quick for him. Edmond had the sure sense when he had won. I was to see it many times again.

"All right then," he said. He dropped the gold pieces noisily back into his pocket, turned abruptly and caught his reins from Samson.

"We'll take it," the woman said.

Petrie nearly choked on his protest. "No we won't . . . we . . ."

She said flatly, "We'll take it. You shut up, Eph. You ain't got no sense and you never had any and the Lord forgive me for ever being fool enough to tie up with you. Here . . ." She stooped low and her hand reached out toward Edmond, looking very much like a claw.

75

Petrie was still fuming but Edmond now ignored him. He walked to the wagon wheel and poured the shining coins into the woman's grasping palm.

She bit into one after another with her stained teeth, then, satisfied of their value, popped them into the large apron she wore over the gingham dress, and motioned to the boy.

"Untie Sadie."

The boy moved stolidly around the wagon. Petrie was now almost hopping in his fury.

"Don't you dare touch that rope. I'll bullwhip you good."

The boy, a head taller than his father, shrugged, untied the lead rope secured to the cow's leather bridle and handed it up to Samson as Edmond mounted his horse.

Petrie screeched, red faced. Edmond touched his hat to the woman and led us off, back through the camp. Not until then, did I see what an interested audience we had. Many of the people from the waiting train had gathered behind us to watch, and most of them were grinning, thoroughly enjoying Petrie's discomfiture.

They parted to let us through and we moved at a snail's pace to where Bob waited for us. He reined forward to take the rope from Samson's hand.

"You go ahead, Mr. Edmond. I bring her."

Samson and Edmond rode on. I stayed with Bob, towing Sadie as she ambled unhurried after us. I was to learn to hate that cow. She was the stupidest, most stubborn animal I have ever known, with the added bad habit of kicking at anyone who tried to milk her.

Unfortunately, the job of caring for her and milking her fell to Sandy and me.

I never learned my aunt's reaction when, weak as a string and wasted almost as thin, she roused and found Myrtle Stoop her nurse. She insisted ever after that Myrtle had saved her life, and while neither approved of the other, a bond was forged. From that day forward Aunt Emiline, whatever her private convictions, would never hear a word spoken against Myrtle Stoop.

I know very little about the convalescence. Caroline and I stayed with the Stoop family, as far away from possible infection as was practical, and unhappily the cow stayed with us. Myrtle disappeared inside our tent and I did not see her again for five days. Sandy took care of the younger children until Black Bob came to her aid, and I spent most of my time moving Sadie's picket rope from place to place. It seemed to

76

me that she could eat a patch of grass almost quicker than I could tie her in the center of it.

Three times Sandy and I managed to sneak off for a swim in a hole we had found up the side creek, and each time little Joe Stoop trailed along to wade and chase the fingerling fish in the shallow water.

A different spirit grew in the camp. It was as if Aunt Emeline's distress drew these people closer together. Nothing was said, at least in my hearing, but where they had been casual, independent units thrown together by the accident of the trail, they now seemed concerned with one another's problems, and gradually more and more of the company shared their food, seated around a common fire.

It could, of course, have been that with the number so shrunken they wanted the warmth of companionship. Or it could have been that they needed one another's help.

The ten days we spent waiting for my aunt to regain enough strength to travel was a blessing in disguise, for the stock, so weary and thin with walking that their heavy hides hung loosely over ribs that showed, rested and began to fatten. Even Joe Stoop's ragtailed team looked as if they might go another mile without staggering to their knees. And the wagons, all of which were trail marked, were repaired, their tires tightened, the wheels soaked in the creek, split reaches replaced, goods overhauled and restored.

Bob kept us in meat with an able assist from Samson. Between them they brought in more antelope than we could use fresh, and some of it was smoked. Then Samson killed the first buffalo we had seen.

My aunt began to take meat broth and then some solids, and her danger passed. The train was reorganized into a tight working group, each man having his own assignment.

It was Edmond who suggested the reorganization and the need for electing a new captain. He nominated my uncle.

Uncle Ben refused, maintaining that there were others better qualified to solve the ever-changing problems that the trail posed. He suggested Ike.

Ike said he was too old and offered Samson's name, and Samson was elected without a dissenting vote. For once Lysander Cox agreed, I think because he was secretly pleased that the choice had not fallen on either Edmond or Donny Scranton. For the three way rivalry for Lisbeth's attentions was now an open contest, to Old Ike's delight. I heard him and Myrtle Stoop making bets on who the winner would be.

"Cox is too dour for that gal," Ike reasoned. "And Jones is too much the hoity-toity gentleman for any female from New England. But that Donny Scranton, now there's the one. He's keeping his head down and letting Jones teach her how to play that piano so she'll be just the wife he wants. The quiet one, that's the one to watch. He'll step in and grab her off and them others won't know what happened."

"Nope," said Myrtle. "It'll be Lysander. She'll get way out here where everything's strange and different to what she knows and Lysander comes from her neck of the woods. She'll turn to him when she gets homesick enough."

For myself, I did not want Lisbeth to marry anyone. I wanted her to wait until I grew up, but if she wouldn't do that, and Sandy assured me that she wouldn't, then I could be reconciled to losing her to Edmond Jones.

Mr. Peyton did not share my view. He made it increasingly plain that he resented Jones' suit, and Lysander stood jealously by, making certain that neither of the others ever had a moment with her alone.

Samson Dohne was the one who surprised me. He went about his business never even looking at Lisbeth, spending his free time squatted beside my aunt's tent flap knotting ropes together into what turned out to be a hammock, and saying very little.

Aunt Emeline continued to mend and our company began to relax. Then one evening Uncle Ben carried her outside the tent and made a place for her beside the supper fire. Samson dug out his banjo and sat down against the wagon wheel and played very softly, the sad, slow songs of his Kentucky mountain country.

I was much heartened. Another wagon train had come in to camp between us and the main river. We had not spent a night there without the fires of a new train in sight. In fact there were few hours of the days when the dust of an oncoming cavalcade could not be seen, and I was becoming extremely worried that everyone in the United States was heading for California, that all of the gold would be picked up from the hills before we arrived.

I went over and sat down beside my aunt, not knowing quite what to say. It was the first time Caroline or I had been permitted to see her. She looked very thin and wasted, all of her plumpness had melted away and the rosy color her soft cheeks had always had was replaced by a transparent gray.

"You feeling any better?" I asked.

She said that she was.

"Gee, I'm sure glad."

She laid one hand on my arm. It was as near a caress as she had given me in a long time.

"Thank you, Austin." She even gave me a trembly smile.

"Everybody's glad you're well. We were all scared."

Her eyes lighted at that. "Everybody's been so wonderful. It's a blessed thing, Austin, to have good friends."

Myrtle Stoop interrupted us, arriving with a bowl of rich soup. She squatted down and fed it to my aunt slowly, and I couldn't help noticing how meekly the patient obeyed her.

CHAPTER TEN

When Aunt Emeline was able to travel again Samson slung his hammock from the bows in our wagon and helped Uncle Ben to lift her into it.

"She'll ride easier," he explained to me, "not jouncing around on the wagon bed.

We advanced to the South Fork, where that crossing marked another milestone in our journey. It was the twentieth of June, with the water still so high that many trains were held up, unwilling to risk the river. Wrecked wagons and dead cattle littered the stream bank for miles below us, and the smell was overwhelming. We learned that the other part of our train had ventured across three days before and had lost three wagons, one of which was George Muller's. But there had been no loss of life.

Our group looked at the swift, deep water and at the stinking near shore, where all of the grass had been eaten to its roots, and decided to try the river.

Ike suggested that we take the strongest wagon box, remove it from its running gear and use it as a boat to ferry all of the goods from the other wagons. The lightened vehicles could then be more easily driven over. It proved a good solution, with the men swimming their horses on the upstream side, towing Edmond Jones' watertight box.

As the first load moved into the current a large crowd

79

gathered to watch, and set up a cheer when it finally grounded on the opposite bank, although it had drifted nearly out of sight below its starting point.

My uncle's press and Donny's piano made the crossing in their own wagons because of their weight and the awkwardness of handling them, and with tempers edged by the competition for Lisbeth's affection, the piano led to an explosion between Donny and Lysander Cox. As Donny's otherwise emptied wagon was being let down to the water Lysander's rope broke and the load nearly got away.

Donny began to yell. "Watch it, watch it, watch it . . . If that piano gets wet . . ."

Lysander's sulky mood, not improved by the labor and soaking of five trips across, flared.

"Put a sail on your Goddamned piano and sail it over. Only a fool would think of hauling that heap of wire clear across the country, and I don't like fools." He dropped the end of his broken rope and yanked his horse away.

Donny's lunge was fluid and faster than I had ever seen his lanky body move. He caught Lysander's bridle.

"Nobody talks to me that way. I'll . . ."

He never said what he would do for Samson Dohne had swung his horse about and thrust it between them, grabbing the wet collars of their shirts and shaking them solidly.

"Cool off or I'll put you both in the river. I'm captain here."

Both were surprised out of their quick anger, but Samson held them a moment longer to make sure they were properly subdued, then said in a milder voice, "Get another rope, Lysander. Let's get these wagons across before dark."

Cox looked at him, shrugged and went for a rope, and the piano reached the far bank without further incident.

And then we lost Samson's own buckboard. Not being watertight, it was run up onto the ferry. The current caught the clumsy boat and swirled it around. The rope holding the buckboard in place snapped and it toppled upside down into the river, floating quickly away from the men, faster than the swimming horses could pursue it.

Samson found it late that night. It had been dashed into a log jam four miles down, its pole broken, the axle bent and one of the wheels broken beyond repair. He came sadly back to camp long after dark, and my uncle went to meet him.

"Never mind. We've got enough for you, and you can help drive. Your mules can help haul the Stoop rig."

"It ain't the buckboard," the big man said, shaking his head, "I had a tintype of Maw fitted under the front seat. I didn't find it."

He touched my uncle's arm with a doubled fist and walked on.

We climbed a mountain then, the highest I had ever seen, and down its other side, over broken, gorge-torn, treeless land to the grove at Ash Hollow, back on the main Platte. Westward from there began a country entirely strange to me, long reaches of flat ground with grass so short it looked like a ragged lawn. Enormous rocks, as big as castles, looking like castles rose abruptly from the plains, as wild as a moonscape.

The river was still with us, a comforting friend when, across the slowly rising vastness, the snowcapped top of Mount Laramie lifted above the horizon. We would pass this single outpost of the Rockies far north of it, but the sight of it was a chilling reminder that we must soon tackle the ascent of the great mountain chain. It was now well into July, and while snow was not expected on these ridges, we had still to cross the desert before reaching the Sierras, where early snows were something to be reckoned with.

I learned this at Fort Laramie, listening to the discussions that ran through the camps there. One of the camps was George Muller's train. They had arrived only two days ahead of us, having lost four more wagons. I heard one of the men tell Uncle Ben that George had tried to bring them down the treacherous descent to Ash Hollow too fast, that the rigs had got away and tipped, teams and all, into the yawning rocky chasm.

There was much talk that the way would get increasingly harder now, and again people were sorting over their possessions and discarding, lightening their loads. Even food was dumped beside the road, some of it dirtied and destroyed by angry wagoners, and other piles with signs on top inviting anybody who had a mind to help themselves.

George Muller came bustling into our camp almost before we had it set up. He didn't look like the portly, cocksure lawyer of Wilmington, Ohio. He had lost so much weight that his clothes hung from his big frame as if they belonged to someone else. He was long unshaven, and behind the scraggly beard his face was drawn. What caught my attention most was his eyes, and the strange intensity that burned there.

He didn't make a speech this time. He walked nervously up and down in front of Uncle Ben and, oblivious that we all listened, poured out a tale of woe.

He had lost all of his gear with his wagon. All he had left was the gold he carried in a belt around his shrinking waist. His wagon train had mutinied, some being so discouraged that eleven rigs were turning back. The remainder had split, one part electing a new captain and pulling off to themselves.

The other part, ten men including George, were selling their wagons and cattle, buying horses so that they could push on at a faster rate.

"It's getting late, getting late." George's speech was jerky and rapid. "I don't want to get caught in them California mountains like the Donners did. We gotta move out."

"They was stupid," Joe Stoop snorted. "They throwed away everything before they started up . . ."

"Stupid, hell," George's voice rose. "They just plain got caught in a blizzard and stuck there and starved until they had to eat each other up. I ain't gonna . . ."

"George Muller . . ." Aunt Emeline reached out to clap her hands over Caroline's ears. "What a terrible thing to say in front of children . . ."

I don't think George even heard her. He had grabbed Uncle Ben's arm and was shaking it.

"You better come with me. The horses can travel twice as fast as these damn wagons."

Uncle Ben freed his arm, making no fuss about it. "Simmer down, George. I've got my family, and I can't haul my press on a horse, nor Peyton his goods, nor Donny his piano."

"Damnit," George Muller sputtered. "What's more important, getting to California before it snows or dragging that crazy stuff? You'll never make it."

"We'll make it," said Samson Dohne. He said it slowly, deliberately, as he said all things. "You know, Mr. Muller, you put me in mind of a fellow I knew back home. Always he and I'd start out for the store about the same time. He was ever in a hurry. Off he'd take at a half-run, up the hill, leaving me loafing along easy. I'd get to the top and there he'd be, plain out of wind and panting. Mostly I beat him to the store by maybe five minutes."

George glared at him wildly puzzled. "What's that mean?"

Samson scratched his head reflectively. "Well, I'll tell you to your head, sir. You couldn't tarry when Missus Emeline got sick, you had to go all-fired busting on to California. So here we all are. Now you're going to dump everybody and get on a horse and go busting off again, and you know something, I got an idea we'll catch up with you somewhere else along the line."

George shook his head as if to clear away the words, and his eyes ranged around our camp. He frowned, then looked back at Samson.

"Where at's your buckboard?"

Samson said levelly, "Lost her."

George's eyes darted around again, ferreting out Samson's mules, now tethered to Joe Stoop's wheel. He licked his lips.

"I'll buy those mules." He was already reaching into his shirt for his money belt.

"Joe's using them," Samson said.

"I'll give you a hundred dollars apiece."

Samson just looked at him for a long minute, then shrugged and walked away. George watched him, open-mouthed, then swung on Edmond Jones.

"What about you, Jones, you going to tag along with these damn fools?"

"I think so," Edmond said in his even voice.

"Then sell me that black horse."

"Sorry."

"Damn you. Damn you all," George exploded, and went rushing off.

Around our fire everybody was quiet with embarrassment for a long while, then Aunt Emeline said nervously, "Is there anything in what he said, that we might get caught in the snow?"

"I'd rather believe Samson," my uncle soothed her. "I guess George was always a fool."

It was the first time I'd ever heard him give up on a friend. Ike laughed and rose from where he squatted, unable to resist a jibe.

"It took you long enough to find that out."

Uncle Ben looked at him sadly, without reproach. "It's a sorry thing to need to learn about any man," he said, and turned to the evening chores.

George Muller and his horsemen took off before the following daybreak. We did not get on the road until nine o'clock, and as had been foretold, traveling was not as easy as it had been east of Laramie, for the ground was rising on the long, uphill slope to the South Pass. Yet the road was wide and open, there was grass and the weather was pleasant. And the great river stayed beside us.

Then it bent away, writhing up to its headwaters in the foothills of the Rockies that now loomed just south of us. We had to cross and work down the west bank to reach its tributary, the Sweetwater, whose valley would lead us into the pass.

It was in this stretch that we learned what the warnings meant, why the loads had been lightened at Laramie. The land began to heave and toss into angular red and yellow hills with tops so flat that they might have been sheared off by a knife. Dark juniper trees grew on them spottily, making me think of a loose herd of buffalo grazing. The hills were made of a rock that seemed to be rotting. Edmond Jones said it was decomposed, stratified shale. Between them were frighteningly deep gullies, as sharp edged and angular as the hills. And the ground we covered was sharp and hard on the animal's hoofs.

We wound around like a snake, avoiding the canyons and detouring the buttes, and came to another flat plain from which a different kind of rock mountains thrust. These were weather worn, rounded knobs, and toward one of these we headed.

Independence Rock, the totem of the trail, was an enormous biscuit on the valley floor, three hundred feet high, five hundred long, its sides too vertical to climb. Everybody who passed that way stopped to scratch his name and the date on the rough surface, and it was difficult for us to find room to add ours.

Donny Scranton beckoned me to his wagon and drew it tight against the giant rock, then held me on his shoulders while I inscribed his mark and mine. And yet there were names out of reach above me. I never was able to figure out how the people got them up there.

We found George Muller's fresh inscription and then went on the little way to another sight that took my breath. One of these huge boulders had long ago been cleaved in two, and through this cleft the whole of the Sweetwater River gushed in a great jet. This was the Devil's Gate which guarded the entrance to the wide, green Sweetwater Valley.

The route up to the South Pass was not, as I had envisioned, a narrow canyon, but instead a gently lifting slope, and as we followed the meandering stream I was not aware how high we had climbed. And then we were on the crest.

It was more like a saddle, fully twenty miles across, with the Rocky Mountains stretching away southward and on the north their continuation, the towering Windy River Mountains whose tops are always wrapped in snow.

This was the top of the world. The fountainhead of the Sweetwater rises here and flows eastward, and close to that spring is another, whose waters go the other way, down the west slope, into the Green River, the Colorado, and out to the distant Pacific Ocean.

Around the springs were camped four wagon trains and, to my surprise, George Muller's band. It seemed that in their hurry they had driven their horses too hard up the deceptive valley and been forced to wait three days here in the thin air while the animals rested.

Sandy and I discovered him, and I thought he wouldn't want to show himself around our camp, but it wasn't long before he came puffing up to my uncle. His delay had him edgy, but his self-importance was back in his manner.

"Ben, Ben," he said as if they hadn't seen each other for a year. "I'm glad you got here in time. We're having a meeting tonight."

Uncle Ben's voice wasn't rude, but it was cool. "You're always having a meeting. What's this one about?"

George waved his arm grandly to the westward. "Why, about the different routes to the gold fields. You see, up to now there wasn't much choice. You had to follow the Platte if you wanted water and grass. But from here we've got to decide which way we go."

The way he said *we* made me wonder if he figured on joining up with our train again.

My uncle sounded skeptical. "Who in this crowd knows much about the country ahead?"

"Oh, we've got an experienced mountain man now. He's with that train over there. Been out here a long time, with Sublette and Bridger. He's been to California twice, once with Frémont, and to Oregon twice. Hickson's his name. John Hickson."

"Well," said my uncle, "that does sound interesting. Some of us will be there."

CHAPTER ELEVEN

JOHN HICKSON WAS shorter than my picture of a mountain man. He was built like a barrel set on short, thick legs. His arms were extremely long and above the elbow were as big around as Sandy's waist. His big head was covered with a graying, uncut thatch and his little eyes and lumpy nose were all of his face that showed above a graying bush of a beard.

He wore a shirt of fringed buckskin so dirty and greasy that it was black, and I could smell him although I sat a good eight feet from the wagon on which he stood.

But when he spoke you forgot how he looked and smelled. His deep voice had a sure tone that built confidence. You felt that he knew intimately all of the secrets of the wild land ahead.

"There ain't no easy way from here," he said, "but others have made it and there's no reason you won't if you keep your heads."

He paused to gnaw off a chew of twist and ponder as he worked it comfortably into his cheek.

"The easiest and safest way is down to Fort Bridger and up to Fort Hall, cross to the Humboldt and follow it to the Sink, then across the desert to either Truckee or Carson and up over the other mountains."

He paused again, lifting a foot booted in a soft, thick moccasin to the dashboard and resting his bent forearm on his knee in friendly absorption with his subject.

"There are shorter ways. The Mormons went down to Bridger, then crossed the Wasatch to Salt Lake. That's as quick a route as there is. Trouble comes between Salt Lake and the Humboldt. It's mean country, mighty little water and less feed.

"Then there's the Sublette Cutoff. You've got forty-five miles of bad desert 'til you hit the Green, you've got a big alkali flat that's damn hot and you've got tough mountain roads, hard for wagons. You join back to the Bridger trail north of Fort Hall.

"Now, there's another road I've heard about but I ain't been over it. Cuts west from Soda Springs. Saves a lot of miles but it's rough and water's scarce.

"You got any questions now I'll try and answer them."

There were a lot of questions, then they let him go and the discussions began. John Hickson jumped from the wagon, disdaining to climb down by the wheel, and came walking toward me. I stood up and fell into step beside him, having a question of my own.

"You ever trap any beavers?"

He stopped and looked down, surveying me as if he'd never seen a boy before. Then he laughed, a shaking of his whole body, exposing a snaggle of stained and broken teeth. He reached out and slapped my shoulder hard enough to knock me backward.

"Did I ever trap beaver? Laddie, I'm known all around as Beaver Johnny. Why, down along the Platte and up in the Medicine Bows there ain't no hoss that's took more pelts than me, and you can ask Jim Bridger if it ain't so."

I wanted to ask him about Indians, but George Muller butted in with further inquiries about the Sublette short cut. I listened until Aunt Emeline called me to supper. There, around our evening fire, I was most flattered and gratified. As our men discussed the routes, Samson Dohne saw to it that I had the chance to repeat all of the information I had picked up. It was the first time I had had a speaking part in these councils of decision, and being listened to by the grownups was a heady excitement.

Samson heard each man out as he had his say, and it was agreed with little argument that we would go on by the longer, surer Fort Bridger, Fort Hall road.

We laid over in Fort Bridger to tighten the wagon wheels again, to repair some split reaches and for Joe Stoop to put a new pole in his wagon. Edmond Jones and I went to look up Jim Bridger. I wanted to ask him about Beaver Johnny Hickson.

"He said to ask you if it wasn't so that he's caught more beaver than anybody else in the mountains."

Bridger looked at me, then squinted his eyes up in a tight wink.

"Son, that Hickson can lie faster than a hoss can run. It ain't really lying, he just gets carried away. Like when he was down Taos way once, he got to shooting off his face to Kit Carson. Kit kind of took himself serious and Johnny annoyed him. So Kit talked him into a shooting match, each man to stand a full jug of whiskey on his head. They was to face each other at fifty paces and each shoot the jug off the other's scalp, the bet to be a hundred beaver pelt. You know what happened? Hickson, he pulled out during the night. Nobody saw him for a full year."

Edmond Jones laughed, then sobered. "So you can't believe what he said about the trails west?"

"Oh sure. There you can. That's one thing Johnny knows, the trails. It's just that he can't resist to brag." He looked at me. "You ever see a beaver, son?"

I shook my head and he thumped my shoulder. "Tell you what, you and me'll go down the creek this afternoon. Seems like I ain't been out with a youngun for years."

All the way down the stream he told me stories about these wonderful animals, how they make a dam and build their houses under water and sink logs so they can eat the bark when the winter ice covers the pond. He said they were great engineers. I didn't know whether to believe him any more than he said to believe Johnny Hickson until we got to the dam, which looked like a brush jam holding a pond behind it.

"Watch," he told me, and walked out on the dam's uncertain top, deliberately breaking an opening so that the water began to drop. Then he clambered back to the bank.

"Watch close now."

Almost as he said it I saw the king beaver surface and swim angrily to the dam. It was fascinating, the way he used his broad flat tail to propel himself, keeping submerged so that only his eyes seemed above water.

"That's Old Smokey." Bridger spoke as fondly as if he were speaking of a pet hound.

The beaver climbed up on the dam, ignoring us, and waddled over to examine the break. Other beaver appeared and I watched them in downright amazement. They seemed almost human as they worked. You could feel their anger as straightaway they began dragging sticks across the flowing water, bringing up grass and mud to plaster against the brush until the dam was whole again. In no time they were finished and again vanished beneath the tranquil little lake.

It was nearing dark when Joe Stoop appeared, ax in hand, looking for a straight sapling to cut for his wagon pole. We stood and watched him as he dropped and cleaned a young tree beside the stream, and as we started back he joined us.

Jim Bridger chuckled. "You better not leave that there overnight if you got a use for it," he said. "Old Smokey'll have it chomped in a dozen pieces and hauled away by morning."

Joe looked at him as if to say quit pulling my leg, and came on back to camp. But in the morning, when I went back with him, sure enough, the tree was gone, entirely gone, and in its place was a string of small neat piles of chips.

"Jim told you," I said. "Those beavers sure are smart."

Joe just stood there scratching his head, muttering, "I'll be doggoned. I'll be dad-burned double-danged doggoned."

It seemed to me that Joe was the only one of our group who could still take a setback in stride, except for Samson and Edmond Jones. Even Black Bob had drawn into himself and was growing more morose by the day. And Donny Scranton and Lysander Cox had quit speaking to each other. Their feud came to a boil that night.

Edmond gave a piano concert for Jim Bridger, and as a surprise for all of us, Lisbeth Peyton sat down and played a piece clear through. She wasn't very good yet, but I was as proud as if I had accomplished the feat myself.

She finished and turned around, flushed and excited.

"How was that?"

I thought she was looking at Edmond Jones, but it was Donny Scranton who scrambled to the wagon bed and reached for her hand.

"Wonderful, beautiful." The way he looked at her, she might have been a piece of cake. "I knew all the time you were the one."

Before the startled girl could withdraw her fingers he bent his head and kissed each one. She pulled loose, gasping and flustered, and I looked quickly at Edmond. He had not moved, nor did he appear displeased. In fact his lips were twisted in the quirk of a smile. Lysander, though, was red faced with fury and he started forward, his fists clenched, but was halted by Samson suddenly blocking his path.

"Get out of my way."

The words came in such a low growl that I would not have heard them had I been ten feet away.

"No." Samson's tone was also low, but solid. "We'll have no trouble here. You'll not embarrass her any more than she is."

Lysander started to speak, then choked it off. He raised a

fist against his hip and shook it toward Donny, then went raging off to his wagon.

Edmond had helped Lisbeth to the ground and she hurried to her own camp. Donny, oblivious, stood beaming after her as if he had just invented her. The others, except Edmond, were silent in embarrassment. Edmond acted as though he had just seen a great show. I edged close to him as the group dissolved.

"I thought she was your girl?"

"Did you? It isn't safe to make such an assumption, Austin."

"But you said you were going to marry her."

"So I did, but have you heard her say anything about marrying me?"

I hadn't, and I admitted it.

"It is a folly to decide that a woman will do anything until after she has done it."

Sandy had hung around when the others left, and as Edmond headed for his wagon I asked her, "What does he mean by that?"

"You're a goose," she said. "You just don't know anything."

"Now what do you mean?"

"You'll understand when you get older."

It made me mad, both of them talking in riddles, and I ran off, down to the creek beyond the wall of the fort's stockade. I stayed there as the short western twilight deepened toward night. I was just about of a mind to go back to camp when Lysander Cox's voice jerked me off the rock where I was sitting.

"You. Wait a minute. I want to talk to you."

I thought he was talking to me, but when I peered through the bushes fringing the stream I saw him facing Donny Scranton, who stood with a water bucket dangling from his hand, apparently on his way to the creek. He looked Cox up and down without expression, then side-stepped. Cox was a head the taller and outweighed Donny by thirty pounds, and he moved now to block Donny's way.

"You're going to listen, man. You embarrassed Lisbeth in front of that whole crowd back there. That's no way to talk to a good woman."

Donny said shortly, "Why isn't it? It's a compliment to want to marry a girl, isn't it?"

"Not when she's spoken for."

"Are you saying she's going to marry you?"

"That's right."

"I'll believe it when she tells me so herself. When did she agree to marry you?"

"I talked to her father before we ever started on this crazy trip. It's all arranged. Why else do you think I'd be here?"

"Arranged by who, Lisbeth or her father?"

"That don't make any difference. She'll do as her father says. She's a good girl."

Donny laughed suddenly. "You know, Cox, you're not only churlish, you're a fool. You think a girl with her spirit will have you just because her father says so, you're dead wrong. I'm going to try to get her to marry me. I give you fair warning."

"You leave her alone or I'll beat the hell out of you."

Donny stepped back. For a second I thought he was afraid, then he said evenly, "I don't think you can. I'll warn you again, I did some prize fighting back home."

"That's fine," said Lysander, and it was the first time I'd heard him sound pleased about anything. "You're asking for it. You're going to get it."

He threw a big fist, aimed at Donny's head, but Donny had danced back, tossing his bucket into the bushes.

I'd never seen two men really fight before. Back home I'd seen drunks get into an argument and swat at each other, but this was different. There was a grimness, a deadly earnestness in the way they went about it that frightened me. I wanted to run to the fort for help, but I couldn't move. They were standing now, Lysander flat-footed, swinging solidly, the way he would swing an ax against a tree.

But Donny was no tree. He took most of the blows on his arm or shoulder and his right fist sneaked in and out with the quickness of a darting snake. I saw that Lysander's lip was cut, and his nose began to bleed. Then one of his heavy blows crashed through, caught Donny on the side of his head and sent him staggering backward.

Lysander followed his fist, jumping in, wrapping his powerful arms about the smaller man, carrying him to the ground. Their fall unfroze me. I raced for the fort's gate and across the hardpacked ground. Lisbeth was the first person I saw, coming toward me with her own water bucket.

I knew that I was crying, but I was too excited to care. My voice wouldn't work as I ran up to her, and I grabbed her hand and yanked, pointing wildly behind me. She glanced at my face and began to run, asking no questions, towing me through the gate as her longer legs stretched against her flapping skirt.

"They're killing each other," I finally managed to gasp as we came up to them.

They were rolling over and over, their legs thrashing and straining for foothold. Lysander had both hands around Donny's throat and Donny was clawing at the strangling grasp.

"Stop it. Stop it." Lisbeth's voice was rough with shock.

Either they didn't hear her or their emotional momentum was too strong for them to react. Lisbeth shook my hand free and stepped in, swinging her wooden bucket in a loop over her head and bringing it down on the back of Lysander's neck and shoulders with her full strength.

The impact drove him forward, breaking his grip on Donny and sending him somersaulting over Donny's prone head. Donny coiled around and up to a crouch, facing Lysander as the big man came up to his knees, poised for another rush.

"Stop! Stop! Stop! Both of you!"

This time they heard her. This time they stopped, standing up slowly, eyeing each other warily.

Lisbeth, still holding her bucket, doubled her fists on her hips, elbows akimbo.

"Which one of you started this?"

Neither of them spoke. I piped up. "Lysander did. He told Donny to leave you alone. He said you were promised to him."

She didn't look at me. She looked at Lysander. "Did you say that?"

Lysander was wiping the blood from his nose on his sleeve. He neither looked at her nor answered.

"You go down and wash yourself. And then go back to camp."

He looked at her then, his eyes like a beaten dog's. "Lisbeth . . . please . . ."

"I don't want to talk to you. Get down to that creek."

He went in meek obedience. Donny stood rubbing his bruised cheek.

"You shouldn't have swung that bucket on him so hard."

"So"—her tone was biting—"I should have stood by and let him kill you. You get out of here too."

"Yes'm," he said and turned toward a track to the creek different from Lysander's path.

In bristling, rigid dignity, Lisbeth watched him out of

sight. Then in a voice of great disgust she said, "Men. Hmph. They're all children," and took herself and her bucket off on a third tangent to fulfill her original mission.

CHAPTER TWELVE

WE LEFT Fort Bridger with regret. The cloud of trail weariness hung over us and the frictions of long, close association bubbled, as charged as the strange waters of the Steamboat Spring. We had completed well over half our journey, but it was the easy half. We were in the mountains, and after the mountains we faced the deserts that so obsessed Lysander Cox, and after the deserts yet other mountains.

Across the Green, across the Divide and up the Bear Valley to the spring that threw its water in an eternally repeating small geyser . . . over the rough, precipitous ridge to the Snake. .

There the campsite was a nightmare of mosquitoes. We all suffered, but Black Bob was in agony. If Myrtle Stoop had not given him grease to rub on his bites I think he would have gone out of his mind, but the grease worked and the next morning, despite his swellings, Bob was in a better humor than he had been since we left Fort Laramie.

We passed the turnoff of the Hudspeth short cut and Samson bet me a plugged nickle that George Muller had gone that way. We passed Fort Hall where we heard the heartening news that we had only another seven hundred miles between us and Sutter's Fort in California. We crossed the Panack River, ascended a steep hill to a plain barren except for sage and greasewood, and plodded on through dense clouds of dust, past American Falls where the river drops over a high dyke of black shiny lava rock.

This was a country of ancient volcanos, the road broken and very hilly as it turned south to the Raft, where the California trail branches from the Oregon. Down this stream a way the Hudspeth route rejoined ours. It was just beyond the junction that we found the grave.

Sandy and Edmond and I were riding ahead of the train

in the hope of finding some game, for we had had little meat in several days. We had passed a number of graves along the way, lonely cairns of stones piled to keep the animals out, but they had meant nothing to me. Death was something that happened only to people I did not know, impersonal, outside my orbit of interest.

But a rabbit broke from this particular little mound. Edmond shot it and I ran the few yards from the trail to pick it up. As I passed the grave the words freshly burned with a hot iron deep into the rough board wedged in the head of the pile rang a familiar bell. I was already beyond it when the meaning registered on my consciousness and I swung back, reading without believing.

GEORGE MULLER

WHO LEFT HIS HOME IN WILMINGTON
OHIO TO SEEK GOLD, FOUND DEATH
INSTEAD ON THIS DESOLATE PLAIN
AUGUST TWELFTH 1815—1850

I read it three times, a feeling of unearthly terror creeping through me. Then I shouted wildly to Edmond, who came running with Sandy at his heels.

The train came up slowly. The lead wagon stopped short of the grave and the others halted, strung out behind, a puny-looking entourage under the colossal, empty sky, a pinpoint in the middle of the vast, dead landscape. The people came forward, hurrying as the word went down the line, and gathered in a little silent knot, each having his own reaction yet no one speaking. Even the youngest Stoop child was quiet. The only sound was the soft-soughing wind scraping through the brittle desert growth, ruffling my hair with a chill touch.

My aunt's convulsive sob broke the stillness at last. In life she had never thought highly of George Muller, but she had known him for as long as she could remember, and he had been a link with her home.

George had been so filled with vitality, so driving, so determined to reach the gold fields, and now he was no more. His loudness did not exist. I felt emptied, as though my breath had been sucked out of me by a sudden vacuum, and I had a picture of George lying beneath this cairn, staring unseeing into the wide sky for all eternity, the shifting gritty dirt blowing over him until no indication of his resting place remained.

Sandy stood close beside me, her slight body trembling as it pressed against me and unconsciously I put my arm around her. Aunt Emeline was crying openly, and then Edmond was speaking, slowly, in a low musical voice, repeating the words of the Twenty-third Psalm.

As he finished Myrtle Stoop gathered her brood, shaking the tears from her eyes, her words choked. "If we hadn't found him just by chance his family mightn't ever have known what happened."

We traveled only a little farther that day. We had to go on, and now the specter of death went with us. And the desert lay ahead.

The City of Rocks, a mountain of decayed and scattered stone, loomed out of the short grass which was like a sea across which you could look as if it were an ocean, and the days grew hot.

The soil grew less fertile, then stony, then sandy. The heat increased and we drove day after day in a cloud of choking dust. We jumped from stream to stream, the Raft, Goose Creek, Thousand Springs, the Mary's River. Not the tree lined waterways of the east slopes these, but naked rivers twisting between barren banks.

The water itself turned bad. Trains that had passed before us had left their exhausted animals dead in the stream beds, and beside the road the heaps of discarded possessions so increased that it seemed we marched between fences of destruction.

The Stoop children cried and whined. Everyone's nerves were raw, and as the temperature rose above the hundred mark the wearying, oppressive heat slowed even Samson's steady pace. Strangely, Lysander alone seemed oblivious of its crushing weight and grumbled the least. Aunt Emeline suffered in perspiring silence.

One of the Peyton oxen died and Peyton's saddle horse was pressed into service. Our cattle grew more gaunt and sore footed as the grass thinned out to small, widely separated tufts. Sadie, the milk cow, lowed miserably all day through and my hatred of her rose with each passing hour.

Then two of our oxen foundered on the bad water, and we were presented with the dilemma of splitting the other team or paring our goods of all but the barest necessities.

Empty faced, Uncle Ben dragged out the precious bundles of newsprint and stacked them meticulously on the ground. With unabashed tears flowing down his dust-caked cheeks, Old Ike bent to help unload the press. They had it half out of the wagon when Aunt Emeline roused from the sleepwalker's torpor that gripped her.

"Ben," her voice rose in a cry. "Benjamin Garner. You put that press back where you got it. Don't you dare . . ."

He looked at her and spoke without unclenching his teeth. "It's got to go, Emmy."

"No," she said. "No. That's our livelihood."

She scrambled into the wagon bed, sobbing aloud, and began hurling whatever she could lift onto the blistering plain. The applesauce dish shivered into a thousand pieces. The root sack bounced down. She was struggling with a bell-topped trunk when Uncle Ben caught her from behind, pulling her against him and pinning her flailing arms at her sides.

"Emmy, Emmy!" I don't think he knew that he was shouting. "Emeline, darling . . ."

Suddenly she collapsed against him, carrying him with her to the cluttered boards.

We made a dry camp where we were, and as my uncle's trembling hand bathed her pale face and overhot neck with a wet cloth, Samson called a council.

Edmond Jones leaned against the high wheel of his wagon. "Tell you what," he said in his soft, drawling voice. "Nothing much in here that either Bob or I need. Chances are the things I'm hauling won't be worth a thing in the gold fields. "Empty us out, Bob, and start loading Mrs. Garner's goods."

"Same goes for me," Donny Scranton cut in. "Seems like I've got a lot of no-account junk. I'll get rid of most of it, saving only the piano."

Samson nodded. You could see that he was very pleased. The idea of Aunt Emeline giving up the least item precious to her had gone almost as hard with him as with her.

"What about you, Peyton? You been selling stuff to everyone you met, just like a traveling store. You must have spare room."

Peyton's nutcracker jaws worked. His voice was drier than the surrounding dust. "We're coming to the desert, Dohne. I'm going to have to fill water kegs and carry extra fodder. And you all better be thinking the same way."

Samson looked baffled. Next to Edmond he was one of the most openhanded people I've ever known. He had lost everything when his buckboard washed away, yet he had not uttered a word of complaint. And it was he and Edmond who had kept the train in almost constant meat.

"Peyton," he said, "I hope you sleep well nights, but I don't know how you can."

Lysander spoke up. "Mr. Peyton has asked no help from anyone."

"No," said Samson, "and Emeline Garner hasn't asked help either. I thought we all was kind of in this together. Seems maybe I'm wrong."

I was watching Lisbeth as he spoke. Her face was a dull red as she looked at her father, but I guess she figured she could not change his mind in this.

Aunt Emeline chose that moment to revive, and Myrtle Stoop climbed to where Uncle Ben had propped my aunt against the trunk.

"Mrs. Garner," she said, "we been gathering in discards all along the way, that ain't worth the hauling. It would break my heart to see you leave your pretty things out here. You ain't going to do it. Anything you throw away, I'll pick up."

Aunt Emeline cried, trying to protest that it wasn't fair to the company, but she wasn't very coherent, and as she sat with her face in her hands her goods were distributed among the other wagons.

Then we continued down the Humboldt. The trip became an unbroken nightmare of heat and dust, of bad water and dead animals. The whole air stank with them. And for the first time we had trouble with Indians.

We had seen the Sioux east of Fort Laramie, and believed their boast that they had never shed the white man's blood, for they were a proud and intelligent race; and around Fort Hall we had met the Snakes. Although they were only half dressed, these Indians had a reputation for impeccable honesty. But the depraved Diggers of the Humboldt were known to shoot poisoned arrows at such travelers as ourselves, and to steal whatever was loose.

We saw them frequently at a distance, skulking along the low sand hills, watching us but keeping out of our rifle range. They did not attack us, but they did steal Edmond's black horse and my Prince.

Black Bob blamed himself, but I think it was my fault. We had them on picket ropes with Sadie. There was almost no grass, but there were reeds growing along the salt marshes which bordered the river, and the animals were disconsolately picking at these.

Bob left me to watch them while he tried his hand at getting the mules to drink. They refused to drink from a bucket and had already gone two days without water, for it was impossible to get them down to the river. Everyone else had given up.

I was hot and very tired and I must have dozed, sitting among the reeds. A commotion made me open my eyes. Half a dozen Indians were closing in around the horses. I jumped to my feet and tried to yell. No sound came out, and I stood paralyzed, not even thinking of my rifle.

They paid no attention to me. I don't think they even knew I was there then. They swung up bareback and started away, and I began to run. One of them saw me and shot at me. I heard the bullet whisper through the reeds close by and dived for shelter.

When I straightened, they had gone. I ran to the camp, crying, but it was too late. We had no chance to catch them.

We walked, everyone save the drivers and young children. Nor were we alone in our misery. Never were we out of sight of other travelers, most of them far worse off than we.

We walked to the Sink, where real tragedy struck us. The temperature was unbearable through the day and by midnight ice skimmed the buckets while we shivered in the desert cold. It was the last of August, with the towering Sierras still to cross.

We had ignored the Lassen Cutoff, and had a choice of crossing the desert to either the Carson or Truckee Rivers. Debating with other people in the trains camped around the Sink, it was decided we should take the longer Truckee route. From what meager reports we could glean, the road was fit for wagons all the way, while the more southern trail was said to have grades so steep that the vehicles had to be taken apart and raised by ropes.

Forty miles separated us from the Truckee and there was said to be only one spring between, a hole of boiling water. It was decided to lay over at the Sink for two days to recuperate ourselves and the animals, to fill our water casks and cut as much of the reeds as the wagons would hold, then set out across the desert at nightfall, pushing to reach the boiling spring sometime during the following morning.

All of us, even the women, fell to cutting reeds. Little Joe

Stoop, Donny Scranton, and I were working fairly close together when little Joe suddenly screamed.

"Snake. Snake."

Donny raced past me and I ran after him. By the time I got to where Joe lay howling on the salty ground Donny had ripped a strip from his little shirt, twisted a tourniquet above Joe's knee and tightened it so that the leg was beginning to whiten beneath the tan and trail grime.

The marks of the fangs stood out starkly on the small calf of the boy's leg.

Donny yelled at me. "Hold his arms, Austin."

I dropped and crawled forward, anchoring my knees on Joe's shoulders, grabbing his thrashing arms and pinning then under my full weight.

Donny had been using his sheath knife to cut reeds. He used the razor-sharp point to cut across the ugly punctures. Blood spurted up and my stomach turned over dizzily. Then Donny pressed his mouth against the cut, sucking out the blood and venom.

Sandy and Black Bob came rushing up. Little Joe was yelling at the top of his voice. Others arrived and there was much confusion. Bob helped Donny clean out the wound, then carried him to the wagon.

Sandy and I stood close together, wide eyed, the younger children grouped fearfully around us. Sandy's chin was trembling and I took her hand, squeezing it. No one said it aloud, but we were all afraid that Little Joe would die.

Night came, but no one wanted to go to bed. They had a tourniquet on Little Joe's leg, and through the wagon flap I could see Myrtle, sitting unmoving beside the boy's bed. Aunt Emeline and Lisbeth had cooked supper for all of us, and we sat huddled around the fire, waiting, no one talking.

I was the first to notice that something was wrong with Donny Scranton. He was next to me, and I thought his face was flushed beyond what the fire would cause. Then he stood up to walk toward the water keg on his wagon. He swayed as though he were drunk, and I saw that his face was swollen. I called to Ike and pointed, and just then Donny fell down.

Ike and Edmond got to him first and lifted him into his wagon. Myrtle Stoop left Little Joe and came hurrying over. No one knew what was the matter until Ike had an idea. He put a finger inside Donny's mouth, pulling down his lower lip exposing the soft pink flesh, and exposing a cut there.

I heard Ike's breath come out in a long, heavy breath. "Saw it happen once on the Santa Fe trail." He said it to no one in particular. "Snake pizon he sucked out of the little feller's leg got in through that cut. Guess that's about it."

Lisbeth's face went very white. My aunt's eyes filled with tears and she moaned softly. Myrtle Stoop said in a funny, flat voice, "He did it for my baby."

Sandy made a choking sound and slid one arm about my neck, whimpering in a shaky whisper. "He's going to die . . ."

Caroline and the younger children were bunched behind us. We all felt the cold, urgent helplessness that came from the grownups, and the kids began to bawl.

Myrtle turned on them savagely. "You brats be quiet. Sandy, take them over to our wagon, and stay there."

Sandy was shaking against me, but she stepped back and herded the children off like a goat girl with a faltering flock. No one paid any attention to me. I didn't want to stay. I had never seen anyone die, and it seemed like something terrible that no one should watch, but I could not drag myself away.

It took a long time. Donny was in agony, squirming and fighting on his bed where Black Bob tried to hold him down. The rest stood by, silent, unable to think of anything that would ease him. Then Edmond brought a bottle of brandy from his wagon, but Donny could not swallow it.

He began to talk, wild words that made no sense, that sometimes weren't even words. Then he got away from Bob's grip and lurched up on one elbow, and very clearly called Lisbeth's name.

Many eager hands reached to help her to the high level as if in some way they were aiding him, and she went to her knees beside his tossed blankets, catching his hand in both of hers.

It was hard to tell what he said. His throat muscles seemed to be stiffening.

"The piano . . . you take it . . . play it good."

Lisbeth was crying so that she could not talk much clearer than he. "Yes, Donny. Yes. I'll take care of it. I'll think of you every time I play it."

He smiled at her, but it was more a grimace than a smile.

They buried him as soon as he died. It was too hot to wait for morning. I crept under our wagon and lay there shivering. I was crying and I did not want anyone to see. I thought of how far he'd come, and now he would never see California. I wondered about the rest of us. Death seemed to join our party. Donny was the first of our little group to go. I didn't count George Muller, for he had split away from us and I had not been there when he died. But Donny, with a smile for everyone . . . it was unfair, it was a dirty trick. I couldn't understand why it should happen

In the morning I stole across to look at his grave. It was heaped with stones to keep the animals from digging it up, and someone had mounted a board from a discarded wagon. It read DONNY SCRANTON FROM PHILADELPHIA. That was all. None of us had even known how old he was.

CHAPTER THIRTEEN

IT SHOULD HAVE BEEN a morning of reverence, of respect for the dead. Instead, when I came back from Donny's grave, Grover Peyton was bawling out Lisbeth.

"Stuff and fiddlesticks," he was saying, "I will not have you drive a wagon from here to California just to cart that piano. It's not fit work for a girl."

Lisbeth was near tears, shaking her head. "But I promised Donny. I promised."

Peyton snorted. "What earthly difference does it make to Scranton now? You are not driving any wagon."

I ran in search of Samson. I did not find him, but I did find Edmond.

"Whoa up," he said as I came panting to his side. "Who set fire to your shirttail?"

"It's Peyton," I gasped out. "He's being mean like always. He won't let Lisbeth drive Donny's piano to California, and she's all upset . . ."

I never finished the sentence, for Edmond was already striding toward Donny's wagon. By the time I caught up he was facing the girl and her father, saying quietly, "I will be glad to drive the wagon on."

Peyton's light eyes were icy. "Mr. Jones, I am perfectly able to make the decisions for my family without interference from you. I have other uses for that wagon."

I had seldom seen Edmond lose his temper, but there was a note of dangerous intensity in his voice now.

101

"You seem to be laboring under a misapprehension, sir. Donny Scranton bequeathed his piano to your daughter, but I heard no mention of a wagon."

Peyton swelled like a rooster. "And what gives you the right to appropriate it?"

Edmond shook his head slowly. "I have no such intention. The disposition of the wagon should be decided by a vote of the members of our train, or by Samson Dohne. Neither, I believe, will find in your favor."

He smiled at Lisbeth, his voice softening. "Don't worry. The piano goes along."

Peyton was breathing heavily through his nose, making an ugly sound.

"Besides, it's valuable," I said. "I'll bet there aren't many pianos in California. I'll bet Lisbeth could sell it for a fancy price."

I watched Peyton's eyes change. I'd heard Old Ike say that he was as close as a cat's behind in a cold January, but I was to learn that no one held the respect for a dollar that Peyton did.

Lisbeth stood looking at Edmond, dabbing at her eyes with a crumpled handkerchief. She managed a small smile, saying, "Thank you, Edmond. I'm most grateful for your help."

He gave her a long, exaggerated wink, then said, "We'll get it through. Now you'd better rest. We move into the desert tonight."

The night drive across the desert was weird. There was no moon but there were a billion stars making an awesome roof over us. Ahead and behind we could hear the clanking of other trains, and see their swaying lanterns, but it did not make me feel any less alone. With Donny's death still fresh in my memory I felt that we were a moving island in an empty infinity, a terribly cold infinity.

It was ten in the morning when we reached the boiling spring, and now the air was stifling. I dropped down under my uncle's wagon and was asleep before the cattle were unhitched, too tired to even want a drink.

The heat finally wakened me and I stumbled over to the spring It was merely a hole in the desert floor, ten or twelve feet long and about five wide.

All the ground around it was littered with discards, and those who had gone before us had heaved much of their debris into the water itself. Black Bob and Old Ike were fishing out pieces of chain, a yoke, a rope bed spring as I came up. Ike stopped to wipe his forehead and curse.

"People," he said. "They foul their own beds. You could kill off the whole human race and the world would be a better place. Look at this stuff. Why'd they have to throw this junk in the only water around?"

Bob shook his head. "They was sore, having to let go of all these nice things."

"You'd think they'd have a care that people coming after them have to drink this water."

He had cleared a place large enough for his purpose and, still muttering, dipped his buckets into the dark liquid.

The water tasted not too bad after it had set for a while. They had waited to let the cattle drink until they had cooled out, remembering the bloated carcasses with their stiff legs in the air that lined the Humboldt. Then they tried to force the mules to drink, but these still refused although they were more dead than alive with thirst. Finally Samson spread reeds on the ground and soaked them with water, and as the mules ate this fodder they took in a little moisture.

I was famished for food, but when it was ready and before me the thought of eating sickened me. Still, under Ike's stern orders, I choked down part of a meal.

Afterward the water casks were refilled, and as the sun burned against the floating western mountains we embarked on the last twelve miles toward the Truckee. Ahead of us the Sierras had been rising from the horizon, taking the shape of mountains instead of clouds, and in the swift, brief twilight they now looked like enormous cardboard cutouts whose ascent must surely be vertical.

The road to the spring had been very rocky, but as we pushed westward we struck a belt of deep sand that deepened as we pursued its eight-mile length. Here the sides of the trail were unbroken hills of dead cattle and abandoned goods, and we passed two parties bogged to their axels, their cattle bawling and collapsing in their chains.

Their appeals for help were pathetic and Uncle Ben wanted to turn aside, but we were in deep trouble ourselves as it was. Samson laid down one of his few commands. We were too small a group to be able to give the needed assistance. There would be larger trains behind that might render aid.

We went on, struggling through the night and the sand, and then as daylight showed behind us, the cattle scented water.

Our wagons were dragging their bottoms in the loose dirt, but the animals lurched in their traces, quickening their pace. Black Bob, in the lead, let out a yell that would have shamed any Indian. Everyone, in fact, was inspired to exert themselves and Sandy and I found the strength to run lamely ahead.

A green-topped line of trees marked the river's course. Behind us the weary, famished cattle broke into a lumbering run and plunged, wagons and all, down the steep bank despite everyone's frantic efforts to stop them.

With sticks we tried to drive them from the stream before they could drink too much of the cold water. We would get them out only to have them swing back again and again.

The wagons took a beating. One of Peyton's poles was snapped, tipping the load so that part of his goods hurtled into the stream, and against all we could do the animals stood belly deep, shuddering, trying to absorb the moisture through their thick hides.

That night one of Samson's mules gave up and by morning the other was too weak to stand. Animals and people alike needed rest and it would take three or four days to repair Peyton's battered wagon. And again we must find things that we could do without—the wagons were too heavy to hope to cross the mountains which were now so close that in the crystal morning light we could see the dark foliage belting their slopes.

Lysander Cox insisted that Uncle Ben's press and the piano must be abandoned. For three days he kept insisting. Uncle Ben, who had been willing to discard it earlier, now set his chin in a stubborn lock and was ably backed up by Aunt Emeline and Ike.

Lisbeth, when it looked as if Lysander would take his ax to the piano, moved quietly and put her hands on the keyboard, and her voice was determined.

"The piano goes where I go if I have to give up everything including clothes. It was Donny's dream, and I will take care of it."

Myrtle Stoop looked at Little Joe. His leg was still bandaged and he had ridden all the way in the wagon, but aside from a marked limp he seemed to have no ill effects.

"We'll take it in our wagon," she said. "The least we can do is to get that piano to the gold fields."

So when we started up the Truckee canyon both articles were still with us. Joe mollified Lysander by repairing Peyton's outfit, the stock had had three days' rest and everyone's possessions were so mixed up in one another's keeping that no one knew what they had or had not.

The canyon road was a surprise, a pleasant one. It was far better than any of the men expected. True, it cut back and forth on itself in sharp switchbacks to climb the upthrusting cliffs behind the little lake, but it was eased by the many who had used it earlier, and again we had water and grass.

Even the snow that swirled in on us as we passed the summit was a token fall, not a blizzard such as had trapped others there.

Samson took no chance on camping at this height, but brought us down the western grade until it was full dark and the white flakes no longer reached us. There we stopped, and having no one immediately behind us, slept in the trail, and in the morning continued safely down the canyon toward Sutter's Fort, at the junction of the American and Sacramento Rivers.

We had crossed the plains and conquered the desert. The golden hills lay just ahead.

CHAPTER FOURTEEN

THE EARTH began to cool and its hardening surface captured the gasses and liquids and flowing metals. The crust heaved and sank under the writhing pressures from within, and a part of it wrinkled into the towering Sierra Nevadas, the snow mountains.

Volcanos blew open, fracturing the inner shell, and the gasses spewed forth, carrying with them in their upthrust a charge of liquid quartz, forcing it into the new fissures and filling them.

There the quartz cooled into brittle masses of tentacles all through the mountain's body, and again the volcanos belched up. The quartz shattered. Escaping gas drove jets of boiling gold and silver in to clog the crazes until the mountain's veins were crammed with solid metals.

Ages weathered and eroded the softer quartz, and great

rivers flowed from north to south, lifting the gold as it was freed from the rotting rock, concentrating it in the water's path. The riverbeds were paved with a deepening floor of the precious stuffs.

Further eruptions followed. The tertiary rivers and their glittering horde were buried beneath a thick, hard cap of lava rock. The earth convulsed, the mountain shook and the waters turned aside, blocked by the lava, and found new paths which cut across the ancient channels, flowing thenceforth westward to the Pacific.

The Feather, the Yuba, the Bear, the American, Cosumnes, Mokelumne, Stanislaus, Tuolumne, and Merced, these new streams washed and cut their gorges through the cap rock, creating deep and narrow canyons, some a thousand feet below the mountain's breast.

As they crossed the tertiary rivers they in turn gathered up the wealth with the fine, heavy particles of iron in which it was trapped. Torrential floods roiled the waters and rolled the bars, distributing it in a downward course, exposing it in the leached quartz outcroppings, laying it in the lap of man.

Gold again lined the riverbeds, slithering, sluggish snakes of it, gathering into pockets behind rock dykes, inching down the mountain, piling and piling and piling on itself.

The first nomadic inhabitants put little value on it.

The Spaniards arrived in Mexico and spread northward, searching for the fabled cities of gold. Not finding the cities, they turned to ranching and raised cattle in the south and along the coast, selling tallow and hides as far up as Monterey and Vallejo. They did not venture inland to look in the rivers. And the lode grew.

The Russian whalers and fur hunters established a settlement on Bodega Bay, a lonely outpost in a largely uninhabited land, but their eyes were turned westward toward home and the rivers continued unexplored.

The Swiss, Captain John Sutter, wangled the grant to a vast, empty empire from the disillusioned, gold-hungry Spanish sovereign, and within its borders the quiet riches lay.

The Mexican War gave over the whole territory to the United States, and bitter arguments raged around the advisability of taking on a country considered a worthless burden.

And then John Marshall, building a water wheel in one of Sutter's creeks, picked up a nugget which had found its way onto the valley floor.

The flood was now of men. It poured in from across the world upon the slopes of the high Sierras. Camps sprung up and became towns and then cities. Camps bloomed and died as their people moved overnight to the greener fields of a fresh discovery, and the miners recovered gold in such quantities that the world literally feared there would be so much of it as to reduce its value to that of lead and iron.

The American River divided the gold fields into the northern and southern mines, with first Sonora and then Columbia becoming the most important camp of the south section.

The first rush came naturally from the few Americans who were in the territory at the time of the discovery, mountain men, adventurers, soldiers left there after the Mexican War, and sailors who deserted their ships and made for the hills.

They were followed closely by Mexicans and South Americans, by convicts from the penal colony in Australia, by Chinese and Europeans and the first arrivals from the eastern states.

Sonora was founded by Mexicans and Chileans, Columbia by a company of American doctors. The population of California became cosmopolitan in the extreme with but two common denominators. Their lust for gold was one. Secondly, all were ill equipped for the venture, and the scantiness of everything in the gold fields made the suffering intense.

I was unaware of any of this as we made our way down the mountain, unaware that I was walking over the ground we had come so far to reach, that Sutter's Fort lay in the middle of a swampy valley from which the miners must backtrack with their shovels and pans.

But the camps along the creeks were no place for women and children and, desolated, I was forced to remain that first winter with Caroline and Aunt Emeline in Sacramento.

Our train dissolved itself there, its members again becoming disassociated individuals and taking off each in his chosen direction with lamenting farewells and assurances that we would see one another again.

Samson Dohne had attached himself to us at the outset of our trip, and he was with us still when the others had departed. Making no pronouncement of his plans, he set to with Ike and Uncle Ben to build Aunt Emeline a one-room log cabin. I began to appreciate his capacities.

I had not gotten to know him well on the wagon train.

Edmond Jones was my hero then. Edmond was older than Samson, more polished and he had a detached humor that could throw an amusing light on a situation no matter how grim the reality was. But looking back, I know that it was Samson, his bulldog stubbornness and unbending honesty that held us together and brought our disparate group to port with fewer mishaps and less anguish than was endured by the majority of the travelers who crossed the country. It was he who made life tolerable for us during the first miserable winter, and who continued to stand by when help was needed most.

By the time we arrived, an embryo town had begun to develop on the high ground around Sutter's Fort. The captain and the earliest settlers had envisioned a sizable city within Sutter's empire, and laid out a network of streets which stretched down to the banks of the river. Already it was being called Sacramento.

It was late in the year. Emigrants were pouring over the mountains daily in varying degrees of exhaustion. Some were afoot and destitute, but all were eager to reach the river canyons from which the flow of gold dust was an ever-increasing tide.

Lumber in Sacramento was selling at five hundred dollars a thousand when it could be found, and the previous arrivals had already stripped the trees along the riverbank until it was difficult to find enough wood for fuel.

Most of the cabins were mere wooden frames over which cloth from the wagons was tacked, and such was our first home. It was little protection from the cold and the penetrating rain. We wallowed in mud.

The days became a kaleidoscope of changes for me, most of them unhappy, and I cannot now put them down in chronological order.

The Stoops settled on a lot a hundred yards below us. Peyton departed downriver for the town of Stockton because he heard that this would soon become the outfitting point for the southern mines. Edmond sold his wagon to Sam Brannan and took passage on a river steamer for San Francisco, saying that he meant to see the Golden Gate and the great bay before he quit moving.

I walked with him and Bob down to the muddy embarcadero, trying to argue him out of leaving.

"Why do you want to go way off there, if you want to marry Lisbeth?"

He looked down at me, his left eyebrow arching as it always did when he was amused. "And that I intend, Austin, but the time for marrying is after I find where I want to settle."

I still tried to hold him with us. "But didn't you come out here to dig gold? It will be all gone before you ever get back from San Francisco."

"If that's all there is, then all of us were fools to come so far. Don't worry, they'll be taking gold out of these hills for years to come."

Desolately I watched him mount the short plank which connected the steamer with the rickety wharf, saw the lines cast off and saw the boat pull out into the sluggish current. It was like the cutting of a cord between us. I felt that I had lost my best friend, and was certain that I would never see him again.

Back at our cabin there was a new threat. Mr. Burnett, Captain Sutter's agent, had been there and told my uncle that our cabin had been built on ground belonging to Sutter, ground not set aside for the town, and that we would have to get off.

Aunt Emeline sat on a stump outside, her shoulders drooping, staring emptily at nothing. Uncle Ben had a driven but dogged look. Then Old Ike came in, huffing indignantly, saying that all of the people who were camped or had cabins along the river had had the same notice, that none was paying any attention to the eviction, and that Burnett had not the force to do anything about it.

Uncle Ben brightened like a sunflower on a summer morning, and announced that with the family thus securely established, it was time for him to think of business. He made no objection when I trailed him into town.

As a bee searches out honey, his steps turned down Front Street, directly toward a small cabin, the office of the Placer *Times*.

The publisher introduced himself as J. H. Giles, and warmly welcomed us. He was a friendly man with few formalities. He had been a printer, he said, with the New York *Tribune* before coming West, and he proudly exhibited his paper.

It was a little sheet, thirteen by eighteen inches, very badly printed on a heavy stock called Spanish foolscap, and my uncle frowned as he fingered it. Mr. Giles explained that the native Californians used it for everything from wrapping their packages to rolling their cigarettes, but as newsprint it took ink very badly.

"I'll tell you, Ben," he said. "If you've got an 'office' I'd like to buy it. I'm using an old Ramage press that was shipped out of Boston to Monterey in eighteen thirty-three. It's the same kind that Ben Franklin used for his *Poor Richard.*"

"This," said my uncle, "I have got to see."

Giles walked us back into the tiny shop, laughing. The press had a wooden frame and the inking roller was home-made of glue and molasses.

"Last summer," Giles said, "I had to bury it in the ground to keep it from melting. And the platen keeps warping. I have to even it with a jack plane every time I use it."

I was looking at the boxes of worn type and thinking smugly of our cases, which Ike kept with fussy care.

"You see," said Giles, "I really need your office. How much do you want?"

"It's not for sale." My uncle shook his head. "I dragged that office three thousand miles, and I'm going to put it to use as soon as I find the right place to set up."

Giles sighed, and a wariness crept into his tone. "You know, Garner, this ain't the best climate for newspapers, and that's a fact. There been better than a dozen started in San Francisco, and the *Alta* is about the only one's got its head still above water."

"Too bad." Uncle Ben was only mildly interested in the mortality of the press in San Francisco.

"So you better sell us your office," Giles pushed on. "We can't pay cash, but I'll give you a thousand dollars for it, one hundred down."

Again Uncle Ben shook his head, smiling.

"You're not figuring to start up here in Sacramento?" There was worry in Giles' voice. "There ain't enough business for one paper."

"No," Uncle Ben told him. "I want to get closer to the diggings. I didn't come over that trail to sit and rot in a swamp."

Giles made no effort to hide his relief, and his friendliness expanded again as my uncle asked, "Where would you suggest as a good place?"

"Now that's a hard one to answer. Sonora's about the biggest town in the southern mines. Most of the camps don't have more than two, three hundred men working. They ain't

110

towns like we knew them back East. I'd say, wait until next year before you start. Maybe something will open up somewhere."

My uncle was very thoughtful all the way back to the cabin, and he said something that shocked me.

"You know, Austin, maybe we made a mistake, coming out here. It isn't the way I envisioned it, at all."

I was feeling let down too. For myself, I'd been here three weeks and had not picked up a single nugget. But I didn't think he meant what he said until I heard him talking to my aunt that night. I slept in the wagon with Samson and Ike, but the cloth walls of the cabin did not close out sound. Ike was snoring regularly, but between his respirations I could hear the voices.

"Maybe I'd better take you and the children down to San Francisco and find a boat that's sailing for the East Coast."

I held my breath. As a boy, the discomforts meant little to me, and I wanted to stay and look for gold.

"What brought this up?" My aunt sounded surprised. "It's not like you to talk about quitting anything."

"I made a mistake. I admit it. This is no place for women and children. I'll take you home."

There was a long silence, and then her voice, sounding very solemn and soft through the night.

"No. No you won't, Ben. Back home you had a call, something very strong that pulled you away. I fought you as hard as I could, but when you stood your ground against all of us, I was proud of you. You're not going to convince me now that it was just a weak man's whim that uprooted us. I couldn't stand that. You haven't even been to the mines yet. What's discouraged you so?"

He told her what Giles had said. "A lot of papers have been tried here, but they all die after a couple of issues."

"Pooh," she said. "They don't know how to run a paper. I've seen that silly thing they call a newspaper. Now when you and Ike . . ."

"I'd like to see the mines," he cut in, and he sounded wistful, "but I can't take you there. The life's too hard, too uncertain for a woman."

To my immense surprise, she giggled. "Oh, my great big strong husband, my dear. Who walked halfway across this continent beside you? I think, Ben, that I shall survive. As for the mines, tomorrow you and Ike and Samson will start

111

off. The children and I will be all right here. You go and look over the camps, so in the spring we'll know where to locate."

"Em"—his voice was thick—"you are the greatest woman a man ever had, and I used you cruelly."

"Stuff and nonsense. You made me open my eyes and look around me. What woman in Wilmington has seen the things I've seen? Now, go to sleep."

And so we stayed in California.

The men left us. All of those who had been with us on the trail were gone. Joe Stoop was the first to return. He tried mining only long enough to find that working up to his waist in the icy waters along the sand bars was not for him. Then he took a job driving a wagon for Sutter, bringing grain and supplies down from Hock Farm on the Feather River.

My aunt and Myrtle Stoop drew closer together from sheer loneliness. I do not know by what feminine logic my aunt eased her conscience.

Between them they decided that we children needed schooling, and my aunt set up a class in our cabin. We sat on the floor, shivering in the damp air, for the sheet-metal stove which my uncle had bought from Sam Brannan seemed never to give enough heat.

I was scornful of the project. With my uncle and the others away I deemed myself the man of the family and the bread-winner. I milked the cow morning and night, though hating her, and what surplus there was over what we and the Stoops used, I sold easily, for a good price.

All prices were high. Food was scarce as the town grew daily. More and more gold seekers came up the river from the ships arriving in San Francisco, and discouraged miners dropped back from the canyons where the rivers had risen and made work impossible.

And then Joe Stoop began his rise to fame.

He had left Sutter to become a driver for J. E. Birch, who had built up the first stage line in the state, running to both the northern and southern mines.

Sandy came racing down the wheel track which served as our street, unable to contain herself.

"Pa shot a man last night," she panted.

I was in the yard, chopping up some oak branches, and no one else heard her. I dropped my ax and gaped at her.

"Why?"

She fought for her breath, gasping out her words. "He was bringing in the Stockton stage. A man held him up. Pa shot him dead."

That Joe had shot a man had sent a bolt of fear through me. That he had shot a holdup artist was another thing, and I saw its worth instantly.

"Who knows about it?"

She shook her head. "Nobody but us and Mr. Birch, I guess. Birch is looking for the sheriff to go out and get the bandit. Pa just come home. He's some shook up."

I ran for their camp. Joe was seated at their rickety table, eating cold biscuits and drinking the black liquid we made by boiling charred corn, in place of coffee.

He looked more skinny and insignificant than ever, and his uncertain eyes shifted when I demanded to be told the story.

"I don't want to talk about it, Austin. I don't rightly like to think I killed somebody, even if he was a robber."

"But look," I argued, "nothing much exciting happens around here. This is real news. You'll be a hero."

Joe blinked, then gave me a derisive snort, but Myrtle, across the table, sat back slowly, folding her fists loosely on her big hips.

"Why now," she sounded pleased. "Austin's right, Stoop. Speak up. Ain't just every man can shoot down a robber, and that when he's holding a shotgun on you."

My eyes bugged. I couldn't believe it. I pleaded with him.

"Tell me, please. I'll write it down and get Mr. Giles to run it in tomorrow's paper."

Joe lowered his head and plucked at a spot on his shirt, glancing sidewise at Myrtle.

"Don't seem dignified, a man going around blowing his own horn . . ."

"How else is anybody going to know what happened?" I said. "You let people start guessing and they'll get it all mixed up."

He watched me a moment longer and then nodded. "Well, I guess that could change things . . . All right. I was coming in with an empty stage, and this hombre steps out of the bushes with a stocking over his head. He points a shotgun at me and tells me to hold up. There's a little grade, not much, but the team was walking, and the first thing I knowed, I was looking right into these twin barrels. Believe me, sonny, they looked as big as cannon. I like to swallowed my Adam's apple and my tongue too. I haul up so hard I near broke the horses' necks."

Myrtle cut in angrily. "Stoop, you are a damn fool. Always have been . . . always will be."

His slack mouth curved, mocking her. "Because I didn't want my ass full of buckshot?"

"Because for the first time in your glaked life you've got the chance to be looked up to, and you ain't got the common sense to take it. You think I want my kids to grow up hill trash all their lives?"

He sighed deeply. "Ma, one thing I ain't is a blowhard liar . . . Anyhow, I haul up and this feller tells me to throw down the box. So I lean down to get it from between my feet, and my hands hits the gun that Birch made me take along. I'd stuck it there because it was heavy in my pocket."

I was breathless. "And then you thought of shooting him."

"Didn't neither. I just took it up and shot before I thought. Had I been thinking I'd never have done it."

"And he hit him right between the eyes," Sandy said.

Myrtle smiled proudly. "Joe always could shoot faster and straighter than anybody else. I've watched him knock the head off more than one turkey at the shoots. It's the reason I married him."

I'd half-wondered why she chose him. At the moment, however, I was impressed by the feat.

"Was there much dust in the box?"

Joe lifted his shoulders. "I don't know. The Reynolds agent who shipped it didn't say. But Birch was some happy when I brought it on in."

"I'll say he was," Myrtle said. "Joe, show him the ring Birch gave you."

Stoop extended one of his knuckled hands. On his little finger was a gold ring with a diamond in it. The diamond wasn't very big and I learned later that Birch had loaned a miner twenty dollars on it and the man never showed up again, but it was a diamond.

I took off for the newspaper office at a dead run, praying that Giles had not yet heard of the robbery and killing.

He hadn't. He had been up at Brannan's store, talking with the Mormon leader, and we arrived at the shop at nearly the same time.

I made no preamble. "I've got a story," I said.

He considered me. "You're Ben Garner's kid, aren't you?"

"He's my uncle."

"Ben send you?"

"He's gone to the mines."

"Well, and what's your story?"

"It's Joe Stoop, the stage driver," I said. "He killed a holdup artist on the Stockton run. There was thousands of dollars' worth of dust in the box, and if Joe wasn't one of the bravest men in California the man would have got it."

Giles looked skeptical. "Stoop don't seem overly courageous to me."

I stood as tall as I could. "Mr. Giles, would you draw a revolver and shoot a man square between the eyes when he was holding a shotgun loaded with buckshot on you?"

Giles spat toward his tin pan, making it ping. He raised an eyebrow and regarded me.

"No man in his right mind would, or I dare say could."

I nodded emphatically. "Joe Stoop did. You can see for yourself when they bring the body in. Joe's the best shot that ever came out of the Ohio hills. He blew the head off every turkey at every shoot back there. And he kept us in meat all across the country."

Giles was listening with a dubious frown. Finally he said, "I'll go ask Birch," and started for the door.

"He's not there," I called after him. "He went out with the sheriff to bring in the body. But he gave Joe a diamond ring."

Giles turned back. "He did, huh? All right, you tell me the story."

I held my breath. "I can set it up in type better."

Both his eyebrows went up. "How old are you anyway?"

"Eleven, going on twelve."

"And you think you can set type?"

"I've been a 'devil' since I was six."

He put a hand over his mouth, but it didn't quite hide his smile. "Well, have at it then. But you've got to break down the form if I can't use it the way it's set."

I jumped to the makeshift "case." I'd never seen such a mess. The type was in three different sizes. Giles had cut out the side of O' to make Cs and managed to tack tails on others for Qs. But by drawing from the full assortment I found what I needed.

I still have a copy of the proof I pulled, for this was my first real story, and I was proud of it. I spent all afternoon at the stone, for I made mistakes and my spelling was not the best, but Giles ran it just as I put it up.

The story read:

BRAVE STAGE DRIVER SAVES TREASURE CHEST

Joe Stoop, late of Wilmington Ohio and at present employed by the Birch Pioneer Stage Line, saved the money box for his employer and Reynolds and Company Express by shooting a would-be robber directly between the eyes.

Mr. Stoop who in his own state was a noted shot and an utterly fearless man, was driving the stage between Stockton and this city last night when a highwayman stepped from the brush and leveling a shotgun on him, commanded him to halt.

Mr. Stoop pulled up his team and the robber, who was masked by having pulled a stocking over his head, ordered him to throw down the money box.

Instead Mr. Stoop drew a revolver which he had concealed beside the box for just such an emergency, and with no thought to his own peril shot the highwayman before the startled robber could pull the triggers of the shotgun.

The shots so startled the four horses that they ran away, and it was some miles before Stoop was able to get them under control.

There were no passengers in the coach at the time.

Mr. Birch was so pleased that he presented the valiant driver with a valuable diamond ring which Mr. Stoop now wears proudly on his little finger.

More honor toward you, Mr. Stoop. It is men like you who will tame this wilderness and bring law and order to these hills, protecting us all.

The Times salutes you, Diamond Joe, and hopes that you will drive many more miles in safe dispatch of your sworn duty.

Anxiously I watched Giles' face as he read the proof. Finally he put it down on his desk, walked around the desk, his eyes still on the paper warily, as though it might explode, and at length sat down before it.

"I don't really believe it. How old did you say you are?"

I repeated my age.

"Where'd you learn all the big words?"

"My uncle makes me read a lot of books, like Dickens and Thackeray and such."

Giles scratched his head. "I'll be double damned. I'll be dadburned, doggoned, hornswoggled double-damned."

I left him sitting there and carried a proof home to my aunt. She read it in neutral silence, then she focused on me squarely.

"Austin, is this exactly the way Joe Stoop told you it happened?"

"Well, no." I scraped the earth floor with the side of my boot sole. "But Ike always says to give the story the best of it, so long as you don't get too far from the truth."

She sighed. "Do you know what you have done? You have made poor Joe into a hero."

"Well, he is, isn't he? He did shoot the robber, just the way it says."

"Yes . . ." She admitted it slowly, thoughtfully. "I only hope that you haven't given him a reputation he can't live up to."

"Oh, he'll live up to it all right. Myrtle's seen him shoot the heads off of flying turkeys."

"I didn't mean with a gun," she said, but she didn't explain what she meant.

I went down to the Stoops' and read the page aloud to them. Not that Myrtle and Joe couldn't read, but I read faster.

Myrtle's face glowed. Joe looked sheepish. Sandy kissed me right in front of everyone, and neither her mother nor father seemed concerned. I was terribly embarrassed, and to cover that I said, "I hope you like it."

Joe squirmed. "The boys are gonna laugh at me."

"No they ain't." There was a dangerous note in Myrtle's voice. She got up and brought Joe's gun to the table. "You shove that in your belt and nobody's gonna laugh at you no more."

"You ought to go down to the leather man and get yourself a holster," I said.

I did not realize what I was doing, but I had created a new Joe Stoop. The day after the paper came out people stopped him on the street to shake his hand, and the next week he bought a full suit of black clothes. Sandy told me it was the first real suit he had ever owned.

Captain Sutter and Sam Brannan began speaking to him. For a while Joe shaved every day, then he grew a beard, and it altered his whole appearance, hiding his slack mouth and thin jaws.

117

There was talk of making him city marshal, but he preferred driving the stage. He would stand in front of the stage office, waiting for time to start, blowing on his ring and polishing it on his sleeve. You could hear the passengers whisper, "That's Diamond Joe. He's killed at least five men."

Giles printed frequent articles about him, and some of them were true. It was the first time I had watched a character being created in newsprint, though not my last, and I watched in awe.

But the impact on the Stoop family was even more startling than the effect on Joe himself. They became for the first time people of importance.

Sandy told me about it one day as we hunted driftwood along the edge of the river.

"You don't know what it means, Austin, to be a somebody," she said in wonderment. "When I go downtown now people say, 'That's Diamond Joe's girl. Isn't she pretty . . .'"

I looked at her. Sandy was changing fast. She didn't look like a kid any more. And she was filling out, for with a steady job Joe was making more money than he had ever seen. There was color in her cheeks and her freckles were not nearly so noticeable.

They had money to buy food, and, to my aunt's deep chagrin, had it not been for the Stoops we Garners would have gone hungry at times that first winter.

CHAPTER FIFTEEN

IN JANUARY Uncle Ben returned. He was shockingly thin, and he'd developed a cough. Samson brought him down while Ike stayed on the claim they were working on the Stanislaus River below Melones. They had disappointing news. They had not made much more than wages for their mining.

Samson was horrified to learn how short of supplies we were. He borrowed a horse and in three days brought in three deer.

My uncle read my story about Joe Stoop and grinned. "A good job, Austin. How's Joe making out?"

"He's fine. They had a shooting match Christmas Day and Joe won. He got a turkey and a gold watch."

My aunt sniffed. "You should see him. When he's home he struts all over town parading that gun. You'd think he'd shot a dozen men, the way he carries on."

Joe got in from a run and came immediately to see my uncle. He sat in a rough chair beside the bunk my aunt and I had rigged, twisting the beaver hat he now wore around and around in his hands.

"You don't look so good, Ben. This mining business, it ain't for the likes of us."

My uncle watched him, fascinated. "Maybe you're right, Joe. California isn't a very soft berth."

"It's been good to me," said Joe. "There ain't a better driver in the southern mines than me. Come spring I might just start a line of my own. Maybe you could run the office for me. I ain't so much at writing and figuring yet, though Sandy's teaching me . . ."

When he had gone my aunt was indignant. "The very nerve of him. I always did say, give trash an inch, they take a mile."

My uncle's smile was weak, though amusement still showed in his dull eyes.

"I'm glad to see him getting on. I like old Joe."

"Of course," said my aunt. "And they've been mighty kind to us. But when Joe Stoop tries to patronize a man like you, that's just too uppity."

My uncle started to chuckle, but it turned into a cough. I've never seen anyone cough harder. It scared me. Two people had died of consumption back home.

I went out to where Samson was squaring a log with a sharp-bladed ax. He'd hired a wagon that day and gone upriver looking for timber, vowing to build us the tightest cabin in California.

"You think Uncle Ben's real sick?"

Samson stopped and tested his blade on his callused thumb. "He ain't well."

"You think he's got consumption?" I hardly dared speak the word aloud.

He shook his head. "Chills and fever, I'd say. There's a lot of it on the creeks. Ben wasn't cut out for that kind of labor, but he's stubborn. Even Ike couldn't do much with him."

I changed the subject, relieved. "What was it like at the

mines?" This was the first chance I'd had to really talk with him since they'd come back.

"Wet," he said, and went on with his work. "It's the wettest rain I ever saw. We got nothing like it in Kentucky. It rains and the chill goes right through you, though it don't often get cold enough to snow."

I knew what he meant. Even in Sacramento when it rained the chill could turn you blue.

"But what's a mine like?"

He thought that over reflectively. "Well, they're all different. Ours is on a kind of sand bar. There's a lot of big boulders, some half as big as this cabin. We dug a trench down close to the river, clear to bedrock. Then we made what they call a dip box. It's like a snubbed-off sluice box. You dump your sand into it, then you hold up one end of the box with one hand and dip a bucket of water from the river and pour it over the sand. That washes off the worthless stuff, down to the black sand. Then you take that out and pan it down to the gold."

"Sounds sort of slow," I thought aloud. "You ought to have a machine like George Muller made."

"Only thing he ever did right." Samson was sour. "They got all kinds of rigs, but it's all hard work and your uncle, he ain't really strong enough for it."

"That's what Aunt Emeline says, and Joe Stoop. Joe wants Uncle Ben to go to work for him."

Samson gave me a long look and went on with trimming the log. That evening I heard him talking to my uncle, as if he were still captain of the train.

"Ben," he said, "you made a mistake coming out here. You ain't properly fitted to be a miner."

My uncle smiled tiredly. "I never intended to be one. I only wanted to get the feel of it, and make enough to buy paper to start my weekly."

"They already got one here."

"I don't mean here. Remember that camp we came through on our way back from the diggin's, Sonora?"

Samson admitted that he remembered.

"I've got a hunch on Sonora," said my uncle. "That town is going to grow. The main road to all the southern camps goes through it. All the supplies the miners need have to go out from there. Come spring, we'll set up a paper there."

So it was that despite Samson's protests, we moved to Sonora the first of April.

It was my first trip to the mining area since we had dropped down the foothills with the train, when I hadn't realized where I was. I had pictured whole mountains gleaming with the yellow metal, but what I now saw was but ugly banks of sand and shallow pot holes strung along the creeks.

We found a cabin north and a little east of town. The town itself was tiny, a few merchants and a sprinkling of cabins inhabited by miners who were working the ground there. But the Sonora area, along Woods Creek and under Table Mountain was a feverishly busy place. There must have been a thousand men scattered unseen out through the brush, maybe more. You couldn't really tell, because they were a restless bunch. Those who were there one day would have vanished the next, the gold on the next creek always looking richer and easier to reach, and onto the vacated claim another eager gold seeker would move.

The day of our arrival was windy and blustery, the mud nearly hub deep as our two wagons turned into the quagmire of Sonora's main street, and I knew by my aunt's face that she faced this new move with less than enthusiasm.

Looking back, I wonder at her fortitude. The single room of the cabin was less than ten feet square, and incredibly dirty. It had been vacant for weeks and the pack rats had moved in. The former occupant had decamped for some new strike in such precipitate haste that he had abandoned many of his possessions, and they were now dragged and scattered about the earthen floor.

My uncle's cough was worse and his cheeks had a fever flush. My aunt mucked out a small space and made him a bed in one corner while Samson built up a blaze in the rock fireplace, that being the only way of heating the cheerless place.

Without complaint she changed from her traveling dress and went to work. She swept the cobwebs from the sod ceiling and pole walls, swept the floor down to clean soil and arranged her meager things as Samson carried them in from the wagons.

That is one of my warmest memories of my aunt. She could be shrewish. She could make life difficult and uncomfortable for those about her when she chose, but when something required doing she was first to grapple with the problem.

She sent me for wood, sent me exploring for the nearest

water, and by evening of the first day she had made the interior of the rough shack into a place of some livability.

Again Samson built her a second room, and then a lean-to kitchen to house the iron range we had hauled up from Sacramento.

Ours was one of the first cook stoves in the camp. It had a well for heating water, and there was a tin bathtub in which I was thoroughly scrubbed every Saturday night. These do not sound like creature comforts now, but in the spring of 1850 on the Mother Lode they were almost unheard-of conveniences.

Next, Samson built the cabin for the print shop, and my uncle, against my aunt's harping insistence that he was too ill to be out of bed, set up the press and the boxes of type.

Debilitated though he was, there was a new life in Uncle Ben, a hopeful urgency and a hint of his old gaiety. He had his office, he had his territory, and he had paper.

Before we left Sacramento, Mr. Giles had come to bid us goodbye. He too was leaving, turning the Placer *Times* over to a new editor, a Mr. Lawrence, and going back East.

"Ben," he'd said, and his eyes had laughed, "I'll bet you I'm the only newspaperman who's taken any money out of this benighted place. I've made me a little pile, and I'm going to run with it. Hope you make out as well."

I didn't hear the rest of the conversation, but somehow Uncle Ben conned him out of enough of his precious paper to print a hundred copies of an issue.

To Sonora he had brought a copy of the San Francisco *Alta*, and had arranged with Mr. Lawrence to send him a news letter once a week. Now he wandered about the new camp, making friends, which he always did so easily, picking up stray bits of fact and gossip.

At last he was ready for business, and the spring looked bright and promising.

The first issue of the Sonora *Clarion* appeared April 20. It was a single sheet, printed on both sides, and I still have a copy of the original press run. It was badly printed, since my uncle had never been the craftsman with the press that Old Ike was, and news was scarce. But it was our paper, and I felt as though we were again complete.

The *Clarion* announced at its masthead that it was a free, liberal, unbiased digest of the world's events, and that it would appear every Thursday afternoon.

My aunt haggled with Uncle Ben about the price until

the day of issue, and this argument she won. As a writer and publisher he had little interest in the financial facts of life. Aunt Emeline was looking for profit. She pointed out that there was no competition, that the isolated miners were starved for news, for any word of the outside world, and made the telling point that with so few businesses yet open in this budding community there could be little advertising revenue. The price, she said, was one dollar.

Samson and I rode through the apparently empty hills, from one miner's cabin to another, with the hundred copies tucked into our saddle bags. Hardly a camp we visited declined our offering.

We had no gold scales and the men had almost no cash. There was very little coinage in circulation in the mines through that first season.

Samson solved the difficulty.

Sonora's one saloon, a plank counter with a broached keg of whiskey sitting at one end with six tin cups ranged beside it, served drinks for a pinch of gold each.

The proprietor, Houser, had an unusually broad thumb and forefinger. In paying for his drink a miner produced his poke, a small chamois bag usually made of doeskin in which he kept the fine grains of gold he had washed from the sand. Houser licked his fingers to wet them and thrust his thumb and forefinger into the poke. Whatever gold he was able to bring out with his pinch was the price of the drink.

Samson's fingers were even broader than Houser's, and for each paper he extracted one pinch. When the issue was sold out and we returned to Sonora, the local gold buyer gave Uncle Ben three hundred and twelve dollars for the dust we brought in. Even Aunt Emeline was pleased.

We also brought Ike with us. We had stopped at Melones on our swing and found Ike deeply disgusted with the business of mining. He vowed that it was the last time he would ever touch either a shovel or a gold pan.

We spent three days at the diggin's while he made his final cleanup. It was my first experience in the art and I've never quite forgotten my thrill when Ike pointed out the bright string of colors edging the fan of black sand in the bottom of the pan.

I'd seen a lot of dust by now, but the colors looked different here, each flake separated from the others. Some were paper thin, so light that they nearly floated. Others were thick and heavy. Some were the size of a small pea.

123

In all Ike had more than seven hundred dollars worth of dust, and I couldn't understand why he was so anxious to leave. But after watching the miners for three days, working up to their knees and waists in the snow water of the muddy river, with rain beating down upon them, I grudgingly conceded that Ike was right in contending that money wasn't worth its cost.

"This ain't California," he told Samson. "This is plain hell, and the Devil never thought up a worse torture than for a man to work a placer claim."

I didn't spend all of my time with them, but went investigating up the shoreline. There was about a hundred men on the bar and their methods of extracting the gold were as different as the individuals. One company had built a ground sluice, digging a trench about three feet wide and twenty long. At the bottom, they had made riffles of flat stone. They threw gravel in at the head of the trench, then with a Chinese water wheel they raised water from the river and flooded it over the sand. This washed out the pulverized rock and left the stones, the heavy black sand and the gold caught behind the riffles. Once a week they shut off the water, climbed down into the trench, threw out the stones, scooped up the silt and panned that out by hand.

The water wheel intrigued me. It was an ingenious contraption, two wheels linked together with a reverse gear. The larger wheel was fitted with wide paddles and was turned rapidly by the swift stream. The smaller turned in the opposite direction. Around its rim were nailed cups which dipped up water and dumped it into a wooden trough. The trough led the flow across to the sluice.

There were gold machines aplenty, rockers, cradles, plain sluice boxes. But the majority were in too much haste to waste time building, and dug sand from small shafts, carted it to the river's edge and squatted in the shallow water, shaking their pans with a circular rhythm so that the lighter stuff sloshed over the side while the heavy particles sank and the tiny precious flecks were gradually exposed.

The problem for everyone was then to separate the gold from the iron sand. First the nuggets were carefully picked out. Those fortunate enough to have a flask of mercury treated the residue with the silver light liquid. The mercury took up the gold, changing in color and becoming a paste-like substance called amalgam.

This was squeezed through a chamois bag. The leather

permitted the mercury to pass through it while it retained most of the gold specks. After several usings the mercury became "tired." It was then heated in a kind of still. The mercury was driven off in a vapor, which condensed again to liquid in a water-cooled tube, while the gold melted into a single button at the bottom of the crucible.

Exciting as it was, I was glad to return to Sonora, deciding that my uncle and Ike were right, that we were newspapermen, not miners.

Uncle Ben was glad to see Ike and especially pleased with the dust he had collected. That, with the money from the *Clarion* sales gave them close to a thousand dollars, enough to buy more paper. But there was no paper closer than San Francisco.

Uncle Ben and Ike set out for Stockton, where they could catch a boat down the San Joaquin River. I begged to go. I wanted to see the city and the bay filled with abandoned ships which everyone was talking about, and mostly I hoped to see Edmond Jones.

But my aunt put her foot down firmly. Something else was being talked about: a rash of robberies and murders on the highways which had led to the formation of the first Vigilante committees. It was no place for a child, she said. She did not even want my uncle to go, but he had a solid argument. How could a man become a publisher without newsprint?

CHAPTER SIXTEEN

THE TOWN OF Sonora had been founded by a party of Mexican miners and named for their home province. Its early population were Spanish-speaking people from Mexico and the west coast of South America who had rushed northward at the first cry of gold.

But by now we Americans were already in the majority, and while the town still had a Spanish flavor which marked its customs and social life, the easygoing Latins were being shoved aside by the single-purposed Yankees.

A foreign mining tax was charged by most districts upon those who had not been born in the United States, and many of the Mexicans and Chileans were leaving for the more remote camps. Still, a lot of them remained, working their claims down the tortured course of Woods Creek and the dry placers along the edge of Table Mountain.

I made friends with a number of them and began picking up their language.

The weather turned warm and the rains ceased. My aunt continued schooling Caroline and me, and I had chores to do, but beyond those restrictions I was free to roam the hills and streams.

The winter rains had sluiced the tailing piles left by the transient miners, exposing small nuggets that had been missed. I hunted these and searched the stream bed for colors. I accumulated a small hoard of gold dust and carried it secretly in a tiny leather bag.

But I felt a strange loneliness. Samson was busy adding to the print shop and my uncle and Ike had not returned from San Francisco. I missed the Stoop kids, especially Sandy, and I missed the comparative activity of Sacramento.

Sonora seemed empty. There were only three or four stores, a makeshift hotel with canvas sides, two saloons, and two fandango parlors. These latter were situated in what we called Spanish Town, on the flats south of the creek, to which I was strictly forbidden to go. Yet I managed to create an occasional excitement.

I was on Washington Street one morning, headed home, having found a small, star-shaped nugget, when a man stopped me in front of the Golden West Saloon. I had never seen him before.

He was full-bearded and his uncut hair was caked with mud, his hands cracked and scabbed beneath gloves of grime. His clothes could have stood by themselves, and he carried a bundle wrapped in a hide, the hair still on it.

He stepped in front of me, his eyes eager.

"Aren't you the newspaper fellow's boy?"

I nodded. "He's my uncle."

"I hear you folks have got a stove with hot water in it, and a bathtub."

I admitted that this was so.

"I been looking for your uncle." He sounded oddly embarrassed. "He in town today?"

126

"He went to San Francisco to find some paper to print the *Clarion* on."

The man's face fell, then he peered at me speculatively.

"You think if I asked her your aunt would sell me a bath? Trying to wash in that creek, with everybody stirring up the mud, and it as cold as ice anyhow . . . I ain't been clean in six months."

I was horrified that anyone wanted of his own volition to take a bath, but everyone had his own oddity. I shrugged.

"Sure, I guess so. Come on, I'll show you our house."

He walked with me up the street, telling me how he had worked a claim alone all winter, his nearest neighbor a mile away. He must have been really lonesome, because he talked a blue streak all the way.

"This is it," I told him as we turned in toward the door. "Aunt Emeline's inside."

I reached the door and opened it just as Caroline, playing in the yard, making mud pies, got one of her cute ideas and let fly with one that caught me square between my shoulders. I swung around to settle with her and left my miner standing on the threshold.

I scooped up a mud ball and hurled it at my fleeing cousin, aware from the corner of my eye that Aunt Emeline had appeared in the doorway, her broom in her hand. Then I heard the miner stammering to her.

"Ma'am, you've got . . . I'll give you five dollars . . ."

Before he could finish I heard my aunt's sharply indrawn breath, and as I ran back toward her I saw her raise her broom and jab it at the man before her. She pushed him backward, swung the broom and batted him over the head.

"Get out of here, you . . . get out," she yelled.

All the while she screamed at him she beat at him. He stood for one stunned moment, then flung his hands up to protect his head and turned, running with long, agile strides for the safety of the street, his bundle falling and rolling in the mire at my feet. Aunt Emeline chased him clear across the yard, then stood with rigid dignity and heaving bosom as he dashed on, out of sight.

"What'd you do that for?" I asked in amazement.

She glared at me, her face flushed and her chin quivering. I shook my head in puzzlement, picking up the bundle and seeing that it contained a set of fresh clothes.

"He just wanted to buy a bath in our tub with hot water.

He asked me downtown. Gee, you could have had five dollars just for letting him."

Aunt Emeline's mouth flew open as she stared at me.

"Bath? A bath? . . . Oh. Oh. Oh." She looked off down the street, then flung herself around and marched back inside the house, slamming the door.

She was upset all the rest of the day, and that night I heard her crying.

I didn't know what it was, but some sound waked me. I wasn't exactly scared, but I did want the comfort of being closer to someone. I slept on a bunk in one corner, my aunt and Caroline in another across the room. I rose and groped my way in the heavy darkness, carrying a blanket with me, meaning to curl up on the floor beside their bed.

But my aunt wasn't there. Caroline was a small ball against the wall, sleeping heavily. I think Caroline could have slept through an earthquake.

Again I heard the noise outside and recognized it with a shock. I stole to the door, which was partly open, and peered out. My aunt was sitting on a stump close to the doorway. There was enough moon for me to see her clearly. Her hands were over her face and she was sobbing.

I didn't know what to do. I started to call out to ask her what the matter was, then I heard the door of the print shop creak open. Samson slept out there in one bunk. Ike used the other when he was home.

Samson stopped, seeing my aunt. I think he hadn't known she was outside. Then he came forward and I saw that he wore only his heavy red underclothes. I guess he forgot how he was dressed in his concern for her.

"Ma'am." He sounded shocked. "You shouldn't be out here this time of night."

She tried to answer, but her voice broke. He stood for a moment, hit by the knowledge that she was crying, then he dropped to his knees on the damp ground and wrapped both his arms around her, pulling her toward him.

"Emmy." I'd never heard him call her anything but ma'am or Mrs. Garner before, and his voice was different, fuller yet shaky. "Emeline. Darling. What is it? Whatever is it?"

She turned against him, clinging, her fingers digging into his back, her face buried in his big shoulder.

"I can't stand it, Samson, I just can't. I've never known anything like this. Only one other woman in town. No one to talk to. Nothing but men, men, men. And all of them dirty.

128

All of them looking at me like . . . and Ben gone most of the time . . ."

"Oh my darling. My poor darling." He was stroking her hair, burrowing his face in it.

"I'll go out of my mind. I've got to get away, a long way away . . ."

"I know. I told him. But the damn fool won't take you." Only her sobs answered him.

Suddenly he held her out, away from him, shaking her shoulders.

"I'll take you." It came out in a burst. "Back where you belong." His arms went around her again, drawing her close. "You know I love you, Emmy. I've tried hard, but hiding it's no good. We've got to do something. Come with me, Emeline."

The rush of words seemed to jar her out of her own anguish, and her words trembled.

"Hush, Samson. Hush. You mustn't."

There was a great savageness in his voice then. "And why mustn't I? It's not wrong. A man's got the right to protect the girl he loves."

"Oh"—she struggled to free herself, but he held her tightly —"Samson, please. I'm not a girl. I'm a grown woman, and married."

"To a nothin'. I'm a good man, Emmy, more a man than Ben Garner is. He's all right in his way, I guess, but he don't take proper care of you. I'll make it up to you. We'll go home. Home to Ohio. We'll take the younguns . . ."

She dropped her head against his shoulder, and hung there, silent, for a long moment, then she drew a sharp breath and sat up rigidly.

"No. Samson. No, no, no."

"Yes, Emmy. Please."

"I love Ben. I married him because I loved him. Right now I'm feeling sorry for myself, but he needs help too. And I believe in him. You're very dear to me, Samson, but I can't abandon Ben."

"Emeline. I love you so terribly."

Again she lay back in his arms, this time as if she didn't even realize it, even snuggled against him, and her words had a dreamy quality.

"I know you do. You were very attached to your mother, I know that from the way you talk about her, and in a fashion I have taken her place."

He looked down at her, shaking his head. "My darling, don't beggar me. I don't love you that way. I want to be your husband, be a part of your body. I want you as my wife. And I want to take care of you."

She put her head back, hanging it over his arm, her eyes closed. Then slowly she moved her head sideways.

"You think so now. And it's a great compliment, my dear. But I'm ten years older than you. When I'm old you will still be a young man, and you'd hate me then. Someday you'll find the right girl, and you'll thank me, believe me."

As she spoke her voice was gaining back its customary certitude, and she finished almost briskly.

"Now, help me up."

He rose, lifting her in his arms, then setting her gently on her feet, still holding her. I heard him choke as if he were crying. I couldn't believe it. The idea that Samson Dohne, to my mind the strongest and biggest man in the world, would weep, especially in front of a woman, sent a chill of fright through me. And then I was shocked further as Aunt Emeline turned her face up, saying, "You may kiss me, just this once, just that we both shall have that much of each other. Then you must go away."

"I won't go without you." His words were thick and fierce.

"Yes, my dear, because I ask it. You have been a great comfort to me. I don't think I could have managed this far without you. But now it's best for us both that you leave. And you will not let Ben know why it is necessary. I want no constraint in our memory of you."

I crept back to my bunk, my head reeling. It made me dizzy to think of Aunt Emeline acting that way.

I watched them covertly all week, but beyond an unaccustomed gentleness in my aunt's manner toward him and a strange, cowed mournfulness about Samson, I could find no sign of the upheaval.

But they did not fill my whole attention, and before my uncle and Ike got back I had called down my aunt's familiar wrath upon my head and felt somehow that my world was back in place.

The miner who wanted a bath stayed in my mind. It still did not seem to me worth five dollars for the doubtful privilege of sitting in a round tub of soapy water with your feet on the floor outside, but I wanted those five dollars.

My chance came when my aunt went to spend the day with

Mrs. Grace, whose husband ran the town's biggest store. Mrs. Grace was expecting.

Aunt Emeline took Caroline with her and Samson had gone over toward the Stanislaus, looking for a bear that had been raiding miners' cabins. It left me in sole possession of the cabin and the print shop.

I fired up the cook stove and made sure the well was full. I dragged the tin tub out to the print shop and filled it a quarter full of cold water. Then I went in search of my victim. I'd seen him twice since my aunt ran him off, so I figured he was still in town.

As I came down the street I saw him just disappearing through the door of the saloon. I stopped. I wasn't supposed to go in there and I knew it, but after all, business put a different face on things. I went in.

The room was long and narrow and close, smelling of wood smoke, tobacco smoke, stale alcohol, and people. The smell of people overrode everything else, for the waters of the creeks were too cold for any bathing other than what the men got by constant working in them.

There were four customers leaning against the plank bar, including my miner. The bartender was a short man who wore a frock coat, very greasy, and a plug hat. I knew him without knowing his name. He did not sound pleased to see me.

"What do you want in here, kid?"

I stood by the door, pointing at my man. "I want to talk to him. I want to know if he wants a bath."

The customer at the far end gasped, then he let out a guffaw that threatened to blow out the cloth sides and ceiling of the room.

"A bath . . . Pete? You out of your head, kid?"

"He asked me the day before yesterday," I said, "and he dropped a bundle with clean clothes in it. I got the bundle and I want to know if he'll still pay five dollars for a hot bath."

"Not me." Pete sounded very mad. "I don't want to get my brains beat out by that crazy woman."

"She didn't understand," I told him, "and besides, she's not there. She went down to Mrs. Grace's for all day. I got the tub out in the print shop. The water's hot and I got a cake of lye soap."

I could see by his eyes that I was making an impression.

"You sure she ain't there?"

"Sure I'm sure."

Abruptly he slammed his fist on the plank. "Damned if I don't do her. Me, I'm leaving this country tomorrow. I've sent my dust out by the express and I've seen the elephant, and boys, I aim to leave clean. Come on, kid." He started for the door.

The man who had laughed so loudly shoved his stained hat to the back of his uncut head, "A hot bath . . ." He was talking to himself. "Say, boy, you got enough hot water for two baths?"

"I can make all you want." I saw a thriving business opening up before me. "There's plenty of wood."

"You just got yourself another customer," he said, and followed Pete.

The other two at the bar looked at each other. "Why not?" said one. "I ain't seen a tub of hot water since I hit this miserable dump."

The bartender didn't like it, my taking his customers away from him, but I didn't care. I ran down the street ahead of them. By the time they arrived I'd lugged two pails of hot water out from the stove and poured them into the tub.

Pete undressed in a hurry and the rest of the men stood around watching while he had his bath. The second was finished and the third was in the tub when my aunt came home. I had no warning. I was refilling the reservoir when I looked around and there she was in the doorway, Caroline by her side.

She came into the kitchen slowly, her eyes on the bucket I'd just emptied and the water I'd spilled on the floor.

"Austin, what are you up to? Who are those men in the print shop?"

A dozen answers flashed through my mind, but I didn't dare lie to her. I'd never yet succeeded.

"I'm selling them baths," I said. "I'm getting five pinches of dust from each one of them." Hurriedly I pulled out my poke and held it open for inspection.

She didn't even look at it. She just kept staring at me until I wished that the ground would open so I could crawl into it. Only it didn't.

Her voice turned dangerous. "And just where are they taking these baths?"

"In the print shop."

"In my tub?" She made it sound as if I had let them sleep in her bed.

"It's the only tub there is."

"You get them out of there. Right now."

I had visions of my gold hoard shifting away. "I can't," I wailed, and started to cry. "I've been paid, and I promised, and anyhow I wouldn't know how to divide up the dust. Why's it hurt? They can't get the tub any dirtier than it already is. I'll clean it up . . ." I couldn't say any more.

She glared at me. "Stop that sniffling. I mean it. Stop."

She seemed to think I could turn off my tears on command. I tried, while she considered. Then she said:

"All right, you promised, so they have to finish. I'm going back to Mrs. Grace's. When they're through you scour out that tub with wood ashes until it shines, you hear? And if you ever invite another of these human hogs up here for any reason I'll have your hide off right down to the bone. You understand, young man?"

I understood. But I did not understand why she was so all fired upset over my making more than twenty dollars and letting four men recapture the dignity of cleanliness.

Neither, I think, did my uncle as she indignantly recounted the story to him as soon as he came home, the following week. He winked at me without her knowledge, and Old Ike had sudden business outside, where he hastened, one hand clamped tightly over his mouth.

They were both very tired, having walked all the way from Stockton, and my uncle still had his cough. He sat listening while she told him everything that had happened while he was gone, with the exception of the fact that she had kissed Samson.

That was her way, for my aunt's world was composed of the small things, the little incidents around the house or within her immediate orbit.

Finally she ran down, and then asked him about the paper.

He shook his head. "We didn't get any."

She was nonplused. It never really occurred to my aunt for years that everything would not work out exactly as my uncle wished, and that they would not own the biggest newspaper in California.

"Whyever not? Surely there must be paper in San Francisco?"

He moved his head wearily. "If there is, we didn't find it."

"Why not?"

Ike had come back in, but he turned again toward the

door, unhappily. "Maybe I'd better go see if the press is all right."

"You stay here," my uncle said, and it was an order.

Ike subsided, twisting his hat nervously in his hands. My uncle rubbed the side of his head as if to compose his words.

"Well, we went down to the *Alta* office and talked to Mr. Kemble, but they had lost a good deal in the fire on May fourth and couldn't spare either paper or material. He told us, however, that several printing offices had been ordered from the East, and he said he'd pass the word that we were looking for paper."

My aunt had moved to the stove as he talked, and begun preparing supper. I'll never forget it, the even tone of my uncle's voice, hiding the despair and chagrin which gripped him.

"A week later a Mr. Hood came to see us. He said he was supercargo on a vessel that had just landed from Panama, that they carried a quantity of newsprint, on which the shipping charges had not been paid. He said the man who was bringing the paper in had died at sea, and the stuff was for sale to cover the charges."

He passed his hand over his eyes. "I guess I was a little greedy. After all, I knew that paper was in short supply, and worth almost any price you cared to ask for it. I jumped at the bait like a stupid fish, came clear out of the water."

The bitterness of his words made my aunt turn from the stove.

"What are you trying to tell me, Ben?"

"That Hood was a crook. He took us down to the waterfront and pointed out the ship, said he'd go and make a deal with the captain if I gave him the money. It never occurred to me that he wasn't honest. He was charging me a ten per cent commission."

"What did he do?"

My uncle stood up and crossed to put his arm about her shoulders.

"He didn't do anything. He just got in the boat and rowed out toward the ship. We waited. The fog rolled in, and that was the last we saw of Mr. Hood."

"You mean he got lost in the fog?"

"I wish it were so. He took us for chumps. The fog was so thick that we thought he couldn't get back to shore. So we kept waiting.

"In the morning when he didn't come we got a boat and

134

rowed out to the ship. There was no paper aboard. And the captain had never heard of Mr. Hood."

She twisted in his embrace. "And he got away with all that money? All the money you worked so hard digging?"

My uncle nodded. "We had just enough left to get back here."

"But . . . didn't you try to find him? Didn't you search?"

"We did. We went back to the *Alta*, because Hood had said that was where he had heard we were looking for paper. Kemble told us Hood had been hanging around the office for weeks, trying to get a job as printer."

"And no one knew where he was?"

"We looked every place we could think of. Ike would have killed him if we'd caught up with him. He was gone from his boardinghouse, and the man who ran that thought he had probably shipped out for Australia."

"All our money . . . all gone . . ." Her face was white. "What are we going to do?"

My uncle started to cough. My aunt began to cry, and Caroline, as if on cue, cried too. Ike couldn't take it any longer. He stalked out of the house, anger in every stride. I followed him to the print shop, echoing my aunt's question.

"What do we do now?"

He turned around, looking at me in surprise. "Do? Why, dig up some more money the way we dug up the last."

His simple assurance heartened me.

"Women," he said in deep disgust. "Women always get upset at the wrong time, about the wrong things. It's Ben's health I'm fretting about. He ought to go to bed and stay there a spell."

"I don't think he would."

"No," Ike agreed. "I don't reckon he will. I ought to have sent him to the Sandwich Islands with Edmond."

Excitement banished my worry. "You saw Edmond Jones?"

"Yes. Ran into him on the street the day after we got to San Francisco. He was sailing next day."

"Then I'll never see him again." Sudden disappointment dumped me into gloom again.

"I wouldn't count on that." Ike patted my head. "Edmond's like I was, kind of fiddle-footed. He wants to see what's on the other side of the mountain, or the other side of the sea. But that kind usually wanders in a circle . . . and

135

there's that Peyton girl. She was asking about him when we come through Stockton."

"You saw them too? How is Lisbeth?"

"Busy." Ike grinned. "Somebody broke into Grover's store and stole more than half his goods. He was fit to be tied. I think it near ruined him."

I wasn't interested in Grover Peyton. "I wonder how Black Bob will like it in the Islands."

Ike shook his head. "He didn't go with Edmond. He took off for the gold fields as soon as spring came. He's up around Mokelumne Hill somewheres. Edmond heard from him once, said he was doing fine, but I'll bet you he ain't doing as good as Joe Stoop."

"What about Joe?"

"Someone tried to hold up the office of the Todd Express, down by Stockton. Joe just happened to be there. Shot the guy dead."

I thought he was joking. Ike was chuckling heavily.

"That Joe, he's just plain got luck. I was talking to him when we come through. And he's got another diamond. If he keeps on killing robbers he'll look like a walking pin-cushion.

I had a quick homesickness for Sandy. "His family still in Sacramento?"

"Guess so. Didn't think to ask." Ike had small interest. "But that Joe. Everybody's talking about him. That hillbilly is about as famous as anyone in California, and all because you did that lying article about him. Funny how things work out."

"It wasn't a lie," I protested. "I just did what you and Uncle Ben taught me, kind of embroidered the story to make it sound good."

"Joe should thank you, but he never will. It's kind of gone to his head. He struts around showing off his diamonds and his big gun, wearing fancy clothes."

"Maybe he'll be Governor," I said.

"And maybe somebody'll gut-shoot him." Ike snorted. "The towns are getting plumb full of rough characters. First when people come out they were too busy trying to get rich finding gold to think of devilment. Last year there weren't more than half a dozen holdups in the whole territory. But that's changing. All them convicts from Australia are pouring in as fast as the ships can bring them. And a lot of the boys got tired of working their rockers and sluice boxes. California was sort of a nice place when we first got here, people helped each other and you could leave things lying around loose. You can't no more. Take this Hood that done your uncle. He probably come out to strike it rich and missed. So he went to thieving. There'll be plenty more like him. We're going to see a lot of trouble before this year is out."

CHAPTER SEVENTEEN

I WAS TOO young to be truly concerned with the wave of crime which swept our embryo society, or with the political jockeying that went on as the first legislature was called to Monterey.

My uncle and Ike and Samson went back to the diggings below Melones, and life settled back into a routine for my aunt, Caroline and me. Somewhere, probably from Mrs. Grace, my aunt got some seeds and started one of the first vegetable gardens on the Mother Lode. She had the stern background that made American women the pioneers they were, but for myself, I looked on the labor of carrying water to nourish the struggling plants, and the night and morning milking of the cow, as chores which interfered with the daily enjoyment of life.

It turned hot, as it can get hot in the interior valleys, and it was hard to recall the penetrating damp agony of the preceding winter. And then, on the Fourth of July, John White and Jack Marvin started the *Herald*.

They had arrived a week earlier with the old Ramage press which was the father of California journalism. It had seen service at Monterey, San Francisco, Sacramento, Stockton, and finally it had come to Sonora.

The first number was printed on foolscap, the type was uneven in size, and I viewed it with a journeyman's disgust. But I could not stay away from the office.

Sonora was booming. The gravels around Woods Landing on the creek below us were proving unusually rich, and the first attempts at drift mining . . . digging tunnels into the layer of tertiary gravel which underlaid the flat lava cap of Table Mountain . . . were bringing out gold in quantities.

Reynolds and Company established a local express office, and five new stores and six saloons joined the straggling line of structures along the uneven edges of Main Street.

What pleased my aunt was the knowledge that there were at least a dozen "good" women in town. I thought I knew what she meant, but was not quite sure.

And then the *Herald* came into being and in a sense my life changed. I got my first job. I was in the newspaper office at eight o'clock on the morning of July 5. I hadn't said anything to my aunt because I was afraid she'd stop me.

Jack Marvin was just getting up. He had his pants on and his suspenders pulled up over his red undershirt, for both he and his partner slept in bunks at the rear of the office.

He was a big man with a friendly smile, and I liked him at once. The office was not yet set up, since they had printed their first edition at the Stockton *Times* and hauled it to Sonora in a wagon.

"Hello there," he said. "And what can I do for you on this bright and unusually hot day in July?"

"You can give me a job," I said.

He rubbed his hand across his eyes as if to clear them. There had been quite a celebration on the Fourth, for the miners took the national holiday seriously, and I suppose Jack still thought he was a little drunk.

"A job? What kind of a job would you like? The editor's chair, I assume?"

I knew he was joshing and it made me angry. "You don't have to be so smart," I said. "You aren't the first paper to set up in Sonora, and I've seen better print jobs a thousand times."

"You have now?" He seemed to find this even funnier.

I pulled the proof of my story about Joe Stoop from my pocket and handed it to him. "I wrote that for the Placer *Times* and set it up in type. If you don't believe me, just ask Mr. Giles."

He read it with growing interest. "So you know Diamond Joe?"

"I named him," I said. "Before I wrote that story he was just plain Joe Stoop, a hillbilly from Ohio who came West in our wagon train. He shot that man by plumb accident, and my uncle says I made him."

"Most celebrities are made by newspapermen." He still held the smudged proof, and studied me with open curiosity. "Who is your uncle?"

"His name is Ben Garner. He used to be editor and publisher of the Clinton County *Clarion* in Wilmington, Ohio. We came West with our press and type, and we're going to start a paper in the mining country. We already started one here. We got out one issue, and if we hadn't run out of paper we'd be here instead of you." My voice had gotten shrill, for I couldn't keep the bitterness out of it.

He sensed the way I felt. He put out a big hand and pulled me against him. He had a good healthy man's smell. In those days people in California had distinct odors, but there was something comforting about it. I had been feeling very small and very much alone with my uncle and Ike and Samson all gone.

He didn't ask how old I was. He didn't query me about why I thought I could hold a job in a print shop. He asked me where my uncle's press and type were.

I told him, but I added quickly, "He won't sell them."

Jack Marvin sighed. "The story of this country," he said, not speaking to me but to himself. "We need everything here, everything." Then as if remembering why I was there, he nodded.

"So you want a job. And what do you think you can do?"

"I've been a devil since I was six."

"I believe you." He smiled. "You're hired. You get one dollar a week. You will be here at eight in the morning. You will build the fire and sweep out the shop. You will break up the forms and clean them, and we will pay you linage for any story you bring in. Children often happen on human interest items that adults would never find."

My aunt took the news more calmly than I hoped. Probably she was glad to have me in a regimen with fewer idle hours for the Devil to make capital of.

John White was neither so kind nor so considerate as Jack Marvin, but I managed to keep out of his way, and the summer passed slowly until John Haverstick gave me the waistcoat.

I was big for my age. I had grown three inches that year, but still Aunt Emeline had to take in the side seams to keep it from hanging on me like a flour sack. And she did not approve of the vest, though she let me keep it because any sort of clothing was hard to come by. This was a fancy red affair with patterns stitched in gold thread.

"Land sakes," she grumbled. "You look like a gambler, and you only eleven."

"I'll be twelve pretty soon," I said.

I'd already told them at the print shop that I was going on thirteen. And I did not tell my aunt that John had won the waistcoat from an Oakdale gambler in a poker game, and had only given it to me because it was too small for him.

John was teaching me to write. He had come out from New York where he had worked for Horace Greeley, and he was regretting his trip, although he never said so. A fair-haired man of about thirty, he was more literate than either of our employers who had hired him as editor, which involved writing most of the items thenceforward appearing in the *Herald*.

I was alone in the shop that morning. Marvin and White had walked over to inspect some claims at the new American Camp, three miles away, which would later become Columbia, the richest square mile on earth. I don't know where Haverstick was, probably playing cards in one of the saloons. As he told me repeatedly, "Nice people don't make stories. It's only from the cutthroats and rogues that you get anything worth writing."

I was reading the weekly newsletter from the *Alta* office and did not see her until she opened the door, then I looked up and gaped at her with open-mouthed curiosity. I knew who she was. In a town the size of Sonora little that went on was missed by anyone.

She was Jason Fox's widow, come out to take over his claim. I had not known Jason Fox; he had been killed in a landslide the winter before, but I did know the miners' edict.

The miners' meetings of the early camps were probably the high point in practical democracy. Based on the format of the New England town meetings, they embraced all men who happened to be in the area at the time, and they filled a vacuum, for there was no law nor any constitutional authority to guide them.

In the period when California was wrested from an unwilling Mexico there were few Americans within the territory. The reins of government were usurped by our military, and these men, trained to sail ships or conduct punitive expeditions, had no knowledge of mining and were wholly unprepared for the flood of humanity pouring into the California foothills.

It is one of the happier phenomena of history that this deluge of treasure seekers managed on their own initiative to establish a self-government which worked efficiently to the benefit of all. In the face of wealth beyond the dreams of man they conceived their self-policing mining districts and made their rules stick.

Fortunately the percentage of educated men who joined the westward rush was out of all proportion to their percentage in our settled states. We had more doctors per hundred population than any other region in America, more newspapermen, and three or four times the number of lawyers. These were the young men, the not yet settled men, the vigorous men, and their vigor gave its strength to the budding camps.

I am still proud that they developed the mining land, and water-rights laws. They were abided by, and they were the basis of this country's first codified mining laws. The legal code was not to be formulated by the Congress for another twenty years.

The rules of each district varied slightly from that of its neighbors, and Sonora was no exception. We had no provision that a man's hundred-foot claim should pass at his death to any of his heirs. It was his only by sufferance from the mining district, to be held only as long as he worked the ground and obeyed the district rules.

The widow had not known this. Few people in the East had any definite knowledge of placer mining, and she had arrived via Panama, believing herself to be the mistress of a flourishing mine. Instead, she was three thousand miles from home, without resources.

Not that she lacked well wishers. I had heard from my aunt all about her, and it was rumored that she could have her choice of half the claims along Woods Creek, for the word had gone out that a widow woman, young and pretty, was in town, and the men tramped for miles just to catch a glimpse of her on the street.

But she had refused all assistance, almost to the point of rudeness, and the few women, occupied with their battle to make a home and take care of children in the face of brutal odds, had given up on her.

And now she was coming into the shop.

"I am looking for the proprietor." She had a quick way of speaking, a decisive, clipped way of dealing out her words. "Is he here, please?"

"They went to American Camp," I said.

She was small, barely taller than I. Her hair had a burnished quality showing through the darker sheen when the sun caught it. Her face was thin, making her dark eyes look larger than they really were, and I sensed suddenly that she was very nervous.

She sounded a trifle exasperated as she said, "Then who is running the office?"

I started to claim that I was. I was proud that neither Marvin nor White hesitated at going away and leaving me alone in the shop. But John Haverstick forestalled me by coming in through the door behind her.

John was a dresser. When most men were content to go around in California pants and red flannel shirts, he always wore a gray suit, fresh linen and a tie around his laundered, starched collar. The only concessions he made to the country were his polished boots and the black slouch hat shading his blond head.

He removed the hat with a flourish. I thought that he was play acting and liked him not too much for it, and I found his usual flamboyant speech offensive, for he seemed to be mocking this woman with whom I was suddenly in love.

"May I assist you, madam? I am John Haverstick, at present engaged as editor of this estimable sheet."

She gave him a slow scrutiny, then said primly, "I wish to insert this in your publication," and presented a slip of ruled paper.

He smiled and the smile lightened his long, ascetic face. He took the paper and glanced at it, saying in surprise,

"An advertisement."

He had a right to be surprised. The *Herald* was not overburdened with paid-for copy at the time.

She nodded, and he read aloud, "Vinegar and dried apple pies. Homemade. On sale at Grace's store. Two dollars."

She listened, concentrating on every word. When he finished she asked quickly, "Is that too much?" She sounded apologetically uncertain. "Everything is so terribly expensive, with flour eighteen dollars the hundredweight and lard seventy-five cents the pound . . ."

He was long in answering, so I said, "It sure isn't. They were getting three dollars for pies in Sacramento last year."

She turned impulsively. "You're nice. What's your name?"

I was not easily stricken dumb, but I stood there tonguetied, my face beginning to burn. John watched me, and he sounded amused as he came to my aid.

"May I present Austin Garner, Mrs. Fox. He's our devil.

142

He's probably the youngest printer's devil on the Mother Lode, and certainly he thinks he's the smartest."

He was making fun of me and a rush of resentment smote me. Then she smiled at me and offered her hand as if I were her equal, and I forgot John in my giddiness. I still could not speak, and she turned again to John.

"The advertisement . . . how much will it be, please?"

John Haverstick's tone was thoughtful. "Dried apple pie. I haven't tasted one since I left Philadelphia. Tell you what, Mrs. Fox, shall we say two pies for the advertisement?"

"Judge Marvin won't like that." I spoke before I thought, and could have bitten my tongue out for uttering the words. I added lamely, "He says you can't pay the paper bill with eggs and stuff . . ."

"I insist on paying." The girl produced a thin purse.

Haverstick never glanced in my direction, but I knew he was displeased. "It will be four dollars," he said.

She opened the purse and picked out a handful of coins. My heart sank as I saw them. The smallest coin I'd seen in Sonora was a quarter, unless you included the Chile reals and the odd French and Spanish pieces brought in by our cosmopolitan population. But here were dimes, half dimes, and pennies lying in a little mound as she counted them out carefully.

When she finished she returned the remainder to her purse. There were not many left and I writhed, realizing what I had done.

After she had gone I said guiltily to John, "She's about broke, isn't she?"

He grunted. "Fool woman, drag all the way out here not knowing what she's doing . . . bake pies . . . how can she expect to make a living baking pies?"

"People like pie," I said.

"Certainly. But where is she going to bake them? How will she pay for flour and filling, and whatever she requires?"

"You were going to help her. You were going to run her advertisement and pay for it yourself."

He gave me a sheepish glance. "Austin," he said, "women make men do foolish things. You're a little young to know, but you'll learn. She was flirting with you just now. You know that, don't you? And you not quite twelve."

I felt my face redden again.

"That's a woman for you." His tone turned bitter. I'd never heard him talk that way before, but then, I'd never heard him talk about women. "They can't help it," he went on. "Every new man they meet they have to test. Maybe he's got something the man they have does not."

I started to say that all women weren't that way, and then I remembered Aunt Emeline and Samson, and a heaviness touched my heart.

"You don't like them, do you?"

"Like them? I love them. But to hell with them. You know why I gamble? Gambling, they say, is a sublimation of sex . . ." He broke off and for one of the few times while I knew him I saw him embarrassed. "Hell," he said in a different voice, "what am I talking? You're so old in so many ways that I forget you're only a baby."

He crammed on his hat and slammed out of the office and I did not see him for two days, but I heard he was drunk in one of the fandango houses.

That afternoon I went down to Grace's store, thinking she might be there. She was not, but I heard Doc talking to the loafers grouped around the cold stove at the rear.

"Come in here and asked me for a job, yes siree. Bold as you please and kind of forward. So I said, 'ma'am, it's not fittin' for a woman to work in a store hereabouts.' And she comes right back with, 'Why not? Women clerk in stores in New York, don't they?'

"Well, I explain that I get mostly men off the creeks, a lot of them have liquor in them and they ain't seen a woman in months. I didn't tell her most of them are headed for Spanish Town."

"Should be good for business, having her around," Bill Huber, the express agent, said. "Wouldn't mind having her around myself." He leered. I didn't like Huber.

"My wife wouldn't think so," Doc Grace said. "Funny thing about women, they can work themselves all up, feeling sorry for a single girl. They're forever matchmaking and the like, but when one of them catches a man she'll do her damnedest to keep the other women away from him."

"You ain't that attractive," Huber said.

"A widow's a widow," said Doc. "Old story is that a dancing girl wants a dancing man, an educated girl wants an educated man, a pretty girl wants a handsome man, but a widow, she just says, where is he?"

"That one shouldn't have any trouble," Huber grinned. "She could whistle up the biggest poke of dust along the creek."

Doc shrugged. He had a story to tell and he was not going to be denied.

"Anyhow, I was feeling sorry for her, even if I couldn't help her out, and then she spied that barrel of dried apples. First thing I know she's wheedled me into grubstaking her to flour and lard and apples and vinegar, and selling her dadblamed pies. She sure can get around a man without half trying. But she ain't found a bake stove, and unless she does, it's no deal."

No one was paying any attention to me, standing just inside the door. I slipped out and hurried off in search of Prudence Fox. I had an idea, and I didn't want my pretty widow to lose her deal.

I found her walking up the far side of the street and ran toward her, calling. She stopped and turned, and her face looked tired and discouraged. Then she recognized me and smiled.

"You want a stove?" I said. "I know where one is. It's a real cook stove with a big oven. There's only three in camp."

Her face brightened, then clouded. "Why Austin, thank you. But a stove . . . here . . . it would be terribly expensive."

"They wouldn't sell it," I said. "They couldn't sell it because it belongs to both of them, and they're not using it for the same reason. But they'll loan it if I ask them. They owe me a favor."

She looked puzzled. "I guess what you're saying makes sense, but . . . who . . . ?"

"The partners," I explained. "They're mad at each other and they don't speak. When they want to tell each other anything they relay it through me."

"Who are they?"

"Bob Ford and Anson Wicks. Everybody in camp knows about them. They've got one of the richest claims on Woods Creek, down near Jimtown."

"And why are they mad at each other?"

"Well, one of them wanted to dig on the east bank and the other on the west. They argued for days. Then they split the claim in half, down the middle of the creek. And one day Bob Ford, he's the tall one, found a nugget in the stream bed. It's a big hunk of quartz. It's all I could do to lift it, all shot through with wire gold.

"Anson Wicks, the short one, claimed half of the nugget was lying on his side of the line. They wrangled over that for a month until folks thought maybe they'd shoot each other.

145

Then George Works, the sheriff, brought them in and made them post a peace bond. But they still can't agree how to split the nugget. It's lying in Reynolds and Company's safe right now."

"That sounds pretty silly, doesn't it? I'd think the camp would laugh them out of the country."

I said slowly, "You see, Anson's from Texas, and he was a ranger or something, and Bob Ford came out from New York with Stevenson's regiment in forty-seven. They're not the kind you laugh at real loud."

But she was laughing. Then she said, "And the stove?"

"They divided everything they could," I explained. "Even the cabin. But you can't divide a stove, so they moved it out to the woodshed and there she sets, no good to anybody."

"Well," she said, "well . . . but I want to pay rent for it."

"That's easy." I was confident. "It's only a little way. I'll show you."

As we started down the street she gave me a slow smile.

"Dear Austin, how did I ever get along before I found you?"

I had an uneasy feeling, wondering if she were flirting with me again, as John had said. She was thinking about him too, apparently, for after a minute she asked, "Has that Mr. Haverstick been with your print shop long?"

"About a month," I said, "but don't waste your time thinking about him. He don't like women."

She flushed and began walking a little faster.

"He likes to gamble," I said. "He won this vest I'm wearing, and a lot of things."

"You mean he plays cards for money?"

"Sure," I said. "He's real good at monte and poker. He plays down in Spanish Town mostly."

Her voice sounded stifled. "I heard about those places. And he seemed so courtly . . ."

"Old Ike says it's the courtly kind a woman should steer clear of."

"And who is Ike?"

"He's our printer." I went on to tell her about Ike and Uncle Ben, and how we'd run out of paper and about Uncle Ben losing the thousand dollars. By the time I finished we had made our way down the creek to the partners' cabin.

It was a long room, and they had added a second fireplace at the north end, and a second door. Bob Ford stayed at the south end. Anson Wicks moved to the new accommodations. We went into his half to find both men at home. It was nearly six o'clock, and they had quit work for the day.

Bob Ford was sitting beside his dead fireplace, reading a tattered Bible. Anson was getting his supper. He jumped in consternation as we came in.

"A female."

Bob Ford dropped his Bible and made no attempt to recover it. His boots were off, so was his shirt, his upper body clothed only in his red underwear. He stood up slowly in his sock feet, too paralyzed to move farther.

"Evening," I said. "I want you to meet Mrs. Fox. She came out all the way from Boston to work her husband's claim, only he don't own it any more because he's dead."

No one said a word, and I rushed on. "So she's got to do something to make a living. She's going to bake pies, and she needs a stove. I thought maybe you'd let her have the loan of yours."

"Rent," Prudence Fox corrected me sharply.

"Rent," I echoed, although I thought she was crazy, because if I worked it right they'd let her have it for nothing.

Bob Ford ran his fingers nervously through his black beard. He had not shaved for weeks. He opened his mouth, but no sound came out.

Anson Wicks coughed. "Austin, I can't speak for a man whose name I won't even mention, but the lady is welcome to my half of the stove, and I'll take a pie for rental."

Bob Ford could not let his partner get ahead of him. "That's right," he said, "although I can't agree with anything that froghead says. The lady can use the stove with my compliments, and if she wants to give me a piece of her pie, it will be more than welcome." He glared at Ford.

"That's fine," I said, wanting to get her out of there before any real trouble started. "I'll have Joe Walker bring his wagon and fetch it in the morning."

I urged her through the door and we started uptown.

"Those two"—she was talking under her breath—"they are perfectly ridiculous."

"They may be ridiculous," I told her, "but they're about the richest men in camp, and neither of them is married."

She stopped walking and looked at me as if she were seeing clear into my head, and a mischievous grin twitched about her full mouth.

"Austin, are you trying your hand at matchmaking?"

I shrugged and said logically, "You haven't any husband, and neither of them has a wife."

"You're not suggesting that I marry them both? I don't think that would work, even if they aren't speaking."

I'd heard tell that Mormons like Sam Brannan could have two wives or more, and I didn't see why it shouldn't be true for women, but I did not say so.

"You could take your pick. Bob Ford's real religious. He reads the Bible morning and night no matter what, but Anson Wicks is younger and stronger. He's about the strongest man I know except Samson Dohne."

"Who's that?"

I told her about Samson.

"If I were going to marry someone because he's so strong, maybe I should marry this Samson."

"He's not rich," I said. I did not tell her that I didn't think she stood a chance because Samson was in love with my aunt.

"Well," she said, "before I can worry about getting married I've got to find somewhere to make those pies."

"I've got a place." I'd already figured that one out. "Alf Higgins went to Doan's crossing to work his claim and he asked me to keep an eye on his shack. It's just off Washington, a hundred yards behind Grace's store."

She lifted her face to the sky for a moment, then she put her hand on my shoulder, giving me a small, comic smile. "You are my guardian angel, Austin. You should be elected mayor. Do you run the whole town the way you run things for me?"

I shook my head. "My aunt says I spend my time sticking my nose into other people's business, but my uncle says a good newspaperman should know everything that's going on in a place, whether it's something you can print or not . . .

"I'll show you the shack in the morning and help you clean it. And we'd better get Walker to draw you a load of wood. How much are you giving Doc Grace for the apples and stuff?"

"He gets a dollar and a half, I get fifty cents."

I did some ciphering in my head. "That don't sound hardly fair. You do all the work."

"But he's giving me the supplies, and selling the pies."

I didn't say anything more. I left her and went down to the store. Doc was in there alone, straightening things up, getting ready to close. He had a thin, nutcracker face that

148

reminded me some of Grover Peyton's. I never liked store-keepers much.

"What's on your mind?" he said. "Emeline forget something?"

"It's not Aunt Emeline," I said, "it's the pie lady. I just got her the loan of the partners' stove, and she can use Alf Higgins' shack and Walker can haul her some wood. But it don't seem right, her only making four bits and you getting all the rest."

He had been using a duster. He laid it down beside the money drawer, and I didn't like the look on his face.

"You're a smart-ass kid." There was a bullying tone in his voice. "And I don't like smart-ass kids. I'm going to tell your aunt to tan your hide, and if she don't, I will."

"Maybe," I said, for I was a little afraid of him, but I wasn't going to show it. "But you hit me and you'll be sorry. How would you like the whole town to know you're taking advantage of a widow lady by gouging her and pretending to help her? I think most of the miners would come in here and do something about it. They kind of respect women, there ain't many around."

His eyes got a little smaller. "And how would they hear about it?"

"They might read it in the paper," I said.

"And who would put it in there? Marvin wouldn't."

"He'll print anything I write," I boasted. It wasn't true, of course, but Grace did not know that, and Grace had never advertised with us. He said it wasn't necessary, that everyone in town knew who he was already.

He took a long, deep breath, then said in a badgered tone, "Kid, what's your interest in this fema . . . this lady?"

"She's an advertiser." I wasn't about to tell him the truth, and hid behind my uncle's business philosophy that a good newspaper takes care of its advertisers.

"All right, all right." He nodded like a bird. "I'll talk to her in the morning. But don't you go spreading stories around about me or I'll have your hide."

I went back to the office. I wanted to write a story about pie, to get people thinking about them, but it didn't come off well.

Two days later John Haverstick found it in the basket when he went to make up the paper. He had showed up at the office needing a shave and his eyes so bloodshot that I thought he was bleeding. I'd never seen him this way, but

149

I didn't comment. Neither did Judge Marvin. Fortunately Jack White had gone to Stockton.

When John finished, the story read:

PIE HONORS SONORA

Pie . . . delicious, savory, sweet, juicy and tender . . . Pie . . . one of the most important symbols of our civilization . . . Pie . . . the emblem which emphasizes the distinction between man and brute. A wolf partakes of meat, a horse of grain, but whoever heard of the beast delicately placing his provender between two delectable crusts of shortened dough?

Through the ages we read of pie in one form or another, but basically these were crude and heavy breads stuffed with a soggy mass of meats.

It remained for our countrymen in their infinite wisdom, properly to create these exquisite shells and grace them with the tasty sweets we exiles recall with lactivation.

Apple pie . . . apples are without question the quintescense of pie . . . and Sonora is indeed fortunate that she now entertains one of the leading concoctors of apple pie.

To say that this superb artist is young, comely, and above all a lady . . . but we have said enough. Citizens, it is in your hands now to discover the rest.

I was in agony to show the piece to Prudence, but my uncle had instilled in me the dictum that you never released a story from the paper until the issue came out, and I was forced to wait.

When it came off the press I had to start at the far end of town, making my deliveries. By the time I reached the Higgins shack someone had already showed her a copy, and her mind was busy elsewhere.

I burst in at the door to find her bent above the stove, her cheeks rosy with its heat. The place was even cleaner than we had gotten it the first morning. The earth floor was swept and dampened and hard, the bench along the wall scrubbed and now adorned with the mixing pans, and the board on which she rolled her crusts covered from dust by a fresh towel.

There was a smudge of flour on her nose and across her

clear, high forehead, and her dark hair was pulled back in two tight braids to be out of the way. She was as pretty as a doll, and she was distraught.

"Austin," she cried, "I'm so glad to see you. Please make them stop."

"Stop?"

"The partners," she said. "For two days they've been bringing wood. The whole back yard is filled with it, and the way they glare at each other when they happen to meet . . . and they're both wearing guns. I'm afraid . . ."

"They won't shoot each other," I promised her. "If they'd been going to they'd have done it months ago."

"I appreciate the wood." She sounded exasperated. "But they hang around here and frighten the customers. Everybody seems afraid of them."

"I'll fix it," I said, and showed her the article.

She read it again, and her face flushed more than it already was.

"Who wrote it?"

"Well, it was my idea, and I wrote it first, but John Haverstick kind of fixed it up."

She was openly blushing now, and flustered. "It's very generous of him, considering how he feels about women. I didn't think he was even aware that I was here. I haven't seen hide nor hair of the man."

"He's been on a toot," I explained.

Her face screwed up in distress and she clicked her tongue. "Poor, foolish man."

I didn't have time to explore that, for Bob Ford was just crossing the creek with a Mexican leading a mule loaded with wood. I hardly knew him as I went to meet him. His beard was gone, leaving his face thin but making him look ten years younger. He wore a boiled shirt and broadcloth pants that looked like they might be the suit he was saving to be buried in. He had a plug hat, too small, slanted on his head. He was about the funniest sight I'd seen in quite a spell, and I laughed.

He looked pained, like he'd eaten something that didn't go down well. "What's funny, Austin?"

"You are," I said. "You look like a Front Street gambler from Sacramento."

"Do I now?" He sounded concerned. "I bought these dudes from Howie Henderson. He said they're what's being worn in San Francisco right now."

"They must be real comfortable to chop wood in."

He flushed at that, and told the Mexican to unload the mule and pile the wood neatly, then go get another load.

"She's got enough wood to last her all summer," I told him. "You're going to make talk and embarrass her if you keep on."

He looked unhappy, but he was stubborn. "I can't let that knothead Wicks beat me out."

"She doesn't want any more wood from either of you."

He squinted at me suspiciously. "This ain't one of Anson's tricks to get me out of his way while he makes time with her?"

I denied that it was, or that I was taking sides.

He nodded quickly, taking the hat from his head and scratching his thick hair thoughtfully. "Guess I shouldn't have said that, shouldn't have doubted you. Seems I'm kind of mixed up. I never saw a woman like her, never once."

"Why don't you tell her that?"

He started. "Me tell a female, right to her face?" He shook his head. "I couldn't never do that. But you maybe could. You could put in a word for me, say I'm a steady man and that I ain't killed no one like Anson has, leastwise not since I come to California."

I agreed to tell her.

"And I got a hundred and twenty-eight thousand dollars with Reynolds and Company. I ain't much, but I'd make her a good, solid husband."

"If I tell her," I bargained, "you got to quit hanging around all the time, and not bring any more wood until she asks for it."

He was uncertain, but he nodded slowly. "Well, if you say so. But you got to make Anson clear out too or it's no deal."

I promised this and watched him go away, arguing with himself, then I went back to the shack. The widow had just taken six pies from the oven, brown and crisp, and their smell was almost more than I could stand.

"I fixed it," I told her, watching as she lined them on the shelf and put another six in to bake. "Bob won't bring any more wood until I tell him."

She turned around and gave me a hug. "You're my boy, Austin. You pick the pie you want and take it home."

I backed away. I wanted one of those pies desperately, but they were worth two dollars each, and that was all I made in two weeks. One thing I'd learned that summer was the value of money.

"You can't afford to be giving your pies away."

She smiled warmly. "If it weren't for you there would be no pies at all. And that article you wrote will have customers rushing in from all over."

I had to be honest. "It was the way John fixed it that made it good. He's the one to thank for it."

Her face changed. "I'd like very much to thank him. But he hasn't given me the chance. Where is he now?"

I suspected that he was gambling, but I did not say so.

Instead I found him at the shop when I got back there, carrying the pie she had pressed into my hands. He wasn't doing a thing, just standing at the high desk, staring out at the dusty street.

"Mrs. Fox gave me this," I said. "She says thank you for the article."

He acted as if he didn't hear me. "You'd better start breaking up the forms."

I went to work, watching him from the corner of my eye. "Bob Ford wants to marry her," I said. "He's got a hundred and twenty-eight thousand dollars with Reynolds."

He spun on me, for the barest instant his face open with dismay. Then it closed again and he said laconically, "You tell her that?"

"I forgot to."

"You'd better tell her," he said. "She might as well have it as some other woman . . . a hundred and twenty-eight thousand . . . How does a man get that much money?"

"By having a good claim," I said, "and by working it. He don't gamble or anything."

His head thrust forward and there was an expression around his eyes that sort of frightened me.

"Austin, are you trying to reform me?"

I hadn't really thought about it, but I guess I had been.

"Don't," he said. "When you get to be as old as I am you will learn that no one reforms anyone else. People will be what they will. You have to live with them or you don't. I don't. There is no one dependent upon me, and no one gives a damn what happens to me. Please have the courtesy to let me go to hell in my own sweet fashion."

I knew then that he had been drinking. It wasn't always easy to tell. He continued to watch me for a long moment, then picked up his hat and stalked out of the building.

I heard Judge Marvin talking about him to Jack White a couple of weeks later. The pie business was thriving. Doc Grace had sent to Stockton for more apples and flour, and the miners were coming in from the creeks just to stand outside the widow's shack and gawk as she lined her pies up on the counter that had been built out front. The partners were nearly always there. I think they had not spent a full day on their claim since the night I had borrowed the stove.

Of course all this made talk. Prudence Fox seemed to be the center of every conversation in camp. But John Haverstick had not gone near her.

"I'm afraid we'll have to let him go," Marvin was saying. I was at the back of the shop, cleaning the press's roller. "He's drunk about half the time."

"He does his work," White said. That was the only thing that ever concerned Jack White, whether a man did his work and whether the paper was making money.

"It isn't only his drinking. He's been losing money steadily at Pete Ranso's, and Ranso is a dangerous man."

Ranso was a ticket-of-leave man from Australia who had come to the Pacific coast the year before. He ran a gambling and fandango house in Spanish Town with the help of a woman known as Squash Nose Kate.

"How do you know that?"

"Ranso had the effrontery to stop me on the street this morning and ask if Haverstick was good for a ten thousand dollar debt."

"What did you tell him?"

"That it was none of his business. You want to talk to Haverstick?"

"It won't do any good. He's a stubborn fool. That Philadelphia girl really ruined him. There wasn't a more promising writer on the Atlantic coast."

"I never heard about that."

"He doesn't talk about it. He was to be married, and she ran off with an older man who had money. That's why he came to California. He's been trying to destroy himself ever since."

"A shame," Marvin said. "But if he knows what's good for him he'll get out of here pretty fast."

Two hours later John showed up at the shop. I was alone and I studied him, deciding that he was sober. He had changed a lot in the last few weeks. He was close shaven and his clothes were still fresh, but he had lost the warm friendliness that had drawn me to him at first.

"Where is everybody?"

"The Judge went down to Jimtown. I don't know where Jack is."

He went over to the cash box under the high desk, where we kept the money from advertisements and job work. He opened the box and lifted out the poke of gold dust, then fingered through the collection of coins.

I watched him. I had a funny feeling in my stomach. He turned and found me there and flushed.

"I was going to draw an advance."

He dropped the poke back in the box and closed it.

"You're in trouble, aren't you?" I asked.

He glanced at me sharply. "What are you talking about?"

"Ranso."

His voice had a sudden dry sound. "What do you know about Ranso?"

I didn't dare tell him I had listened to Marvin and White. "It's all around town," I said. "You'd better get out of this country before Ranso gets mad."

He wet his lips. "I can't, Austin."

"Then you'd better get the money to pay him."

"Where? I couldn't get it for her, how could I get it for him?"

"What her?"

"The pie lady." He laughed shortly, with no sound of mirth. "The story of my life. Women. I am destined to be haunted by them. They never brought me any good, nor I them."

"Was that why you gambled with Ranso?"

He took a long time to answer, but he had to talk to someone.

"That's why." He sighed. "I had nothing to offer her. She can take her choice of any man along Woods Creek. Bob Ford or Anson Wicks with their hundreds of thousands of dollars . . . how can I compete? If I could have won . . ."

"But instead, you lost."

He slammed his right fist against his other hand. "I lost. I lost. All my life I've lost. At everything. I've always lost."

I kept very quiet. I was scared.

"Fool. Fool." He was talking to himself. He took a pacing turn of the shop and then continued blindly out of the door.

I went back to work half-heartedly, puzzling over what

John Haverstick could do. I wasn't aware of Anson Wicks coming in until he called my name.

He was carrying a paper-wrapped package and I could tell by the way he handled it that it was heavy. He came toward me with the air of a conspirator and laid the package on the floor behind the high desk.

"Anson, you want to see something pretty?"

He bent down and unwrapped the paper. You could have heard my gasp clear to Stockton. He had the Woods Creek nugget.

I'd seen it only once, still muddy and sand encrusted from the stream bed, and I was not prepared for what I saw now. It was about ten inches long, a jagged chunk of rotten quartz intershot with layers and wires of gold that laced through it like filigree.

I stooped to pick it up, but found it was all I could do to lift it.

"Pretty, ain't it?"

"It's beautiful," I said fervently. I'd seen hundreds of nuggets since coming to Sonora, but I'd never seen anything to equal this. Few people in the gold country had seen its like.

If a nugget weighed half a pound, quartz and all, it was considered a phenomenon. This chunk of rock must have weighed close to twenty. There was no way of judging its worth, but one man had offered the partners five thousand dollars and they had refused.

"Think a woman would like it?"

"Who wouldn't?" I said.

"Then you tell her, the widow, I mean. Tell her it's hers."

I couldn't imagine anyone giving away the nugget, but I said, "She won't take it from you. She wouldn't even take the stove for free."

He rubbed the side of his nose with a crooked index finger. "You tell her. See, women are scarce in this country, they're sort of worth their weight in gold."

I thought of something else. "But it isn't yours to give. It belongs half to Bob Ford."

He shook his head. "The polecat claims that, but it ain't so. I found it on my side of the line. Then he says the hole it come out of was half on his ground. He even took the sheriff down to show him, but that hole was dug after I pulled out this nugget, and I don't care who hears me say it."

"I hear him." Bob Ford was standing in the doorway,

with a rifle in his hand and a look on his face that said he meant to use it.

"He's a thieving skunk. He's trying to steal both my half of the nugget and the woman I'm fixin' to marry."

Even in this extremity Ford would not directly address his partner, but at the moment it did not strike me as funny. Anson Wicks had a Navy Colts in his belt, and Sonora boasted that he was the fastest gun out of Texas.

"Please . . ." I begged. "Please . . ."

But neither of them heard me. Anson was turning slowly. Ford was bringing up his rifle. The next instant the printing shop was filled with sound and smoke and curses.

I dropped down behind the desk, trying to drop clear through the floor. I didn't know how long they would keep shooting.

But there were no more reports and after a minute I stuck my head around the corner. Bob Ford was lying in the doorway. Anson Wicks was twisted on the floor a couple of feet from me, his shirt front soaked with blood. Neither was moving nor making a sound.

I was frozen on my hands and knees. Then I began to shake so that I nearly pitched onto my face. Then I heard Aunt Emeline's voice screaming, "Austin, Austin," as she flew through the door, jumping straight over Bob Ford's body. She had been on the other side of the street when she heard the shots, and knowing that they came from the print office, was certain I was dead.

I began to yell, as if the loudness of my voice could undo the terrible act. "They shot each other . . . they shot each other . . ." I blurted over and over.

Aunt Emeline skirted around Anson Wicks' grotesque form and her arms closed about me. She pulled me up and held me against her, tight.

"It's all right, baby." She clasped my head against her breast and kept rubbing it, hard, as though she could rub away the picture in my mind.

The shop was suddenly filled with men and I heard George Works' voice as the sheriff took charge. Then he was beside us.

"What happened, Austin?" the sheriff asked.

The direct question broke loose my tears and sobs, but I tried to tell him.

My aunt's voice had a fierce sound above my trembling

words. "Let him alone, George Works. You hear me? Let him alone."

I managed to turn in her protective arms. "Anson brought the nugget to give it to Mrs. Fox, and Bob came in. Then they shot each other."

Dr. Topper pushed through the crowd. He was a tall, very thin man who looked more like an undertaker than a doctor, and, in fact, doubled as one when the need arose. He made a ticking noise with his tongue as he looked at one and then the other of the quiet figures.

"Both in the stomach. Not much to do."

My aunt was steering me out of the shop. I wanted to go and tell the widow what had happened, but Aunt Emeline wouldn't let me.

"That woman has caused trouble enough," she said sharply as she piloted me home. "You keep away from her now."

The town appeared to agree with her. For the next three days, while we waited for Anson and Bob to die, no one went anywhere near her. Her pies sat invitingly on the outside counter, but no one came to buy them.

On the fourth day I finally managed to get back to the print shop. My aunt had insisted that I quit, but I won the argument that the fight between Anson and Bob had no connection with my job or the shop.

Both of them were still alive, although the doctor kept saying they had no chance and that there was nothing he could do.

John Haverstick was alone when I came in, and he looked sicker than either of the partners. He was standing at the composing stone, doing absolutely nothing, his mind far away until I spoke to him. Then he blew out his breath in a gust.

"They're animals to treat her this way. They've no right to blame her."

I guessed that he was talking about the widow, and I felt a kinship with his distress. It was my first experience with mob cruelty. But my aunt had issued strict orders that I keep away from her.

"Have you talked to her?"

"I tried, but I can't do her any good. I'm in bad trouble myself."

I knew he was talking about Ranso. "You'd better skip out of the country."

"And leave her at the mercy of these idiots?"

"You just said you couldn't help her. And getting yourself killed won't fix anything."

"I just don't know what to do." He wandered out of the shop almost in a daze.

I had a short battle with my conscience, then I went down to the bakery shack. Prudence Fox was sitting beside the cold stove, just sitting. When she saw me her face brightened.

"Austin. I knew you'd come. I haven't talked to a single soul in three days."

I felt guilty. She looked so alone, so helpless. But I could not tell her why I hadn't come sooner.

"John Haverstick is very worried about you."

She was startled. "Why should he be worried?"

"He likes you," I said, "even if he doesn't trust women because a girl in Philadelphia ran away with somebody who had a lot of money."

She was listening now.

"He says the people are animals to blame you for the partners' fight."

She drew a slow breath. "How are they?"

"Alive. But Doc Topper says they don't have much chance."

She shuddered. "Austin, why do they blame me? Those men were feuding long before I came out here."

"It's the nugget," I explained.

"What nugget?"

I was surprised that she did not know about the Woods Creek nugget. I told her about it, how it had caused most of the trouble between them and how Anson had brought it in to give to her.

Her eyes grew wide and pained. "But he must have known I wouldn't accept it."

"He said you were worth your weight in gold. He wanted you to marry him."

She put her slender fingers against her cheeks and pressed her temples up. "You'd better go now. I must think."

It was the next day that my aunt told me Anson wanted to see me. She did not approve, but she said that Mr. Wicks was dying, and you just couldn't refuse the request of a dying man.

I went to their cabin. Bob Ford lay in his bunk at the far end of the room. Anson was huddled under his own blankets and Mrs. Grace and my aunt and the other ladies were taking turns nursing them.

Anson looked small and shrunken, his face wax-like and warped with pain.

The first thing he said was, "Get them out of here."

My aunt and Mrs. Grace did not appreciate the demand, but again, it was a request of the dying, and they left. When they had gone he lifted his head a little and looked down the room.

"That polecat not dead yet?"

I said that Bob Ford was still alive.

Anson fell to cursing. "I wish he'd hurry up. I hurt. But I'll be damned if I give him the satisfaction of dying first." He was quiet for a moment, then his voice changed. "The widow ain't been near here, has she?"

I shook my head.

"All the rest of the fiddle-butted females been buzzing around like flies in August, but she ain't come."

"It isn't her fault," I said. "It's theirs."

"What do you mean by that?"

I told him how everyone was blaming her. "She's having it bad. Grace won't give her any more supplies and no one is buying her pies. She's got no place to go and no money."

He shut his eyes. I thought he was asleep or maybe dead, he was so long in speaking. Then he said:

"I'm twenty-seven years old, and I been a lot of places and known a lot of people. But I never felt about anyone the way I feel about her. Tell you what . . . where's that nugget?"

"George Works impounded it."

"You tell George to give that nugget to the widow."

"He won't listen to me."

"You tell him to come here with it and I'll tell him. Guess a dying man has the right to do what he wants with his own nugget."

"But it's only half yours," I reminded him.

He grimaced again. "You'd think that polecat would have the decency to die and let a man do the one thing he wants. You go tell him how they're treating the widow and that I want her to have the nugget."

I went to the other end of the room. Bob Ford did not look any healthier than Anson. He opened one eye, then grunted.

"Wicks dead yet?"

"Not yet," I said. "He claims he won't die until you do."

Ford grunted again. "You tell him I could lick him in a

160

fair fight any day there was, and I'll lick him on this." He closed the eye.

"He sent me with a message."

The eye opened. There was pain, but also suspicion. "What message?"

I gave it to him. He listened without comment. When I finished he took time to think about it.

"It's all right with me to give her the blamed thing," he said finally. "It never did us no good. But she's got to think it was my idea."

"He'll never agree to that."

"No, he won't, the stubborn mule. But he ain't going to head me while I'm breathing."

"So she don't get it," I said. "Then what happens to her? What difference does it make whose idea she thinks it was? You're both going to die anyhow."

He had both eyes open now, watching me intently.

"How about," I said, "if she thinks it was my idea? That you both agreed. That way you'll be even."

Ford considered this at length, then nodded. "You tell Wicks that. If he agrees, she gets the nugget." He closed his eyes.

The news spread like fire through the town. George Works must have told it, for I hadn't, but the people gathered along the street as he carried the heavy chunk of quartz toward the bakery shop.

Prudence Fox had no warning, and she was not alone. John Haverstick was with her. I had followed George Works. We came into the shack to find Haverstick and the girl talking so earnestly that neither of them heard us until we were in the room. John had his hands on her shoulders, and their voices were very low.

They started guiltily, and I saw that the widow's cheeks were flushed and that Haverstick looked very unhappy. If George noticed anything out of the ordinary he gave no sign. George was not very observing, and he took himself with great seriousness.

He bobbed his head, saying, "Ma'am, it is my duty as sheriff to carry out the dying wishes of two of this community's citizens. This nugget belongs to both of them, and they want you to have it."

He laid the chunk on the pie shelf where a ray of the late afternoon sun came through the window and struck glinting color from it. Then he stepped back, removing his hat and fiddling uncertainly with it.

Prudence Fox looked at him, at the nugget, at Haverstick, and then at me, her eyes wide and dark.

"You mean those poor men are dead?"

"They're still trying to outwait each other," I said. "But they know they're goners and they want to get things straightened out. They both want you to have it."

She walked in fascination to the shelf, catching her breath at the stringers of gold. Haverstick said something under his breath which I did not catch.

"It's beautiful." She touched it with her fingertips.

"Unbelievable." Haverstick's voice was choked.

"But I can't accept it."

George Works jumped. The idea that anyone would refuse that nugget was beyond his comprehension.

"Why in tarnation not? Them two are headed for the great beyond, God rest 'em. They can't take that baby with them, and I never heard that either of them had kith nor kin."

She was still fingering the nugget. The fascination made her eyes bright. I'd seen the same look on other faces. Gold does something to people unlike any other metal.

"Thank you," she said. "I'll have to think."

George Works heaved a sigh of relief. He had been afraid that she would create a situation which he did not know how to handle. He put on his hat, bobbed his head to the girl and hurried from the shack. The girl still stood, tracing the filigree lines with her fingertips.

Haverstick came forward, and his voice was more relieved than I had heard it in many days.

"You're all right now. I don't know what that is worth, but I'd guess at ten thousand easy, maybe more. You can go back where you belong."

She did not seem to hear him. She said to no one in particular, "I've got to thank them. The poor dears. Imagine them thinking of me while they're dying."

She walked out of the door without even glancing back. John looked after her, and then at the piece of quartz.

"She's damn trusting to leave a thing like that lying around."

"Everybody in camp knows it," I said. "A man wouldn't dare steal it."

"Austin," he said, shaking his head, "you're as innocent

as she is. Anyone could break that up with a hammer, and who's to prove any piece was once a part of the Woods Creek nugget? Gold has no identity. It belongs to the one who possesses it."

He gave me an odd look, and then almost ran from the shack. I stood, thinking about what he had said. There were plenty of men in Spanish Town who would cut a throat for half an ounce, and here lay an unguarded fortune, more than most people in Sonora had ever seen.

I glanced out of the door. It was beginning to get dark and most of the people had disappeared from the street. Reynolds and Company Express was closed. I thought of taking it home with me, but I didn't know how to get it there. I wished I knew where George Works was. I looked at Grace's store, but he had closed also.

I considered the dirt floor, but if I dug a hole it would show. And then I thought of the firebox in the stove. I removed the lids and dug in the thick layer of ashes until I had room enough for the quartz. Then I wrestled it from the shelf and managed to carry it across, laying it on the grate and covering it carefully.

But I still was not satisfied. I got some kindling and built a small fire, figuring that no one would think of looking for a nugget under a bed of hot coals.

Then I went home. I had milked the cow and was just having my late supper when someone pushed open the door and came into the cabin. My aunt was at the stove, cleaning up the pans. Caroline was already in bed.

I looked up. There were two men, with stockings pulled over their heads. Both were carrying guns.

I almost swallowed my fork. I guessed what they were after, and I felt sick inside. My aunt turned and gasped, and then she was perfectly quiet, as if any words she might have were caught in her throat.

One of the men said harshly, "What did you do with that nugget, boy?"

I gulped twice, then I told the truth. "I left it in the pie shack."

"It ain't there."

I was having difficulty in saying anything. My throat felt as though someone had hold of it with very powerful fingers.
"Then someone must have taken it."

"There's ways to make you talk." The voice was dangerous. "So don't get too smart."

He glanced around and saw Caroline staring at him wide eyed from her bunk, and started toward her. My aunt held an iron skillet in her hand. She ran forward, swinging it.

He gave her a back-hand slap that sent her stumbling to fall over one of the rawhide seated chairs. I jumped up, but the other man caught me by the shoulder and pushed me down.

"Don't make us hurt the little girl."

The first man pulled Caroline from the bunk, and she let out a yell that seemed to tear off the roof.

"Let her alone. Let her alone. I'll show you where it is."

My captor shook me roughly. "Tell me."

"I'll have to show you." That wasn't true, but I had to get them away from the cabin. And maybe I would see George Works downtown. I stood up and started for the door.

The other man hesitated. "What do we do with them?" He shook Caroline and nodded toward Aunt Emeline.

His partner laughed, but the sound was chilling. "Lady, if you ever want to see this boy alive again you'll stay right here, and you won't talk to anyone. Understand? Anyone."

Aunt Emeline was still on the floor. She got up slowly. She looked at me, and there was great pleading in her eyes.

"Austin." Her voice was steady, with all its familiar authority, but I knew that the tone was directed at the men. "You show them just where it is. And then you come straight home or I'll paddle you."

The man who had my shoulder shoved me out into the night. There were no street lamps in Sonora, and most of the people went to bed early. Few of the cabins showed light. I had never felt so alone, and I was scared. We moved over the uneven ground, feeling our way in the half-glow from the sickle moon.

The lamp was burning in the bakery shop and the door was ajar. The man pushed me through and I saw Prudence Fox sitting beside her mixing board. Then I saw a third man standing in the far corner. He stepped forward quickly, saying in a hoarse whisper,

"Did he tell you . . . ?" Something about the voice was familiar, giving me a creepy feeling, but I could not place it, for the widow had given a little cry when she saw me, and jumped up.

"Have they hurt you, Austin?"

I shook my head, not knowing what to say now.

"Do you know where the nugget is?" Her voice was strained and her face very white.

I nodded.

"Tell them, child. No gold is worth your getting hurt." I realize now that what I heard in her tone was contempt, but I didn't know it at the time.

I pointed to the stove. It was her nugget, to give up if she wanted to. "In there."

The whispering man swore. "How can it be?" And again I had the eerie sense of familiarity.

"In the firebox, underneath the ashes."

The man behind me jumped forward and raised the lids. They had built up the fire and it was blazing brightly. They dashed it with water.

They dug the lump out of the ashes. The fire had done it no good. The rotten quartz had fractured so that it came apart in their fingers. Some of the gold stringers had melted, but it was still gold.

They clawed at it like three animals fighting over the carcass of a deer, and the girl watched them, loathing on her face.

"All right, Mr. Haverstick. You have your gold. Now get out of here."

Every motion in the cabin froze. I knew she was right. I think I'd known it too, without accepting it. One of the others began cursing.

"That does it. Now we've got to kill her."

Haverstick said in his normal tone, "No you don't, Ranso. You made a promise that no one would be hurt."

Ranso's voice was cold. "Before she guessed who you are. I ain't leaving her here to talk, nor the boy either."

I guess Haverstick knew the man. I guess he knew that the whole thing was finished for him. But for once in his life he did not quibble or hesitate. His gun came up and he shot Ranso through the head.

The third man had taken no part in the argument, but he moved now. His first bullet struck Haverstick in the chest, his second went over John's head to tear through the shack's thin wall, for Haverstick had staggered under the first impact. Then he steadied and shot the man squarely.

Haverstick stood for a long minute, perfectly still, then he swayed. His knees crumpled. He sat down and then went over on his side.

Prudence Fox was screaming. I didn't know it, but I was

165

yelling. She was down on her knees beside Haverstick, trying to cradle his head in her lap.

"John. John. Why? Why?"

His eyes were open. His voice a fainting whisper. "I owed Ranso a lot of money."

"You could have had it. You could have had it all." She was crying, smoothing her hand over his yellow hair.

His lips twisted in pain and bitterness. "Yes. And had you too. And always you'd have wondered if I wanted you for the gold."

He was dead before George Works and the rest of the camp got to the shack. My aunt came running with them. I can still feel the comfort of her arms as she held me close and wept on my tousled hair.

The widow left Sonora the next day. She went to the partners' cabin and tried to give back what was left of the nugget.

"I give it to you," Anson Wicks insisted, "and I ain't no Indian giver."

"I gave it to you." It was Bob Ford, yelling from his end of the room. "You take it and clear out of here. Ain't no use you hanging around, waiting for two damn fools to die."

She kissed Anson, then she kissed Bob Ford. Maybe it was the kisses, or maybe their contrary natures, but neither died. Or maybe it was just that neither would give up first.

As soon as they were up and around they sold their claim to a company of doctors just in from Illinois, and took off East, looking for the widow. They still weren't speaking, but they were traveling together. As Anson told me:

"I gotta stay with that polecat and make sure he don't ever get ahead of me."

I don't know whether they found the widow, for they didn't know where to look.

CHAPTER EIGHTEEN

WE MOVED TO Mokelumne Hill in the spring of 1851. The Mokelumne River winds a tortured descent through a deep, sharp canyon from the higher reaches of the Sierras to its junction with the San Joaquin north of Stockton.

There is nothing lovelier than the California foothill country in the spring. The ever-green oaks freshen, wild grain sprouts through the mat of pale dried straw that softens the rocky ground. The streams quicken to floods, fed by the melting snows of the upper slopes.

No matter how dull, how miserable the winter has been, the breeze of new life stirs everyone to increased activity.

My uncle was particularly susceptible to this spring surge. After a long time my aunt became resigned, but in '51 she was still fighting his restlessness with every wile her woman's mind could conceive.

I was very excited at the prospect of moving to the Hill. Sonora never was a very stimulating camp. For one thing, it was not on a river. For another, the placers along Woods Creek and on the edge of Table Mountain were not actually in town. I had come West to dig gold, and until this time I had had little chance.

Moke Hill was different. Although it sat on the canyon rim, high above the rushing water, it was only a short way to the actual diggings.

"I won't go." My aunt used a tone which brooked no argument. "I gave up my home and my people to cross this country with you. I put up with the misery of winter in Sacramento. I came here and tried to make you a new home of this."

She looked around the cabin with real fondness. It was much enlarged. My uncle and Ike had returned from the Melones claim in early December. Samson had not come with them. We had no idea where he was, for he had sent no word. All winter my uncle had labored steadily, improving the place. We had three rooms and a lean-to kitchen, without question one of the best houses in Sonora.

Ike had gone to work for the *Herald*, but this had required only two days of the week. The rest of the time he worked with Uncle Ben or hunted, with the result that we ate as well or better than anyone in camp.

"Sonora isn't much, but it's growing. There are more than twenty women here, and five doctors and four really good stores. And a church. I won't go."

We moved to Moke Hill the first of May. My uncle sold the cabin to two of the men who had bought the partners' claim, and who were getting wealthy. He bought a team of horses, loaded the press and type and some paper he had been able to buy in Sacramento, and started north. Ike and I

167

went with him, leaving my aunt and Caroline to follow by stage, for there was now a thrice-weekly service between Sonora and Hangtown.

The road was hazardous, made doubly so by the slides and washouts of the waning winter. It dropped down the towering wall of the Stanislaus canyon, crossed on a ferry raft which ran along a cable stretched between the two banks of the swift stream, climbed the far wall through Volcano, Murphy's, Angels', San Andreas, and on up to Moke Hill.

This was the road through the heart of the so-called Southern Mines, alive with wagons and pack trains, and every creek and gravel bar we crossed was dotted thickly with sluice boxes and rockers.

The air was soft and warm. Flowers were everywhere, and I think it was from that spring that I began to have a love for California which I have never lost, which is in a sense the strongest love of my life.

I was almost thirteen. I had grown over four inches since we arrived in the state. I was beginning to fill out and, as Ike said, getting to the point where I could handle the business end of a shovel.

Children on the frontier developed faster than those in the East, from sheer necessity. Whatever comforts and improvements we had we made ourselves. Supply points were distant, and haulage made everything to be brought expensive.

It was not nearly so bad as when we had first arrived, for ships were now arriving with increased regularity at San Francisco, and a constant stream of river vessels brought their cargos up the wide waterways to Sacramento and Stockton. But it was still a long, tedious haul over cruel roads to transfer the necessities of life to the camps and foothill towns. I had learned to pretty much care for myself.

Moke Hill proved a disappointment after my imaginings. Fresh from the rapidly growing Sonora, its lack of nearly everything that went to constitute a town distressed me. There were four stores, but compared to Grace's well-stocked establishment they looked rude indeed, merely shacks with wooden shelves sparsely laden and planks laid across empty kegs for counters.

What goods there were were fundamental in the extreme, and I wondered how Uncle Ben could hope to secure enough advertising that a paper could survive.

The town itself had fewer than five hundred inhabitants,

but of course this did not include the miners strung along the main stream in the canyon below, nor those in the side gullies diverting from it.

My uncle's first concern was living quarters. He and Ike unloaded the press and printing office on a level piece of ground at the head of the single street, then drove north along the canyon rim, searching out trees with trunks straight enough for their purpose. We built a two-room cabin with a sod roof, and the lean-to printing office.

The town looked on with interest. A number of the citizens stepped in to help, for there was a strong rivalry between the mining camps, and my uncle's promise of a paper for Moke Hill was an advantage for which they were eager. He was at once the hero of the hour.

Ike was characteristically sardonic, bucolic of my uncle's business acumen. The relationship between the two men took me years to comprehend. To Ike, my uncle, with his education and writing proficiency, was one to be admired, and he treasured the association more deeply than anything in his rather empty life. But when it came to such practical matters as printing the paper and attending the business details, Ike believed, and with some justification, that my uncle was slightly retarded.

Some of their arguments were classic, with business fact and business theory at loggerheads. It always seemed strange to me that although my aunt's and Ike's views on logic were usually identical, in these arguments she took my uncle's side.

I was much older when I realized that her basic emotion was a fierce loyalty, totally unreasoning when one of her own was involved. This applied to Caroline, to my uncle, and to me. Although Ike was very nearly a member of our family for forty years she did not approve of him or welcome him to the inner circle.

But at thirteen I was not this perspicacious. I only knew that Ike was worried over the move and grumbled constantly to me. I shared his uncertainties, but I had no desire to leave the Hill.

I worked hard physically during the building. My particular job was peeling the logs for the walls. Ike taught me how. He was skillful with an ax, and under his tutelage I learned to slit the bark neatly and peel it away in circular chunks, some of which were ten feet in length.

Above us on the ridge Uncle Ben found a Mr. Cooper,

who owned a whipsaw, and contracted with him to cut out enough lumber for a floor. It was an unheard-of vanity, and people came to stand around and admire as he laid the rough boards on the log mud sills, setting them squarely with the hand-forged nails.

When the roof was on my uncle took the wagon and started back to Sonora to fetch the stove and household furnishings. Ike set up the printing office, and for the first time since our arrival I was free to explore the canyon below us.

For a week I roamed the banks of the rushing stream, from bar to bar, making friends as I went. Most of the miners knew that I was "that newspaper feller's kin," and the distinction made me welcome among them.

There is no thrill quite like watching a man clean up his sluice or rocker, turning the fines into the pan, squatting beside the stream, filling the shallow receptical with water, then swirling it gently, flooding the lighter sand over the edge until nothing remains but the rim of black sand heavy in the bottom, and the shining border of colors. No paper money nor minted silver will ever seem of any great value to me. Nothing except the yellow glint of gold has any real meaning.

Some of the men permitted me to jump down into their trenches, dug to bedrock, and fill a pan for myself, and wash it out in the icy river. In a week's time I accumulated two ounces of dust.

Mostly the miners were young, but those who had been more than a year in the diggings showed the effects of the grueling work and bad diet. There was a lot of land scurvy, a high rate of consumption, and always the danger of cholera. But in all they were a carefree lot, given to much horseplay and heavy drinking. The three saloons did more business than any other establishment on the Hill, barring the five girls who occupied a tent at the north edge of the straggling town.

The miners came from every state in the Union, and were for the most part homesick. I saw hundreds of pictures during that period, faded, bent, and torn. Only a few of the men had their families with them.

The majority of those on the Hill came from the southern states, and there were long debates about the slavery question and arguments in favor of California being admitted as a slave state.

My aunt and Caroline arrived on the northbound stage and I was thoroughly glad to see them, being terribly tired of Ike's cooking, but this pleasure was nearly lost in my excitement when I recognized the stage driver. It was Joe Stoop.

I had not seen him since we left Sacramento, and he was a different being. He was heavier, his scrawny skin now comfortably filled. I suspect that this was the first time of his life when he had consistently had enough to eat.

But the principal metamorphosis was in his manner. Stage drivers were a breed apart, and reveled in it. It was not everyone who could handle a coach and four to six horses under any condition, and the roads which snaked up and down the bottomless canyons were at best narrow shelves cut into the rocky walls.

A knight, a jehu, a whip, they were a swaggering company, very conscious of their worth and not at all averse to letting the general public know it.

Joe swaggered with the rest, and he had the added distinction of being rumored an exceptionally fast gun. To add to his reputation he had continued his purchase of diamonds. He wore a ring with a heavy stone on each little finger, and his shirt studs glittered in the sun. His shirt was frilled, his suit of broadcloth, perfectly cut. His boots shone as though glazed.

It was his boast that although he wore his precious stones in plain view of a treasure-hungry populous, no bandit would venture to hold up the stage he was driving, and those few who in ignorance made the attempt had died peremptorily.

He greeted me with the dignity of an emperor. He stepped down over the wheel while the hostlers held the restless horses. He moved to the coach door and helped down my aunt and Caroline and two other women passengers. While he supervised the unloading of the baggage he condescended to converse with me.

"You're getting a real good size on you, Austin."

"Am I bigger than Sandy?" It had always irked me that Sandy had been taller than I.

He squinted at me, measuring. Sandy was Joe's pet, his special pride. He loved all of his children. I think that if Joe Stoop had one quality which endeared him to everyone, it was his feeling for his children. But Sandy was something special, and he was now trying to decide whether if he admitted that I was larger than she he was being disloyal.

He apparently decided that he was not, for he said, "No, you're bigger than she is. I'd say maybe a couple of inches, but then, she's a girl. Never did hold with large women."

I wondered what he considered Myrtle, who could not be considered diminutive.

"She all right?" I was asking about Sandy.

"She's fine. She took herself honors at school this year. She won the spelling bee."

I said that was great.

"And she's singing in the church and at the socials. One of the women down there says she's got a voice should be in opera."

I was impressed, although I was hazy as to what opera was.

"Tell her hello," I said. "Tell her I'd like to see her."

"I'll do that." He nodded. "I'll just do that."

He saluted my aunt, waiting on the boardwalk before the stage station, mounted the wheel, turned to make certain that all of his charges were in place, motioned to the hostlers to jump clear, and took the six horses clattering down the curving grade at a dead run.

You could not help thrilling to the performance, and I said so as I joined my aunt.

"Joe's some driver."

"He's a madman." She expelled it forcefully. "Why the wheels didn't fly off that coach I'll never know. Whoever thought that a namby-pamby like Joe Stoop would turn out like this."

"He's sure important now," I said.

She gave me a frosty look. "Seems like in this heathen country men like Joe Stoop, who were trash back home, become important, while people like Ben . . ." She stopped there, almost biting her tongue, then she said in a different voice, "All right, show us where we live."

My uncle did not come with the household goods for three days. Ike welcomed my aunt uncertainly, knowing that she would not be happy with the new home.

"It's the best we could do," he said. "Not as nice as the Sonora place, but it's about the best house up here. Ben, he labored long and hard on it."

"And what right have you to criticize it then?"

He sighed helplessly. "I wasn't criticizing, ma'am. I just wanted you to know we tried . . ."

Caroline and I ducked away. Caroline was growing too.

She was over ten, and I began to think of her as a human being. I showed her my gold dust and bragged a little.

"I know how to pan now. Some of the boys say I'm as good as anyone on the river."

"Will you teach me?"

"It isn't for girls," I said. "You've got to work in the water. It's cold."

"I can stand as much as you can. Let's go downtown."

We went downtown. It was hardly a block long and Caroline was critical.

"It's not as big as Sonora. Why did Papa want to come way up here?"

"Because a man told him the bars here are the richest in the mining country."

"Are they?"

I didn't know, but I wasn't going to admit it. "Sure. Bart Spicer says Moke Hill will be the biggest town in California, bigger than San Francisco and Sacramento together."

"Who's Bart Spicer?"

"He owns the store, that one." I pointed across the street. "He's buying up lots. He's going to be a millionaire."

Caroline let out a squeal. "Look . . ."

"Where? What?"

"Over beside the store. It's Black Bob."

Sure enough, there he was. He sat with his back against the store wall, his head bent forward, his face shielded by his broken hat.

"Bob. Bob." We were both running, yelling at the top of our voices.

Bob had been asleep. His head came up as we pelted toward him, and his mouth split in a big grin.

"Mr. Austin. Missy. Where'd you drop from?"

"We live here," I said. "Uncle Ben's going to start a newspaper here next week. Come on over and see Aunt Emeline and Ike. Uncle Ben isn't here. He went down after our things at Sonora."

I was shocked, looking at him. His clothes were worn and patched and his big body was shrunken until the flesh hardly hid the bones. He hesitated.

"You sure they'll want to see me?"

"Of course," I said. "Why not?"

Still he hesitated. "Don't want to embarrass them. Folks hereabout aren't so friendly to my people, seems like."

I didn't stop to tell him that my aunt's two brothers were

173

rumored to run a station on the Underground Railroad, helping runaway slaves to reach Canada.

"You come," I said, and grabbed his hand.

He had a small bundle, a pick, a shovel, and a gold pan. Apart from the color of his skin he might have been just another of the thousands of miners swarming along the canyons.

My aunt was already busy arranging the things she had brought in her trunk, cleaning up our men's disorder, readying this latest in her growing succession of homes, marking it with her special warmth.

She was surprised to see Bob, and she was pleased. I think any familiar face would have been welcome on that day, for she sounded very much alone and not a little homesick.

"Tell us about you, Bob. Where have you been?"

He stood in the middle of the room, twisting his hat in his powerful hands.

"Sutters Creek," he said, "and down south of Placerville. It ain't been so good. I thought I'd try up here on the river."

"You haven't found any gold?"

"I found some, a couple of places." His tone was restrained.

"I'll bet he's hungry," I said.

My aunt looked startled. Then she examined him more critically. "When did you eat last?"

He smiled lamely. "Well, I had me a rabbit yesterday. Right tasty, too."

"Land o' Goshen." She turned toward the door. "Ike, you bring out some of that meat."

Ike had a quarter of venison hanging in a well between the print shop lean-to and the cabin. One thing I remember, we were usually short on fresh vegetables and fruit during the early days, but we never lacked for meat. Ike was a dedicated hunter.

While she fried the meat and warmed a kettle of beans over the open campfire, and set out some of Ike's pan bread, she cross-questioned Bob. At first he was reluctant to talk, but anyone who thought they could keep anything from my Aunt Emeline was deceiving himself.

"What have you heard from Edmond Jones?"

Bob shook his head. "Haven't heard in a long spell. Not since he went off to the Sandwich Islands."

"How is it you didn't go with him?"

"Well, ma'am, I kind of hankered after getting me a little gold. Mr. Edmond, he didn't care very much. Money never meant a real lot to him."

174

"He's an idler," my aunt said. She had never been too admiring of Edmond.

"No ma'am." Bob was very polite. He was always polite, but he had a majestic dignity within him. "Mr. Edmond isn't lazy. He just don't see the sense of breaking his back to get something he already has. Me, I'm different. I like money. Yes ma'am, I like it very much."

"We all need it," my aunt admitted. The meat was done and she filled a plate, setting it on the plank table Ike had built. "Fill yourself up."

Bob ate slowly, deliberately, but something in his manner told me that he had been very hungry indeed.

"This," he said as he finished, "was mighty good, Mrs. Garner."

"You were starved." She had refrained from her questioning while he ate, but her curiosity was unabated, and she renewed the probing. "You must have found some gold, to have lasted this long?"

"Oh, I found some. I guess maybe I found too much."

"I don't understand."

"Well"—for one of the few times Bob sounded discouraged —"when you're the only black man on a creek, and you find a little more than the other fellow, they kind of get jealous."

"You mean they took it away from you?"

He stifled a sigh. "They made things a bit unpleasant, you might say. So, I'd move. I'd find me another spot where no one was too close, and then pretty soon more people would come and I'd have to move again. I'm kind of running out of places."

"Why, that's criminal."

Bob's smile held a trace of sadness. "That's the way the world is, ma'am."

"They won't do that to you here." I was indignant. "I know all the miners down along the river. They're nice people."

Bob looked at me. I was too young to sense the tragedy in his eyes. "All people are nice, Mr. Austin, except when you got something they hanker after. Then they're not so nice."

"You'll see," I promised. "We'll find you a piece of ground that's richer than any you've had."

Bob stayed with us for two weeks, and in that time he fleshed out again. I never saw anyone eat as he did, but I guess he had some catching up to do.

My uncle arrived with the furniture. Bob helped unload and set up the stove and carry the heavy pieces into the cabin. He cut wood and stacked it neatly, and finally he helped Ike with the press.

He was not our only visitor. Sandy arrived the week after my uncle.

We were all surprised to see her. I don't think my aunt appreciated her coming, but she made her welcome and kept her with us. Joe brought her up from Sacramento on his run and dropped her in front of the cabin with a flourish.

She seemed much older and at first I was a little afraid of her. She was beginning to look like a woman, not a skinny girl, and while I was a quarter head taller she was still more mature.

The first thing she did was kiss me, there in front of everyone. I could have died of embarrassment. Then she kissed Caroline, and finally kissed Aunt Emeline on the cheek.

She was bubbling as always, and she was all dressed up. I remembered the faded calico she had worn on the trip West. This had vanished, and she looked like a prim young maid in bright gingham, her hair done up in two tight braids.

I found out the first day that Sandy had not really changed. True, she was Diamond Joe's daughter and holding her head high that her father was now such a figure, but she was, in Ike's words, still a hellion who got into everything. She explored the print shop and then the town and finally the river, dragging me with her.

Two days after her arrival we climbed up the canyon, skirting the rushing water until we had passed the upper workings by half a mile. It was a hot day, the sun baking the chasm's depths, and we threw ourselves on a patch of grass in the shade of a twisted oak.

"I saw an orange tree this morning." Sandy was never one to be too attentive to the truth when she had a point to make, but this came clear out of the blue.

I laughed at her.

"I did. Mrs. Curtiss got three of them. They came in on the morning stage."

I didn't believe her. "What did it look like?" I'd seen oranges, but only one or two, and I had no idea where they grew nor how.

"Like a tree, silly. They came clear from Spain, or somewhere."

"You're crazy. Oranges won't grow up here, if they come from Spain."

"Wait and see."

She had the ability of provoking me with the simplest statements.

"You're funning."

"All right, wait and see."

"You say that again and I'll hit you."

"You aren't big enough. I can still lick you."

"I'm bigger than you are now."

"So what? You want to Indian rassle?"

I jumped up. We faced each other, setting the outside edges of our right feet together, grasping our right hands. The object was to make your opponent move his left foot before you moved yours. Sandy gave a quick twist of her lithe body as I pressed forward. I wasn't ready and I stumbled past her, plunging to my hands and knees.

I got up, frustrated and mad. "You didn't play fair."

"I did too."

I made a grab for her and missed. She was still faster than I. I started after her and she ducked around the tree and a pile of rocks.

"Slow poke, slow poke. Try and catch me."

I was trying and having no luck whatsoever. We ran back and forth across the grassed little meadow, she ducking and twisting like a fawn. Then she caught her toe on a stone which shoved a jagged tip through the carpet of grass, and fell headlong. The next moment I plunged on top of her, holding her down with my superior weight.

She lay a moment, panting, then she tried to squirm out from under me, but I held her.

"Let me up."

"Say uncle."

She squirmed harder, but I had a firm grip on both of her arms, holding her spread-eagled with her face digging into the grass.

"I can't breathe."

"Say uncle."

She said it finally, faintly, but she said it. I relaxed my hold and rolled free. She sat up, rubbing the dirt from her nose.

"That wasn't fair."

"That's not true. . . . Let's go down along the river."

We walked down the path beside the stream, jumping

from rock to rock, waving to the miners scattered along the shore.

"We've got to find Bob a place to work."

"We'll bring him down here. I know all the men and I know a claim that nobody's using."

But when we told Bob our plan he shook his head and gave us an argument. "No call for you kids to get mixed up in this."

"But I can help," I said. "I know where to go. It would take you a long time to find as good a place for yourself."

"I guess so," he said finally, then he went into the cabin and I heard him talking to my aunt.

My uncle was not there. He and Ike had printed up a handbill that read,

ANNOUNCING

The Mokelumne Hill Clarion.

A non-partisan journal standing for freedom and justice, with correspondents in Sonora, Stockton, Sacramento, San Francisco and the major cities.

Our first issue will appear on Thursday, the twenty-fifth of May.

One dollar the copy.

He had taken one of the horses and was riding up and down the canyon, passing them out to everyone he met while Ike was preparing the run.

My aunt followed Bob out of the cabin, Caroline holding onto her dress.

"You come back," she told him. "If there's any trouble. You understand, Bob?"

He nodded. He carried a packet of food wrapped in his clean shirt, his pick and shovel and pan. I took the pick, Sandy took the shovel, and the three of us moved along the trail down the canyon.

We made a strange group of gold seekers. I went in the lead, since I knew the shortcuts. Bob was in the middle, Sandy tagging along in the rear. I had in mind a place called Hoffman's Point, for I knew a claim whose owner had died the week before.

It was about two miles below the town, and all along the

way men stopped their work to stare after us. I waved to several of them but only two waved back. I did not take note of this oddity. I was too busy telling Bob of the superior advantages of his future claim.

"There aren't any big rocks," I said, "and there's an eddy in the river where you can build a Chinese water wheel to lift water into your sluice, and Hoffman had a ditch halfway to bedrock before he got the fever."

Bob listened in silence, but his dark eyes carefully studied the bar as we passed. We reached the point well before noon. There was one company of four men working above the abandoned ditch, three parties of two each working below. I knew them all.

I jumped down into the ditch and used the pick to loosen some of the cemented sand at the bottom. Then I motioned Sandy to pass down the shovel. I filled the pan and held it up.

"Go try it," I told Bob.

He took the laden pan and went to the river's edge, scooping it half-full of water to soak the sand. He used his strong fingers to break apart the lumps. Then he swirled it slowly, just beneath the surface of the running stream so that the current carried the lighter sand away.

It took him a quarter of an hour, working with practiced efficiency, until very little remained on the bright bottom of the pan save the curve of black sand rimmed with the feather glint of gold dust.

"See!" I was excited. "I'll bet that will give half an ounce anyhow."

Bob nodded, but he had no chance to answer. The scratch of boots on gravel caught our attention and three men came around the bend in the trail, crossing the spit of sand toward us.

The man in front was named Crouse. He had long red whiskers and a narrow, ferret face.

"What you doing, nigger?"

Bob looked up at him, saying nothing, quietly holding the pan.

"This ground's took. You got no business here."

"It's not," I said. "I looked in the claim book last night. Hoffman's dead and no one else has filed on it."

"Keep out of this, kid," Crouse said. "This ain't your business."

"It is too." I was beginning to get mad. He had no better

179

right there than we did. "I brought him here. He's going to file on this claim and . . ."

"He ain't going to file on no claim, not along this river. We don't need no niggers here."

There was a concurring mutter behind him. Two more men had come around the corner and Crouse appealed to them.

"This is for Americans." He said it loudly, as if taking comfort from his own voice. "We ain't having no Mexes or Chileanos, and we sure ain't having no niggers."

I felt that I was going to burst inside with sudden anger. I was afraid that I was going to cry. I used to cry when I was very mad.

"You've got no call to act this way. Bob is free. He's got his papers and he can go anywhere in the United States. He came clear across the country to dig for gold."

Crouse sneered at me. "I don't care where he digs, so long as it ain't along this river."

"That's not fair." I happened to glance at Sandy. She was white faced, her eyes enormous. I couldn't tell whether she was mad or scared or what. "If you won't let him dig on the river, where can he?"

Crouse turned slowly to the group around him. Others had joined the crowd. I'd been so upset that I hadn't seen them arrive. He grinned and they returned the grin. They were enjoying the sense of power it gave them to pick on a defenseless individual.

"Let him go find his own place." Crouse raised his head. Above, up about three quarters of a mile, was a hill. It is still known as Nigger Hill. "Tell him to go up that hill yonder. Maybe he'll find some real rich gravel up there."

The men broke into cawing laughter. "Maybe he'll find a big spring to run his sluice. But I'm telling him, he's got five minutes to be off this claim and stay off."

Crouse turned and swaggered away, the men following. He looked back, savoring his moment. "Five minutes, or we'll strip the black hide off his back and beat him to death with it."

They were gone, and we could hear their continued laughter as they pushed through the brush.

Sandy and I stood mute. Bob rose. Without emphasis he threw the black sand with its streak of colors out of the pan. He bent above the water and rinsed it clean. Then he straightened and slowly gathered up the shovel and pick and his small bundle.

He was big, bigger than any of the men who had just left, and I knew he was no coward. I had seen him on the trail, not hesitating when others had wavered.

But he had not opened his mouth under Crouse's abuse. I sensed that this was because his skin was black, that he knew from long experience that this was a game in which he could not win.

I sensed this, yet my mind refused to grasp it. In our home, in our community, there had been little bigotry. True, there were social levels and patterns, but this was ny first consciousness of discrimination.

"What are you going to do?" My voice sounded guilty, for I had promised, and I was at a loss.

"It ain't no use." He spoke like an old man. "A body's a fool to keep trying when it ain't no use."

Sandy moved quickly, catching his hand in both of her own. "You can't quit," she said. "You just can't quit. Nobody can. Look at my paw. Paw never amounted to shucks until he shot that robber and Austin wrote that piece about him. Even then he was scared, but Maw made him get out and live up to what Austin wrote."

I had not realized that she was this aware.

"Now Paw's one of the best-known men in California. Sure, he gets a bit foolish at times, but who don't? You go on up that hill and dig."

Bob looked up at the hill. "No use, little missy." His soft voice still held the hopeless note. "Ain't no gold up high like that. It's all down along the water. Maybe I go up north somewhere. Maybe I find a creek nobody's found yet."

"You're running away," she kept on. "Me, I'll never run. When we first moved up to Wilmington I knew we were different from those town folk. I was just little, and Paw went around apologizing all over the place. But I wasn't going to do that. I was going to make people like Austin notice me, even if I had to pull his hair."

Bob was listening intently, an expression on his face of wonder and hardening resolve.

"All right, Miss Sandy. I go up there and dig." He began to climb the canyon wall.

Below us I heard the men laugh.

In two weeks they had stopped laughing. Bob had found the richest claim in the whole district. Not only gold, but there was a little spring with a running stream directly below the deposit, making Crouse's whole irony come true.

Years later a mining engineer named Shinn explained it to me. The old tertiary rivers of the Mother Lode country had run north and south. Then the land buckled and the modern streams developed, flowing east to west. These new courses sliced down through the old channels, and what Bob found was a cross section of one of these, exposed in the high canyon wall.

We came upon the streak of sand about three o'clock. We had paused at the spring to eat the food Bob had brought, and I climbed on up through the brush and stunted trees, for no reason except to prove to Sandy that I could maneuver the nearly vertical wall.

I reached a bare patch where the brush was sparse and there were no trees, and started across it. Instead of the rocky ground I had been covering I found that I was walking across sand.

It was so lightly cemented that the crust broke under my feet and I slid down half a dozen yards before I came to a jarring stop against the shoulder of a jutting rock. I was frightened, for the steep slope dropped straight to the far-off canyon bottom.

I reached for a hand hold to steady myself and picked up the nugget. It was the size of the nail on my little finger, a twisted, knobby piece of gold, but gold nonetheless, freed from a quartz chip that had broken away from some distant fractured vein and been carried here by the prehistoric stream.

I choked. Then I yelled down the hill. "Bob, Bob. Come on up here. I've found it."

They came scrambling up, slipping and sliding, and stared at the little nodule in my hand.

"Glory be." It was Bob. His eyes ranged up the sloping sand as if he could not believe it.

The area was about eight feet wide and twelve from top to bottom, a sheered face betraying a sand-filled tunnel through the rock below the crest of the hill Crouse had sent us to.

"How you think this sand ever got up here?"

None of us knew. I was too excited to care. "Get your shovel and let's fill the pan."

It was hard going. The hill was so steep that we had to cling to the small trees and bushes to keep from falling. But

Bob got the pan filled and we retreated safely to the spring where he squatted to wash it. Then everything but the black sand was gone, and there was a crescent of color all around the edge of the heavy iron particles.

"Must be an ounce there." My voice was shaking. "An ounce out of one pan."

Bob was standing as if paralyzed. He said slowly, "You found it. It's yours."

I shook my head quickly. I didn't realize what I was giving away. Maybe I wouldn't have done it had I known. How can anyone tell what he would do in a moment relived?

"No," I said. "Crouse sent you up here. We were hunting a claim for you."

He thought for a long minute, then he nodded his head solemnly.

"Yes sir." He was speaking to himself. "That's the way it was. I guess it's mine."

He looked up the hillside, studying it, planning. "Got to do this right."

And he did it right. I don't think I've ever seen one man put in as much work singlehanded as Bob did. Oh, Sandy and I helped. We spent more time up at the claim than we did anywhere else. He cut steps up from the spring to the gravel. He built a trough to slide the sand down to the water. And only then did he begin to drift in on the channel.

The rock around the old river bed stood without timbering, and he made a remarkable hole. He built a rocker down by the spring, and the trough dumped the sand into this. Sandy and I dipped water over it with a bucket and tipped it back and forth, agitating the sand.

The rocker worked like a baby's cradle, with an upper and lower compartment. We picked out the larger stones and an occasional nugget, then the residue was scooped into the pan for Bob to finish by hand.

The first week he accumulated a coffeepot half-full of gold. He let me take it down the hill to our cabin, sending word for my uncle to buy him a flask of mercury.

Bob had warned us not to breathe a word about the richness of his claim. I don't know how the story got out, for certainly Sandy and I kept the secret, but one morning, two weeks after we got the mercury, I was just cleaning out the rocker when I heard steps on the path below us.

Crouse came around the shoulder below the spring. Then two others appeared. Sandy had stayed at home to help

Aunt Emeline with the washing and I stood there alone, watching them.

Crouse stopped. He had eyes too small for even his narrow face, reminding me of a pig. He looked at the chute, at the steps carved in the face of the bank, at the opening of Bob's tunnel. Then he walked forward and stirred the sand in the bottom of the rocker with a grimy finger.

"Doing pretty good, huh?"

I was cautious and somewhat scared. Something about his manner made me nervous.

"Fair," I said. "Some is better than others."

Bob was out of sight in the tunnel. I knew that he could throw all three men off the mountain if he had a mind, but I knew that he would not.

Crouse reached for the gold pan. He scraped the fine silt from the rocker into it, hunched beside the spring and began washing.

Then he whistled a long note. "Hey, Jake. Look at this."

The other men pressed forward, edging me out of their way, but even where I stood I could see the necklace glitter in the pan.

"Jesus Christ," Jake gasped. "I never seen nothing like that."

"And a nigger's got it." Crouse sounded sour. Purposefully he tossed the pan on the ground, upside down. He rose and started up the steps.

As he climbed Bob emerged from the tunnel with a bucket full of sand and started to dump it down the chute. He stopped, holding the bucket in his big hand.

"What you want?"

Crouse had halted instinctively. Now he started up again. "Just to see how you're doing."

"You got no call to come up here. This is my claim."

"Thought maybe I'd stake one next to you."

"Ain't no more sand. I got it all covered."

"No harm to look." Crouse continued climbing.

"You stop right there." Bob hadn't raised his voice, but his tone made the man pause.

"Now wait a minute . . ."

"You wait," said Bob, letting the loaded bucket swing a little on the bail. "You get down them steps and go away, or I let you have this right on top of your head."

"You throw that at me, nigger, and I'll cut out your heart."

"Get off them steps." The bucket was swinging in a wider arc. "I mean it, man. You get away fast."

Crouse eyed the bucket. It was heavy. If it struck him it would surely knock him off the steps and send him plunging down the canyon wall. Slowly he retreated until he again stood beside me at the spring.

"I'll be back," he called up to Bob. "I'll be back, and when I come you'll wish you never seen any gold."

They left, cursing among themselves. I ran up the steps.

"This is trouble," I told Bob when I could no longer hear Crouse's voice. "They will come back."

Bob was still swinging the bucket, unconsciously. Slowly he spilled its contents into the chute.

"Kind of figure they will." He didn't sound frightened, exactly, only resigned, as if he knew there was nothing he could do about it.

"You'd better come down to town with me."

"No sir. You go on along, Mr. Austin. You take the gold down with you. Me, I ain't going to move off this mountain for any man, not until I is dead."

I didn't know how to argue with him. I wanted to get to town and tell someone about Crouse. I carried out nearly four pounds of gold. Every time I came to a turn in the trail or a clump of brush I expected to run into the trio.

But I saw no one. Still not reassured I ran from the point where I climbed over the canyon rim all the way into town. I was so winded by the time I reached our cabin that I could not speak.

At length I got it out. "They're after Bob," I said. "Where's Uncle Ben and Ike? They've got to make them let him alone."

Aunt Emeline looked puzzled and concerned. "Who's after Bob? What for?"

I was still gasping. "Crouse came up and saw the gold. He's going to rob Bob. I know he is."

"He has no right to do that." My aunt sounded positive. "You can't throw a man off his claim."

"They can Bob," I insisted, "because he's black. They wouldn't let him dig down along the creek. Now he's struck it rich, they'll take it away from him."

"We'll see about that." My aunt's mouth set in a grim line.

"You can't do anything," I told her, agonizing. "When will Uncle Ben be back?"

"Tomorrow. He and Ike went down to Sonora."

My heart sank.

"You stay here." She was reaching for her bonnet. "We'll just see about this."

She saw. She talked to everyone at Moke Hill, almost, even the bartenders. No one felt that it was any of their business. Crouse had a bad reputation as a saloon brawler. I think a lot of people would have been glad to see him get his comeuppance, but no one would go against him in defense of a Negro.

That evening Sandy and I went down to the store. Caroline trailed along. A crowd had gathered in front of the saloon, and Crouse was haranguing them. He had been drinking and his voice was thick.

"What's this country coming to when a black nigger won't let a white man stake out open ground?"

There were growls from the crowd. It was the first mob I ever saw get started, and its ugliness was like a threatening storm.

"Personally"—Crouse's words carried up and down the street—"I don't know what you boys are going to do, but I ain't going to stand for it. I'm going up there and stake me a claim, and if that nigger so much as looks crosswise I'm going to hang him to the nearest tree."

I eased back along the street, Sandy at my heels and Caroline behind her.

"You think they would, Austin?" Sandy sounded breathless.

I nodded. Fear made me certain. "You and Caroline go on home. I'm going to warn Bob."

"I'm coming with you." She swung around and grabbed Caroline by her skinny shoulder. "You run and tell your maw where we went."

We did not wait for Caroline's usual argument. We were both running.

I was ahead of Sandy as we climbed the hill. For once I had beaten her at one thing. Bob heard me coming. He had a camp set up on the little ledge beyond the spring, and he was just getting his evening meal.

"Mr. Austin. What you doing here this time of day?"

I yelled as I panted toward him. "Crouse is bringing a bunch of drunks. They want your claim. He says he'll hang you to get it."

I'd reached the fire. "Come on. Let's get away from here while we can."

"I ain't going."

I stared at him, seeing the set of his jaw in the light of the flames. "You . . . you've got to."

"I ain't got to do nothing." He said it firmly. "Mr. Jones' daddy gave me my papers and set me free. I ain't never had anything in my life that really belonged to me until I got this hole. I ain't going to leave."

"They'll hang you."

"Worse things than being hung." He said it as if to himself. "Man's got to stand sometime."

Sandy had clambered to the shelf and stood panting. I looked at her helplessly.

"He won't go."

Sandy was more intuitive than I. She always had been. There were some things she comprehended about the basic tenets of life as I never would.

"Of course he can't." It was a flat statement, not an argument.

"You kids scoot on back to town." It was Bob. "Don't want you to get hurt, whatever happens."

"I'm not going," Sandy told him. "I'm going to stay right here. They aren't going to hang anyone with me here."

Bob shook his head and his voice tightened with authority. "You do like I tell you. You climb on down this mountain right fast. You ever see a man hanging up to a tree by his neck? It ain't right pretty."

"I'm not . . ."

She did not finish the sentence, for suddenly we heard them coming up the trail below us. They sounded like wild horses, thrashing and stumbling through the brush. No one needed to tell me they were drunk. It was plain in their voices, in their noisy progress.

"We can't go now."

Bob looked about wildly. The canyon wall above the tunnel was impossible to climb in the darkness.

"Get up to the tunnel. Get way back inside. Don't you either come out, nohow."

"You come too." Sandy started up. "When they climb up the steps we can throw things down and stop them."

Bob hesitated for a moment.

"You come," she threatened, "or I ain't going."

"All right, all right. You climb."

We scrambled up the steps, Bob following. At the top, in front of the tunnel's mouth, was a flat place about eight feet where Bob had excavated and dumped the boulders and waste soil not worth putting down the chute.

We paused on this and stood watching down the slope The men were having difficulty, but they were coming, their way marked by the angry flames of their pitch torches.

We saw the first weaving figure reach the fireside by the spring, then he was joined by another and another.

Crouse looked upward. "You there, nigger?"

"I'm here." Bob's voice was heavy, level.

"You ain't got no right to keep us from staking the ground on both sides of you. I'm coming up."

"Better not," Bob said.

He picked up a discarded boulder and heaved it down the mountainside on the far side of the spring. It went crashing and bounding down the steep wall, its noise lessening as it flew. A stillness fell on the men until a distant click of rock told us it had reached the bottom.

"That's just a warning." Bob still showed no feeling. "You come climbing up here, somebody's going to get hurt."

There was a conference around the spring. We could hear Crouse shouting at them.

"He won't dare. He knows if one of us gets hurt we'll string him up. You going to let a black devil steal all this gold that belongs to you?"

Someone yelled, "No."

A man started up the steps, holding his torch high. He climbed compulsively, warily,. Bob picked up a boulder. It was about all he could do to lift it. I heard him muttering to himself and knew that he was praying. Then I saw him roll rather than throw the rock down the steps.

The man heard it come. He looked up quickly. He tried wildly to get out of the way, scrambling out of the steps, going crabwise across the rock face.

He did not make it. I saw him slip and grab frantically at the scant brush. I will never forget his high, piercing scream as he fell backward, nor forget the way his arms waved, reaching and reaching for the support that was not there.

There was silence in the canyon. The men beside the fire stood shocked into a kind of sobriety for a moment, then Crouse yelled:

"The nigger killed him. He killed him. Hang the bastard."

Bob was more shaken than the men below him. He said in a choked voice, "I didn't mean he should die. I didn't . . . you kids get back in that tunnel. I'm going down there."

"You aren't either . . ." Sandy was crying. She caught his arm and hung on. "No . . . no . . ."

"Ain't no other way. Can't stay up here forever. They'll starve us out. I'm going down."

"Someone will come and help."

"Who's to come? Who cares to help old Bob?"

As if in answer to his words we heard a new voice, a strident, commanding voice.

"What do you fellers think you're doing?"

Looking down, we saw a figure scramble up to the little level area beside the fire, and Sandy gasped.

"It's Papa."

It was Joe Stoop, although I would not have recognized him except for Sandy's word. He carried a rifle and he was all dressed up. He looked mighty small, facing the grouped men. He raised his voice.

"Sandy. You up there?"

"I'm here, Papa."

"You all right?"

Her voice broke. "I guess so."

Stoop had not taken his eyes from the mob. He stood, his back to the steps. "I hope you're all proud of yourselves."

Crouse pushed forward belligerently. "I don't know who you are, stranger, and I don't give a damn. That nigger up there just murdered Al Tingler, and we're going to hang him."

"No you ain't," Joe Stoop said. We could barely hear him, his voice was that low. He wasn't blustering or arguing. "You're going back down that hill and you're going to leave Bob alone. Not only tonight, but from now on."

"Who says so?"

"I do. I'll kill you if you don't."

"And who in hell do you think you are?"

"Diamond Joe Stoop."

Now you could hear him a mile. It was as if he said, I am the King. The assurance, the self-confidence, came from a total stranger to me.

They backed up. They knew who he was, and they were afraid of him.

Crouse tried one more thrust. "What gives you the right . . . ?"

Joe swung the rifle to level at Crouse's chest.

"You've got just one minute to get started down before I blow you off this hill."

In the weird light of the torches they hesitated no longer. There was a sudden surging for the trail.

The story was all over Moke Hill in the morning, how Aunt Emeline had met the stage, wringing her hands and shooing Joe to the rescue. Joe's reputation had grown a thousandfold.

We were in the print shop, Bob, Ike, Uncle Ben, Joe, and I. I was making myself as small as possible for fear they'd run me out.

"That was a great thing you did last night, Joe," my uncle said. "I thank you. But there's going to be feeling."

"Let them feel." Joe sounded indifferent. "They aren't going to tackle Bob as long as I'm around."

"No," my uncle agreed, "they won't tackle Bob. They're leary of your reputation. But people like Crouse don't give up. You hurt his pride. You made him quit, and it'll gall him."

"Hope it does."

"He may try to drygulch you."

"Let him try."

"Take care. Now the question is, what do we do about Bob? I hate to admit it, but popular opinion is already running against him. Three or four people stopped me on the street this morning."

"What do you want him to do?"

Uncle Ben was patient. "It isn't what I want him to do. I consider he has as much right to his claim as anyone else. But I can't remake human beings and I can't alter prejudices and greed. The best thing would be if he could find someone to buy the claim."

"Got it," said Joe Stoop. "The Pells."

My uncle raised his brows questioningly.

"The Pell brothers. There's four of them. One's a doctor in San Francisco, one's kind of a half-baked politician, but Sam and Elam, they're go-getters."

That was the first any of us had heard of the Pells, but as the years rolled out the state and the mining business as a whole came to know them well.

My uncle wrote the letter, and four days later Elam Pell showed up at Moke Hill. He was a slender man with black hair and very dark eyes set in an angular, stubborn face.

He listened to what Uncle Ben and Joe had to tell him, looked at the gold in the now full coffee pot. Nothing in his expression changed to show whether or not he was impressed.

"All right, show me the mine."

Bob started toward the door. Aunt Emeline stopped him. "You aren't going out of this house."

Joe stood up. "I'll show him."

"You aren't going to leave either, with Bob here, not the way this town is acting. Austin, you show him. They won't bother a stranger and a boy, I reckon."

"I'll just mosey along." Ike reached for the rifle he kept in the corner.

"No you don't." My aunt had taken control. "You go out there with a gun and some fool man will figure he has something to prove. Men haven't got a bit of sense."

"Can I go?" Sandy was uncommonly meek.

My aunt considered, then nodded. "Be a good idea. Two children, even that Crouse knows better than to pick on children."

Sandy and I led Elam Pell down the canyon side. We passed the miners who had been my friends. They watched us silently, but no one made a move.

We climbed to the spring. By this time the path was pretty well beaten and we made good time. I noticed that Pell did not pant nor hold back. We reached Bob's camp and found that someone had been there. The shack was wrecked and his few things thrown down the bank.

But they had left the pick and shovel and pan in the tunnel. Pell looked at the steps and watched the water running out of the spring, then we climbed to the tunnel. He lit one of the pine knots Bob had used for light, and went back along the hole. I stayed at his side, explaining that this was a drift mine.

He glanced at me, saying in his dry voice, "I know. We are mining down under Table Mountain now."

He was thorough. He dug out cemented gravel to be certain no one had tampered with it, salted it. Some people in selling a claim would dig into their gravel and plant a few nuggets to make a purchaser think the mine was richer than it really was.

He took ten different panfuls from the face, carrying them down one at a time and washing them out at the spring. The gold and black sand he scraped into a leather poke, and although he did not speak and his expression never altered, I judged by the eager way he worked that he was getting more and more excited.

191

It was almost dark when he stopped, and he said not a word on the way back to town. Not until we reached the cabin did he open his mouth.

Aunt Emeline had supper waiting, and I was starved. None of us had had any dinner. But Elam Pell did not seem interested in food.

"You've got quite a mine," he said to Bob. "How much do you want for it?"

Bob looked for help to Uncle Ben, but it was Aunt Emeline who spoke up.

"He's been making better than two hundred dollars a day, working the mine all alone. If you were to put in several men you should make a lot more, maybe a thousand.

"We don't know how far the gravel runs, and it is pockety," Pell said. "The real values are only in the two or three feet at the bottom of the strata."

"And it probably runs clear through the mountain, which is three or four miles."

Pell laughed. There was no humor in the sound. "You are a good advocate, ma'am. But you forget that he can't work it himself, not the way this camp feels about him."

"But he can hire it out to anyone, maybe Ike."

I was standing where I could see Ike's grimace. There was not enough gold in California to make Ike want to go mining again.

"Well," said Pell, "I'll give him five thousand dollars and an eighth interest in what we take out. We can use the Express shipping records as a tally."

"You're very generous." Aunt Emeline could play the great lady when she chose, and she put a lot of contempt into her voice. It was the first time I'd seen Pell show any emotion. Now it was annoyance.

"What do you think he should have?"

My aunt never hesitated. "I will not let him sell for less than ten thousand dollars and one fourth of the profits."

Pell picked up his hat. "I'm afraid you have a rather warped imagination, Mrs. Garner. Maybe you had best look for another buyer. Thank you all." He did not even stay for supper.

As soon as the door closed Uncle Ben said, "What did you want to do that for? It is Bob's business."

Bob was looking crestfallen. Five thousand dollars was to him an undreamed-of sum, but he said loyally, "Mrs. Garner says something, that's all right with me."

"He'll be back." Aunt Emeline sounded positive. "I saw him looking at that coffeepot."

She was right. I learned later that Pell went down to the Express office and used the company scales to weigh what he had taken from the claim that afternoon.

Sandy and I were clearing the table when Caroline, playing outside, came rushing in.

"Someone's coming."

Ike got up and reached for his rifle. Joe Stoop crossed to where he had put his belted gun on a chair. Everyone was jumpy, looking for trouble. But it was Pell. He did not waste words.

"Where do you want the money paid?"

My uncle looked at Bob. "San Francisco," Bob said. "Mr. Edmond will be coming in there shortly."

We all looked at him in surprise. "You hear from Edmond? He's coming back from the Islands?"

"I didn't hear from him, but he's coming back."

"How do you know?"

He sounded a trifle puzzled. "How do I know? I just know." Which was all we got out of him.

Pell was all business. He had a paper and pen on the table, waiting.

"You sign here. What's your name?"

"Bob Jones."

"Robert Jones . . ."

"No sir, just Bob. That's the way it reads on my papers."

CHAPTER NINETEEN

BLACK BOB WAS right, although how he knew was never satisfactorily explained. Edmond Jones was back in California.

He walked into the print shop just a month after Bob had sold out to the Pells and taken off with Joe Stoop and Sandy for San Francisco.

Things were not going well on the Hill for my uncle. There was still a hot resentment against him for taking Bob's part against Crouse, and Old Ike had spent more than one night on guard for fear they would burn the shop.

The Pells had moved in, Elam and Samuel, with a crew of eight men. They had recut the steps, enlarged the chute, put a coffer dam around the spring, and were working the tunnel methodically.

Some of the jealousy the men along the creek had felt toward Bob was transferred to the Pells, but they were not dealing with a lone black man now. In all my experience at the mines I was never to run into two more determined, fearless and single-purposed individuals than the Pell brothers.

They were Scotch, dour, seldom smiling, seldom speaking, but they knew what they were doing and how to keep their crews laboring.

I visited the mine three times, but did not go again, feeling that I was not welcome. Not that anyone said anything, but that was the trouble, no one ever stopped to talk.

It was different with Edmond. Edmond was always ready to quit anything he was doing for a conversation.

He came walking up to the print shop in the morning. Ike was scraping the stone and my uncle had gone out in a forlorn attempt to drum up some advertising. But the merchants were afraid of Crouse's bully boys and would have nothing to do with the *Clarion*. Already my aunt and uncle had been discussing the advisability of changing location, and we would have left a couple of weeks back had not Uncle Ben been so stubborn. Now, at the time Edmond arrived, even my uncle was ready to admit defeat.

Edmond had not changed at all. He sauntered in and sat down in a corner of the shop, merely nodding as if he had seen us the day before.

I let out a yell you could hear across the canyon. "Edmond. Bob said you were coming. How did he know?"

Edmond scratched his head, looking bland. "Back home the people said he has second sight. I long ago ceased to doubt it."

"Did you see him in San Francisco?"

"He was down at the wharf when my boat came in."

"And you didn't write to him, or anything?"

"I didn't even know I was coming. I met a ship's captain who was sailing, and suddenly I'd had enough of the Islands."

"You'll stay here now?"

"Think I'll go up on the American River, a place called Murderer's Bar."

I was astounded. I could not imagine him mining. "Whatever for?"

He smiled, the quiet, turned-in smile I'd always found so friendly.

"Because Bob says Lisbeth Peyton wants to see me."

"She's up there?"

"So Bob says."

"Did he talk to her?"

"I don't know. He just said for me to go up there and see her. I've been doing what Bob says ever since I was little."

My uncle came in then and I knew from the way he walked that he hadn't had any luck. He shook hands, and I think he was glad to see Edmond, though they never were as close as Edmond and I.

"Where'd you drop from?"

Edmond told him.

"How'd you like the Islands?"

"Wonderful." Edmond was enthusiastic. "Those people know how to live, eating fruit, dancing on the beach and singing."

Ike growled. "Then why'd you come back to this bone breaking place?"

Edmond turned to look at him. "Ike, you're one who ought to comprehend this weakness of the human race. None of us knows when we're well off. We have to go off hunting something better. I came back because something inside me said that it was time."

Uncle Ben wanted to know where Edmond was going, and I watched his interest spark as he heard about Murderer's Bar.

"A new camp?"

"I guess so. Joe Stoop was up there once. He says it's in the canyon, right down on the river."

"They got a newspaper?"

"I don't know about that."

"Maybe I'll ride up with you and take a look. We've been having a little trouble here."

"That's what I understand. You people were very good to Bob. I appreciate it."

"That's all right. He's as fine a man as I know. What's he doing down in San Francisco?"

"He's opened a gambling house."

My uncle had been filling his pipe. He nearly dropped it. "He what?"

Edmond laughed. "Bob's smart, don't discount that. He looked around and saw that the gamblers and saloonkeepers were making most of the money. He said to me, 'Mr. Edmond, it ain't fitting for a member of your family to run a gambling house, but if I could find a white man to kind of hide behind . . . ain't no good for a nigger to get nothing. Those tough boys would just try to take it away from me.'

"Well, it seemed to me a good idea. San Francisco is getting to be quite a big town, and Bob knows how to run a dining room and bar. So I told him why not open an exclusive place, keep the riffraff out.

" 'How am I going to do that?' he asked me.

" 'Get a fighting man,' I said.

" 'Like Joe Stoop . . . sure . . .'

"That was the first I knew that Joe had turned into a fighting man."

My uncle laughed aloud, his depression gone. "You know how that happened?" He told Edmond the story. "Funny, how a man sees his name in print and right away his character changes."

Edmond winked at me, but he had more to tell. "I asked around and found that everyone knows Joe and they're afraid of him. So, they opened Diamond Joe's. Right now it's the plushest restaurant in town. Joe's running it, strutting around in a frilled shirt and broadcloth coat, greeting everybody like a baron and keeping order.

"You really should see it, Mr. Garner. If there's no upset they'll both wind up millionaires."

Ike was dancing around the floor like a satyr, in a paroxysm of vengeful laughter. Uncle Ben's laugh was silent, but it shook his whole body.

"Edmond, you're good medicine," he said. "When do you leave for Murderer's Bar?"

"Tomorrow."

My uncle took a turn of the shop, looking more light than he had in many weeks, then he slapped his leg in decision.

"Austin, run along and tell your aunt to start packing. We're going up on the American."

The day we arrived at the American River was the day Lisbeth Peyton promised herself to Lysander Cox.

I couldn't have been more dismayed if she had announced she was going to marry a red Indian.

All the way across the country we had known that Cox

196

was in love with her, but none of us had taken it very seriously because we did not like the big, slow, plodding State of Maine man.

Along the river, where miners outnumbered women a thousand to one, Lisbeth could have had the rich, the handsome, the educated, the wise or serious or gay. But she had made her choice and she announced it at a party at her father's store.

I knew how Edmond felt about her, and why he had come to the Bar, and when I heard the news I expected him to get drunk. He didn't. He did something he had never done before. He went to work.

We had pulled in three days before, but Ike and my uncle had been too busy putting up a cabin with canvas sides to take much part in what was going on. My aunt had set about establishing our new home. She had not uttered a word of protest. I think she was relieved to get away from the trouble at Moke Hill, and too, she was very glad to see Lisbeth again.

Maybe Lisbeth told her what she intended, but if so my aunt did not pass it on, for my uncle was as surprised as I, and Old Ike went around shaking his head and muttering, "Women," over and over. His inflection left no doubt of his opinion.

Edmond took it better than the rest of us. He attended the party and congratulated Lysander, making it sound as if he meant it.

The next morning I found Lisbeth alone in the store. I liked the store. It was clean and neat and the earth floor swept smooth.

The stock was not large, but it was the only store in town and the closest supply point was Auburn, twenty miles away by twisting mountain trail, for Murderer's Bar was a remote camp.

The story was that it got its name because a man wanted for murder had hidden there and made the original discovery. But no one seemed to know his name or why he had left.

Lisbeth was arranging the stock on the shelves. She turned and saw me and smiled.

"You're out early, Austin. Why aren't you helping with the cabin?"

"It's up," I said. "Ike got the canvas stretched across the

197

frame last night, and Aunt Emeline told me to keep out from under foot."

"So you came down to see me. Did you enjoy the party?"

"Not much." I could not keep the way I felt out of my voice.

"Why, I thought it was nice." She sounded hurt.

"Oh, the party was all right, and the cake was good. But why did you promise yourself to Lysander?"

"Austin." She gasped and her cheeks flooded with color, then she managed a short laugh. "You beat all, Austin Garner. No one asks a girl a question like that. And why shouldn't I marry Lysander? I've known him all my life. He's a good, hard-working man with one of the best claims on the bar, and when he makes his stake we'll go back to Maine, away from this wilderness, and buy a farm."

She was talking too much, I knew, and I heard a hungry loneliness in her voice.

"You didn't say you loved him."

She sounded exasperated. "Child, when you're older you'll understand more about such things."

"What about Edmond?"

She drew her breath in sharply, then she put her hands on her hips and leaned toward me, looking mad.

"And what about Edmond?" She mimicked my tone. "Edmond Jones is a grasshopper. All he does is play the piano and sing and amuse himself."

I glanced at the corner of the store where Donny Scranton's piano stood.

"You like to play," I said. "He taught you."

"That's different."

"And why should he work? He's got enough money."

"People have to work." She said it with conviction. "What would this world come to if nobody worked?"

It did not sound like Lisbeth at all. I walked out and down to the river, feeling very sad. I knew that I would never go East, and I did not like the idea of Lisbeth, married to Lysander, going back to a Maine farm.

A perverse magnet drew me toward Lysander's claim. The layer of sand was only six feet deep here, but the seepage water was so bad that the big man had trouble cleaning the bedrock where most of the gold lay. He was down in his hole, knee-deep in the thin mud, lifting buckets of sand up to ground level with a homemade windlass, and dumping them there. I stood watching until he had quite a pile heaped up and crawled up his crude ladder.

He threw some sand into his rocker, then began to dip water from the river with his bucket.

"Why don't you build a Chinese water wheel?" I asked.

He spoke without stopping, his tone dogged. "It would take two days to build a wheel. On a good day I can make six ounces. I don't think a wheel is worth twelve ounces."

My resentment against him almost gorged me. I said, "Edmond claims that's the trouble with all you miners, you don't stop to plan ahead. You'd rather use your back than your head."

He straightened up, his own anger that Edmond had come to the bar goading him.

"Jones certainly never uses his back, and as far as I can see never uses his head either."

It gave me a little satisfaction to see him flare up. I left and went on down the bar and found Edmond near the end, where a rock slide which had fallen into the canyon years before had created a natural dam and backed the water into a lake.

Edmond was sitting with his back against a boulder, staring at the slide as if it were telling him something.

"Hi," he said, without turning his eyes. "How's the cabin coming?"

"About finished." I looked at him carefully to see if there was any change. I thought he would be all broken up, crying maybe. But he wasn't. He seemed just the same.

"I was talking to Lisbeth," I said. "I asked her why she's going to marry Lysander."

He pursed his lips and raised his eyebrows. "Did she say?"

"She said he was a good worker and you were a grass-hopper. She said everybody should work."

He looked toward me then and gave me the little half-smile that lit up his eyes but barely touched his mouth.

"She's right, Austin. When a man sees a job that ought to be done, he should get at it. I've been looking at this rock pile for two days now. It is time, I think, to go to work."

I looked at the rocks doubtfully. To me it was just another jumble of stones. The country was filled with them.

"What's so special about it?"

His face lost its dark brooding and he smiled, an honest-to-goodness smile that made me warm to him as I always did.

199

"That slide," he said, "has probably been there more than a thousand years. I saw you go swimming down here yesterday. How deep do you think the water is?"

I was used to the way his mind switched from one thing to another. "It's over my head. Maybe six feet deep, maybe eight. You going swimming?"

"The lake is only six feet deep, yet the slide is a good twelve feet high on the lower side. Do you know why?"

I understood then that Edmond had some kind of an idea cooking in his head, and that he would tell me about it when he got around to it, so I stayed silent, waiting.

He did not speak for nearly five minutes, then he said, "Those rocks fell down a long time ago. They made a dam and closed off the current and created the lake. And the river keeps washing sand down from the higher hills. When the lake was first made it was twelve feet deep here, but through the centuries it has been gradually silting up. Now there's a layer of sand five or six feet deep on the bottom."

I still did not say anything, and his voice grew as excited as I had ever heard it.

"There's gold in that sand, Austin, probably more gold than sand. Sand is light. It would wash over the dam in flood times. But gold is heavy. It would sink to the bottom. Why, Austin, that pond is literally paved with gold."

I caught the idea and my voice trembled. "Lysander says they tried to work the river bed but the water's been too high. They're praying for low water come August."

"That's the blindness of people." He was full of impatience. "Always waiting, for low water, for something to happen. That water is never going to drop low enough to work here unless they lower it."

I looked at the slide. "How can you lower it? You'd have to move the river."

"That's it, boy. Move the river." His eyes flashed with excitement. "There's a job to challenge the caliber of a man. What about it, Austin, shall we move the river, you and I?"

I gaped at him, then I turned and looked up along the narrow bar.

"But where would we put it? There's not enough room in the canyon, unless we took it through the air."

"That's the idea. You always had a head on you too big for your years." He stood up, folding his fists on his hips, looking up the canyon wall, studying each foot of it with careful attention. "I think there's room. Come on, Austin, we've got a job ahead."

That evening I heard my uncle talking to my aunt. "Jones wants to build an earth-fill dam at the head of the still water above Buckner's Bar, and divert the river along the far wall of the canyon in a twelve-foot flume."

Aunt Emeline sniffed. "And how long would this flume have to be?"

"A mile, at least." Uncle Ben sounded awed, but at the same time intrigued. "It's a tremendous undertaking without proper machinery, without someone who understands engineering."

"It's insane," said my aunt. "Who would listen to Edmond on such foolishness? There isn't a flume that large anywhere."

"There's a first time for everything." Uncle Ben's interest was coming up as he talked. "And they are listening. Edmond went all up and down the river this afternoon, talking, and when that man really talks, he's got magic."

"I thought you didn't like him."

"I never said that. I said I don't understand him. I don't. But maybe that proves he's a genius."

"If you ask me," Aunt Emeline said tartly, "he's a fool. He says he loves Lisbeth, and then he sails off to those islands and stays over a year. I don't know what men expect of women."

My uncle crossed the room and put an arm around her shoulders. "You came West with me when you didn't want to."

"That's different. I was married to you, and . . ."

He stooped and kissed the nape of her neck. She pulled away from him. "Stop your silliness. Are you going into this idiocy?"

His eyes were bright and his breathing a little shallow as the vision took hold of him. "I think Edmond is right. Gold has been piling up behind that slide for centuries. It's there for the picking up, if we get rid of the water."

"But think of the cost."

"It will cost a lot," he agreed easily. "It will take all the dust everyone along this river has collected, maybe more. But these people all came a long way because of a dream. Only the adventuresome come to California. They're used to taking a chance. And it's the people with dreams who will make this country grow."

"The dream of a lazy man trying to get out of honest work."

My uncle laughed. "Most human progress comes out of laziness, because someone dreams up a way to do a job easier and better."

"At least I'm glad Lisbeth had better sense than to tie herself to that kind."

My uncle refrained from commenting on that. He said, "There's a meeting to consider Edmond's idea at the store in a few minutes. Do you want to come?"

My aunt came. Much as she disapproved, her curiosity would not permit her to remain away. I loved the miner's meetings. I loved the feeling of the crowd, the excitement, the speeches. I have never lived where I thought the people shared their responsibilities as broadly as did the miners along the rivers and creeks of the Mother Lode.

It was the largest meeting the Bar ever held. The crowd filled the store and fanned out through the open front door to jam the level ground to the river's edge, a spine-tingling sight in itself in this lonely, isolated canyon.

I crept behind the stove where I could see and hear. Lisbeth joined me, sinking down at my side, out of sight, sitting with her hands tightly folded in her lap, tense and withdrawn.

We had no *alcalde*, since the camp had never been formally organized, and my uncle was voted temporary chairman. He called the meeting to order and made a short speech outlining the project before them. This was, of course, redundant and unnecessary, since Edmond had already stumped the river, but at the meetings the rules of order were strictly adhered to.

The crowd noise had quieted when Edmond climbed to the board counter and began to talk. Most people liked Edmond, whether or not they agreed with his ideas.

"Congratulations, all of you." He drew them all to him with a wide smile. "You are a most fortunate community. True, all spring you have been working in ground no better or worse than that along our other great rivers. True, it's a wet camp, you've been working in water up to your waists, water seeping from the river into your shafts. It's cold work, and hard work, and sometimes discouraging work. But most gravel bars are wet, and if there's gold enough a miner accepts the hardship as the price of his gain.

"You've been content with that, but now it appears that

you have barely scratched the fringe of a horde sufficient to make every man here a fortune.

"The channel of your river is paved with solid gold."

A murmur rose, quaky with nervous laughter.

"It's a fact," said Edmond. With a flourish he bent and lifted a bucket from behind the counter, holding it high. "I waded out in the pond and ducked under with this bucket. Lysander, take a pan and wash out what I brought up."

Cox was standing beside the door, saying nothing, and from his dour face it was obvious that he was not pleased with the attention Edmond was getting. He shouldered away from the jamb heavily and pushed through the crowd, accepting the bucket with little grace.

Edmond gave no sign that he noticed. "Naturally," he said, "I did not go down to bedrock. I nearly drowned as it was."

It brought a roar of hooting laughter and a spate of joshing as Lysander stumped back toward the door. I had a chance to peek into the bucket as he passed, and saw that there were five or six inches of wet sand in the bottom.

Then Edmond was going on, talking while Lysander panned, telling how the gold had got there and how much of it there should be.

"I'll venture it runs five hundred dollars to the ton," he said, and drew another shout.

Excitement was rising and the room was noisy, and over it Edmond drew the picture of his vision.

"I'm no engineer, but there are those among us who have been builders and mechanics. They admit the plan is feasible, and the plan is simply this. Build a dam of earth and rocks at the head of still water. Carry the river in a flume along the canyon wall to the curve below the slide. Then break the slide and empty the lake downstream. With this done we can work the lake bed without so much as wetting our feet."

A rising sound of shouting voices outside stopped him, then Lysander shoved through the door. He had to fight his way, carrying a dripping gold pan, as men pressed around him to look. Then someone had taken it from him, and it passed from hand to hand, gradually working toward the rear counter as the clamor grew.

As it crossed by the stove I stood up to see. There was black sand, rimmed with the widest fan of gold that I had ever seen.

Edmond stood watching and laughing silently, and then Grover Peyton tugged at his arm, climbing to his place as Edmond jumped down. The storekeeper's vinegar voice fell like a drizzle on the room.

"I'll not deny there may be some merit in Jones' notion, but just you think of the almighty cost. A flume, twelve feet, he says, with three-foot sides. And the canyon wall is rough, you'd have to dig out a shelf. There's one stretch that's all rock, straight up from the river. How you going to get around that? It ain't worth the risk. It's too big a gamble, and for myself, I am not a gambler."

A hundred voices growled agreement, but twice that number yelled in favor of the flume, and to my surprise, Lysander was one of these.

Major Harry Love pushed to the counter and clambered up. An ex-Army officer who had served with the engineers, he was solemnly listened to.

"I'll build the dam," he cried, "and not one drop of water will come down that channel. You fellows that want to join in stand aside and let the ones who don't want a part of it go on out. Then we can organize."

The crowd began to shift, but my uncle held his hands above his head, waving them for attention.

"No, no, not tonight. This is too important a decision to be taken without careful thought. We will now adjourn. You all think it over properly. Another meeting is hereby called for Wednesday afternoon."

By Wednesday everyone knew that the preponderance on Edmond's side assured that the immense project would be tried. I was enthusiastically in favor of it, and shocked that Lisbeth held her father's view.

"You've a right to your personal foolishness," she snapped at Edmond, "but no one has the privilege of dragging everyone else down with his folly."

I backed away a step. I had never seen her that angry. But Edmond did not retreat. He smiled the lazy smile that so infuriated people.

"Why, as to that, the very fact of living is a gamble. When nothing is risked, little is gained. But even gain is not the real importance. It's the doing that counts. Here we have a chance to challenge Nature's strength, to change a river's course and wrest her horded treasure from its hiding place. I had hoped that you, of all people, would understand."

There was a note of sadness in his voice that I had never

heard there before, but if it touched the girl she gave no sign.

"Empty words," she said. "You're very free and easy with words, but nothing gets done with talk. And your talk is dangerous, Mr. Edmond Jones."

But few shared her doubts, for the golden lake was beckoning. The company was organized. Along the channel were five separate bars and the men were divided into five parties.

With Harry Love building the dam, Lysander volunteered to head the grading crew, cutting the shelf along the flume's course. The men on New York Bar would build their section of the flume, we on Murderer's Bar would be responsible for ours. Edmond Jones was general construction chairman and my uncle treasurer.

Ed Leffingwell, who had been a builder in the East, and Sam Tyler offered to build the Murderer's Bar section for six dollars the lineal foot.

When my aunt heard the price she gasped. "And a mile long? That's over five thousand feet." She did some quick mental arithmetic. "Thirty thousand dollars for just the flume."

"More than that." My uncle was giving her no help.

She was horrified. "And what about the dam? What about the grading?"

"The gold in the bottom of that channel will make the cost as nothing."

She sighed in resignation. "Well, you'll do it. That man has you all hypnotized. I can only hope it works. What is the flume to be made of?"

"Lumber. There's plenty of pine in the canyon. Tyler and Leffingwell went to Sacramento this morning, looking for a sawmill."

The two had come back a week later with a circular saw blade, a handmade shaft and a "horsepower" which had been shipped around the Horn by a man who thought grain grew on the timbered ridges and meant to use it for a threshing rig.

They also brought a hundred Spanish horses with Mexicans to drive them, and I spent hours watching the horses as they paced on their treadmill track, turning the saw as the spinning blade ate through the soft pine logs.

It was for me my most exciting summer. I had no time to loaf in the store and I saw little of Lisbeth, who seemed quiet and removed in the midst of all the activity.

There was so much to see. Harry Love and his crew cut logs and dragged them to the dam site. The cribbing rose, and as it grew they filled it with shattered rock and earth, packed solidly with heavy tamps.

Lysander sweated his men, hacking out a shelf twelve feet wide along the canyon wall. Ahead of them rose the sheer face, and I was fascinated as they drilled holes into the face to set the huge logs which would serve as a bridge to support the flume. One end of each log was wedged firmly in the wall, the other supported by an upright whose footing was in the river.

Everyone worked as if the Devil were driving him. The aim was to finish in time to clean the channel before the winter rains would halt all mining for the season. And they were making amazing progress. Everything was going according to schedule. And then disaster struck.

The mill had sawed out three thousand feet of four-inch puncheons before they started to build the flume. Then it was discovered that because of warping and the roughness of the lumber, the boards had three- and four-inch cracks between them.

Edmond and I got the word from Lysander's crew and climbed the canyon wall to where they stood, staring at the crooked planks in dismay. They had worked hard and long, and to have it all go for naught made their tempers ragged, their mood sullen.

"That'll never hold water, damnit." Lysander sounded thoroughly disgusted. "I knew this crazy idea would never work. The time's wasted. The money's thrown down a gopher hole."

I thought for a moment that he would cry. Edmond hardly glanced at him. He sent me running to the sawmill for Tyler.

Tyler was short and squat, with legs like kegs and long, gangling arms and a round, bald head. He had been a sawyer all of his life.

When he came puffing up the grade Edmond merely pointed at the cracks. Tyler pulled off his battered hat and wiped his sweating skull with a piece of rag. He kicked at a board viciously, spat on the ground and then kicked again.

"It ain't my fault. It's this damn sugar pine. It's green and as soon as we cut her she begins to warp. The more it lies in the sun the more it warps."

"Can't we straighten them?" said Edmond.

"Don't know how, unless you got a planing mill, and then it ought to cure for a year first."

We did not have a planing mill, and everyone knew that we did not have a year. Lysander turned ugly, but he was only saying some of the things the others were thinking.

"So now what do we do, Mr. Edmond Jones genius? You got so many wonderful ideas, let's see you come up with one that will work."

Edmond ignored him, frowning at the twisted boards. "If we had something to calk the cracks with . . ."

One of the men I didn't know snorted. "No calking's going to hold in them cracks, when you've got all that water pouring down on them."

Edmond was talking on as if he had not heard. "If we had enough cloth to stuff them with . . . . or if we had canvas we could make a liner." But even he sounded discouraged.

"Hey," Jim Bosh exploded from the edge of the crowd, "that's an idea."

Lysander swung on him furiously. "And I suppose you know where we could get enough canvas to line a mile of flume?"

"Sure. San Francisco Bay is full of abandoned ships. The crews all deserted and went off to the mines, just like I done."

We were all looking at him. Edmond snapped his fingers. "Of course. I've seen them." A trace of excitement came through his voice. "Do you know how to use the 'palm'?"

Bosh nodded eagerly.

"Anyone else in camp know how?"

Bosh laughed. "There's half a dozen sailors here who come up with me."

Edmond did some rapid calculating. "We need about seventy-five thousand square feet of canvas. Bosh, you and I are going to San Francisco."

His spirits, down but a moment before, were flying again. And mine soared even higher with a quick hope.

"Can I go too?" I could hardly contain myself. "Please, Edmond, please, please, please?"

He was taken aback for a moment, then he laughed aloud. "All right, if your aunt has no objection."

I ran all the way down the canyon to the Peyton store. I knew better than to ask Aunt Emeline first. If she once said no, that would be the end of it. But if I could get Uncle Ben's permission, then maybe I stood a chance.

He was working on the company's ledgers in the corner of the room. Lisbeth was behind the counter when I burst in. I was so excited that I didn't even see her.

"Edmond's going to San Francisco to get canvas and he'll take me with him if you'll let me go."

My uncle looked up with a puzzled smile. "What's this all about?"

"The flume leaks," I told him. "The boards are too warped to hold water . . ."

Behind me I heard Lisbeth gasp. "Oh, no."

"But it's all right," I yelled, "because Jim Bosh was a sailor and there's tons and tons of canvas just rotting on the deserted ships in the harbor, and he knows how to sew them together and they're going to make a liner for the flume and can I go, please, please, please?"

At least I had his whole attention. "You sure you've got this all straight?"

I nodded vehemently. "Edmond's coming down to get dust to buy the canvas with, then he's going, right away."

Lisbeth had come around the counter, her face stricken. "Do you think it could possibly work, Mr. Garner? They've tried so hard."

My uncle gazed out through the doorway. "I don't see why not. I'd say it's worth trying."

"Then I can go?" I cut in quickly.

"You'd better ask your aunt."

"But if she lets me?"

Uncle Ben laughed. "All right, if she lets . . ."

I did not hear the rest of the sentence. I had already dashed out toward the cabin.

CHAPTER TWENTY

I LOVED San Francisco from my first view of it, the great bay stretching between the wooded headlands, the rising hills, the new buildings crowding along the dusty streets.

I had seen Cincinnati on our way West, but it was nothing like the bustle through which we now drove. We had brought three wagons on which to carry the canvas, and it was well that I had the middle one, for I was far too busy gawking to pay much attention to the road.

Bosh had not lied. The bay was litterly filled with idle, empty ships. Some had been so hastily deserted by their crews that fragments of their torn sails still hung from the yardarms.

I don't know how large the city actually was at that time, for so many people were passing through, but it seemed to me a metropolis. Neither Bosh nor Edmond knew where to go or who to see about purchasing the canvas, but Edmond headed at once for Diamond Joe Stoop's.

The building was large. It had been built as a warehouse, not far from the Embarcadero, about a hundred feet off Market. It was two-storied, of logs and frame. Below it someone was building a three-story structure of cut stone which we learned had come all the way from China.

We put two wagons in a livery and drove the other through Portsmouth Square, pulling up at Joe's door.

Joe welcomed us with a warhoop, clapping Edmond on the back with a resounding blow and stretching out a long arm to tousle my hair. He wore a long-tailed coat and a ruffled shirt with lace at the cuffs, and two large diamonds for buttons.

He stood back, teetering on the heels of his polished boots, thrusting his thumbs inside the waist of his striped trousers. I noticed that his fingers, barely brushing over the stocks of his fancy revolvers, were white and clean, the nails shining like a woman's.

I knew that Edmond did not like anyone to put a hand on him, but after a slight start he just stood, smiling and watching Joe chew the corner of his full mustache with his snaggle teeth.

"Well, now, Edmond. What do you think of her?" He waved an arm expansively at the room behind him.

It was early in the afternoon, but already the big gambling room with its ornate bar was well filled. I was openly dazzled by the crowd. Most of them were gentlemen certainly, tailored for the city in lavishly fine shirts, tight pants, and slim-wasted coats. Some wore their stovepipe hats even though they were indoors. There was a sprinkling of men from the mines, but even they looked important.

They turned to glance at us in polite curiosity as Joe piloted us through the gleaming tables to the bar. There must have been three hundred, gathered around the monte layouts, the faro banks and roulette wheels and clustered along the bar. This was a sight in itself, its mahogany top at my shoulder height, a thick, polished brass rail at its foot and behind it an enormous mirror framed in dark, carved wood and shelves of crystal glasses.

Joe slapped it and chuckled to Edmond. "Got her off a fellow who went busted bucking a faro bank. Pretty, ain't she?"

Bob was behind the bar, making drinks for a group at the far end, looking majestic in a white jacket and black tie. He saw us and hurried his drinks, then came toward us, his white teeth gleaming in a smile that threatened to split his face apart.

"Mr. Edmond, Mr. Austin. Now this is really fine, just fine."

Two other bartenders were also working, and Bob left to join Joe in taking us on a tour of the whole sumptuous establishment. I was kept silent in open-mouthed astonishment. The place seemed totally unreal after the single-roomed cabins and shacks of the mining country.

Pride of ownership glowed in Bob's dark eyes, but I noticed that he had adopted an attitude of deference to his customers.

Edmond listened and looked and said nothing about canvas until the tour was completed. Then Joe told him importantly that he knew just the man, a ship's chandler named Hughes, and they disappeared with Bosh trailing at their heels.

Bob took me to the rear of the big building and knocked on a door. Sandy opened it. She gasped, then threw herself into my embarrassed arms.

"Austin. Austin." She was laughing against my shoulder, shaking me until my teeth rattled. "Hey, Maw, kids, Austin's here."

The whole Stoop tribe descended on me. If it had not been for Bob I think they would have completely smothered me. Little Joe was nearly as big as I. The rest were growing like beanstalks.

I hardly knew Myrtle. She had on a purple dress with a yoke of lace, and she led me into the parlor with the pride of a queen showing off her throne room.

I stared around the room incredulously. It looked very

like my aunt's parlor in Wilmington, but I had never seen anything like it in California.

To add to my amazement there were two Chinese house boys in quilted jackets, with pigtails bobbing down their backs. Sandy told me there were five, employed as cooks and houseboys by the club.

Bob went back to work, Myrtle had to go downtown for something, the kids drifted away and Sandy hauled me down Montgomery Street to show me the city.

But the minute we stepped outdoors she ceased to be the girl I knew and became a young lady, quiet of voice, demure of manner. I could not understand the change and asked her.

"Everybody knows I'm Diamond Joe's daughter," she said. "I can't do anything to disgrace my father."

I laughed at her, remembering the girl I had known on the trail, even the girl at Moke Hill.

"You're making fun of me."

"I'm not!" She sounded exasperated. "I'm not a child anymore, Austin. I am learning how to act as a lady."

"And just how does a lady act?"

She thought about it. "Like your Aunt Emeline, I guess."

I could not think of Aunt Emeline with anything except a very personal picture, so I did not learn much there, and I was too interested in the rising city to pursue the subject.

She led me the length of Market Street, down to the blue bay, and we stood looking out across the water. The multitude of raw new buildings, the construction projects in progress, the wagons and horsemen and pedestrian traffic milling through the wide streets had my head in a whirl, and Sandy seemed to guess it.

"This is going to be the biggest city in the world," she said. "That's what Papa says."

"Your paw must be getting rich, if he's got a share in Bob's place."

She looked around quickly at the people near us on the wooden sidewalk.

"Shh. No one is supposed to know Bob is anything but hired to work for Papa. Remember those men at the mine."

I remembered well.

"So Papa acts like he owns everything, but Bob pays him every month. Twice as much as he used to make driving the stage."

Such a salary was impressive enough, for the stage drivers were the elite of the mining communities.

"Is Bob making a lot?"

Again she glanced around, then she almost whispered. "Over a thousand dollars a day. Maw keeps track of it for him. That's where she's gone now, down to the express company."

It was a fantastic sum. I knew how hard my uncle and Ike worked to try to start a paper, and how many men it was taking to raise the money for the flume.

"What's he going to do with all of it?"

She shook her head. "That's the problem. It doesn't matter how much money he has, he's still a black man, even if he's got his free papers. I heard him talking to Maw about it just the other day. There don't seem to be anywhere in the world for him to be like other people."

I had thought that in San Francisco it would be different, and I felt hurt and let down by this city that I began to love. We returned to the gambling club and went into their apartment through the entrance on the rear street.

Edmond and Bosh and I spent five days there, and I hated to leave, but finally our business was finished. The canvas was loaded on our wagons and they were driven aboard the *River Belle,* a side-wheeler which ran up to Sacramento.

The boat was not so large as the one we had taken down the Ohio, and it drew only about four feet of water, but at that time of the year the river was low and the channel studded with snags.

All the Stoops came down to see us off, and Myrtle handed me a bundle of dress material for my aunt.

"Tell her to come down and stay with us. It must be hard on her, stuck up in those hills."

It did not seem strange to me at that time that Myrtle Stoop and my aunt had in a sense changed places, that Myrtle, who had come barefoot out of the Ohio hills, should be the wife of one of San Francisco's best-known citizens while my aunt lived in a canvas, earth-floored shack on the raw banks of the American River. Children do not think much on such perplexities.

I was kissed by Sandy and both the younger girls, then Myrtle wrapped her arms around me and hugged me until I could hardly breathe.

"You come back. You hear?"

I said that I would, and walked up the plank, Edmond

and Bosh following. The lines were cast off and the left paddle wheel began to churn, taking us crabwise away from the wharf. It would be over two years before I saw San Francisco again.

The canvas liner worked. The sailors sewed together a hundred-foot section, and we turned water into it, just to see if it leaked too much, but it leaked very little.

The pace along the river increased day by day as completion of the great project began to seem a reality. Edmond Jones, I think, never slept. He was everywhere at once, urging the sailors, commending Lysander's herculean effort, joshing with the Mexicans at the sawmill, watching the dam rise above Buckner's Bar.

By now I could see the shape of it. Abutments ran out from the canyon wall on either side, leaving a space in the center. At this gate two heavy posts were driven firmly into the river bed against each abutment, creating a vertical slot. When all else was ready, four-inch planks would be dropped into the slot to shut off the stream's flow.

At the east end of the dam the flume's mouth yawned, and the wooden serpent stretched along the shelf hacked from the rock wall, ready to receive the diverted river when the water rose behind the dam.

As Bosh's crew finished each section of the canvas liner it was spiked in place, and Lysander's crew, finished with the shelf, now had a final project.

They were engaged in placing shots of powder in the old rock slide. When the dam was closed they would blow a hole in the slide to let the lake drain off, to lay bare the accumulated golden sand.

And then it was done. Looking back, it seems incredible that three hundred men working with the crudest tools could have accomplished the task at all. But the last section of canvas was down. The gate boards were dropped into the dam. The water rose six feet behind it and flowed over the board spillway into the flume.

The river was turned.

I ran through the flume, ahead of the trickle as it found its way the full mile and spilled back into its old course below the slide.

The full complement of the Bar was gathered, standing in an awed silence as the water swelled to a lapping tongue, and I will never forget the cheer that filled the canyon as the waterfall poured forth.

The men were bearded and dirty. Some had been working in water to their waists for months. Their clothes were ragged, they had not had proper food nor enough of it, but every face shone with the deep satisfaction which only accomplishment can bring.

It was Saturday noon. We took a luxurious idle hour, laughing and whooping and congratulating ourselves. Then Lysander's crew moved down to light the fuses of the powder charges.

We all took shelter and I literally held my breath, watching the powder crew scramble away, waiting for the first explosion. It came with a puffing roar, followed by a second, a third, and then a fourth as the kegs let go.

Rocks flew in every direction, spewing up like a geyser of stones, pelting down where Caroline and I crouched behind a large boulder. Three of the men did not retreat far enough and were struck by flying fragments, but none was seriously hurt.

Another cheer welled up as the lake which had been trapped behind the slide began to drain.

We all crowded down to the shore to watch. A roiling, roaring spout of white water shot through the gap. All afternoon it raged, and by dark the level was low enough to ease the pressure. Then Edmond jumped down into the water, throwing out debris, deepening and widening the gorge. He was joined by a dozen others and they worked feverishly in the light of pine torches, trying to clear a space to drain the remaining lake without disturbing the precious sands.

Some of the rocks were too firmly wedged to be moved by hand, and bars were brought. Even we kids turned to, pulling out the smaller boulders and rolling them ashore.

Finally a halt was called and everyone retired to the store, bone weary but too exhilarated to go home to bed, joyously comparing plans to what they could do, now that they were rich.

Edmond made the speech. He praised them all for their efforts and cooperation.

"It will take all night and most of tomorrow to complete the drainage. Sunday is traditionally used for cleaning camp, washing clothes and a little rest. I suggest we keep the Sabbath as usual, and begin work on the lake bed Monday morning."

The suggestion was greeted with uncertain silence, and Lysander spoke from the rear of the store.

"Why should we put it off?"

"That gold has been lying there for thousands of years," Edmond said. "A few hours won't make any difference. We are all exhausted. By Monday we will be in shape to work. Shall we take a vote?"

The majority voted with Edmond, and after the meeting I walked with him to the hut where he lived.

"Why didn't you want them to work tomorrow?"

He stopped, filling his pipe and gazing up at the arch of star filled sky far above the canyon's rim, and his voice was very tired.

"The water won't be low enough to work properly before tomorrow evening at best. If we try to go in there tomorrow we'll merely stir up the gold and the lighter flakes will be carried down the stream."

I nodded.

"On Monday," he went on, "we'll divide up the work, start at the slide end of the lake and move up. All the gold will be turned over to your uncle to hold until we're finished, then it will be divided according to the number of shares each man holds."

"You'll be famous," I told him. "When the other camps hear how rich we all are they'll want you to go tell them how to do it."

He gave me his sleepy, mocking smile. "Wait until we are all rich."

"You mean you think that sand maybe isn't as rich as you said?"

"I mean, you never can tell about gold, Austin. They say it's where you find it, and I hope we aren't wrong. We'll see." He turned away from me. "Good night. I think I can use some sleep."

I was disappointed. I'd have liked to stay and talk, but I knew how tired he was. I went back to the store, surprised that everyone had gone with the exception of Lisbeth. The lamp was still burning and she was sweeping up the litter the crowd had left behind.

I slipped through the door and stood watching her for several minutes before she turned and saw me.

"Why, Austin, I thought you'd gone to bed."

I shook my head. "I was talking to Edmond. Sometimes

I can't understand him. He thought up this whole idea, and now it's done and he isn't even excited."

"I imagine he's excited enough."

"Anyhow," I said, "he's proved one thing, that he can work as hard as the next one when he's got something to work for."

"He worked, all right."

"Harry Love says he's the smartest man he ever knew." I was watching her from the corner of my eye. "He still likes you."

She tossed her head. "I'm promised to Lysander, Austin."

"You don't love him."

She started to get mad, then changed her mind and talked to me very solemnly.

"Austin, you're getting big enough that you should realize there are some subjects you should not pry into. I know your uncle tells you that you should know all that's going on, but people's personal lives are excepted. But I'll tell you this because I've known you so long. I am promised. Lysander needs me and Edmond doesn't. When he gets through here he'll go charging off, back to the Sandwich Islands or Asia or some place. A woman is different. She can't just pick up and go every time she has a mind to. She needs a settled home, a place to raise a family."

I thought of my aunt, who had picked up and gone with my uncle not once but several times. And standing there I knew that she would do it again and again as the need arose. But somehow I could not say this to Lisbeth. I knew that Edmond needed her as much as Lysander did. I liked Edmond and I did not like Lysander, but I knew no way to tell her. I went home depressed and puzzled.

Sunday morning I was up early, in time to surprise Lysander and Grover Peyton making their way toward the head of the lake. They carried a shovel and a gold pan, so I followed.

The canyon side was heavy with brush and they did not see me as I trailed them up the river to the foot of the new dam.

The lake was not fully drained, but the upper end was out of water, exposing the sand and boulders of the stream bed. The sand was still soft and waterlogged, and they sank in halfway to their knees as they waded out to the center of the old channel.

Lysander began to dig. He went down three feet before

he got to bedrock. Water drained into his hole and I heard him cursing it as I picked my way toward them. Both were so intent on their errand that they paid no attention to me.

Lysander was down at the bottom of the hole, knee-deep in muddy water. Peyton stood above him, holding the pan. Carefully Lysander ran his shovel over the bedrock, bringing up a scoop of sand and carefully dumping it into the pan. He put in three shovelfuls, then climbed out and discovered me.

His heavy face darkened with anger. "What in hell are you doing here?"

I didn't answer. I had always been a little afraid of Lysander Cox.

"Get out of here."

I found my tongue then, for he touched my temper. "Edmond said no one was to dig until tomorrow."

"Edmond said, Edmond said." He shook his fist at me. "I'm damned tired hearing what Edmond Jones said. Whoever elected him God? You'd think the way he gives orders that he owned this river. Well, I worked as hard to drain it as he did, and if I feel like finding out what we've got, I have the right."

I did not argue. I was as curious as he to know how much gold was in the pan.

"You going to wash it?" I said.

"Why do you think I went to the trouble of digging it up?" He took the pan from Peyton, turned and climbed the breast of the dam.

Peyton watched me, his nutcracker face looking like an annoyed squirrel. "You won't say anything? We just want to see what the sand looks like."

I shook my head, feeling that I had no more right to be there than they did.

"You're a good boy."

He had a sour way of saying anything. I knew he did not like me. I'm not sure that Grover Peyton ever liked anyone. I've always wondered how a girl like Lisbeth could have such a father.

He turned and climbed the dam after Lysander. I was at his heels.

We found Cox squatted down at the water's edge, holding the pan just under the surface, stirring the muddy sand with his thick fingers. I never knew anything that took quite so long. It seemed that he took hours to wash out that pan of gravel, though it was but a few minutes, for I was practically holding my breath.

Lysander Cox was a slow thinker and a slow mover, but as he slopped more and more of the dirt and sand over the edge his motions quickened. Still, he was extremely careful not to spill out any of the heavy matter.

Finally he grunted in satisfaction and straightened. I had my first look at the result. There was a core of black sand perhaps a sixteenth of an inch thick in the center of the pan's gleaming bottom, and rimming it lay a fan of gold flakes a full inch wide.

I had never seen anything nearly like it. Few had. Bob's gravel mine had been extremely rich, but nothing like this. It would go at least a hundred dollars to the pan, likely more.

Lysander was in a better mood than I had ever seen him. Even Grover Peyton was smiling broadly, his thin lips stretched back across his small jaw.

"Lord, lord, look at that."

There were several nuggets in the pan. One was a chip of quartz about half an inch across, shaped roughly like a heart, with wire gold stringing through it. I reached in and picked it up.

"You keep it, kid," Lysander said. "Just to remember you had the first piece of Murderer's Bar gold."

He pulled a leather pouch from his shirt and very gently began to work the black sand and gold flakes into it.

"You going to pan some more?"

They looked at me, their greed shining in their eyes. Regretfully Lysander shook his head.

"Guess not. Guess maybe Jones is right. The whole crowd get out here and stir things up with it so soft, we're liable to lose a part of the gold."

I did not go back to camp with them. I slipped back through the bushes, ridden by a guilt that I should have been there at all. My aunt was getting breakfast when I came into the cabin. My uncle and Caroline were already at the table. My aunt saw me and almost screeched at my muddy boots.

"Land sakes. Get out of here and take off those boots. Wherever have you been?"

I retreated hastily outside and pulled off the boots, coming back in my stocking feet. I had not intended to say where

I had been, but when she asked me again I did not dare lie.

"I went up by the dam," I said.

A quick smile touched my uncle's lips, then was gone. "Water gone down much?"

I nodded and started on the corn-meal mush my aunt had forked onto my plate.

"Anybody else up there?"

Again I could not lie. "Lysander Cox and old Peyton."

"Panning, huh?"

I was startled. "How'd you know?"

"Figures." He was not looking at me, but concentrating on his breakfast. "Always one or two who can't wait. How'd they do?"

My excitement boiled over. I gulped. "There was more than a hundred dollars in the one pan."

"What pan?" Old Ike had just come through the door.

I told him while they all watched me. Ike blew out his cheeks.

"Well. So now everyone's dirt rich. What you going to do with your share, Ben, buy the biggest paper in San Francisco?"

My aunt said very softly from the stove, "Maybe we can go East."

All of us looked at her quickly. She wasn't facing us. She was standing there apparently not looking at anything, and I noticed how bent her shoulders were. Maybe it was my imagination, but I thought there was a catch in her tone.

"Sure," my uncle said immediately. "Do us all good to go for a visit."

She flung around then. "Visit? You intend to stay in this outlandish country?"

Uncle Ben was innocently astounded. "What's the matter with this country? Where else can you have a river of gold in your front yard?"

He stood up abruptly and went to her, putting his arm around her back, ignoring us all.

"It's a good country, Em. It's growing so fast. It's rough now, but there'll be fine towns, I promise you. As soon as this gold is divided I'll take you down and build you a real home. We'll send East for furniture." He was talking low and fast, very earnestly.

I saw that my aunt's fingers bit into his shoulder as she turned out of his arm. She tried twice to speak, but no words came.

It made me uncomfortable. I pulled out my nugget and laid it on the table.

"Look what I've got."

Caroline let out a squeal and reached for it, but I jerked it away. I knew better than to let her get her fingers on anything I wanted to keep.

Aunt Emeline stepped forward with a burst of her old animation and peered at the nugget. "Why, it looks like a heart."

On a sudden impulse I said, "When I get rich I'll have it put on a gold chain for you."

She caught her breath sharply and flushed, giving a shaky little laugh. Then she did something she seldom had done. She stooped and kissed my cheek.

"You're a dear, Austin. But you keep it, save it for your best girl."

I felt my own cheeks turn hot. "I'm not going to have any girl."

"You've got a girl," Caroline giggled, then she began caroling, "Sandy's Austin's girl. Austin loves Sandy. Sandy loves Austin."

"You shut up," I shouted. "I don't love any girl."

"You do too." She jumped up and ran around the table, trying to snatch the nugget from my hand. In the scuffle my chair tipped over, my nugget spun across the floor and Caroline was quick to grab it.

I caught her before she reached the door and wrenched it from her grasp.

That brought my aunt back to her normal role. She thumped me on the head and whacked Caroline's behind, ordering us to sit down and finish our breakfast.

My uncle put out his hand for the nugget and sat fingering it, thinking.

"Just like Peyton and Cox to jump the gun. If this news gets out every man on the bar will be out there before noon."

The news got out. There is no way of keeping such a secret in a gold camp. Four men with a rocker cleaned up nine and a half pounds of gold in three hours, and the camp went wild.

But the men were too busy celebrating to pan out much that Sunday afternoon. And Edmond and Uncle Ben called a meeting to try to keep order. They divided up the whole river bed into claims, assigning one to each man, and as the water receded they waded out to erect monuments.

Then a party developed around Peyton's store. The whiskey keg was broached and the singing and shouting rang through the canyon.

My aunt and Lisbeth and the other few women in camp withdrew to the shelter of our cabin, and I had strict orders not to go near the store for fear of trouble.

But there was no trouble. The most quarrelsome of men could find little to fight about in the face of prospective wealth beyond their wildest yearning.

As it began to get dark the men turned back toward their cabins. It grew exceptionally hot, and there were black clouds and sheet lightning in the upper mountains. We gave it little thought. We were used to the summer storms high above us, and they seldom affected us down below.

The thunder and the brilliant, stabbing lightning did not keep me awake, but it played through my sleep like an approaching ominous giant. I roused with the first light and heard outside a faint shouting of men.

At first I thought the party was still in progress. I dressed and went outside, seeing the pale streak that etched out the canyon's east rim. Then I saw the line of men standing along the river's bank.

I ran toward them with an apprehension of trouble. I did not know what it could be, but as I came up the flume seemed to have come alive. Then in the dim dawn light I saw that water was spilling over its top, up and down its length as far as I could follow it, as if it were not large enough to contain the river.

I heard snatches of words . . . cloudburst in the hills . . . and knew a sickening terror.

Flash floods were common in the country. I ran upstream to where I could see the river above the new earth dam. It was a torrent, a raging, wildly tossing sea, beating against the upper edge of the dam.

Men were running up the stream. Men were running out along the top of the precious dam. They brought sacks from Peyton's store, hastily filling them with earth, and piled them in a dyke atop the dam, but it was too puny an effort.

The American River at that point is one of the larger streams, and it had gone on a vicious rampage. The churning tumult of water was bringing down trees, stumps, debris of all kinds. And the water was licking over the dam.

Edmond Jones ran up with an iron bar and began to pry at the gate, shouting at the others to help. If they could get the gate open and relieve the pressure they might yet save the dam and flume.

But the thousands of tons of water surging against the gate defeated their efforts. They could not budge the heavy planks.

There was a sudden shout of warning. I discovered my uncle at my side and heard him yelling at my aunt to get Caroline and me back to our cabin. He had built it on the rise of the hill, well above the level of the bar proper.

There was a rush from the dam top as the men abandoned hope and raced toward their camps, rushing to haul their possessions to higher ground.

Only Edmond Jones still struggled with the gate. Now water was gushing over the full length of the dam. A tree trunk heaved high into the air and plunged like a battering ram against the earth bulwark, skidding over the sloping surface and flying into the dry lake bed.

Then Lisbeth Peyton, her skirts gathered above her knees, ran teetering through the swift sheet of water, across the dam toward the gate, and caught hold of Edmond's arm.

Even had I been standing at their side I doubt that I could have heard what they said above the echoing roar that shook the canyon, but their motions were plain. He waved her back wildly, but she shook her head and kept tugging at his arm.

He fought her, then suddenly cast away his bar, caught her under her elbow and began to run with her toward the shore.

The water was now pouring a foot deep over the dam. I watched them splash awkwardly through it to the bank and scramble to the higher ground, and I ducked away toward them.

Suddenly a great cry filled the canyon, a cry of protesting voices, a cry of timber shattering and boulders rolling, and I looked up in time to see the dam burst open as the gate went out.

The angry brown flood tore the earthwork away as if it were built of fluff, sweeping all down the lake bed, down the old channel. It struck the rock slide with resounding force, spreading wide the cleft we had blown, shoving the huge boulders before it, ripping out the golden sand we had worked so hard to uncover.

Nothing escaped. Not even the flume, for the flood ate away the posts which supported the bridge around the rock face. They gave, tilting outward, one after another, until with a shriek of tearing timbers the whole bridge section splashed into the tumbling river.

I expected the flume to break in two, but the stout canvas lining held it together. Instead of breaking, the weight of the sagging section dragged more and more of the mile-long box sidewise from its shelf, into the hurrying water, until it floated like a writhing serpent, its whole length bobbing and tugging at the fastenings which held it at the upstream end.

It hung so for one awful, eternal moment, then with a rending, tearing sound which reached us clearly above the constant high growl of the flood, it wrenched free and went twisting and slithering down the waves, past the old dyke and out of sight around the bend.

For years after, miners making camp along the river searched the driftwood piles, coming up with scraps of canvas to roof their shanties with a remnant of Edmond Jones' flume.

You could laugh at the majestic gaiety of the flume bouncing over the current, or you could cry. But no one on the bar had time to do either. The river was still rising at a threatening rate.

Everyone turned in a scrambling rush to save their camps, their rockers and sluice boxes, their stores and possessions. Few were quick enough. The brown water ate across the rising breast of the bar. It crept into Peyton's store, where Grover Peyton and Lisbeth were trying to carry out their goods.

Edmond Jones was running up and down the hill, helping them get the stuff to safety, and I had my hands full helping Ike and my uncle to drag the press and type cases up the slope.

By nightfall we had saved what we could. Nearly the whole of the bar was covered with water, and we clung like half-drowned rats to places along the canyon wall. It was in all respects the end of Murderer's Bar.

I found Edmond Jones seated all alone high up the hillside, his back against a tall pine, staring emptily at the still-raging river. He had worked harder than anyone, helping the Peytons, helping my aunt, abandoning to the flood his own possessions while he assisted others to safety.

"Some flood," I said and settled at his side.

He gave me a rueful sidelong glance, a burning inner anger smoldering in his eyes.

223

"And to think that a man as smart as I'm supposed to be would overlook the possibility."

"It wasn't your fault. You shouldn't have to think for all of them."

"Yes I should." He was not looking at me. "I talked them into risking everything they had. They trusted me, and I didn't protect them. Austin, I'll never try to build anything again. From now on I'll get down and dig like the rest. I won't even use a windlass."

"That would be a mistake." Lisbeth Peyton was standing behind us. Neither of us had heard her come.

Edmond Jones jumped up. I rose more slowly, noticing the flush on her cheeks.

"You mustn't quit because of one setback. You've proved the worth of your dreaming, that your ideas are sound, that you can lead people to accomplish them. There are not many like that. The world needs you."

He shook his head. "You were right in the beginning. A man is privileged to make a fool of himself, but he has no right to involve others. Look at this bar. Because of me every man here is ruined."

"No," she said. "You take too narrow a view. They have lost money, yes, but they have learned something of great value, that by cooperative effort they can do anything. There will be a thousand successful flumes built in this country because you proved it possible."

"You're sweet," he said, "and kind. You take some of the sting out of my disaster. I'm glad you and Lysander . . ."

She looked straight at him. "And there's more proof that all of us can make a mistake. I thought Lysander needed me, that married we could work together as partners. I learned this afternoon how wrong I was. He was very bitter. He said that if it were not for you he could have taken his dust back to Maine and built a house with the finest horsehair furniture for me to sit on in a parlor.

"I don't want to sit, Edmond. I've watched you these past weeks, dreaming, creating, building. You were right. It is the challenge that counts. May I dream with you?"

He caught her to him then, with a fierceness that I thought would hurt her, but she did not seem to mind.

"You mean it," he said. "Oh my darling."

He kissed her then, oblivious that I was watching. I turned and fled.

CHAPTER TWENTY-ONE

EDMOND JONES' flume had cost the miners of the five bars all of the dust in camp, and had left us once again destitute but for the press and type and what little household paraphernalia we had rescued. Of the preciously culled necessities with which my aunt had departed Wilmington, only blankets and a few cooking and eating utensils remained.

We were all stunned, disbelieving. Perhaps that is why no real retaliation was attempted against him, or perhaps it was the normal gamblers' acceptance of fate. There was some muttering that the debacle was his fault, but by the following night most of the men had packed their horses, accepted their loss and headed off for other diggings. A few elected to stay, reasoning that the flood must perforce have washed new deposits of gold down the stream.

My uncle chose to return to Sonora. At least it was a familiar scene, and winter was approaching.

Edmond's vast project in the isolated, heavily pine-timbered hills turned out not to be a solitary feat of men raising themselves by their boot straps, but a piece of a spontaneous combustion of development by the entire California community.

Sonora itself was all but dead, its bright promise flickering out, but five miles away American Camp, after a faltering start, was on the brink of an unprecedented explosion.

Of all the gold camps on the Mother Lode, Columbia became the largest and most prosperous, and to my often uprooted aunt, dispirited by her Odyssey of dragging from hovel to shack to tent, it became home; home, to be jealously guarded and tenaciously clung to and fought for.

Until we moved to Columbia in the fall of '51, she had disdained to consider herself a Californian, homesick for the comforting bosom of Ohio, doughtily marking time while my uncle had his fling at Adventure, surviving on the vision of one day returning East.

But Columbia captured her. Without her years in the rude

225

camps she would have viewed its birth as rough and uncouth, but from the day of her arrival she saw it as a blessed city.

Set in a sandy bowl surrounded by gentle hills shaded by great, spreading live oaks, softened by lush fields of wild grain and in the spring gay with such a profusion of wild flowers that it looked like a prize-taking garden, it had beauty from the start. Its single lack was of water. Being a "dry" camp had retarded its development, and made mining a problem for as long as the place existed.

Despite this, though other towns along the Lode made rightful claim to size and fame, none ever approached Columbia in richness, in improvements or in civic pride.

Out of the square mile on which the town sat, over a hundred million dollars in dust was shipped by the express companies alone in a ten-year period, and the unrecorded treasure carried out by individual miners undoubtedly doubled this figure for total production.

This jewel in the necklace of the southern mines had been founded in March of 1850 by a party of doctors lead by Thaddeus Hildreth, and was called Hildreth's Diggings.

The first strike was made in a dry gulch leading to Kennebec Hill, and one month later the district had an estimated population of six thousand, becoming American Camp.

But the following winter proved highly disappointing. Water was scarce and costly, and the foreign mining tax passed by the new legislature drove out many of the Mexican and Chilean inhabitants who had made up the bulk of the miners.

Not until a water company was formed and a ditch dug the following summer did the camp begin to really grow, now as Columbia.

It was that autumn in Sonora that my uncle, fresh from the misadventure at Murderer's Bar, met Captain Avent, who had dug up two and one half pounds of gold in his first day on his claim.

Immediately my uncle and Ike headed over the four-mile trail to Columbia. As yet there was not even a wagon road, and they rode the work horses which pulled our wagon south from the American River.

My uncle came back the following week, bringing with him half a pound of gold. We were living in a tent pitched beside the wagon which still held the press, the cook stove, and all else we owned.

"We've struck it at last." He did a jig around my aunt. "Our luck has changed. Emeline, you'll wear diamonds and pearls for the rest of your life."

She looked at him across the open campfire and told him bitterly, "I'd be satisfied with enough to eat."

He was jarred, saying in an abashed tone, "I'm sorry, Em. I'll have to admit that things haven't gone well for us, but now it's different. You'll see."

As always after she had hurt him, she relented. "I shouldn't have said that. We've never really gone hungry. But Ben, not another wild goose chase to another awful camp. Ben, winter's coming. We haven't a house. Please, can't we stay here? At least there are some women here, women I know. . . ."

She did not say it, but even I could tell that she was near the end of her fortitude. Uncle Ben's enthusiasm, though, was running free.

"Sonora's dying," he argued. "And there are women in Columbia, at least a dozen nice women. There are over two thousand people already, and more coming every day. It's not a camp, Em. It's a town. They've even piped in water from Matelot Gulch, through hollowed out pine logs. You'll be surprised. You'll love it. We'll leave the wagon for now and take the kids . . ."

He sailed off to the livery to rent horses to transport us, and past argument, Aunt Emeline mounted and turned into the narrow trail. Her face said that she knew she would not love it. Her reluctance and her doubts were valid enough, for it was a strange way to come into a town of two thousand.

Yet my first glimpse of Columbia told me that there was something here to set it apart from any other camp we had seen.

True, the streets were deep-churned red dust and the houses lining them were built of any material the owner could come by: shakes, stone, clapboard, and adobe, but they were houses, not cabins or shanties even if their floors were still earth, and there was an air of permanence such as I had not sensed even in Sonora.

My uncle piloted us to a boardinghouse run by A. W. C. DeNoielle and his wife. Mrs. De Noielle had come across the plains from the Midwest, and my aunt all but collapsed in relief on meeting her.

Ike and Uncle Ben had staked a claim under Kennebec

Hill, almost in the center of where Main Street now runs. He was making better than three ounces a day even though he had to load his sand into sacks and carry it half a mile to the water that flowed from one of the wooden pipes.

The camp was indeed booming. Two weeks after we arrived, Al Hunnewell established a post office, and the Chain Lightnin' Express riders brought in mail and papers by way of Knight's Ferry.

By Christmas a wagon road to Sonora was finished and my uncle went after our press, and Van Arsdale and Kelty inaugurated rival stage lines which made the trip to Sonora and return four times every day.

Uncle Ben worked the claim with Ike four days a week. The rest of the time he spent building a house on the oak ridge directly across town from Kennebec Hill. He had chosen the location with care, with the deliberation of a man who had some intuition that here he would stay. There was plenty of timber for his building. There was a small spring running out of the hillside behind the house, and it was a good mile and a half above the budding town it overlooked.

"This is one place that's going to keep growing," he told my aunt. "I feel it in my bones. It will be twice the size of Wilmington at least, and I don't want you living downtown among the saloons and gambling halls and things."

In January we moved to the new home. It had three rooms, a floor in the living room, which was an extravagance with the cost of lumber, but was in the nature of a precious gift from Uncle Ben to Aunt Emeline.

And in March we brought out the first issue of the Columbia *Clarion*, whose forebears had been so fragile and mortal.

The old press had once again been set up, in a building on Fulton. A lump rose in my throat as Ike pulled the first proof and passed it across to me.

Aunt Emeline and Uncle Ben hovered over my shoulder and Caroline was exploring the shop. It was like old times in Wilmington, and yet it wasn't. It seemed a long, long time ago that I had read that first story about California gold.

The front page was entirely given over to advertisements. There was a quarter page extolling the virtues of Bixel Beer, brewed locally at the head of Matelot Gulch. There were notices from five of the forty saloons which now graced the town. There were half a dozen of the gambling-halls, who were said to house forty-three faro banks, and a dozen merchants were represented.

No longer a town, Columbia was a full-fledged city. Now she boasted eight hotels, three theaters (one a Chinese playhouse), a private school, a free library in which my aunt took a major part, two bookstores, Methodist, Presbyterian and Catholic churches, plus a Jewish synagogue.

My aunt was already teaching Sunday school, and the paper carried the church notices free.

There was plenty of news. I was watching a city literally spring from the plain, and it was breathtaking. Solid trains of freight wagons wound up the new road from Stockton and Stanislaus City, bringing mountains of supplies yet never satisfying the voracious appetite of the exploding growth. Even the firm of D. O. Mills, bankers and dealers in gold dust, established a branch of their Sacramento bank to compete with the ensconced Adams & Company, Reynolds, and the new Wells Fargo Express.

To a newsman, the *Clarion* was a beautiful, lucrative paper with a promise of success.

My aunt cried that night. I don't know what started her. We had delivered the first issue. I had carried a bundle under my arm and visited a list my uncle had made out, the merchants and advertisers, the hotels, saloons, theaters, and gambling rooms, even the bawdy shows and sporting houses.

It was dark when I climbed the path up the ridge to the new house and found them all gathered around the slab table my uncle had made. I lifted the bag of coins I had collected and dumped it on the table in front of Uncle Ben.

"Sell-out?"

"Every one. I could have sold a lot more. People stopped me on the street."

He nodded slowly and I knew that he was pleased, and suddenly my aunt was crying.

It took us all unaware. Caroline made a small whimpering sound and ducked her head. Old Ike was so embarrassed that he dropped a forkful of food into his lap.

"Now what?" Uncle Ben said, and got up from his place to round the table and put an awkward hand on her shoulder. "There, there, Em. What's wrong?"

"It's been so long." She was snuffling and trying to check the tears. "So long, Ben. But now we're home."

She stood up. She had her handkerchief wadded in her hand. She pressed it against her mouth, then she ran for the door.

My uncle went out after her, closing the door behind him, and they were gone for a long while.

Caroline stared at me with round eyes. She had turned eleven the week before and was growing fast.

"What's wrong with Mama?"

I did not know.

"She's happy," Ike said.

Caroline looked at him. "She's happy? She's crying."

"Sometimes people cry because they are happy. You kids eat your supper."

I ate. I was hungry, and the stewed rabbit tasted good. Ike had not lost his knack for hunting, and we seldom lacked game in the house.

The *Clarion* prospered. The winter of 1852-53 was good to us. I worked full time in the print shop and we were increasingly busy. I was nearing fourteen and had attained one goal that I had long yearned for. I was as tall as Uncle Ben, a fact that annoyed him, although he would not admit it.

Columbia continued to grow electrically. By December we had seventeen thousand people. The saloons, gambling halls, fandango parlors roistered around the clock. A gambler named Hunt told me that he took in over a hundred thousand dollars during the month.

Even though I watched it from the print shop daily, even though the stories and rumors and reports and facts flooded through our office in a constantly swelling tide, I had trouble keeping pace. Blink your eyes and there was a new street, new buildings. Stores, assay offices, theaters, restaurants sprang into being.

The Jenny Lind served squab under glass and oysters shipped in in ice. The French restaurant featured a Gallic chef. All of the refinements of a metropolis were ours, supported by the enormous output of gold dust, and the ground level itself was dropped ten to twenty-five feet as the miners dug out and hauled away the heavily mineralized soil. Stripped to bedrock, the limestone outcroppings and pillars were left to stand like gravestones, naked, indecent.

To the east of town, Sewell Knapp's forty-acre ranch yielded forty thousand dollars to the acre and some of the largest nuggets to come out of the country. One chunk worth near five thousand was found in April of '54.

New strikes were so numerous and frequent that we all became jaded by them. Columbians did not go rushing off at the shout of "gold" rising in the hills. Others rushed to us.

Even James Marshall, the original discoverer of gold at Sutter's Creek, arrived, to join our Masonic lodge.

I had been thrilled by the word and by the yellow metal in the early camps. Now a new interest took its place. I discovered the theater.

Colonel Thomas Cazenau's Exchange Theater was the first. Its builders left a sapling pine tree to grow up through the stage, and beneath its graceful branches I heard the renowned lyric soprano Signora Eliza Biscaccianti sing. I understood then what the Sacramento woman had meant in saying that Sandy Stoop should study opera, and wondered if Sandy was doing so.

I watched as Edwin Booth brought Shakespeare's brooding Richard the Third to life, and saw Mrs. Alexina Fisher Baker, Henry Coad, Catherine Sinclair perform.

There were always passes at the print shop, and I was early established as critic for the paper. This happened more by accident than design, for Ike cared little for the drama and though Uncle Ben took Aunt Emeline and sometimes Caroline to each new presentation, he had far too much to do to include personally writing the reviews. And in a town whose cemetery never received a soul over thirty years of age, I was not made to feel too young for the job.

Several fires razed the wooden town, but after each one new buildings rose immediately, more and more of brick and stone.

Charles Cardinell's Terpsichore Hall was rebuilt more lavish than the original after the first big fire. A two-story structure with stores and saloons below accommodated the theater above, one hundred feet wide and fifty deep, elaborately appointed with a dress circle around three sides. And John Leary's Modern Theater rose again from ashes.

But of all the greats, it was to Alicia Mandeville that I gave my fourteen-year-old heart, sitting enraptured, talking to her in her dressing room after the show as she played with the chips as tossed to her by admiring audiences. It was with grief and horror that I heard the news when the steamship *Republic*, on which she was returning to New York, burned and sank off the Farallones and took her away from us all.

The theater, though, did not claim all of my time or attention, for Columbia was a roaring, brawling, laughing bawd, and awesome news broke every minute, ranging from the grim business of the miners' strike against the water company to the amazing funeral of Paddy Dorn.

Paddy had made one of the richest strikes along the whole Mother Lode and with much fanfare had opened the Beacon Mine. A flamboyant Irishman in his late twenties, he had a mellifluous tongue and a beguiling manner. Merry and popular, he was one of Ike's favorite drinking partners and when he wasn't working the mine he spent many hours loafing in the *Clarion* shop.

Uncle Ben was away in San Francisco and Ike and I, with another reporter we had taken on, were running the paper when the surprise letter and photograph came from Michigan. The tintype was sharp and clear, showing a man and woman in wedding costume, staring rigidly into the camera. The man's left arm was bent, the woman's fingers slipped through the crook of the elbow and his right hand was spread over the crown of the stiff bowler hat clutched against his breast.

The letter was inscribed in a round schoolgirl scrawl, badly misspelled, but its jist was clear enough. Four years earlier her groom, one Michael Dougherty, had set out to make his fortune in the California gold fields, and she had had no single word from him since. She was writing to all the papers along the Lode, hoping that someone had known him and could tell her of his fate. Could we, she pleaded, give her any help?

Her description and the bearded portrait might have fitted a hundred men in the town, but one betraying distinction caught my attention. Michael Dougherty had six fingers on the hand that held the bowler. I got out the reading glass and studied the evidence to make sure.

Then, excited, I carried both letter and photograph to the back of the shop where Ike was setting a handbill for an up-coming bear and bull fight.

"Who," I asked him, "do you know who has six fingers on each hand?"

"Paddy Dorn," Ike said without looking up.

I flourished the give-away picture under his nose and then handed him the letter, watching him intently as he read. He held the paper gingerly between an ink-smudged thumb and forefinger, and when he had finished he opened them, letting the sheet flutter to the floor.

"Poor Paddy." He shook his head sorrowfully. "Just when he'd got the world by the tail his past catches up with him. Sad thing."

I nodded sympathetically. "Well, what shall I do about it?"

Ike looked off into the distance and sighed. "No rush I guess. Wait until he shows up."

That same evening Paddy came breezing in, juggling a pair of nuggets as big as marbles and whistling happily. "Lookee here, boys," he crowed. "After all them years I froze and starved I finally got me a mine, oh, I got me one sweet mine."

Ike hadn't the heart to tell him the news. He made me get the letter and picture and I handed them to him wordlessly, and it was a sorry thing to watch the sparkle, the joy of life leak out of Paddy Dorn. The ruddy skin above his luxurious whiskers blanched to a dirty gray and his voice was a hollow croak as he turned from one to the other of us.

"What are you going to do?"

Ike looked as harrassed as if he himself were caught in this trap. "You're not the first runaway husband I ever heard of. What do you want us to do?"

"Just write her you never heard of me."

"Won't work, Paddy boy. Those extra fingers are a dead giveaway, and next she'll be writing to the sheriff's office or the county clerk. Believe me, I know. I moved out on a wife once . . . and those county butt-ins don't have the high ethics we got at the *Clarion*."

He looked at his hands as if he would like to chop them off. "I'll have to go away . . . I could go to the Sandwich Islands, or Australia maybe . . ."

"And take your mine with you?" Ike snorted.

Paddy shriveled further. Then to my astonishment he dropped into a chair, crossed his arms on the desk, lowered his face onto them and began to sob. I had seen few grown men cry and the experience gave me nothing but embarrassment, but Ike was unimpressed.

"Come off it, Paddy Dorn, I know you. You had nerve enough to kill that claim jumper down on Sutter's Creek and you've held your own right along in this brutal land. You sure can't be that afraid of a frail little woman?"

Dorn lifted his head in anguish. "Eunice frail? That harridan's got the tongue of a rattlesnake and the disposition of a tarantula."

With unassailable logic, I said, "Then why did you marry her in the first place?"

"Who thinks when he's eighteen?" Paddy's misery overflowed into such a flowery rhetoric that Ike and I gaped at each other. "At eighteen your feelings soar beyond the realm

233

of reason and your beloved appears an angel sheathed in the bright aura of desire." Then his tone turned to injured indignation. "The woman and her mother trapped me. I had a good job driving a horse car. They plied me with their cookery . . . oh, they were fine cooks . . . they fed me up until the knot was tied, and then they dropped their wiles and changed to jailors. Oh, Ike, I wish I was dead. I wish I could just die and be shut of everything."

He sounded so sincere that suddenly it was the only answer. I said, "Now you're talking sense."

Paddy started, looking at me with a fresh pain. "Now Austin, that was a metaphor. I'm too young a man to die. I've got a lot of good years ahead of me if . . . no, that's too radical."

"You know any other way out?"

He just looked at me, a dull apathy overwhelming him.

"It's simple." My idea was setting me afire. "Michael Dougherty has to die if Paddy Dorn is to live his good life."

"Come again?" Paddy was bewildered. "We're one and the same person. One of us can't die without the other."

"Ho." Ike understood me and a fiendish delight broke through in a wide grin which I returned. "You were born independently of each other, you may die independently. If you have the wherewithal to handle it. Everything is possible when you have such riches as your mine is raining upon you."

Paddy's eyes narrowed suspiciously. "What are you two hatching up here?"

Ike winked at me. "Farewell, Michael Dougherty. May your afterlife be sweeter than was your stay in this vale of tears." He had caught Paddy's extravagant eloquence maliciously but the Irishman paid no heed. He put one hand on the chair back and rose uncertainly, keeping his hold, prepared to defend his life.

Ike abandoned himself to his building vision, gazing into far places and gesturing as he talked. "I can see the coffin . . . the handsomest one in town . . . you lying in it pale and still, your hands crossed piously upon your poor breast . . . And the funeral, oh it will be grand . . . a marble headstone . . . Columbia marble, rising in St. Anne's Cemetery . . . the inscription reading . . ."

Paddy picked up the chair and held it threateningly over his head. "You've got to kill me first."

Ike watched him with a benign smile, letting the moment drag on, then he lifted a finger. "Not you, Paddy boy, not you . . . It's Michael Dougherty we must do in. Of course you'll have to substitute, lie in for him for the pictures, and the viewing, which may tax your patience, particularly if there are flies to light on your nose . . . there'll be a lot of mourners . . . but freedom and peace are surely worth the price."

Ike's eyes were dancing. I hadn't seen him enjoy anything so much since before we left Wilmington. Then when Paddy looked as if he firmly believed we had both gone mad, Ike spread his hands and offered up his dénouement.

"When everyone has paid his respects, looked his fill and departed, you climb out, we close the coffin and bury it. Austin will write the story of your passing and we will send it with your last picture to your grieving wife."

It took a while for Paddy to readjust himself, then slowly he began to grin.

"We'll have to send her some money," I said casually. "Say ten thousand dollars, as your estate."

Paddy spun on me, yelling. "Ten thousand?"

Ike picked up my cue. "Everybody believes in money if they believe in nothing else. I presume your wife knows you well enough to be sure you would not consciously part with a lead dollar if you were alive. The ten thousand will cinch it that you're dead."

Paddy wet his lips. "Wouldn't a thousand do?"

"If you want to be cheap about it." I said it loftily.

Ike looked at the ceiling as though calculating. "Well, we might get by . . . the funeral will cost something . . ."

The funeral cost a lot. It was the grandest ever held in Columbia, and we had some fine ones. They were a favorite entertainment, satisfying the consciences of those who seldom saw the inside of a church and eliciting all the finery and fanfare of a parade. The brass band in full regalia was an essential. It mattered not whether the subject was a leading citizen or a swamper from a lowly saloon, the town turned out to mark the passing.

In the case of Michael Dougherty all the stops were pulled. No other memorial service ever had more enthusiastic, dedicated and active stage managers than Ike and I. Paddy's Irish imagination took fire and in the throes of composition crocodile tears coursed down his leather cheeks. The zest of his sympathy for the deceased overhauled his penury and the plans advanced from excess to excess.

But we had to be careful to avoid disclosure. We decided

that we needed one other confederate, an undertaker, and Ike settled upon Aaron Spaulding. Aside from his artistry in preparing a cadaver for a critical public, Aaron had been previously known to Ike at Rough and Ready. Ike swore that at that ungentle camp Aaron had found it necessary to deliver the coup de grace to a mortally wounded customer who nevertheless refused to succumb, and that Aaron knew Ike was privy to the act. It was good insurance that Aaron would hesitate to risk Ike's displeasure by any lack of cooperation.

That being settled upon, it was next necessary to create the personality of Michaël Dougherty, a name as yet unknown in Columbia. To that end I wrote a story for the *Clarion*. Since I had given the world a living idol in Joe Stoop, I saw no reason why I could not build a dead hero out of Michael Dougherty. The story read:

HORRIBLE ACCIDENT AVOIDED BY BRAVE MAN'S SACRIFICE

The road between Vallicedo and Douglas Flat was the scene last night of one of those unselfish acts of heroism which all too often pass unappreciated in the modern day of hustle and bustle.

The evening stage, carrying three ladies and four young children was held up below Point of Rocks by three masked men.

Captain Barlow, the fearless driver, whipped his horses in an effort to run down the bandits, and for his pains received a ball through his head, which was fatal.

The lone male passenger, Mr. Michael Dougherty, formerly of Michigan, grasped the reins from the dying driver's limp fingers and despite having received two shots through his own body, stayed with the coach as it rocketed down the perilous grade, bringing all safely into Douglas Flat.

There this paragon of chivalry expired, though all efforts were made to save him. His last words were for his loving wife whom he had not seen in four long years.

The thanks, not only of those he succored, but of all God fearing men who honor bravery go with him to his reward.

Services will be held at Mr. Spaulding's Funeral Parlors on Fulton Street on the afternoon of Thursday next.

That no stage holdup had been reported, that no one in Columbia had ever heard of a driver named Barlow did not matter. Fifty percent of the stories which filled the papers of the Mother Lode had little foundation; everyone knew this and no one cared. All the miners asked was that the press amuse them.

Uncle Ben was the exception. He was pretty much a stickler for the truth at the core of anything he printed, and both Ike and I were thankful that he was away while we perpetrated our good deed.

The best way to spread a word through Columbia was to tell the bartenders, and Ike took over this chore happily. Within two hours after the paper appeared with the tragic tale Ike had visited every bar, embellishing the bare reported facts with the unprinted details which only the intimates of newsmen ever hear, and the name of Michael Dougherty burst through the scrubby hills like a heavenly trumpet's call. The dead man became the very model of Irish virtue, a martyr who had fled the English and the shortage of potatoes to seek peace and freedom on our beloved shore. Within twenty-four hours half the men on the street were claiming to have known and loved this paragon well, and told soul-stirring incidents of his illustrious career. As Ike remarked, it was a shame we had to kill him. We might well have elected him Governor of California.

The day of the funeral was a holiday for Columbia. We had privately photographed Paddy laid out in his silver casket, his odd hands prominently displayed, then we had barbered him, shaved his lush beard and restyled his hair and laid him out again with a wreath to cover the distinctive fingers. Ike insisted that the thing should be done properly, that the box should be sealed in the presence of the onlookers, buried, with a tube to furnish air, and only exhumed after dark.

At this Paddy reneged. He lay in agonized state, his head pillowed on an ice pack to keep down his nervous perspiration, while the great and small of the community filed respectfully by, the casket was removed to the sanctum at the rear of the parlor, and the lid was sealed on a hundred and ninety pounds of country rock, wedged so that it would not rattle in transport.

Then the slow procession set out, led by the Sonora band, followed by Columbia's own, and fifteen hundred Loyal Sons of St. Patrick marched by twos in honor of their fallen countryman.

In the front row, laved in glory, marched Paddy Dorn. His face, freshly denuded and suspiciously white, was now swathed in bandage, this being wholly inconspicuous by virtue of the frequency of bodily damage suffered by those who engaged in the normal Saturday night melees.

He wept genuine tears at the graveside as the costly silver casket was lowered, as the symbolic clod of earth was cast and echoed dully on the still crowd. He was the stellar celebrant at the wake held later in the Ferguson saloon.

The obituary was flowery and highly complimentary, and I sent it with the account of the stage holdup, a photograph of Paddy in the coffin on his bed of white satin and a picture of the marble monument to the widow. I also enclosed a Wells Fargo draft for nine hundred and eighty-four dollars which I regretted was the extent of the estate. In this I had some difficulty, for the cost of the funeral shocked Paddy, but Ike at length convinced him that this must be borne separately if the success of the hoax was not to be jeopardized by his lady's becoming suspicious of a penurious legacy.

Like many of the best jokes we were denied garnering its full worth by the need of not sharing it, and the widow had the last laugh. Four months later we received a second letter from Michigan, thanking me profusely and bubbling with happiness. She had married again, taking to husband a Reverend Clay August, they were moving to Kansas, using poor Michael's pittance to establish her groom there in a more felicitous congregation.

I never showed the letter to Paddy, for it was Ike's opinion that Paddy would have a stroke at the thought of a Protestant clergyman fattening on his money.

CHAPTER TWENTY-TWO

MY UNCLE did not share our amusement. When he got back from San Francisco he carefully read all of the issues of the *Clarion* we had run in his absence. The prominence of the Paddy Dorn story stuck out like a sore thumb and he interrogated me with such artful probing that I had at last to confess. His reaction was scathing anger.

"A newspaper," he thundered, "is a sacred trust. Its readers have a right to respect it. It is robbed of its worth when it is used as a tool to any man's private purpose. It is not a toy, but a beacon light to spread the truth . . . the truth. You destroy its whole sanctity when you give it over to such a bare-faced fabrication . . ."

I had never heard him shout so, and I was thoroughly cowed. "We didn't hurt anybody," I tried to defend myself. "Paddy is free and his widow is happy and everybody feels better for honoring a noble deed."

My uncle swung on Ike. "I can't expect the boy to know the difference yet, but I did think you were more responsible."

Ike did not say a word. He just turned around, picked up his hat and walked out of the shop. Neither my uncle nor I thought much about it. Ike was always walking out when he got angry or bored. At heart he never ceased to be a tramp printer. But this time he stayed away longer than ever before.

Finally a letter came. I opened it eagerly. It was written from Strawberry and said that he had stumbled into the little mountain camp to find in surprise that Samson Dohne was *alcalde* there.

As soon as I read it I knew that I was going to Strawberry. Ever since the Paddy Dorn episode my uncle had found fault with everything I did. But I didn't ask his permission. I went to Aunt Emeline with the letter.

"Please," I said. "I haven't seen Samson for a long time and he wants me to come and Ike says the hunting and fishing are good."

Her face softened as she read. "Yes," she said. "I think you should go. It's getting hot down here, and you and Ben have been snapping at each other like two animals ever since your quarrel. A change might clear the air for all of us. I'll talk to him."

Actually I think he felt relieved to be shut of me for a while. He had gotten over his anger but he did not know exactly how to make peace. Neither did I, and I felt a load lift from my shoulders as I joined Jack Strange's pack train and headed up the trail that wound eastward along the Stanislaus canyon toward the higher hills.

It was rough country and Strange ran a dozen burros, supplying the upper camps, carrying mail from the Columbia post office and bringing out the miners' dust. Strange was a taciturn man, slow to anger but dangerous when aroused, and he said not over a dozen words throughout the twenty-five mile trip.

Strawberry never was much of a camp. Ike had said in his letter that it was not even formally organized, that the boys had elected Samson the *alcalde* as a joke. But if that were so the joke had turned on them, for Samson took his new office with deep seriousness. When I arrived I found that the camp had only one center of congregation, Bryce's store, standing at the head of the small high valley where the trail came up over the top of the canyon wall. It was a solid log building of two rooms, the larger one in front used for business and the rear for living quarters.

Ike had moved on by the time I got there, but Samson was almost pitifully glad to see me. He appeared larger than he had on the trail, not that he was fat, but his big frame had fleshed out with magnificent muscle and his face had lost its hungry look.

He took me immediately on a tour of his domain, introducing me to the men and pointing out proudly the characteristics of the terrain. The camp lay astride an ancient tertiary channel through which the Stanislaus had cut its new canyon at right angles, exposing the lower strata. The lava cap which had covered the whole area had been eroded away by Strawberry Creek as it flowed through the valley to drop over the canyon rim and cascade down to the Stanislaus, now far below.

The miners dug their shafts ten to twenty-five feet through overburden to reach the ancient gravel, fitting their holes with ladders, single pine poles with cross slats nailed on as steps. This coyoting, as it was called, was extremely dangerous, for the shafts were not timbered and slides and cave-ins were frequent. Also, water was short. The creek ran low during the summer months and the valley was five hundred feet above the level of the Stanislaus. After the luster of Columbia the camp seemed picayune and quiet, with only about fifty cabins scattered among the pines, each occupied by three or four men.

As befitted the dignity which Samson ascribed to his office he lived alone and wrapped himself in an august, solemn air. From dawn until three o'clock, when he cleaned up the residue in his rocker, he kept a methodical pace, descending to the bottom of his shaft, filling his bucket, hoisting it, tripping it into the rocker and ascending to wash away the dirt, stones, and sand with water from his trickling ditch.

At three he knocked off, changed his clothes with meticulous care, donning a white shirt, clean pants, and boots of soft kid. Then, his long yellow hair crowned by a flat, wide-brimmed hat, he paraded to the table-sized pine stump beside Bryce's store and declared in ringing tones that the *alcalde's* court was now in session.

Every afternoon the miners clustered around the stump. Most of their complaints were trivial, largely contrived. It was not law they needed so much as a break in the monotony of labor and a little social relaxation with their fellows. The court was about the only diversion Strawberry had. There was not a woman in camp and they took their recreation in horseplay, baiting Samson unmercifully, without any intent at malice.

Samson's idea of law was rudimentary. His findings were based on common sense, but he was a stern and impartial judge who accepted the tormenting with an aloof grace, brushing it off as he would a gadfly.

After a week of hunting and fishing I grew bored and joined the court as a pretense of something constructive to do. I arrived just as Samson pulled his Navy revolver from its holster and used the butt as a gavel on the stump.

"Quiet, quiet," his voice rolled out. "The honorable court of the *alcalde* of Strawberry Hill is herewith declared in session. Any of you have business with this court, now's the time to say so."

A man named Hibbs stood up, a long, thin man with the sad expression of a spaniel.

"If it please Your Honor," he said in a high nasal voice, "I spent all last Sunday chopping wood, and when I went out to get some for my morning fire, it was all gone."

Samson fixed him with a piercing glance. "You mean somebody stole it?"

Hibbs was uncomfortable. "I ain't putting it that strong, Samson. I'm just saying it ain't there. And Bud Atkins has got a whole pile of fresh-cut wood behind his cabin, though I know personally that he busted his ax handle last week and it ain't fixed yet."

Samson's gaze sought through the assembly. "Bud, you stand up."

A little man with red hair and an extremely pointed nose

got slowly to his feet. He was holding an open can of peaches. He took time to drink of the syrupy juice before he answered.

"Yes sir."

"Have you got wood piled up behind your cabin?"

Atkins nodded. "Near a cord."

"Where'd you get it from?"

"I cut it, where'd you think?"

"What with?"

"I borrowed Palmer's ax when he wasn't looking."

Someone at the rear of the crowd snickered. Samson glared. "Order in the court. And you, Bud, you be mighty careful or I'll fine you for contempt."

The redhead ducked his chin contritely, although I guessed that he felt no such emotion. There was a gleam in his green eyes which told me he was baiting Samson.

But the joke was on him, for Samson deliberated briefly, then announced:

"Since no one can prove who that wood pile belongs to, you boys can just haul it over and stack it up behind my cabin. For lying to the court about chopping it, Bud is fined one ounce, and Hibbs is charged an ounce court costs for bringing the charge without substantiating evidence."

There were squawks from both of them, Hibbs demanding his wood and protesting the court cost, Atkins disputing the fine.

Samson was unrelenting. "That's to teach all of you not to trifle with this here court. Now, if there's no further business, we will adjourn to the store for a drink."

A yell greeted this pronouncement, and everyone seemed highly pleased with the verdict save the two contestants.

Later, when Samson and I were sitting at the table in his cabin, after the evening meal, I said, "You were a little hard on the boys this afternoon."

Samson drew himself up. There was a new imperiousness about him that I had not noticed on the trail. Perhaps I had been too young, or perhaps he had been overawed by my uncle, Ike, and the others.

"There have to be rules," he said. "You gotta make people obey rules."

"The miners in other camps make their own rules," I argued. "One man isn't supposed to make all the decisions."

"They elected me," he said. "So they've got to do what I say."

"All right. But then the rules should be written down so they stay the same, and so everyone can see them. That's only fair."

He thought about that for some time, then nodded dubiously. "I guess you're right, that's only fair and square. But there's one trouble . . ."

"What's that?"

He took a long time to answer, and finally said in a tone little more than a whisper, "I can't either read or write."

"Why, I'll teach you that," I said.

"Nope," he said. "Got no time for such right now. But I don't want this camp to know about it. They wouldn't have any more respect for me. That would be bad."

The deep and unreasonable pride that gripped him was a shock to me.

"Then I'll write it down for you," I said.

That was the start of the Code of Strawberry Hill. And all the laws that Samson Dohne laid down were remarkable in their simple logic.

Claims must all be marked and registered with the *alcalde*.

A man who stole from another forfeited his claim and was banished from camp.

All quarrels over claim lines would be settled by the *alcalde* or a committee appointed by him.

If a man injured another in a fight he must care for the injured one and work his claim until his victim should recover.

These and other, less important rules I wrote down in a ledger which Bryce got for me from Columbia. I did not consider any of them to have the stature of legal sanction, and on my insistance Samson agreed that in the case of murder or highway robbery the accused was to be arrested and held for the sheriff from Sonora.

But to Samson his ordinances approached the sacred, and he looked out over his valley with deep seriousness.

I amused myself by writing the Code in a fancy script with many curlicues and flourishes, such as I had once seen on a copy of the Declaration of Independence, and on the face of the ledger I inscribed:

Laws and Bylaws of the District of Strawberry Hill laid down by His Excellency Samson Dohne, Alcalde by the Grace of God and the Vote of his fellow citizens.

243

He looked at the design in proud approval, and when I read it to him he nodded emphatically.

"I'm sure glad you came up here, Austin. I just don't know how I ran this place without you. I sure enough don't."

Actually there was little in camp that required judging. Most of the miners were well behaved, too intent on wresting what gold they could from the gravel beneath us to get into much devilment. But there are always, in every group, a few who cause trouble for the majority, and Strawberry was no exception.

There were perhaps a dozen men, two of them rumored ex-convicts from Australia, who were constantly in difficulties of some kind. Their unofficial leader was Merril Haig. He was a handsome, arrogant man of about thirty who spent more time running the poker game in his cabin than he did in working his claim.

Samson did not approve of cards. His mother had been a devout Methodist, and he gave me a detailed lecture on the evils of gambling. However, he had the sense to realize that his views were not unanimously shared, and he left Haig and his followers alone as long as they stayed within bounds.

I had been at Strawberry over two weeks before Samson got up the courage to ask about Aunt Emeline. We had talked about the family generally when I first arrived, but now he singled her out for further questions.

"Your aunt," he said one night as we cleaned up the supper dishes, "is her health all right?"

"It's fine," I said, glancing at him and noting his increased color. "Since we moved to Columbia she's like her old self."

He filled his big chest and let the air out slowly. "She's got no business being in this rough country."

"Columbia's not rough." I was indignant. "We've got everything San Francisco has and more."

I knew that in some perverse way he found this displeasing. I guess that all these years he had dreamed of rescuing her from the hardships to which she was being exposed, and hearing that her life was eased spoiled the illusion.

"What's she do with herself?"

"Well, she helped start the first public school, and the free library. It's got over two thousand books now."

He was impressed by this. I have found that uneducated people are often impressed by the sheer number of volumes in a given place.

"And she's the head of the Methodist Women. They give socials and such at the church."

He smiled his approval. "She would be doing all that."

"Oh, she's busy," I said. "She's got a rose garden, the best in the Southern Mines. Then, Uncle Ben planted an apple orchard and some grapes that came clear from Italy. You ought to go down and see them." I stopped abruptly, knowing that I should not have said this. But I was too late.

He looked stricken. "I couldn't do that." He swung away and hung up the dish towel with a vicious fling.

I changed the subject quickly, telling the story of the rise of Joe Stoop, and how Black Bob had found his mine. But Samson's mood was spoiled and soon he forced a yawn.

"Time for bed," he said, and unceremoniously turned down the lamp.

It did not seem to me that we had been asleep for more than a few minutes when someone was pounding on the door, yelling Samson's name. I heard him get out of his bunk and grope across the uneven floor through the darkness.

"What's wanted? Who's there?"

"Lem Bryce." The little storekeeper sounded breathless. "Merril Haig took a shot at Stoner Sutton. He's got him treed in his own cabin, and Haig's gang won't let us go help Stoner."

Samson had the door open and was fumbling to light the lamp. "How come you know all this?"

"McReynolds just come to the store. They'd beat him up, and he ain't in too good shape."

I jumped from the bed, pulling on my pants. Bryce was jabbering.

"We got to do something about that Haig. He's dangerous. He's downright dangerous."

"We will," said Samson. "Hand me that shotgun, Austin."

I got the shotgun down from its pegs and watched him pour in a charge and set the wad. Then I picked up my revolver and shoved it into my trousers' band.

Samson waved me back as he went through the door. "You stay put here."

I had no intention of staying. He might think of me as still a boy, but as far as I was concerned I was fully grown. It was the first excitement since I had come to Strawberry, and I was a newspaperman.

But I knew better than to argue with Samson. I waited until he and Bryce had crossed the clearing and disappeared into one of the paths leading to the upper end of the camp, then I followed.

Men were running in all directions, some with flaming torches, others with guns. Sutton's cabin stood on the rim between Strawberry and the canyon, and it was ringed with Haig's friends. But Haig was not there. Someone had warned him that Samson was on the way and he had vanished into the heavy timber.

Samson walked forward to where the group waited sullenly. He looked enormously big, powerful, ominous in the jumping light of the flaring torches. The smell of their pitch filled the cool mountain air and I shivered, more from excitement than from the chill.

"Clear out." Samson's voice was as huge as his shape. "If I hear of any of you bothering Sutton again I'll gut-shoot you."

He had not raised the shotgun, but no one doubted that he would use it, given the occasion.

"And you listen to me. The first one sees Merril Haig, you tell him I'm going to hold a hearing this afternoon and he'd better be there. If he ain't, he's spent his last night in this camp."

He did not wait for an answer, but pushed through toward the cabin, calling, "Sutton, hey, Sutton. It's Samson Dohne. Come on out."

The door opened hesitantly and Stoner Sutton appeared. He was a small man in his early thirties with prematurely gray hair, and he carried a rifle nearly as large as he was.

"You come on back to the store. They ain't going to bother you any more tonight."

Sutton showed relief. He walked back with Samson through the hostile circle, and most of the camp followed them.

The story Sutton told on that walk was simple. He and Haig had for months been feuding over the water of a small branch rivulet. Haig claimed he had bought the rights from the man who had originally located Sutton's claim, the man whom Sutton had bought out six months before.

At first there had been no real difficulty, for with the spring run-off there had been water enough for both. But as the summer progressed and the creek dropped to a trickle, the feeling grew more tense.

One of the first problems the early miners' meetings had worked out was the right to water. Merely because a spring or stream ran through a man's property did not give him title to the flow. That belonged to the first person who filed for it, and in the bigger districts each claim was allotted so many miners' inches per day. A miners' inch was figured on the discharge which would take place through a round hole one inch in diameter, under the pressure of a four-foot head, and amounted to about a gallon and three quarters a minute.

In camps the size of Strawberry, discord over water seldom rose, but it had risen now. On the preceding day Haig had closed the gate in the small wooden flume which carried the precious trickle from his to Sutton's workings, stranding Sutton.

Sutton had protested and Haig had thrown him bodily off the ground. Sutton had gone to Bryce's store and filled his bottle with whiskey from the keg at the end of the counter, then returned to his cabin to brood upon his wrongs.

About one o'clock in the morning he had ventured out, made brave by the alcohol he had consumed, and in the dim starlight had torn the gate from the water ditch.

Haig, playing cards inside, heard him, grabbed his gun and rushed out, snapping a shot at the befuddled Sutton as he came.

Frightened sober, Sutton ran for his own cabin, pursued by Haig and his poker companions. Had McReynolds not happened to witness the chase and tried to interfere the chances were that Sutton would not have survived.

At daylight everyone fanned out through the timber hunting Haig, but it was I who found him. It was by accident, of course. I had gone directly to the upper end of the valley with half a dozen men. We had fanned out in a skirmish line and were beating back toward the store. A man named Boyer was nearest me and as we came to an abandoned test shaft we stopped.

We were both winded and neither of us spoke as we half-sat, half-lay against the pile of valueless gravel beside the hole.

And then we heard voices, low pitched. We looked at each other and then at the undergrowth surrounding the little clearing. Boyer started to speak but I put a finger against my lips, at the same time drawing the gun from my belt.

And then it dawned on me. The voices were coming up from inside the shaft on the far side of our tailing pile.

I got to my feet as quietly as I could and moved around

the pile gingerly, holding my gun ready, for I had heard that Haig had a volatile temper when he had been drinking. Boyer was also cautious, lagging behind although he carried a rifle.

As I came from behind the tailings, which were six or seven feet high, the voices were plainer, and I thought I recognized Haig's voice. I crept to the edge of the hole, seeing the protruding end of the pole ladder.

I reached out, trying not to expose myself to those below. I heard someone laugh and knew that it was Haig. Then I caught hold of the pole and yanked it up.

A yell followed it, then someone shot up the shaft, the bullet whizzing harmlessly by my head. Immediately Haig called, "What the hell? Who's up there?"

"Austin Garner."

There was a moment's silence, then the voice came easily. "Oh. The kid that's staying with Dohne. All right. You put that ladder back down right now. If you don't I'll skin you alive as soon as I get out of here."

"Don't do it." It was Boyer and his voice was shaking. "Don't trust him."

I had no intention of trusting him. As long as that ladder was above ground I knew where Merril Haig was, and I didn't think he could skin anyone. I turned to Boyer.

"You run get Samson. I'll stay here."

"What if some of Haig's friends show up?"

I waved my revolver with far more assurance than I felt. "I'll take care of them."

He did not wait to debate it with me. He took off through the tall trees at a quick trot. I climbed up onto the gravel pile and sat down.

From there I had as good a view of the country as you could find. I was very pleased with myself, but I have to admit that it was with intense relief that I saw Samson swinging up the valley, trailed by a dozen men.

Haig was left where he was until four o'clock. Samson refused to be hurried, and even let an extra half hour creep into his work schedule before he sent a heavy guard to take the prisoner to Bryce's store and himself went to change his clothes.

The hearing was just begun and Samson had called McReynolds as the only friendly witness to Haig's shooting at Sutton, when Big Jack Strange and Little Jack Little came up the grade over the canyon rim at a half-run.

I was amazed to see them in each other's company. Both ran pack trains out of Columbia to the high camps and were deadly rivals.

"Samson"—Big Jack was gasping for breath—"you gotta do something."

Samson was so preoccupied in questioning McReynolds that he did not see their approach. At the interruption he swung around in shocked anger, almost bereft of words by his amazement at their audacity.

"Can't you see that this honorable court is in session?" His voice rolled out at them, threatening to shake the log walls of Bryce's store.

I was sitting on the ground beside him, the court ledger open on my knees, noting the important points of McReynolds' testimony.

Merril Haig stood to Samson's left, between two burly miners appointed deputies for the purpose by Samson. Haig's friends made a tight group behind him, and I watched their faces, more than half-expecting trouble.

McReynolds finished his testimony and Samson called Stoner Sutton to give his version of the affair. Both Little Jack and Big Jack fidgeted, but neither could find the nerve to again break into the proceedings.

Stoner's account was wrathful and punctuated by many gestures. He told how Haig had harassed him all of that summer, shutting the gate and cutting him off from water a dozen times through the dry season.

"I just had enough." He was suddenly deflated, run out of emotion. "Just had enough. A man can stand so much. I bought my claim from Willis Ellis fair and square. I give him one thousand dollars for it, because it had a ditch and seemed a lot of water. And then that hog"—he pointed to Merril Haig—"he come and said I didn't have no right to the water. And what's a man to do with sand if he ain't got no water to wash it in?"

This was, of course, the nightmare problem which hung over all placer miners. You had either too much water or too little. Water was at the base of most of their difficulties, and every man in the crowd understood it. Plainly most of the audience sympathized with Sutton.

He told of sitting at home, drinking and brooding over his wrongs, of finally getting up the courage to go out and smash the gate.

He had barely finished the task when he heard sound behind him and turning, saw Haig with a rifle. He had started to run. His voice squeaked upward at this juncture.

"I heard him laugh," Stoner said. "He sounded exactly like the Devil. He said, 'I'm going to kill you, little man.' Then he shot, and the bullet went whooshing past my head. If McReynolds hadn't jumped out and grabbed him I'd be dead right now."

"You got a paper says Ellis sold you water rights?" said Samson.

"Course not. And I don't know anyone else up here has a paper."

Samson looked down at me. "You got all that wrote up?"

I'd been scribbling furiously. I nodded without looking up.

"That's important," Samson said. "That wasn't no accident. Haig really meant to kill Stoner." He looked at Merril Haig. "You better start talking, Merril, and you better make it good."

Haig had been standing jauntily, listening with a sneering half-smile on his handsome face. "This is such an absurd game." He had a smooth, cultured voice that told of education. "I've watched you, Dohne, playing at being a judge, but I'm not permitting you to judge me, nor for that matter anyone else to this extent."

Nothing ever touched Samson so much as someone questioning the authority of his court. He walked forward until he towered over Haig.

"The miners' meeting elected me *alcalde*, and I am going to serve. Now, you got anything to say before I sentence you? For after I do it's going to be too late to talk."

Some of the arrogance went out of the smaller man. Samson's might was impressive no matter what you thought of his abilities as a jurist. Haig was a little cowed, but he dredged up a further insolence.

"All right. I'm a little tired of arguing about this water. Let Sutton and me flip a coin, the winner takes the water, the loser clears out of camp."

Samson was getting madder by the word. "There will be no coin flipping. This case has two sides. First, who owns the water, second, attempted murder. Now, you got any proof you bought them water rights from Willis Ellis?"

"I paid him in gold."

"Proof, I said."

Haig was losing his suavity and getting angry. "Are you doubting my word?"

"I wouldn't take your word on a pile of Bibles a mile high. We all know you're a gambler, a cheat, and a liar."

They stood glaring at each other like two snarling dogs backed into a corner. If Haig had had a gun he would have shot Samson where he stood. But Haig was not armed.

For myself, I thought Samson was going a little too far. It was all right for him to play judge, and he had kept order in the camp and it had been fun to draw up a bunch of laws and set them in the book. But the charge of attempted murder seemed a matter too serious for amateurs.

I had seen the attempt made on Black Bob. I had seen the operation of vigilance committees, with Barclay hanged from the Tuolumne flume. I feared mob violence as only one who has experienced it can fear it.

But there was no stopping Samson. He was thoroughly roused, and he passed sentence sternly.

"The water belongs to Stoner Sutton, and if you dare to interfere with its flow I will have you flogged ten times and exiled from this camp.

"You are hereby ordered not to carry arms, and the next time you attack Sutton or anyone else, they are herewith given permission to shoot you. If they can't, I'll do it myself."

"The cost of this trial is five ounces, payable to my clerk, now."

There was not a sound from the crowd. This was the showdown, the test of Samson's authority. If Haig refused to pay, what action could Samson take? Would he kill Haig? And would the miners back him up in the action?

I held my breath. I do not think Samson even realized the position into which he had put himself. Most courts are backed by the strength of established government, but here in the higher hills there was no real government, no law. Only Samson.

But Haig backed down. Slowly he swaggered forward. Slowly he placed a leather pouch of dust on the stump. Then without a backward glance he turned and pushed his way through the crowd, followed after a moment by his coterie.

I stood up and moved to Samson's side. "There goes a bad man." I said it under my breath, by way of warning. "He's lost face, and he won't be content until he kills you."

Samson did not even look at me as he said, "He's got no stomach, boy. If he could hire me killed he would, but he won't do it himself. No sir, he don't like the idea he might hang."

He turned around, spreading his hands. "Court's adjourned."

The court moved to break up, but Big Jack and Little Jack pushed in angrily.

"Hey, what about us?"

Samson was still fuming about Haig. "You heard me. Court's adjourned. You'll have to come back tomorrow." He started on, but Big Jack caught his arm.

"You gotta listen, Samson." I had never heard Big Jack sound so desperate. "I'm carrying a female passenger. Little Jack won't let my burros up the hill and the female can't stay out on the trail all night."

Samson stopped. He turned slowly, as though he did not believe his ears. "A female lady, did you say?" He sounded incredulous. "What's a female doing with you?"

"She ain't with me." Big Jack was flustered. He was a very thin man who stood a good two inches over six feet and had never weighed over a hundred and fifty pounds in his life. I had known him for three years and I had never seen him smile. Samson took life seriously, but not half so much as Jack Strange did. "I'm trying to tell you. Her name is Eve Chatham, and she come all the way around the Horn to marry with Merril Haig."

For an instant heavy silence blanketed us all, then Samson let out one of his better roars.

"Big Jack, you'd ought to be horse-whipped."

The pack-train owner looked stunned. "Me? What did I do now?"

"Bringing an innocent female up into these hills where there ain't another lady in miles, and expecting her to marry a skunk."

"It ain't my fault." Big Jack was indignant. "When she first come to see me in Columbia I told her Merril was a no-account."

"You shouldn't have brought her."

"Mr. Hayes at Reynolds Express told me to. She come to their office from San Francisco, and they'd sold her a ticket clear through to Strawberry and they ain't got no line running up here cause there ain't no road a coach can get over. So, he gives me a lot of business and I couldn't say no."

"You should have made her understand."

"I tried. Did you ever try arguing with a female? That's

why I come to Californy. I never could argue with my wife. They just plumb don't listen."

"But . . . Merril Haig."

Jack swayed his head and shoulders back and forth in frustration, and mimicked a woman's voice. "Merril Haig comes from one of the best families in Baltimore and he is a gentleman. I do not expect a person like you to understand a gentleman."

"Hmmm," said Samson. "Did you tell her there ain't no other woman in Strawberry?"

"I told her. I explained it real plain. But she's redheaded and she's willful and she just don't listen. My burros, they listen a lot better than she does."

Samson looked from Big Jack to Little Jack, and from his expression I saw that he considered this an emergency of the first magnitude. He motioned me to reopen my ledger, and court was again in session. I could not entirely keep from smiling at the picture of Big Jack, usually without speech, arguing with a woman.

"Now, Little Jack, what's this all about? I thought you had some manners. What's the idea of holding up a lady?"

Little Jack was much more voluble than his rival. Like many small men he was fiery, quick to anger and loud-mouthed. He told his story in sharp, short, jerky sentences.

He had just delivered a load of flour, bacon, beans, and canned fruit to Bryce and was heading back down the canyon for Columbia, carrying a thousand dollars in dust and nothing more. His eight jacks were traveling light and fast when halfway down the twisting grade they rounded a sharp curve and met Big Jack's train, heavily loaded, toiling up the steep trail.

The lead animals of both trains halted, eying each other warily. They stood on a ledge, four feet wide at most, too narrow to allow them to pass each other.

Maude, Big Jack's lead, was a mean burro. Her neck and shoulders were scarred with the teeth marks of past fights, most of which she had won. She put her forefeet together, surveying the situation, then shoved her nose against the steep canyon wall and edged forward, crowding Little Jack's leader toward the sheer edge of the two-thousand-foot drop.

When she had worked him into a satisfactory position she flipped her butt sidewise and her luckless opponent plunged kicking down into the Stanislaus River.

Not only had Little Jack lost his valuable lead burro, but the animal carried with it the gold from Bryce's store.

Little Jack was now bouncing in indignation. "I ran down waving my Navy Colts. I yelled, 'Stop that jenny or I'll shoot her off the trail.' 'You do,' he hollered at me, 'and I'll roll you over after your donkey.'

"We wrangled a while, then we see we ain't going to settle it ourselves and we recall that that trail is kind of in your jurisdiction and that you don't cotton to no unauthorized shooting. So we come up for you to decide the argument. I didn't even know he had a female with his train until he said so just now."

Samson nodded at Big Jack, who took up the story. He stressed the fact that his burros were loaded while Little Jack was traveling light. He had his passenger to think of, and besides, he was headed upgrade.

"Mountain law," he pointed out, "says that when two wagons meet on a narrow road the one going downhill should back up to a turnout and let the other pass."

If this applied to wagons, why then did it not apply to burros? And as for Maude knocking Little Jack's leader from the ledge, Maude was smart. She knew her rights as well as a man, and better than some he knew. He said this last while staring directly at Little Jack, and the fuss became noisy all over again.

Samson cut them short. "The court will decide," he told both of them. "And a man can't think with you screeching so. You be quiet."

They both fell silent. He glanced at me with a harried expression, then cleared his throat.

"You are right, Big Jack. Little Jack has to back up his string to a turnout and let you pass. But the jenny Maude was wrong in taking action on her own and causing the death of Little Jack's leader and the loss of Bryce's gold.

"Therefore this court fines Maude one half of the value of the goods she is now carrying."

There was a moan from Big Jack. "Samson, those goods don't belong to the burro. They belong to me."

Samson did not hear. "As for you, Little Jack, you back up your string like I said. And because you didn't follow mountain law without being told, you are assessed court costs. Three ounces."

It was Little Jack's turn to squawk. "Who's going to pay for my animal? Who's going to pony up Bryce's gold?"

Samson was surprised. "You don't expect the court to pay it, do you? Who ever heard of a court paying for anything?"

Little Jack bowed to this in sorrowful resignation.

"And you'd better back up them burros quick, before I hold you in contempt."

Little Jack was galvanized. "Now Samson, wait a minute. It's all very well for you to give that order, but I can tell you, it ain't going to be done."

A sound, the volume of which shook the trunks of the lofty trees, issued from Samson's throat. Never since he had been elected *alcalde* had his authority been questioned as often as it had this day.

"Do you dare to stand there and defy this sovereign court?"

"I ain't defying nothing." Little Jack stood his ground. "Only thing is, we all know that trail's too narrow to turn a fool jack without him going off the edge, and I never yet seen me a donkey that would back up unless you wanted the critter to go the other way. I can't do nothing. You come reason with them. But if they don't listen, don't you go blaming me."

Samson considered this as he slowly recaptured his poise. Then as if realizing the logic of Little Jack's words he nodded.

"Court's adjourned. I gotta go see that its judgment is carried out."

I went along. I wouldn't have missed it for the world. I knew Samson. He was too stubborn to back down on anything once he had taken a position. I also wanted to see what the girl who would come so far to marry Merril Haig would look like. No one thought to go tell Haig that she was here. None of us gave him a thought.

The burros were waiting patiently where they had been left. I have known burros for most of my life, and the small beasts never cease to amaze me. They can go anywhere that a mountain goat can go. They can subsist where even a goat would have difficulty in securing enough food. They will protest and groan and bite, but once loaded they can carry far more in proportion to their weight than can either a horse or a mule.

They had turned inward, their heads against the rising wall, their rumps overhanging the abyss. The rock face was at this point almost vertical, broken only here and there by shallow crevices out of which grew a few stunted trees.

The situation looked impossible, and I wondered what Samson could do to save his face. I certainly saw no chance that he would persuade Little Jack's train to back up, and the bank could not be climbed by any animal save a chipmunk.

The girl was not in sight, and I concluded that she must be waiting below us, around the bend.

I spotted a tree some six feet above the trail, and managed to scramble up and squat behind it, so that I could watch and yet be out of the way.

Samson had stopped in the middle of the trail and stood studying the problem. Then without a word he pushed past the two Jacks, reached the near animal and untied it from the others. I thought he intended to try to urge the beast to back up, but I was wrong. He shoved it against the wall until he had room to stand on the rim of the firm rock beside it. Then he stooped and slid both his arms under the startled creature's belly. The next instant he straightened his knees, lifting the burro clear of the ground.

It kicked wildly as it felt its hoofs leave the security of the rocky trail. Then Samson pivoted until his back touched the wall. As he swung, the burro was for a moment extended over the edge of nothing, and looking down at the distant river it brayed piteously and redoubled its frantic efforts to free itself from the man's grip. But Samson held it firmly, completed his turn and set the animal again upon the trail, now headed upward.

He handed Little Jack the lead rope and smacked the furry rump. The burro trembled for a moment, then regained its composure and plodded sleepily toward the rim above.

Big Jack swore in admiration. "Never see anything like that, Samson. Ain't a man I know could turn a trick like that."

Samson was above answering. He repeated his turntable operation down the string, and when the last of the blockading animals had been started uphill he followed with never a backward glance.

Big Jack disappeared around the curve below, inching cautiously past his animals. I stayed where I was, waiting as he drove the string toward the camp. Not until the last burro had gone by me did I see the girl.

She came around the bend, picking her way with elaborate care over the sharp stones, looking neither to right nor left, unaware that I crouched behind the small pine.

She went on and I waited until she had reached the canyon rim and passed into the valley before I moved.

I felt an unaccountable disappointment. For one thing, she was older than I had expected. In my mind I had pictured her as a girl, maybe a couple of years older than Sandy. This was a woman in her mid-twenties. And she wasn't pretty, not in the way Lisbeth was pretty. There was nothing soft about her. Her hair was a reddish brown, piled high in unruly, springy curls, without the golden highlights to illuminate it. Her face was angular, even bony in its thinness.

Still, there was an appeal in the alert and vital way she moved.

I reached the canyon rim in time to see her mount the porch and step lightly into Bryce's store. Big Jack, Little Jack, and Samson were standing beside the drooping burros, and I headed for them. As I came up Big Jack breathed deeply.

"Am I glad to get that female off my hands. From now on, Samson, she's your responsibility."

"Mine?" Samson reacted as if he had been struck. "Oh no you don't. You brought her up here, and you look after her."

"You're the *alcalde*," Big Jack told him with unflinching logic. "As long as she's in Strawberry she's in your jurisdiction."

Though Samson nodded unwillingly, there were many men in camp who would have been glad to relieve him of the burden. Most of them had not seen a woman in months, and no one who had attended the late court session had budged from the little meadow. In fact the crowd had grown as word of her coming had spread. They stood about in groups, twittering like schoolboys.

Lem Bryce was as flustered as the rest. He vacated his living quarters hastily, moving in with Stoner Sutton, because his own sleeping room was the most comfortable in camp. The scene was but a forerunner of the impact Eve Chatham had upon Strawberry. It revolutionized our lives there.

She might not be beautiful, but she was a woman, and single. I think that every man in camp with the exception of Samson immediately began to entertain hopes regarding her that in no way included her betrothed. And the effect of her presence on Merril Haig was something to watch.

He had no idea that she was in California. Her letter

257

apprising him that she was on her way had mis-carried, and in the excitement over the Jacks' impasse, we had forgotten to tell him. He had left Samson's court and retreated to the poker game in his cabin, and he was still there when Ab White burst in with the announcement that she awaited him at Bryce's store.

I did not see the meeting between them. Samson was trying to ignore the fact that there was a woman in camp, and we were eating our supper quietly when Merril Haig thrust open the door without even the civility of knocking.

He stood in the entrance, big and handsome and very confident of himself. If he was bothered by his chagrin of the trial he hid it well.

"*Alcalde*," he said in his condescending tone, "I have a duty for you. Miss Chatham and I wish to be married, and I think an ounce is a fair price for a ceremony in this God-forsaken hole."

Samson looked up to see who was there, then lowered his head and went on eating.

"No."

Merril was silent for a moment, and I knew suddenly that it galled him to have to come here, and ask Samson for anything.

"All right, if that isn't enough, name your price."

"I wouldn't marry you two at any price. You ain't good enough to be the husband of any woman."

Haig was furious. He took a quick step forward, grabbed the front of Samson's shirt and tried to jerk him out of the chair.

Samson was too heavy. The shirt tore.

"You buffoon." Haig was beside himself. "You've played your stupid game long enough."

Samson got up. He moved with the slow deliberateness that characterized all his actions. He reached out and took hold of Merril's coat. He spun him around until he faced the door. He lifted him as easily as he had lifted Little Jack's burros, and threw him into the darkness. Then he came back to the table, sat down and continued his supper.

I was disturbed. I agreed with Samson that no woman ought to marry Haig, and my mind jumped to the logical assumption.

"They'll just go down to the justice at Columbia."

But I guessed wrong. We had a second visitor within

minutes. This time there was a knock, and Samson called to come in.

She opened the door and came in, shutting it solidly behind her and walking imperiously directly to the table. She ignored me, her green eyes fixed on Samson.

"You are the mayor, or *alcalde*, or whatever?"

Samson put down his fork and stumbled up, embarrassed. "Yes," he said, "I'm the *alcalde*, ma'am."

"You refused to marry my fiancé and me. You have the authority, haven't you?"

He thought about it. "Guess so. You're the first people wanted to get married since I was elected."

She gave him a birdlike nod. "If you were elected you have the right to perform a civil ceremony. And you have no right to refuse simply because you and my future husband have had difficulties."

She radiated energy, and although her voice was soft she had a positive way of speaking that told you she was used to having her own way.

Samson fidgeted uneasily. "Now hold on, ma'am. You got no business up here in these hills alone. But you're here, and you're in my jurisdiction, and you're my responsibility. Big Jack turned you over to me to protect."

She was flabbergasted. "Turned me over to you . . . ? Well I never . . . I am not a piece of baggage to be passed from hand to hand. I am an adult woman. I have the privilege of going where I please and marrying whom I choose."

"Yes ma'am." Samson was profoundly uncomfortable.

"And I demand that you fulfill your duty as an elected officer of the people and marry me to Merril Haig."

Samson looked at her in frustrated silence, then without a word he walked past her and out into the night. She stared after him, nonplused. I could see her redheaded temper burst loose inside, then her face set in an obvious determination to bend him to her will. I made a small noise as I choked on the bite of food I had been holding in my mouth. She swung on me, her eyes sparking.

"What are you laughing at?"

I was discomfitted. "I wasn't laughing, ma'am."

"Well . . . get out of here. No, wait. Who are you?"

"I'm Austin Garner, a friend of Samson's."

She was suspicious. "How old are you?"

"Sixteen."

"You're a little young to be a miner."

"I'm not a miner. I'm a newspaperman. I'm visiting up here, and . . ."

But she was not interested in what I was doing in Strawberry. "How long have you known that big idiot?"

"A long time," I said. "And he's not an idiot. He was captain of our wagon train, and he did a good job. Since he's been running this camp it's one of the best-kept in the hills."

"A ward-boss," she railed. "A self-important, ungrammatical, self-righteous, hypocritical, ill-bred, bullheaded hillbilly. Tell me, please, how long His Excellency has been reading law?"

"He doesn't read." My own temper flared. "He's not a lawyer, but the rules he's laid down make good sense . . ."

Her eyes flew wide. "He writes his own legal code? How very convenient. I've heard of bullies, but this is beyond belief."

I wanted to come to Samson's defense. I wanted to show this criticizing woman how remarkable a man Samson Dohne was. What I accomplished by my outburst was his undoing.

"He doesn't write his laws because he can't write. I write them down for him. But they're good laws, and they keep bullies like Merril Haig and that gang of loafers from making trouble for everyone. And he doesn't play favorites. He treats everyone fair and square."

In my tempestuous ardor I almost missed the change in her expression. Almost. Her eyes narrowed and her head thrust forward intently. Her voice was very soft.

"Mr. Dohne neither reads nor writes?"

I was horror-stricken at having revealed Samson's lapse of accomplishment.

"It's a secret," I said hastily. "It doesn't matter anyhow. It's how he thinks that counts."

I might as well have talked to the wind.

"Oh," she said, and there was venom in her tongue. "This is very interesting. I can use this. I'll fix that highhanded oaf. I'll make his life miserable. I'll drive him clear out of Strawberry. Before I'm through he'll beg me on his knees to let him marry Merril and me."

I was appalled. I had never seen a woman act this way. I had never seen anyone show such hatred as she showed of Samson.

"Wait, please," I said, trying to repair the damage. "Samson is only trying to help you. You don't know Merril like we do."

She gave me a startled frown, a brittle laugh. "Child, I grew up with Merril Haig. We have been engaged for many years. I know him quite well enough."

"Then why didn't you marry him before?" I was searching wildly for some way through to her reason.

She smiled with a strained patience. "He is a man of imagination. He wanted to take advantage of the fresh opportunity of this new land. And I agreed. I believe that men of culture and intellect should help direct the growth of California.

"He came ahead to establish a home for me, and I was to follow in a year. The year has passed, and I have come."

That puzzled me. "He sent for you to come here?"

"Well, not specifically . . ." Her voice trailed off and for the first time she did not sound so certain. "But he was glad to see me . . . glad."

"Anyone would be." I had sense enough to say it, although it was far from the way I felt. I wished that she were anywhere else in the world. I was scared. I could picture her accusing Samson of being illiterate, and no one but I could betray him.

I thought, Please, please, don't let him learn. If he doesn't find out I'll never say anything about anyone again as long as I live.

Through my agony I was surprised to see her smiling at me. "Why, Austin," she said. "That was a nice thing to say."

When she smiled this way, when she wasn't looking so grim and violent, she was a different person, and a new thought struck me. It occurred to me that she was a very long way from home, alone, and I saw Aunt Emeline in a like position. Unused to the empty hills, in the midst of what must look like a society of ruffians, and now refused the security of the marriage she had counted on, she was entitled to be shocked out of composure.

I stepped forward, rather startled to find that I was taller than she.

"Miss Chatham," I said, "Samson is my friend, and sometimes he listens to me. If you're really sure you want to marry Haig, I'll talk to Samson. I guess it isn't really his place to decide you can't."

Her head came up as she bristled again. "You're quite smart for your age, Austin. But I don't need your help. I'll take care of Mr. Alcalde Dohne in my own way."

The following afternoon she showed what her way was.

I held my breath as she approached the group gathering for court, fearful that she would say something that would tell Samson I had abused his confidence. She did not. Her tactics were more subtle.

Deliberately she walked to the stump and perched herself upon it, sitting with her hands folded in her lap. Samson asked her to move, explaining that this was his official bench, but she did not budge. She did not refuse. She pretended not to hear him.

The miners were delighted. I do not know how many of them were aware of the tension between the two, but they were all happy just to have her there to look at. Most of them had shaved for the first time in weeks, and they all wore whatever finery they possessed.

Samson took time to decide that her behavior was intentional, then he moved six feet away, picked the ledger from my hands and banged his homemade gavel on its stiff cover. He passed the book back to me and I squatted beside him as he declared his court open.

There was a boundary dispute between two claim holders. Samson dispatched it quickly, pointing out from memory that the natural terrain made it possible for either man to work the contested ground profitably, dividing it down the center in the interests of peace.

The girl listened quietly, following every word. Not until he had finished and was collecting the court costs did she say in an even voice,

"Now that was silly, gentlemen. You could have come to that solution by yourselves. Why should you pay what he calls court costs? What costs? And who gets the money, may I ask? Does it go to the mining district, or does the *alcalde* stick your hard-earned dust into his own pocket?"

The contestants looked from her to Samson. The other miners pressed forward, interested. The question had not entered anyone's mind before.

Samson appeared unperturbed. He accepted the dust, pulled out the leather poke and shook the fine into it.

"Write them a receipt, Austin."

I scribbled the receipt.

Eve Chatham waited until Samson had heard the only other case to be presented that day, and just before he closed the court she spoke in a loud, clear voice.

"Mr. Alcalde. I have here an announcement which I wish you would read to the gentlemen."

There was a half-smile on her lips as she held a folded sheet of paper toward him.

Without a change of expression Samson walked to his stump and took the paper from her outstretched hand. He glanced casually at it, returned to my side and passed it down to me.

"Read it aloud for the lady, Austin."

The girl's smile widened, and she called, "Mr. Alcalde, it was my request that you read it. I wanted you to have the honor . . ."

I dropped the ledger in my haste to gain my feet and raise my voice above hers, and my words fell over themselves. It was an invitation to the camp to attend a party around the store that evening, to celebrate the engagement of Eve Chatham and Merril Haig.

It was a malicious thrust by the girl but it missed its mark, for the shouts of the miners drowned her words, and Samson summarily closed his court, then escaped by stalking off to his claim.

Eve slid from the stump and sought the seclusion of Bryce's back room, but she left her sting behind. The miners were jubilant at the thought of a party to break their monotonous existence, with a live female as their hostess to boot, but some had her earlier jibe on their minds. There was a small group around Pete Houser, near me.

"What has he done with all them costs he's collected?" I heard Pete say.

Bob Barber laughed. "Like she said, stuck it in his pocket."

Others joined the laughter, but I did not like the sound. With the ledger under my arm I walked out to where Samson was loading gravel into his rocker.

"You'd better give in," I said. "That girl is going to cause you all the trouble she can until you do."

He did not stop shoveling. "Long as I don't allow her to bother me, what can she do?"

I could not warn him that she was using as a weapon the fact that he could not read or write without involving myself. I squirmed.

"She's already got the boys talking about what you do with the fines and costs."

He straightened then. "Most *alcaldes* get paid a regular salary for their work. My fines are figured to make a man think twice before he tries something illegal again."

I understood the merit of that reasoning, but with Eve

263

goading them, the boys were not thinking on that high level.

"The easiest thing is to marry her off and get rid of her," I told him. "It's not your fault that Merril's no good and she won't believe it. Let her find out for herself. It's her business, not yours."

Samson shook his head doggedly. "It's not right for her to tie up with that hound dog. If her father or brother was here to take the responsibility, that would be different. But they ain't. She's all by herself and helpless. Merril Haig is slick, and he can sweet talk when he has a mind to, but I'm not going to be a party to his hurting her. I just ain't going to do it."

I was more interested in saving Samson from her vengeance than I was in saving her from Merril, although I heartily agreed that she was making a mistake. Then I had a thought that might solve both problems.

"You could banish Merril," I said. "You could run him out of town for something. Then she'd leave."

"Run him out for what?"

"Well, maybe for taking that shot at Sutton."

"I already passed judgment on that. Someplace the law says you can't try a man twice for the same thing."

"Then how about the poker game? I've heard some grumbling that he cheats."

"Have to catch him at it." Samson considered. "Banishing him's a good idea. He's a disrupting influence, for sure. But we got to catch him at something fair and square. The girl's got to know this court is honest. And a man's got to shoot straight. If he once starts conniving, there's no end to it. I wouldn't be fit to run this camp, acting tricky. You got to catch Merril doing something wrong or it won't work.

I had to admit that he was right, and I was not too concerned. "All right," I said. "I'll watch Merril. He's bound to do something. He just can't help himself."

But I was too optimistic. The girl's arrival seemed to have wrought a deep change in Merril Haig. He stopped drinking and even though I watched his cabin for a full week there was no disturbance, not even a card game. Instead, he put in full hours in his shaft, as though desperately trying to collect enough dust to take them from the hills.

And after the day's work he and Eve could be seen strolling through the trees, arm in arm. At the end of seven days I was forced to report my failure to Samson.

He sighed, his mind not on my words. "Never did see

such a provoking female. I haven't had an uninterrupted court session since she came to the Hill."

I was discouraged. "You've got to get rid of her, Samson, or you're going to have to leave yourself."

He looked at me moodily. "Me leave? This is my camp, Austin."

"It was your camp," I told him. "She's spent her whole time talking against you. She's gone from one claim to another, preaching how you exploit the miners."

"Do you think I'm doing that?"

I was uncomfortable. "Well, you're kind of rough on the boys sometimes, and like Uncle Ben says, people set up governments because they claim they want law and order, but they don't want to obey the laws themselves. And they're always ready to suspect the very men they've elected."

He kept on automatically pumping the rocker handle without being really aware of what he did. "I'm doing the best I can, and the boys know that."

"You've got to figure this, Samson"—I must have sounded very earnest and pompous, but I was worried—"you've ruled on a lot of cases, and you've levied a lot of fines and costs. Every man who's paid one is asking what you do with the money."

He started to speak, then closed his mouth and stood looking down the valley, a badgered misery in his eyes.

"They're listening to this girl," I said, "mostly because she is a girl, and they haven't had the chance to listen to one for a long while. She's spiting you good, Samson."

He acknowledged my words with a slow nod, but he said, "She's in a hard spot, Austin. She ain't seen Merril acting like we know he usually does, so she don't believe us. And some of the things she says at court are right, even though she puts a mean twist to them. She's got a good thinking head, so maybe after a while Merril will get used to her being around and make a slip, and she'll see for herself what he is."

It sounded like a forlorn hope to me, and I was amazed that Samson could be so generous and patient. Also, I felt a little guilty, for I found myself liking her in spite of what she was doing to Samson.

It was as if she were two people. One I admired and was charmed by. Obviously she was well bred, used to nice things and comfortable living, yet she never complained of the difficulties here. She never asked for help. Though firewood appeared miraculously at her doorstep, she did everything else for herself, and even kept the store clean for Bryce and helped him in it. She even insisted on paying him rent, though I knew that he would rather have had his room back.

Bryce was too polite to say so. She flattered him as she flattered the rest of the miners, even me. I think she was trying to win me away from Samson, trying to strip him of every friend he had, flagrantly using feminine wiles to do so.

This was the second person. Beyond disrupting his court, beyond dripping her poisonous inferences through the camp, she pressed her campaign to her enemy's doorstep.

She selected a jack pine close to Samson's shaft. There she would sit by the house, and every time he poked his head above ground she mocked him. She would quote from the great poets, perhaps half a stanza, and ask him innocently for the next line. She would talk solemnly about the Constitution of the United States, then ask his opinion on a specific article. As expertly as if she used a scalpel she probed him, exposing his vast ignorance of man's written accumulation of knowledge and beauty.

Her own reading was extremely broad, and secretly I thrilled at the glimpses of new vistas she gave me. But I could take no open joy in it, for every word had malice behind it.

Samson never deigned to answer her nor admit his consciousness of her presence. He endured her at his claim, he endured her at his court without protest.

At the end of the Wednesday session, when she had baited him unmercifully, he turned and stalked away as usual. I watched him go in helpless anger. I wanted to stalk off after him, but I still had notes to finish entering in the ledger.

I was not conscious that she had come up beside me until she crouched down, peering over my arm at the book. I closed it quickly in resentment, although it was supposed to be a public document. She did not appear to notice, but put out a slim finger, running it over the elaborate scrollwork with which I had decorated the cover, and her voice was soft as silk.

"That's a beautiful job, Austin. It's a shame that Samson can't read it."

"He can," I said shortly. "I've taught him that much."

She sighed convincingly. "I don't understand how a man smart enough to fool all of these miners, to boss them around and milk them, can have avoided even the rudiments of literacy."

I had tried to follow Samson's lead and not let her rile me, but all at once I could no longer hold my indignation.

"He's not milking anyone," I said. "And you've no right to go around talking about him, turning the men against him. You ought to give him credit for what he's done. He never had a chance to go to school. He was raised back in the Kentucky hills, with a sick mother to take care of until she died."

She might not have heard me for all the reaction she showed.

"He might have made something of himself if he had chosen."

She completely frustrated me. I found it unbelievable that she could think of marrying a man like Merril Haig and be blind to the worth of Samson. Only if women thought with their emotions, not their minds, did it make any sense. But I was mad enough to again try to reach her reason.

"I think he's doing fine. He was hardly nineteen when we elected him leader of our wagon train, and he brought us through in good shape where a lot of outfits foundered. He's smart, and he's good and unselfish. He stayed and helped my family through a lot of trouble before he started out to make his own fortune.

"And look what he's done up here. The boys elected him as a joke. They hadn't even had the gumption to organize the camp. But it was no joke to Samson, and you may not know it because you haven't seen other camps, but this one is more orderly than any I've been in." I reached for a higher authority to cap my argument. "My uncle Ben says Samson is going to go far."

"A mule can go far," she said perversely. "Your smart Mr. Dohne just outsmarted himself when he refused to marry me. I'm going to really fix the big ox."

She had already fixed him, although she did not know it. Samson had been the most placid of men. Now he was jumpy and haggard, and I suspect that he might have broken and married her to Merril in desperation to get rid of her, for she exhibited the patience of Job and the swift accuracy of an adder in striking at the man's weaknesses. Then too, he was acutely conscious that she had turned the camp against him, and it had been Samson's pride to be friendly with nearly everyone.

In fact I advised him to surrender when, like a cry for help, he asked me what to do.

"You might as well dump her into Haig's arms," I said. "It will serve her right."

"I hate to do it."

"It's almost too late," I said. "She's pretty well ruined you in this camp. Why don't you give up? Your claim isn't paying very well. Why don't you go somewhere else?"

"No one's ever run me out of a place."

"A woman never tried before, I'll bet."

He set his jaw then and I knew that I had said the wrong thing. "I won't go. They need me here."

"They've forgotten that," I told him. "You'll see. They may need you, but they don't know it any longer."

The business of the court had indeed fallen off, and for many days no one had brought a dispute before it. Yet habit is strong, and it was to Samson that they turned when the big emergency struck.

Little Jack was robbed as he took the monthly cleanup down the hill.

There were nearly two hundred pounds of dust in the consignment to Reynolds and Company. Every man in Strawberry owned a part of that shipment.

The first we knew of the loss was when Little Jack labored up the trail in the early morning, his head wrapped in a bloody bandanna.

He went straight to the store, where Eve Chatham washed his face, cleaned the ugly gash in his scalp, applied ointment and a fresh bandage. Then he and Bryce and the girl headed up the valley, gathering miners along the route. Others ran ahead, spreading the word, and it was a noisy, angry, shocked crowd that milled around Samson's claim.

I was at the windlass and saw them coming and called down to Samson. He scrambled up the ladder and stood listening, unconsciously still holding a loaded - bucket in his hand. His shoulders were streaked with dirt from their contact with the low roof of his drift, his yellow head was bare, his long hair stirring in the breeze.

Little Jack had trouble telling the story. Between pain and wrath his words were so thick that they were difficult to make out.

"I left Bryce's after sundown last night, figuring to camp along the river and go on into Columbia in the morning. I hadn't gone more than a mile, but it was half dark in the canyon, when they come sliding down the wall on top of me. I didn't have no chance. There was three of them, and they grabbed my gun before I even knew they were there. They had stockings pulled over their faces, with eye holes cut in them like stage robbers been using down along the coast.

"Two of them cut loose the gold sacks while Merril Haig held a shotgun in my back. Then he bashed me on the head like he wanted to kill me. I guess he left me lying there thinking I was dead and couldn't tell about it."

He was looking at Samson and did not see Haig smiling superciliously beside the girl. In the sudden silence I heard the girl catch her breath, then Samson was saying, "How do you know it was Merril if his face was covered?"

Little Jack hesitated. "Well, it sounded like him. You know that ugly laugh he has, and he said, 'Little man, don't you move a muscle.'"

Samson looked over the heads. "Merril, I'll take your gun now." He exchanged a quick glance with me.

But Eve Chatham came through the crowd with the speed of wind, stopping before Samson, her hands on her hips, her shoulders shaking with fury.

"How dare you? The man just said he couldn't see. Talking through a stocking distorts a voice, and you know he was frightened, excited, not thinking clearly. You've no right to connect Merril in any way with this terrible business."

Samson kept his eyes on Merril Haig, who pushed forward, still smiling, and casually tossed the gun on the ground at my feet. I picked it up as Samson told the girl, "We'll find out if there's a connection at the trial."

I noticed obliquely that the men had pulled back, giving Samson and Eve and Little Jack plenty of room, and she held the stage, ignoring them, her whole angry attention focused on Samson. It was as if no one else existed, that this issue was solely between them.

"A trial?" Her tone was contemptuous. "A trial before you? As biased as you are? What kind of a trial is that? You can decide squabbles between miners and line your pockets with your fines, but you're not going to rule on a man's liberty, his reputation, his future. I'm going to send for the sheriff."

She whirled and flew through the press of bodies that parted hastily, looking frantically to right and left. At the outer rim of the circle she spotted Dean Redman, and caught his arm, shaking it.

"I'll pay whatever you ask to ride to Sonora and bring back the sheriff."

Redman was a big, florid man, one of those who had sat regularly in Haig's poker game. He grinned.

"Why, ma'am, I'd do it for Merril even if you didn't ask." He started at a jog trot down the valley toward the corral where he kept his horse.

Eve Chatham stayed where she was, folding her arms across her breast and standing rigid, defying anyone to take any further action.

Samson went ahead questioning Little Jack, but the man had nothing to add to what he had already told. Then Samson turned to the crowd.

"You men here"—he selected a guard of five—"take Merril over to his shaft and put him down it, and haul up the ladder so's we know where he's at."

I expected Merril to object, but to my surprise he offered no protest. Instead he seemed hugely amused. The others followed, even the girl, and Samson and I were left alone.

Merril's behavior made me uneasy, and I said, "If he isn't guilty and George Works proves it, that girl will really have it on you."

"If he isn't guilty he'll be acquitted." Samson's tone said that he did not believe this would be the case. "I'm right glad I don't have to make the decision."

I misunderstood him. "Yes. Let them take him down to Sonora and try him before a real judge."

Samson winced at the words, but he nodded nonetheless. "It's not that I don't think I have the authority." He was stubborn on this point. "The authority in this country comes from the people, Austin, and they voted me *alcalde*. But a judge, he should be impartial, and I kind of don't like Merril Haig very much. But that yet ain't all of it. When George takes him down the hill the girl will go with him, and we'll be shut of her."

I hadn't had that happy thought.

"So we'll have a hearing, and if there's enough evidence we'll turn him over to George, and then we can all go back to mining and minding our own business."

He said it firmly, but he did not sound as happy as I was. He stood staring down the valley for a moment, then said more to himself than to me,

"I got half a mind to go try to talk to her . . ." Then he

shook his head and turned up the slope toward the head of the valley.

I sat down on the tailing pile. I knew that Samson was unhappy about something, but I could not figure out what. I also knew that he had lost his grip on the camp, that no matter what happened after Eve Chatham left, things would never be the same again on Strawberry Hill.

The day dragged. I got tired of waiting for Samson to come back. I worked in the shaft until court time, and wandered down to the store. But no one was there. It was as if the miners who usually clustered there were purposely keeping out of sight. And Samson did not appear.

It grew dusk. The woods were quiet, with a waiting, watching silence. Then there was movement and I saw Eve Chatham step from the rear door of the store building. On impulse I followed. She went soundlessly on the carpet of needles, down through the shadows beneath the trees, straight to Merril Haig's cabin.

Without even looking around she pushed open the door and walked in. I came in a moment later, stopping on the threshold.

She was pulling blankets from the single bunk and folding them neatly. As she lifted the bottom blanket some sheets of paper fluttered to the floor. She stooped, retrieved them, and tucked them absently into the front of her gray dress. As she straightened she saw me.

"Austin. You gave me a start."

"I'm sorry," I said, and stepped into the dimness of the room. "What are you doing?"

"Getting some covers for Merril. He'll catch his death of cold in that miserable shaft."

I said, "What did you find . . . ? Those papers?"

"Some letters, I expect." She picked up the pile of blankets.

I took them from her and she made no objection. Together we walked toward Haig's claim. It was nearly dark, and a sickle moon hung in the eastern sky.

The guards at the shaft permitted her to lower the blankets to the man below, and we all drew back so that she could talk with him without being overheard.

Samson was not at his cabin when I got there. I lighted the lamp and fixed some supper, but he still did not come. Finally I went to bed.

I was wakened at first light by Samson talking to George

Works. They sat at the rough table, drinking coffee and speaking in low voices.

"The best way is for you to hold a hearing, I guess, and then swear out a warrant for his arrest," George Works said. "You don't have any doubt that he did it?"

Samson was being very careful. "I didn't see him. I only know what Little Jack said. But Little Jack's word is good, and Haig is a troublemaker. He's caused a lot of disturbance here all summer."

George was a stocky man with a round head and sharp blue eyes that missed little of what was going on. "I've talked to Miss Chatham." He watched Samson thoughtfully. "She seems to have the idea that you are persecuting Haig."

Samson frowned but said nothing. I threw back my covers and crawled from the bunk. George turned around.

"Hello, Austin." He said it in surprise. "What are you doing up here?"

I reached for my pants. "Came up to visit Samson for a while."

"Going to start a paper in Strawberry?" He was joking.

"I don't think the camp's big enough," I said solemnly.

He chuckled. "What do you know about this Haig?"

I told him all I could think of as Samson made some breakfast, then we all went to Haig's claim and Samson told the guards to bring him up from the hole.

They tied his hands behind his back and led him to the stump beside the store, seating him on an upended bucket.

Redman, who had gone for the sheriff, volunteered to serve as Haig's attorney, and they put their heads together, whispering while Samson called the hearing to order.

There were over a hundred men present, and from these Samson instructed me to call a jury. While I was doing that he conferred with George Works, and from the few phrases I caught I gathered that George was coaching him on procedure.

The meadow was noisy with ominous growls from the miners who had lost dust in the theft, and Samson used his gavel heavily to open the session.

"This here is a preliminary hearing," he told the selected jury. "It's our job to decide if there's enough evidence against Merril to swear out a warrant and have George take him down for the Grand Jury to set on his case."

Many times I have watched the cause of justice being processed through the courts, and to me there is always a thrill and a grateful reverence for our judicial system. The idea that free men can band together to protect not only the rights of organized society, but to protect the accused as well is both comforting and overpowering.

And I never saw it better demonstrated than in Samson's court that morning. It was a solemn and moving experience.

Everyone present had suffered considerably from this robbery, and without Samson holding a level course by his personal magnetism there would have been no court hearing, only violence.

I watched, the ledger open on my knees, feeling very proud of Samson, when suddenly the picture changed, became distorted and ugly.

Lem Bryce, the oldest man in camp, had been appointed prosecutor. He called Little Jack as his one and only witness, and we heard the story repeated, how the three robbers had dropped down on him in their masks, taking the gold, clubbing him unconscious and leaving him lying there on the darkening trail for dead, as he expressed it, like a mangy coyote. This lack of respect offended Jack's sense of propriety.

"And what made you think the one was Merril Haig?" Bryce asked him.

"Sounded like him," Jack insisted. "You know that laugh, like he thinks he's better than the rest."

A threatening murmur rose, and Samson used both his gavel and his big voice to shout them to silence.

Then from the canyon rim came another shout, high and thin because of the distance, and Connie McGuire appeared out of the trail stumbling and running toward us, waving a paper in his right hand.

We watched him come, watched him shove through to the stump, throw a strange glance at Samson and stop before George Works.

"Look here what I found," he gasped, thrusting the paper forward.

He breathed deeply several times as Works accepted the soiled, folded sheet, opened it and studied it, then looked at Connie, a silent question in his cold eyes.

Connie spoke in disjointed sentences. "I went down to look . . . where they jumped the trail. Must have dropped it before he jumped . . ."

George watched him for a long moment, weighing him, then he looked at Bryce.

"Who's this?"

Bryce was startled. "Connie? He belongs here. He lost more than anybody."

Works stood a moment longer, watching his hands, creasing the paper with his fingernails. He unfolded it again, read it again, then slowly turned on his heel to face Samson squarely, and held out the paper.

"You recognize this?"

Samson took the paper in both hands, squinted at it, turned it over, and handed it back.

"Never saw it before."

George's lip curled. He stepped back to put Samson between himself and the crowd.

"Let me read this to you," he said. "It's a letter, addressed to Walter Kite."

Bryce grunted excitedly. "Why, Kite was one of the sluice box robbers we ran off last spring."

George Works read slowly, in a loud, clear voice.

"Friend Walter: Little Jack is taking out a big shipment on the twenty-fifth. If you were to hold him up it would be worth our while. Even if you should get caught it would not matter, as I am in control of the hill and would turn you loose."

The sheriff paused. He should have been an actor, savoring the drama of the situation. Then he added, "It is signed, Samson Dohne."

It took a full minute for the crowd to understand. When it did, its sound began, querulous with disbelief at first, changing and growing, hardening with conviction.

George Works pulled his gun and swung its muzzle slowly over the men, speaking to me without looking down.

"Austin, let me see that record book."

I was too stunned to move, but he reached down quickly and took it from my hand. He lifted it before his eyes and studied the name, Samson Dohne, on the cover. Then he nodded in satisfaction. He passed the book back and in a quick movement brought his gun around, sticking it into Samson's side.

"Same hand wrote that letter as wrote that name there. Samson, I arrest you for robbing Little Jack and this camp."

Samson stood unmoving, and from his face, unable to

think. As if in some bad dream, he looked slowly around the faces encircling him.

These men had been his friends. These men had elected him *alcalde*. He had ruled them for months and they had accepted his rule. Now there was a viciousness pulsing through them that had not been there moments before, nor even when Merril Haig had been first accused. It looked as if they actually enjoyed pulling down this man who had been their leader. All the petty grudges that Eve Chatham had been playing on rose in their minds.

"Let's hang the bastard."

I don't know who said it. Someone in the back of the crowd. What few voices still protested their disbelief were lost in the rising howl of the pack.

I had seen mob action enough to be frightened of its senseless power, and I had never seen its face more brutal than this one before me.

I tried to shout that Samson could not have written the letter, but a big hand closed on my shoulder and I looked quickly up into his face.

What I saw there dried the words in my throat. Suffering and resignation and a deeply wounded pride contorted it. That these people on whom he looked as his children, whom he had guided and helped, should turn on him so completely, seered into his soul. And I knew with shock that he would rather die than admit before them now that he could not be guilty for the awfully simple reason that he could not write.

I caught a glimpse of Merril Haig, of his secret smile as he stood, his hands bound behind his back, abandoned by the guards who had surged forward with the rest.

I saw George Works leap onto the stump, raise his heavy revolver and fire it into the air in warning.

The shot silenced them for a second, and in the silence his voice cut sharply.

"Go back to work. The prisoner will be taken to Sonora for a proper trial."

"No he won't." Again I could not tell who was yelling. "We'll try him here. We'll give him some of the fine justice he's been laying on us."

There was a roar of laughter that frightened me more than the earlier threats. I pulled my own gun. I was going to stand with Samson and George no matter what happened, and I did not really expect help from any other quarter.

Then I became aware of Eve Chatham, moving without haste, deliberately, between the men. She reached the stump, sat down upon it and then swung her legs up, rising to stand beside the sheriff.

Her red head was high and her green eyes were like ice. She lifted one hand above her shoulder and said in a clear, carrying voice, "Listen to me."

She did not seem excited, and her appearance stilled the men in confused surprise. As the only woman in camp, each miner identified himself with her.

She raised the other hand, lightly brandishing a clutch of papers in it, then turning majestically, she extended them toward George Works.

He took them with a puzzled frown. The crowd, equally puzzled, kept its silence, watching.

Works sorted through the sheets and his frown deepened. He looked up at her.

"Why, these are copies of the note Dohne wrote to Kite."

"Copies, yes." Her voice rang clear. "But Dohne did not write them. He is a proud man, Sheriff. I did not realize how proud until just now. He would rather hang than admit to these wolves that he cannot write, cannot read."

There was not a sound below her, and George Works was as bewildered as any man I have ever seen.

"But the script is the same as that on the court ledger."

"Of course," she said evenly. "Excellent copies of Austin Garner's fancy illumination of the book."

Works was stricken dumb. I heard Samson's low groan. Then Eve was speaking again, her voice breaking once as she began.

"Last night I went to Merril's cabin to get blankets for the poor, cold man. These papers fell out of his bed. I believe they must be discarded, practice copies, unsuccessful attempts to duplicate Austin's hand. I think it is a fair assumption that he planned deliberately to implicate Samson."

It was easy to understand. A minute before the crowd had been ready to lynch Samson. Now they turned savagely on Haig as he panicked and tried to break free. A dozen hands grabbed him.

Samson's bull roar froze all movement.

"Stop it. I am still *alcalde*. The prisoner is herewith turned over to the sheriff. Bryce, you and Sanderson will ride with them down to Sonora. But first, Merril, where is the gold you stole?"

Haig glowered at him. "I don't know anything about it. Somebody else must have framed us both."

Samson stood watching until Haig dropped his eyes, then he said, "All right, if that's the way you want to act. Take him out, boys. I'll keep the sheriff here until you get through."

He lifted his pistol and pointed it at George Works. "You keep out of this, George."

Works' face flushed very red. "Samson, I warn you . . ."

"Take him out, boys."

They lifted the struggling Haig and began to carry him away. Then his voice came up out of the melee.

"No . . . no . . . It's hidden under my tailing pile."

Samson stopped them again. "Austin, you and McGuire go and look."

Connie McGuire and I ran to Haig's claim. It took us an hour to locate the cache of bags. When we came back Haig was seated on the stump, his hands still bound, guarded by George Works. No one, it appeared, had left his place except Eve Chatham, who was not in sight.

We took the gold into Bryce's store and weighed it, making sure that it was all there. Eve came from the rear room to watch, and George shoved Merril through the front door, followed by as many men as could crowd into the small space.

Haig was no longer arrogant. He stood sullen and silent until he saw the girl, then he made a final effort at his old swagger.

"It was for you, Eve. It was the only way I could take you out of here. If that damn Dohne had married us when he should . . ."

The girl did not hear the last of the sentence. Without looking at him she had again retreated to her room.

George Works took the gold and his prisoner, and with an extra guard started back for town. Merril had implicated two other men, but they had disappeared from camp when he was first arrested, and they never were located.

The miners drifted off to work. Samson had ducked away as soon as the gold was weighed, and I headed for the cabin. I found him there, just tightening the ropes on his bed roll.

"You going with George?" I asked.

His shoulders drooped as he folded his knuckles on the table's edge. He did not look at me.

"Going the other way," he said. "No use staying here. Nobody's going to listen to a man when they think they're smarter than he is. They know I can't read or write, and they can."

It was true, I knew. Memory is short, and soon this camp would be ridiculing him.

A heavy pouch lay on the table beside the bedroll. He wiped it toward me with the back of his hand.

"There's the fines and court costs I collected. It belongs to the camp. I figured to build us a town hall when the place got big enough. You turn your book over to the miners' meeting. I'm going someplace where I can learn to write my own."

"You big, prideful ninny."

I jumped as Eve Chatham spoke from the doorway behind me.

"What makes you think you can learn that by yourself? And what are you going to do about me?"

Samson's head came up. He had been no more aware than I that she was within a mile of us. He dampened his lips, his head moving from side to side, searching for escape like a bull, baited at one of the bear and bull fights so popular in all the camps.

She came into the room. "I'm your responsibility," she said, and I felt that she was laughing at him inside, although it did not show on her face. "Big Jack turned me over to you, remember. You can't just walk off and leave me here all by myself."

His face fell open, then it stretched in a grimace of some kind of pain. He took one step toward her, and I thought he would wrap her in his arms. He didn't. I should have known that Samson would never do the expected.

"Get your stuff together," he said, and there was the old note of authority in his voice. "We two got a long way to go."

"Ten minutes." Suddenly her inner laughter broke through, and for the first time since I had known her, Eve Chatham was beautiful.

CHAPTER TWENTY-THREE

IT WAS Jim Coffroth who first had the dream of making Columbia the capital of the state, and it was a valid, logical dream. We were at that time the second if not the first largest California city. And Coffroth, a noted orator and consummate politician, could manage it if anyone could.

Ever since the state had been admitted to the Union there had been a running battle as to where the permanent capital should be located. Benicia had grabbed it from Monterey and now rumors were rife that Sacramento had raised a huge purse and was circulating petitions to be presented to the legislature.

Coffroth came to my uncle in the print shop the day after I got home from Strawberry. I had missed all of the preliminary discussion, so I listened carefully.

"We have to face facts," said Coffroth. "We're bigger than Sacramento and we've got a lot more money now, but the time will come when the ground here will be worked out."

It was heresy to me that one of our leading citizens should talk this way of the richest square mile on earth, but I was too excited about what he was proposing to dwell on his prophecy.

"If we're not to fade into oblivion like the other camps," he went on, "we must find a more lasting reason for existing. Now my idea is to convince the miners and merchants that their only future lies in bringing the capital here. The state is growing, and it will continue to grow long after the last ounce of gold is washed out, but that won't help Columbia unless we have the capital."

"That makes sense." My uncle nodded. "How do we swing it?"

"You keep running editorials, play on people's civic pride. I've set up a committee with Senator Mandeville, Tom Cazneau, Gillespie, and Sewell Knapp. We can't advertise it, but we want to raise a hundred thousand dollars."

My uncle stirred uncomfortably. "I don't like bribery, Jim."

Coffroth laughed. "Who does? But it's cold reality that there's no other way. There hasn't been a bill pass that legislature since it was founded that wasn't paid for in hard cash."

"I know . . . I know . . ."

"You've got to fight fire with fire. But money isn't going to be enough. We've got to give the assemblymen a way to justify a decision in our favor. We need a petition with more signatures than Sacramento can collect. We're having an organizational meeting in the Fallon House ballroom tonight."

The ballroom was not so elaborate as either the Terpsichore Hall or the Clark Hotel, but it was pretentious enough to accommodate the hundred leading men who listened to Coffroth, who cheered him and haggled over the wording of our petition. Uncle Ben was authorized to print the forms and I made up a list of everyone I could corral to help in the circulation of them. The glittering honor leaped from possibility to probability to certainty, and when the meeting broke up we all adjourned noisily to Ferguson's Saloon to celebrate and spread the thrilling word.

Ferguson's was the showplace of the town, the finest such establishment east of San Francisco, for Peter Ferguson had spared no expense. The big area was flanked by brilliant Florentine mirrors from floor to ceiling and two ornate billiard tables filled the rear, overshadowed by the huge mahogany bar and its sparkling array of crystal. The place was mobbed and I pushed through the crowd pressing around the bar toward the more open corner where Putt Stone, our own miner-minstrel, sat strumming lightly on his guitar, his mellow voice answering requests for "Hangtown Girls" and others of his Mother Lode songs.

He winked as I came up. "You big enough now to start salooning, Austin?"

"I'm with the committee. We're starting the petition to get the capital for Columbia."

He cocked his head, looking at me from the corners of his eyes. "Always somebody stewing and stirring . . . why can't they just live and let live?"

That was Putt's attitude. He never worked when he didn't have to. He just lived along uncaring, and I did not try to argue. I didn't really know why it was so important to me that we should be the capital city, but it was, and I didn't want him discounting it. I left him and wormed through to where Uncle Ben was talking with the bartender, J. B. Douglas, our leading steward.

I was surprised to see Elam Pell beside them. I had not seen him since Moke Hill and said hello eagerly. I got a tight nod of recognition, which was considerable, coming from him.

"How's Bob's claim working out?"

He turned deliberately, with a catlike, aloof grace. His dark lean face was already lined and his eyes were as cold as obsidian.

"Fair enough, lad, but we have better. We've taken over the Dutch Boy properties here."

My uncle heard and looked around, smiling. "Glad to hear that, Mr. Pell. We need men like you and your brother . . . need all the help we can get if we want the capital."

Pell gave a short, derisive laugh. "You've got a fight on your hands. Sacramento won't stop at much to beat you." He nodded again, pushed away from the bar and thrust through the crowd, out of the room.

"Queer bunch, them Black Pells."

Uncle Ben looked back at Douglas. "Black Pells?"

"What I call them. Ever see the four of them together?"

My uncle had not.

"You ought to. They're black Scotch, and there's no meaner breed of man. I should know," he chuckled. "I'm one myself."

When we had left the cheerful saloon, turned up Fulton to drop the copy off at the print shop and were climbing the hill toward home I stopped to look back. Below us spread a checkerboard of lights completely filling the bowl of the valley.

"You think Columbia can be worked out, ever?" I could not believe it.

My uncle did not encourage me. "The limestone's already showing in a lot of places. They're stripping off a good twenty to thirty feet of ground and washing it clear away."

The bleak prospect brought me another thought. "How much does it take to buy a legislator's vote?"

He laughed unhappily. "That's a brutal question to have to ask, isn't it? It's a shame to have to admit we have such venal lawmakers."

Venality or no, I was in favor of using any means necessary to secure the capital for Columbia, and in the next few weeks I bent my every effort to that end. We placed our petition in every store, saloon, hotel, and gambling house.

We proselyted the surrounding camps, gathering signatures wherever there were men. It surprised me that not everyone was as ardent as I. Arguments flared and two men were shot over the issue, but no one was arrested since the arguments were considered fair.

The murder of Captain John Parrot was a different matter. I did not see it happen, being two blocks away checking petitions, but I heard the shot and arrived on the run as a group of citizens arrested Peter Nicholas and started him toward the jail. I knew Nicholas slightly, an Austrian who had been in Columbia about a year, and as far as I could learn he and Parrot were strangers.

I hurried through the crowd looking for eyewitnesses, and was told that Nicholas had been drinking in one of the smaller saloons and had had a bitter argument with the woman proprietor, then rushed out, furious to find John Parrot by mischance blocking his way. He had shouted at the man, then pulled his gun and shot the unfortunate Parrot dead.

The jail was a small building, and into this Nicholas was wrestled and clamped in the leg chains stapled into the cell floor. I crowded in, trying to get a statement, but the prisoner was too drunk or too frightened to say a word, and by the time I struggled outside again a large group was forming in the street.

An ominous, angry clamor warned me of trouble and I ducked back, calling to the constable who was still inside. He ran forward, trying to stop the mob that now surged through the door, but both of us were shoved aside. I was pushed to the floor and stepped on a couple of times before I could fight again to my feet and had only just made it when the tide swept back. They had simply yanked the staples from the floor and now dragged Nicholas into the street trailing his clanking chains, and headed for the high framework of the Tuolumne County Water Company's flume trestle.

I ran along behind, my clothes torn and my face dirty, wanting desperately to talk to the man whom I figured had only minutes to live, but I could not force through the growing throng.

Someone climbed the trestle and threw a rope over a heavy cross beam. A wagon was hauled up, the prisoner lifted into it and a noose flung around his neck. I could see him above the weaving heads, looking young and alone, his arms pinioned at his back, terrified as a summary court was organized.

Tom Cazneau stepped forward to prosecute and Jim Coffroth leaped to the wagon in defense. Cazneau's speech was short and demanding but Coffroth seemed carried away and argued long and desperately for a formal trial with an unprejudiced jury.

The mob let him talk, amusing themselves before they hung their prey, and that cost them their fun, for Sheriff Soloman and two dozen armed men arrived, running up behind them and forced a way through to circle the wagon. It was one thing to lynch a lone and unarmed man but quite another to challenge Soloman's special deputies. Grumbling, the mob gave back and watched as Soloman loosened the rope and drove off toward the safety of Sonora's jail.

I went with them, climbing up the wagon, shouting. "I'm Garner of the *Clarion*," when a deputy tried to push me off. Soloman saw me and waved me on.

"Okay, okay, the kid wants an interview," he said.

But Nicholas would not talk. He did not talk until his lawyer told him to.

It was my first murder trial as a working reporter, and while justice is theoretically dispassionate, I found the emotional climate electric. My uncle had had doubts about my competence for the job, but he had little choice. He and Sewell Knapp were committed to attend a strategy meeting in San Francisco with the Speaker of the legislature.

When I took my place at the press table with Joe Aldhouse of the *Herald* and Don Bates of the Sacramento *Union*, Judge Charles Creamer had not arrived although the prisoner and his attorney, Horace Bull, were already seated at the council table and the district attorney was fiddling with a pile of papers before him.

Horace Bull was a small man, quick, nervous, restless, a born competitor known well in the camps of the southern mines. His glance in my direction showed his disappointment that it was not my uncle covering the case, and he came over, leaning above me to whisper.

"Where's Ben?"

"In San Francisco working on the capital fight."

"All right." Bull shrugged. "But remember, boy, a man's life is at stake, and a newspaper is important to a fair trial."

Then the judge came in and the clerk called the District Court to solemn order. I could not help comparing this with

Samson Dohne's hearings at Strawberry, and in the end I believe that Samson's findings came closer to true justice. The prosecution called twenty witnesses. There was no question but that Nicholas was guilty.

I wondered what form Horace Bull's defense would take. He called only two men, the citizens who had seized the prisoner immediately after the shooting and asked each a single question.

"Was Peter Nicholas drunk at the time he shot John Parrot?"

When both had sworn that he was, Bull put Nicholas on the stand and asked one question of him. Had he ever seen or spoken to John Parrot before the fatal hour? Nicholas said that he had not and Bull dismissed him.

"The defense rests, Your Honor."

Even the judge was surprised, and the room stirred restlessly, the spectators whispering and a sympathy rising for the accused man. The prosecution wasted little time in summation. Nicholas shot Parrot down without provocation. The district attorney demanded that Nicholas hang.

But when Bull began to speak you forgot how small he was. "We do not deny that Nicholas shot Parrot," he said. "We do not deny that he should be punished. But he has been charged with first degree murder. Under our law first degree murder involves premeditation. The killer must have planned the crime beforehand, deliberately, in cold blood.

"Gentlemen of the jury, such is not the case here. Peter Nicholas was drunk. Even the honorable prosecutor has stressed this point. Peter Nicholas had no previous acquaintance with the deceased. It is beyond the bounds of reason that he could have planned this fatal shooting. It was a spur of the moment reaction, triggered by alcohol. My client did not even know what he was doing.

"Convict him of manslaughter, yes. To this charge we will enter a plea of guilty. Manslaughter is not a capital crime, and carries a penalty of one to ten years in prison. But if you send Peter Nicholas to the gallows you will be guilty of legalized murder. Do you want to be a party to that?"

I tried to guess the jury's reaction as it filed out. To my mind Bull had certainly made his case. I did not consider that the country was filled with friends of Parrot while Nicholas had very few acquaintances. It took less than an hour to reach a verdict and Nicholas was pronounced "Guilty of first degree murder."

A week later Creamer sentenced Nicholas to hang, setting the date for the first week in October. Bull filed notice of appeal, but no one supposed the higher court would reverse the conviction and it upheld the decision in September.

Bull's last recourse was the governor and he made two trips to Benicia. I was there on both occasions, for the capital fight had developed into a deadly struggle between Columbia and Sacramento.

I had never before attended a session of the legislature and I was appalled at the careless, cynical method by which our laws were enacted. At least half of the assembly were uneducated, several could barely read or write, being for the most part petty politicians come up through the scattered mining camps. Liquor was drunk openly on the floor, and one of the San Francisco reporters made up a sardonic list of names with the price of each man's vote noted beside it.

The Columbia delegation was jubilant. Our petitions surely carried more signatures than Sacramento could have obtained, our war chest was oversubscribed and our leaders were confident that they had the necessary votes.

I had returned to the hotel after one session, and walked into Horace Bull, who had been pleasantly surprised with what I had written about the trial and made no objection that I accompany him to the governor's office. He brushed aside as unimportant my interest in the capital for Columbia, being solely concerned with the plight of his client.

"He's got to listen to me, Steve," he told the governor's secretary. "He has got to commute Nicholas' sentence."

The secretary shrugged. "He won't do it, Horace. You know it. If Nicholas had a lot of friends he might listen. Friends vote."

"It's no less than murder!" Bull was shouting.

"How many people will agree with you on that?"

Bull started to say something else, then stopped, stared at the man, then swung on his heel and strode out.

The next day as I came into the assembly press gallery I sensed the excitement in Sewell Knapp and my uncle.

"They've just voted to bring the capital bill out of committee," Knapp said. "Mandeville wants the petitions brought down from Columbia. He'll read it into the record during the debate on the floor."

"Austin and I will go up and get them," my uncle said. "You and Coffroth had better stay here and watch, you can't tell what those Sacramento people may try."

Knapp laughed. "Better take an armed guard to keep them from stealing the things."

Sacramento did not steal the petition. The papers had been left with the Mills Bank for safekeeping and my uncle gathered what committee members were not down at the temporary capital to call at the bank. We marched down Fulton, people joining us all along the way until we had a parade.

Ceremonially the cashier moved to the big vault, spun the knobs and opened the door, then opened the drawer labeled PETITIONS. But the drawer was empty.

The cashier was aghast. Uncle Ben pushed by him and searched through the vault, through the heaped bags of gold dust on the floor waiting for shipment to the new mint, through the drawers above. Edgar Mills hurried from his office and there was a hasty conference. But no one could guess where the petitions had gone and nothing else was missing. The shocking news filtered out to the street and within minutes had flown through the town.

Hastily my uncle put Ike to printing new forms and we passed them around as soon as they came from the press, but it was a vain, forlorn effort. The word spread to the capital and the Sacramento boosters heard. They managed to cut the floor debate short and the new law was rammed through.

Columbia's chance was lost. Never would she reign as capital of California.

CHAPTER TWENTY-FOUR

WE WERE a stunned city. Charges and countercharges flew and the bank came in for a full share of invective. In the turmoil I almost overlooked the announcement that the governor had issued a stay of execution for Peter Nicholas and commuted his sentence to ten years in Folsom prison.

The message came in a telegram over the new wires to the sheriff, who relayed it to our office by a stage driver. My uncle was again in Benicia for a last-ditch protest at the steamroller tactics by which Sacramento had cheated us of the time to gather the new signatures. I rode to Sonora, to ask the sheriff what he knew.

He showed me the wire and shrugged. "Bull told me ten days ago that he was sure he'd get a stay. I don't know how he did it."

With an emptiness at the bottom of my stomach I thought I knew. Horace Bull was an officer of Mills bank, with access to the vault. I went to his office, but he had returned to Benicia. I went back to the print shop and told Ike what I suspected.

"I'm going to Benicia," I said. "Uncle Ben ought to know about this. You tell Aunt Emeline."

In anguish I rode to Stockton and caught the boat downriver. The country on either side was changing rapidly, farms were springing up to supply food for the expanding population, a population that should keep Columbia glorious as its capital even if her gold production did one day fall away.

In Benicia I failed to find Uncle Ben soon enough to satisfy my haste and went myself to the governor's office.

Steve Ewing, the secretary, recognized me and grinned maliciously, being a Sacramento man. "Thought when you yokels lost the capital we wouldn't be seeing so much of you."

I held my hot answer and said, "I'm just here on a story. What prompted the governor to change Nicholas' sentence?"

"He didn't have much choice. When thirty thousand people sign a petition a public official had better listen."

"I'd like to see that petition," I said, and my mouth felt as dry as cotton.

He led me into the file room and brought out the sheets with the thousands of names. I had been angry on suspicion, and now with proof before me I was raging inside. Horace Bull had cut away our request that our city be made the permanent capital of the growing state and substituted a new heading, pleading for the life of a single man. I recognized the paper, the line forms Ike had set, the signatures on the sheets that I personally had circulated.

"Very impressive." I hid my feelings. "Is Bull around? I want to congratulate him."

"No, he went down to San Francisco. He's at the Hampton House."

I went again in search of Uncle Ben, but found Jim Coffroth instead, who told me my uncle had caught the boat upriver only that morning. I poured out my tale of woe and was shocked that he took it calmly.

"Pretty smart trick." He gave me a crooked smile. "Too bad for us, but there's nothing we can do now. The Governor has already signed the bill giving Sacramento the capital, and he'd look like a damned fool if he revoked the Nicholas decision."

"I'm going to find Bull and make him tell the truth anyway," I blurted.

"Why whip a dead horse? Learn something about politics, Austin," he warned me. "Don't waste time on lost causes. Save your energy for something you can do something about."

But I was in no mood for such counseling. I took a coach down the shore, so filled with indignation that I found it difficult to speak.

The hotel was on Market, a two-story building with a long upper hall off which some twenty rooms opened. The clerk at the desk downstairs looked at me curiously when I asked for Horace Bull but offered no comment, saying merely that he was in room eighteen.

I climbed the stairs, paused before the door and knocked. A mutter came from inside, something unintelligible, but there was no sound of movement. I knocked again, then tried the knob and found the door unlocked.

I pushed it open and stepped in determinedly. Bull was on the bed, struggling to sit up. He was not the dapper, glib attorney now. He wore rumpled trousers but no shirt, and the heavy underwear was grimy. There was an unkempt growth on his lean cheeks, his eyes were bloodshot and he had difficulty in focusing them on me. The room reeked of alcohol and vomit.

He was in no condition to talk, and I was nearly inarticulate with frustration.

"Why did you steal our capital?"

He blinked at me, trying to concentrate. "What's that, son?"

"Our petitions. You took them. You cheated us out of the capital."

He began to shake his head slowly, his whole upper body turning. "Never had a chance." The words were slurred together, all but incoherent. "Too much money in Sacramento. Bunch of amateurs, Columbia."

288

"You hadn't any right."

"Won my case . . ." He gulped in air and straightened, raising his right hand and shaking his fist. "I saved that man's life. That's the important thing. The dignity of man. The sacredness of individual life. Isn't it? . . . Isn't it?"

His jaw was thrust out belligerently. He glowered at me. Then his senses slid away again. He swayed and fell over sidewise on the bed. The next instant he was asleep.

I stood helplessly, then I went away. But I intended to come back when he was sober. Columbia, my beautiful city. I had all but seen her born. I had watched her grow. I loved her fiercely and was fiercely proud of her. She had every right and reason to be the capital. Hundreds of outstanding men had lectured and labored hard to bring her to this fruition. And a cheap, drunken, lying trickster had raped her, had ruined her. I meant to have a revenge upon him. I considered using my new gun, which I had not brought to the city with me.

I gave in to an old emotional reaction of my childhood. I was crying as I walked down the hotel stairs.

CHAPTER TWENTY-FIVE

WHAT DID IT MATTER that a drunken saloon brawler lived? My city was denied her crown. I had bitter time to kill while I waited for the despoiler to get his wits back.

I felt very much alone, and turned toward Black Bob's gambling house and my spirits lifted a little as I thought of seeing Sandy.

I spotted Joe Stoop as soon as I walked in the front door. He had put on weight and was prosperously rounded, and was even more elegant in a flowing black tie. He wore a diamond stickpin, at least five carats, and diamond rings on his fingers. He stood at the end of the long bar, and I stopped at his side.

"Hello, Mr. Stoop."

He had to look up at me, but the eyes which ran over me questioningly were not the uncertain eyes of the handy man

I had once known. This man had power, and savored it and used it. I had grown so much that he did not recognize me.

"Hello there." His voice still whined with the nasal quality of the Ohio hill country. "Ain't you a mite young to be in here?"

"I'm Austin Garner."

He was blank for a moment longer, as if the name failed to strike the cord of his memory, then he grabbed me by one shoulder and clapped my back.

"Why, so you are. So you are. How's a man to know, when kids grow up like that? You're most a man, I declare." He shook me as he talked. "How's your folks? Where you living?"

"They're fine," I said, and for the first time that day I smiled. "We've got a paper in Columbia. I'm the reporter."

"Sure, sure. I ain't surprised at all. That piece you wrote about me was about the best writing I ever read. You come on back and see Bob and the folks."

We attracted considerable attention from the gamblers and even the dealers as he piloted me between the faro banks and spinning roulette wheels. I recalled Hunt's huge take in Columbia, and my head spun as I guessed what this place was making.

"Seems like you're doing all right."

Joe chuckled. "We are that. Bob's a positive genius. Every month he thinks up some new way to fetch more people in here."

Beside the hallway door a lookout now sat on a high chair. I guessed that he guarded it as much as watched the games ranged around the hollow square of the pit. Joe stopped before him, laying a protective hand on my shoulder.

"This here's Austin Garner," he announced in an overloud voice. "He's mine and Bob's friend. Any time he comes in he can go where he wants. Any time."

The man nodded a salute without smiling. "Yes sir, Mr. Stoop."

We went through into the corridor. Two rooms were now fitted as offices here, and the living quarters door had been moved to the far end.

Myrtle Stoop was seated at a desk in the first office, sheets of figures spread before her. She was a lot heavier, a good two hundred and fifty pounds.

"Austin Garner." She did not take a second to know me.

She heaved herself out of her chair and wrapped me in her powerful arms, laughing up at me.

I answered a hundred questions about the family. I told them that Caroline was going to school, that we now had a five-room house with floors in every room, that the paper had a circulation upward of a thousand copies a week and was still growing.

"Lord sakes, I'm glad." Myrtle's face was puffed with her smile. "Your poor aunt. I've worried about her time after time. She wasn't meant for a rough life like them camps, not a lady like her."

I said that Aunt Emeline was happy at last. "She's busy with her garden and her roses and the free library, and she helps the Reverend Lockley run the Methodist church."

"I just know it. What's Caroline like?"

"Getting big. She doesn't like the public school much."

"My kids neither. I got to near skin them to make them go, all but Sandy."

It was the first chance I'd had to ask about Sandy. "How is she? Is she here?"

"She'll be back pretty soon. She's taking dancing and singing lessons. You ought to hear her now."

As I said that I'd like nothing better there was sound behind me and Bob came in. He looked big and competent and easy, still wearing the white jacket and black dress pants, but the hair above his ears showed a fleck of gray.

He stopped still, then gave forth a high "Heehee," and stepped forward, reaching for my hand.

"Mr. Austin." His face broke into its infectious grin and he was shaking me harder than he realized. "Just lookee at you. It sure is good to see you."

I said truthfully that I was mighty glad to see him, and had to repeat everything I had already told Joe and Myrtle.

"And Mr. Edmond?" he said. "Mr. Edmond, he had trouble up on the American River? What was it?"

"You know about that? He told you?"

Bob shook his head. "I ain't seen him since you all were down here after canvas. Don't know where he is. Whatever happened up there?"

I remembered what Edmond had said about Bob having second sight where he was concerned. I told him about the Murderer's Bar flood, and he shook his head in sorrow.

"That's bad, real bad. First time he ever tried himself out.

But it won't get him down, not Mr. Edmond. He's all right now."

"He's fine," I agreed. "He and Lisbeth are living in Sacramento. He's working for a stock seller. They're real happy."

Bob nodded vigorously. "Yep, yep. I was sure wrong there. I didn't figure she was good enough for him." He was silent for a moment, thinking back, then he caught my arm. "You come into my office and talk with me. I got to work, come evening, and the kids will be home then, and we won't have a chance to talk. Just wait a minute."

He turned to Myrtle and I waited while they discussed the money spent on the bar and restaurant the preceding week and how much she would need for the next. Then he led me into the second office and sat down at his roll-top desk, waving me to a leather chair against the wall. He sat studying me as if he had never seen me before, his powerful hands clasped over his knee.

"Your uncle Ben doing all right?"

I nodded. "No one ever gets rich running a weekly paper, but the *Clarion's* doing fine. There's a lot of money in town and the advertisers pay their bills regularly."

"Ben Garner's a good man." He was talking more to himself than to me. "So's your aunt a fine woman. They was most considerate of me." Again he thought back. "And you. You going to school?"

"No," I said. "I'm working all the time. I'm the reporter. Ike takes off now and then to go prospecting. We've got an extra printer and two devils. I handle most of the news stories and the exchanges. Uncle Ben writes the editorials and sells the advertising."

Bob twisted on his chair and pulled out the center drawer of his desk, bringing up a handful of papers. "How old are you now, Austin?"

"Going on seventeen."

"Think of that. What are you doing in San Francisco?"

For a while I had forgotten my deep anger, but it rushed back over me now and filled my voice as I told him about Bull.

"I've got to stay here now until he's sober enough to talk to. I'm going to get that whole story and spread it all over Columbia. He won't be welcome up there again."

Bob was sympathetic, letting me run down, but he was thinking on another track.

"You're a smart boy, Austin, and you're learning fast. But you should get some schooling. Everybody ought to."

"I can't," I said. "I haven't the time and there's no money for it. We're still building on the house. Uncle Ben wants Aunt Emeline to have the best one in Columbia."

Bob appeared not to hear me, searching through the papers before him. With a grunt of satisfaction he found what he was looking for.

"There's a school over in Oakland, across the bay. A preacher named Durant opened it last year, and he came around to all the businesses, raising money. Joe give him a hundred dollars. He's going to send Little Joe over there next year. It's called the Contra Costa Academy."

I had a wishful twinge. The only schooling I'd had since coming to California was what my aunt and uncle had given me. I shrugged.

"I'm learning a lot at the print shop."

Bob was argumentative. " 'Tain't the same. I can read and write. The old Mistress taught me. And Myrtle, she's showed me how to figure, she and Sandy. But Lord, Lord, how I wish I'd had some book learning."

"Well, you seem to be doing all right."

He watched me sharply for a moment, then stuffed the papers back in the drawer and gave me a secret grin, lowering his voice.

"I'm going to tell you something. I got to tell someone and I don't want Joe to know. Not that I don't trust Joe, but he likes to brag sometimes when he's had his drinks, and I don't want it to get around." He paused, studying me intently. "You won't tell no one?"

I shook my head.

His voice trembled just a trifle. "I've got a million dollars. A whole million dollars." He was barely whispering. "Got it down at Mr. Wells and Mr. Fargo's bank. Yes sir. I been down there talking to the man this afternoon. One million dollars."

I was as awed as he. Huge sums did not usually affect me. Wealth was too common in Columbia. Hardly a day passed without my hearing of some struggling man like Putt, the likable, lazy spinner of songs who had spent his life singing in one saloon after another, cadging his drinks and food from the lonely miners.

Putt had taken a pick one afternoon and gone down along Woods Creek. He had come back next day, asking help to haul his find to the Mills bank. The nugget he had un-earthed was worth fifteen thousand dollars.

Such were the twists of fortunes in the mines, but Bob's revelation stunned me. That an ex-slave, who had been hounded from claim to claim by such people as Crouse, had actually accumulated a million dollars through a business, seemed impossible.

When I got my breath I asked, "What are you going to do with it?"

The smile faded from his brown eyes. "That's the rub, Mr. Austin, the rub. I was talking to the man at the bank. He says to buy real estate. A lot of smart men are buying lots and putting up buildings. But that's not for me."

"Why?"

"It's not so simple, boy. It's all right, me having this place and Joe Stoop holding it in his name and pretending to run it. Me and the Stoops, we understand each other, and they're kind of family to me. But I don't want to put a lot of real estate in Joe's name."

"Why not put it in your own?"

"You know better than that, now. A nigger's got no rights. Say I buy me a house and rent it out and the people wreck it. I go into court and try to collect. You think I got any chance?"

Thinking about it, I did not believe he would.

"People ever find out what I've got, they won't rest until they get it away from me. Not even Joe Stoop's gun is going to stop them."

Helplessly I felt the terrible injustice.

"Never mind," he said. "It's just aggravating, just aggra-vating. A man's got something, he likes to do with it as he can. But I can't do nothing."

He was interrupted by a knock on the door. We looked at each other, startled as two conspirators discovered.

"Who is it?" Bob called.

"Leon, Mr. Jones."

"Come on in."

A man whom I recognized as one of the roulette dealers sidled through the door. He glanced back at the corridor, then closed the door and turned, uneasily pressing the rind of his thin mustache with one tapered finger.

"This is Mr. Léon D'Aubrey, from Paris, in France," Bob said. "He deals for us."

I bobbed my head and D'Aubrey studied me with prominent black eyes. His face was unusually white even for a man who spends most of the daylight hours indoors, a chalk white with veins showing bluish through the skin. When he spoke it was with an accent.

"*Enchanté.*"

"Mr. Austin is one of my oldest friends, and a remarkable young man. He found a mine for me, and he saved my life."

This last was of course not true. It had been Joe Stoop who had run off Crouse, but the Frenchman accepted it.

He made me a quick bow and spoke to Bob. "So Mr. Stoop has just been telling us outside. It is why I am here. I hope to enlist him in understanding something I wish to say."

Bob glanced at both of us inquiringly. "About what?"

The man bowed again. "First, I apologize. I listened *un petit moment* at your door . . . Only to ascertain that you were alone. What I heard has given me courage."

Bob's eyes changed, then he settled back and said evenly, "You're not making much sense."

"It is because I am embarrassed. For months I have wanted to speak with you, but I did not know quite how."

"Any time you've got anything to say, I'll listen," Bob said. "I'm a right good listener. I'm about the best there is. Everybody in San Francisco tells me his troubles across the bar."

"That I know of course. But I do not wish to offend. I cannot afford to offend you or Mr. Stoop."

"You aren't going to offend anyone. Just say what's on your mind."

The man took a deep breath, touching his mustache again. "For months I have worked here. It has been a godsend to me, a haven. I came out to dig for gold. I did not have luck, and I do not have strength. I wish only to return to France, to escape this barbarous country."

I saw Bob's hands tighten just a little, but otherwise he showed no reaction.

"So you want a loan."

D'Aubrey shook his violently. "Not a loan. I am offering you a service."

Bob was suspicious. "What kind of a service?"

The man wet his lips and his nervousness increased. It dawned on me that he was afraid of Bob.

"It is this," he said. "Working here, I have observed. This club, it is supposed to belong to Mr. Stoop."

"It does." Bob's voice was short and there was a note of danger in it.

"No, sir. I have seen him take your orders, even though you pretend to be his servant. I have seen you make decisions."

"You see too much." Bob started up from the desk, then dropped back. "All right, is that what you're trying to sell? How much to keep quiet?"

D'Aubrey looked ready to cry. He spread his thin hands that were as white as his face.

"You misunderstand me, sir. I was aware of your problem before . . ." He waved uncertainly at the door. "You have, I think, made a great deal of money here. I am a trained gambler. I do not need to see your books to guess the percentage you take."

Curiosity fought with Bob's quiet anger, and he said nothing. D'Aubrey hurried on, as if he must get it all out before he was interrupted.

"In this country I understand too that as a man of color you may not enjoy your wealth. I wish to offer a solution."

I started out of my chair, but Bob spread his fingers, softly motioning me down. D'Aubrey's eyes flicked between us and again he took a breath of relief.

"Come with me to France. She is civilized. She accepts everyone. One of our greatest authors, Monsieur Dumas, is in part a Negro. And if rumor is correct, the Empress Josephine too. The fact is not important. They are taken for their worth."

Black Bob's face lost all expression. He sat looking at the Frenchman, looking through him, as though seeing a patch of blue sky from the bottom of a mine shaft. Finally he said, very cautiously, "Who's this Josephine?"

"She was Napoleon's wife," I said. I had learned that much from my uncle.

Bob continued to stare through the Frenchman. The gambler said quickly, "And the current Emperor, Napoleon's nephew, is the grandson of Josephine."

"He's a nigger too?" There was a vicious bite in Bob's tone.

D'Aubrey nodded with his whole body. "It is the rumor. Yet he is considered one of us."

Bob began slowly to drum on the desk with his big fingers, reluctant to trust what he heard, then at last he forced out a tentative question.

"You mean if I went to France I could hold up my head and live like white people?"

D'Aubrey smiled for the first time since entering the room. "With your wealth, sir, you could live like a prince, a house in Paris, a chateâu in the south . . . servants, carriages, everything."

The picture sprung up quickly before me, but Bob was taking his time, exploring the idea.

"I don't know French. I don't understand their money. I don't know how they act."

D'Aubrey coughed discreetly. "That, sir, is where I emerge. As your secretary I can guide you. I will serve as your interpreter until you acquaint yourself with the language. I will make certain that you are not cheated. I can present you in the proper places."

Bob put his hand to his face, rubbing the black cheek. "It's an idea." He sounded short of breath. "I'll think about it."

D'Aubrey swung immediately to me. "You are his friend, monsieur. You will advise him that what I say is true?" Then with excellent timing, he turned out through the door.

Bob and I were left gaping at each other in silence. After a long moment Bob whispered, "You think they are colored, this Dumas and the ladies?"

I spread my hands, not knowing.

"Could you find out? Somewhere it's got to be written down."

I was as breathless as he. "I could go to the Mechanics Library . . . or better yet, to Mr. Washburn. He's editor of the *Alta*, a friend of Uncle Ben's."

Bob tried to control his grin, but it was getting away from him.

"You do that, Austin. You find out. If it's like he says in France, that's the place I'm going to."

"Do you trust him?" I asked, for I did not.

"He ain't doing me no free favor, but he's smart, and he wants to get back home."

"But if you go with him you'll be at his mercy. He's liable to steal your money and get you in all kinds of trouble."

The grin broke free. "No he won't. He's scared to death of Joe Stoop. Every time Joe sneezes he jumps like a bee stung him. I'll just take Joe with me. Mr. Léon D'Aubrey's not going to try nothing with Joe around. He knows Joe would shoot him smack in the eye." He screwed his face into a deep wink. "It's kind of nice to have a fighting man. You run down and find out if what he says is so."

I got up, but before I could reach the door it opened and Sandy was standing there. I knew who she was, and yet I did not. It was not just her growth, it was her clothes and her manner.

She had on a pert sailor hat and a full skirt, flouted out with hoops and crinoline. It was the first time I had seen her dressed as a grown woman, and I stood rooted, gaping.

She hesitated for the barest moment, then came forward, offering me an outstretched, gloved hand. I don't know whether or not she expected me to kiss her fingers. Then she curtsied.

I'd seen women do this at some of the dances in Columbia, but none of the girls I knew, and Sandy was the last person of whom I expected it.

"Dear Austin. It's so good to see you."

I still hadn't recovered. All I could manage was, "Sandy . . ." I knew that I was blushing, for my cheeks felt hot, and the knowledge angered me.

"Ain't she something?" There was pride in Bob's voice, the pride of a father. "A real upstanding lady, that's what she is."

Sandy had risen. Her hair beneath the saucy hat was more gold than red and I had to admit that she was beautiful, even with the spray of freckles still showing faintly across the bridge of her narrow nose.

"You may kiss my cheek."

"For gosh sakes," I said. "What's come over you? You used to smack me on the mouth."

Her voice was prim. "That was before I grew up, Austin. Professor Boyer says no lady ever kisses a man on the mouth unless he is her husband, and then only on special occasions."

"And who is Professor Boyer?"

"My dancing teacher. He's danced before all the crowned heads of Europe. He's very elegant."

This was getting too much for me. I was at the age when I refused to be impressed by anyone. I had met the Governor of California and Senator Gwin and Senator Mandeville, and already I had acquired the newspaperman's contempt for posturing humanity.

"Quit it," I said. "This is Austin Garner, remember?"

Behind me Bob laughed. I thought for a moment that Sandy would blow up, then she broke into a peal of giggles.

"Austin, don't you think I'm a good actress?"

"I think you're silly."

She charged me then, flinging her arms around me heedless of her billowing skirt, kissing me savagely.

"There. That better?"

Another knock rattled the door, rapidly, urgently, and a voice called through. "Bob, Bob, Mr. Stoop wants you in the gambling rooms. There's trouble."

Bob stood up quickly. "I'll see you children after a while." He was gone, leaving us alone.

Sandy examined me critically. "You've sure grown. You used to be such a little runt. How tall are you now?"

"Near six feet." I was five-ten, but to me the other figure sounded better.

"How come you're in town by yourself?"

There was a breath of superiority in her tone and I bristled.

"Business," I said brusquely, "and to do some investigating for Bob."

"Oh? How important you sound. What kind of investigating?"

I hesitated. He had not told me to keep the France topic quiet, only not to talk about the million dollars, and I needed something to cut her down to size.

"Bob's thinking of going to Europe, and he wants me . . ."

"Europe?" She cut in with a gasp.

"France," I said laconically, and told her what D'Aubrey had suggested. "I've got to go downtown and see if it's all right."

I was pleased to see her eyes go wide and her mouth come open. Then she moistened her lips.

"Is he going to take us with him?"

I shrugged elaborately. "Your paw anyway. And I don't imagine he'd leave Myrtle and you kids here alone."

She pivoted around the room in a flashing swirl. "Oh . . . oh . . . Mr. Boyer's told us about it . . . the courts and kings, the queens and princes . . . Maybe I won't be an actress. Maybe I'll marry into royalty."

Suddenly I did not like the idea of her going away. I was not old enough to know what I really wanted, but I did know I didn't want Sandy marrying anyone and staying in Europe.

I couldn't think of anything to say against it, but I did think of something else. I reached into my pocket and drew out the small leather sack in which I carried my heart-shaped nugget from Murderer's Bar, and handed it to her silently.

She took it and shook out the chip of quartz with its lace of gold, holding it in the cup of her hand.

"It's beautiful."

"It's the first piece of gold from the bottom of the lake at Murderer's Bar. It's for you."

She looked up at me with a new, faraway expression.

"I was going to have it drilled and hung on a gold chain . . ." I said.

She closed her fingers over the piece. "Papa will have it done. Mr. Telfero will do it. He's the leading jeweler, and he plays here all the time."

She dropped it back into the pouch, closing both hands around it. Then she raised her face to me fully.

"Gee, it's good to see you. I want to go to France, but I don't. If I go, maybe I'll never see you again."

I nodded dumbly. "Oh, Sandy."

She was in my arms. She was crying against my shoulder.

"I'll come back, Austin. I swear I will. And I'll write to you every week. Kiss me. Put your arms around me and kiss me as if I were the best girl you ever had."

CHAPTER TWENTY-SIX

MR. WASHBURN WAS flatteringly glad to see me. I sat in a corner of the busy *Alta* office and looked around, thrilled by the constant flow of activity, by the rumble of the big presses in the next room.

The sound of a press will always move me as nothing else, and this was the biggest paper in California, a daily read by at least four thousand people.

We had exchanged amenities and the editor was in effect interviewing me about Columbia. He had complimented the *Clarion*, saying that he saw it every week, and he was alert as to what was going on in the foothills.

He leaned forward toward me. "Whatever happened to that move to make Columbia the state capital?"

My frustrated anger boiled up again, and I caught myself only just in time. "The petitions disappeared," I said. I did not tell him how, nor that Bull was in San Francisco. That story was mine, and I certainly did not want another newspaperman to get it before it appeared in the *Clarion*.

Washburn put his head back and laughed. "Wonderful game, our politics . . . So what brings you to San Francisco?"

I said that I had come down to visit friends. "I want some information," I told him. "About France. Do you know anything about France?"

He smiled. "A little. What do you want to know?"

Suddenly I was uncomfortable to show such ignorance, but I could not back out now.

"Is it true that Alexander Dumas is a colored man?"

His interest sharpened. "What makes you ask a question like that?"

"I have a friend, a free colored man," I said slowly. "He can't do what he wants in this country, and somebody said he could in France."

"I see."

"You won't tell anyone I asked?"

"I'm a newspaperman," he teased me. "But within the fraternity we do have our secrets. And whether or not you know it, I agree with Senator Broderick that California should be free, that slavery should be abolished everywhere in the nation."

I heaved a sigh of relief. "And Dumas?"

He nodded. "It's said he is, in part."

"And Josephine. I mean Napoleon's wife?"

"Who told you all this?"

"A man from Paris."

"She was born on the island of Hispanola. That used to be a French colony before the blacks revolted, and there was a lot of mixed blood. Josephine is reputed to have a Negro strain."

"Then a black man can live in France as if he were white?"

"Hold up a minute, son. You're going too fast. As far as their laws are concerned, yes. He can hold property and become a citizen. But you can't legislate social standing. Then there's the economic factor. It takes money to live anywhere. Money affects acceptance everywhere."

"Oh, he's got money," I said.

"You wouldn't be talking about Bob down at Joe Stoop's gambling house?"

301

I must have looked stricken, for he laughed. "Don't worry about it. Now I understand why this is sub rosa. Didn't I hear that Bob struck a rich claim two or three years ago?"

I made a mental note to look up sub rosa. "At Moke Hill," I said. "And now he wants to go someplace where he can use it safely."

Washburn nodded, tilting his head on one side, raising his brows, considering the idea.

"Tell him to watch the French. They're worse than the Syrians or the Jews when it comes to treating a dollar with respect."

"He'll be all right. He'll take Joe Stoop with him."

A ribald laugh began in his stomach, moved up through his chest and out his throat. Then he checked himself.

"I'm sorry, Austin. It's my picture of the impact Diamond Joe would have on Paris. I doubt that those people have ever experienced anything like Joe. The great thing about San Francisco is that we take everyone at the value he places on himself, but Paris . . ." His laughter bubbled again, then he stood up and offered his hand. "Well, good luck to them. Give my best to your uncle."

I had already turned to leave, but I stopped in stunned surprise, for the office door had opened and the governor was coming through it.

I stared, and then, unable to stop myself, my anger and chagrin boiled out, the story of Horace Bull, the stolen petitions, the lost capital poured forth.

The governor, caught unaware, was too startled to halt the rush of my words. He listened, first in amazement, then in his own growing anger, and when I ran down he said sharply, "Where is Bull now?"

"At the Hampton House, dead drunk."

"Let's go see him."

Mr. Washburn came to his feet with alacrity, and together the three of us paraded down Market to the hotel.

Never before or since have I seen a man whipped, cut down and annihilated by words as the governor rained his wrath upon Horace Bull. Bull was not sober, but he was in better shape than when I had seen him earlier. He sat on the bed as the governor strode up and down the little room, raging, stopping to shake his fist an inch before the man's face.

Bull tried once to defend himself, shouting that Nicholas had been falsely charged, falsely tried and falsely convicted, that he had used the only possible way to save his client from an execution he did not deserve. I knew that this was true, and for the first time I suddenly doubted. Which was more important, really, the capital or one man's life?

The governor was not concerned with either choice. In that hour I saw what a consummate politician he was and glimpsed the enormous power that a chief executive can wield.

"You are an attorney"—his roar slashed at Bull—"you are an officer before the court. You know better than to take the power of the court into your hands. You are not a judge. You are not a jury. And whether that verdict was wrong or right you have debased your profession. Trickery, theft are grave offenses. You are not fit to be called a lawyer. And when you pull such treachery on the governor of your state, sir, you make a mockery of that office. You have frauded me, sir, and that you shall not get away with. You will never practice in California again, I promise you. If you try I will have you disbarred. Get out. Get out of the state and stay out or I'll have your hide."

I stood rooted, my head spinning as the governor laid on charge after charge that I had not even thought of, until I could not tell what was right and what wrong. And I watched a man who had fought to the utmost for what he believed die before me. No matter what became of Bull in the future this day would be with him, destroying his worth. Already weighed down by his act to the point that he had drunk himself sodden to escape it, he would now carry the added burden of the governor's accusations. I saw it in his eyes as pain filled them and then dulled beneath despair.

And I knew that I had done this to him.

Columbia would not become the capital and Coffroth was right, there was nothing to be gained by fighting for a cause after it is lost. I had actually accomplished nothing but revenge.

I felt sick. I would have given anything to take back my talking to the governor, to undo this scene. The only restitution I could think of was in writing a newspaper story that would make people understand Bull's reason. But even that was denied me.

As we left the hotel the governor made it abundantly clear that the story was not to be made public. At the very least it would make him look the fool, at the worst it could destroy him politically as he had destroyed Bull.

Washburn went along and to my astonishment so did Uncle Ben when I returned to Columbia and reported the whole thing to him. I felt guilty and bewildered.

"The harm's done," he said. "And no purpose would be served by disclosing the story. It would only stir up discontent. People are angry enough now about losing the capital. If it were told how we were tricked those who didn't want it would ridicule the others and we could have serious trouble."

"But it's news." I couldn't tell him how I felt.

"You're right, by a strict interpretation of the phrase. But look at it this way for a moment. Bull had justice on his side in that Nicholas should never have been charged with first degree murder. The governor acted in good faith. What would be gained if he reversed himself and Nicholas hanged? And the legislature can hardly change its mind now and take the capital away from Sacramento without appearing dupes."

I was near tears. "But Bull is ruined. He'll never be good for anything again. He was a good lawyer, and I as much as killed him."

"No." My uncle looked at me keenly. "He did that for himself. You can't help him. Austin, there are many stories a newspaper does not print, simply because they accomplish no purpose."

"It's my fault that he's run out of California." I was heartsick and helpless. "If I'd just kept my mouth shut he'd be all right. Uncle Ben, I haven't got sense enough to be a newspaperman."

He raised his eyebrows and nodded slowly. "When you discover that, you're making headway. You've learned a lot out of all this." He leaned across and patted my knee, giving me a warm smile. "There's hope for you, boy."

I didn't believe it. I lived under my dark cloud for weeks, unaware that the biggest story in Columbia's history was taking shape under my nose.

Every mining camp has one peak day, the pinnacle of its growth, from which it turns downhill. Columbia was no exception, and its highest point was reached on November 18, 1858, but no one foresaw that the end of its greatness was so near at hand.

Its rise had not been steady. The camp had almost flickered out before it was really born, that first winter, for lack of water, yet it was too much water that hastened its end. Water was a constant problem, and the first attempt to solve it had started when twenty-five early miners banded together to dig an open ditch from Five Mile Creek. But the effort bogged down for lack of money and they appealed to D. O. Mills, the leading Sacramento banker.

Mills came, liked what he saw and spent three hundred thousand dollars, extending the ditch to the south fork of the Stanislaus for a larger supply, and sending his brother Edgar to open a branch bank in the new camp. It was this bank that laid the foundation for one of the greatest American fortunes.

But as the years passed and the town grew the miners tired of paying six dollars a day into the coffers of Mills' Tuolumne County Water Company, and gradually the temper of the town grew tense.

The richer ground was worked out, the yield from the average claim dropped, yet the price of water remained six dollars for a sluice-full stream. A petition to the company brought no relief and the miners began to talk strike. With this, Edgar Mills made the mistake of importing "fighting men" to guard the water property. Tempers were further inflamed and there was talk of running the banker out of town.

The suggestion of a strike frightened the merchants, a meeting was called and Sewell Knapp phrased their quandry with the quip, "No mining no money, no money no business in town."

My uncle regretted aloud that there was no competition to force Mills' rates down and Jim Coffroth laughed sourly.

"Sure there's another company," he said. "The Stanislaus and Columbia Water Company. Great outfit, not controlled by Sacramento bankers . . . rights to plenty of water on the north fork of the Stanislaus . . . Only it's sixty miles away, they've got no money and no dam and no ditches."

I did not see that this was an impossible hurdle. "Why don't the miners build their own dam?"

My uncle frowned at my interruption, but Coffroth picked up his ears. "What's that, Austin?"

I was embarrassed, still almost afraid to open my mouth after the Horace Bull episode, but I stammered out, "If they're going to strike they might as well use their time building a dam like we did on the American River."

"How was that?"

I began to come alive as I told him about Edmond Jones, and Coffroth's eyes lighted.

305

"Where's this Jones now?"

"In Sacramento."

"I'll go talk to him," he said with instant decision. "Do you suppose he would come up here?"

I felt a sudden eagerness to see Edmond again, to be involved in another project with him. "Sure, I know he would."

He cocked his head. "What do you think, Ben? You were there."

Uncle Ben looked at his face, and I watched his humor rise until it matched Coffroth's own.

"They did it up there, all right, with a lot fewer people than there are here, and nowhere near the resources that Columbia has."

Coffroth snapped his fingers sharply. "This camp"—his voice swelled with emotion—"is the richest spot on earth. It must not die beneath the heel of the tyrant. Wire Jones. Ben, I'll pay his expenses out of my own pocket. Send for him today."

Edmond came, welcoming the chance to be out of doors again, free to wander across the hills. He brought Lisbeth with him, plump and pretty, and it was a festive time for her, my aunt and Caroline. Caroline was growing into young womanhood, and the three of them twittered endlessly over the clothes now in fashion in such centers as Sacramento and San Francisco.

Edmond spent three days with Coffroth, then he and I were left on our own. We spent several weeks tramping up and down the slopes, working out a possible route.

The more we investigated the more discouraged I became. Between the canyons of the north and south forks was a high ridge, half a mile wide.

Sitting on top of it, beside our small supper fire, I looked toward both sides.

"We'll never make it. Me and my bright ideas."

Edmond gave me a quick look, then fished in his pocket for his pipe. "What's wrong with it?"

"It won't work. They never work. I'm going to quit having them."

He laughed at that, the same warm laugh that had first drawn me toward him on the Ohio riverboat nearly six years before. Six years, I thought. Six years is not an extended time when you are older, but at my age it stretched back like eternity.

"You're a little young to swear off having ideas."

I shrugged despondently. "There's no way to take a ditch around this ridge."

"You told me once to take a river through the air. Why can't we take this one through the mountain?"

I thought he was joking. "A tunnel, half a mile long?"

"If you can dig a tunnel a hundred feet you can dig one a mile. Let's go back and talk to Jim Coffroth in the morning."

We breakfasted early, and I caught up the horses and saddled them while Edmond collected his surveying instruments and packed our gear.

Three days later my story appeared, announcing a mass meeting in the Plaza to discuss the proposed strike. It was one of the last stories I would ever write for the *Clarion*, but I did not know that at the time.

The strike committee had erected a platform of rough boards in front of the Presbyterian church, and the miners began to gather in mid-morning, though the meeting was not scheduled until three o'clock. There was no building in Columbia large enough to accommodate the throng that filled the street.

Jim Coffroth insisted that my uncle and I and a member of the Sonora *Herald* staff sit on the platform, representing the press. A great showman, he was in top form that day.

He opened the meeting bareheaded, his ruffled shirt glistening white, his black coat and gray trousers immaculate. By the time he finished his coat was off, his collar open and large sweat patches stained his armpits.

He had an audience to challenge the best he could deliver. They had come in from the surrounding camps, Saw Mill Flat, Woods Creek, Running Springs, Shaw's Flat, Springfield . . . twenty thousand men, standing silent, grim-faced, listening.

"Members of this community"—his voice began as a low, unhurried growl, climbing gradually to a crescendo as he told off his points—"we are oppressed. We have long been oppressed, by a heartless, all devouring monopoly. So short-sighted is this giant that it willfully chooses to destroy . . . destroy, I say, the very well springs of its own terrible power.

"Well and good, if it only destroyed itself. But that is not the case. You are the source of its power. It is you who are being ruined.

"How are we to reverse this vicious process? How shall we extricate ourselves from this strangulation? A strike?

What will a strike accomplish? Bring down the water rate?

"Yes. For a time. For a time during which all of your production will stop, your capital will be eaten up. Your city will languish. A strike can bring these bankers, these spoilers from Sacramento to their knees, for a time.

"But as long as the monopoly itself continues to exist, Darius Mills and his brother will have their hand at your throats.

"A strike alone will not break that monopoly. And if we are to have a future worthy of Columbia, that monopoly must be broken."

"How?"

The voice came out of the silent crowd. I never knew for certain, but I suspected that Jim Coffroth had planted the miner to shout the question. Whether or not it was arranged, it was very effective. The word spread like a tide and became a chant.

"How? How? How?" The miners began to stamp their feet to the rhythmic beat. "How? How? How?"

Coffroth let it run on for a full three minutes, then he waved his hands, and kept waving them until the echoes died on the air.

"With another company. With another ditch, our own ditch, built with our own hands. A little band of men on the American River showed the way. There is water for us on the north Stanislaus. It needs but your hands, that will be idle while you strike. For your work you shall receive stock in your own company. Who will join me in working for ourselves?"

His own voice led the cheer that shook me in my chair. Then he raised his hands again.

"And your gold. All deposited in Darius Mills' bank. He is using your money to maintain his grip on this camp. Draw it out. Put it into your own water company. With our gold and our labor we shall set ourselves free."

A crowd loves to yell, and this one outdid itself. In the tumult Coffroth swung to the men lined along the rear of the platform.

"We have here five hundred shovels. Who will be the first five hundred to volunteer? Step forward."

Edmond Jones, grinning in delight, leaped up, grabbed the first shovel and shook it above his head like a tomahawk. Laughing men surged up from the street, each eager to be first. All five hundred were gone in five minutes, and

Coffroth herded the men into a column of twos, each with a long-handled blade shouldered like a rifle.

Then, led by the Columbia Brass Band, they marched out to the line of stakes that Edmond and a crew had set along the course of the ditch, and the dirt began to fly.

It was probably the greatest cooperative effort that was ever attempted in the Mother Lode country.

I was not there to watch it for a week after the strike began I received a letter from San Francisco. It was from Sandy, and it read:

> We are going to Europe in two weeks. Bob has sold the gambling hall, and all of us sail on the steamer Margaret, for Panama. Bob wants to see you before we depart. He says to tell you it is of the utmost importance that you come. Please, please, dear Austin. I want to see you too. So do Mom and the kids and Pa.
>
> *Sandy.*

I carried the letter quickly from the post office to the print shop. Uncle Ben was deep in writing an editorial. The Tuolumne company had surrendered to the miners and were offering the four dollar a day rate, and in an effort to halt the rival company they were offering work to any miner who would help to widen their own ditch.

Already some of our volunteers had quit, and my uncle was trying to coax them back, pointing out that if they abandoned the new enterprise it would be only a matter of time before the Mills brothers returned to the six-dollar rate.

I did not usually interrupt him, but I was full of my own news.

"Bob and the Stoops are going to Europe. They want me to come down before they go."

My uncle looked up, pulling his thoughts back to the shop. He had a spot of ink above his right ear, for he was in the habit of jabbing his quill there to rest while he thought out his next sentence.

"I know."

"You know?" I was disappointed.

"I had a letter from Bob yesterday. So did Edmond. Yours must have been delayed."

"Then I can go?"

"Of course. You'd better catch the four o'clock stage."

The stage took me to Stockton. I caught a riverboat and

all the way down the twisting stream I sat on the deck, staring glumly at the tule swamp and rangy willows. Sandy was going away. I had only vague, storybook ideas of what Europe was like. I'd seen pictures of the young Queen Victoria of Great Britain and of the French and German Emperors, but it was a faraway, unreal place.

I found the Stoop home in profound confusion. Myrtle had acquired a great many possessions during her stay in California. Having done without for most of her life, she had an insatiable appetite for things, and she was having as much difficulty discarding them as Aunt Emeline had had in Wilmington.

I found Bob at his office desk and gave him the letter Uncle Ben had sent with me. He read it while I fidgeted on the edge of my chair, then he looked up, smiling.

"You know what's in this, Austin?"

It struck me that there was some mystery here, and my face must have showed it.

"Your uncle didn't tell you why I wanted you to come?"

"No, he didn't."

His smile widened. "Well, before I told you what I have in mind I wanted your uncle's permission. He grants it in this letter." He laid the paper on his desk.

"I'm going to France. You know why. I want to leave knowing you'll get the kind of education you should. You still want to stay in the newspaper business, I think?"

I nodded. I had rallied from the shock of Bull's death, and returned to the fold. "But Bob, I can't afford any more schooling."

He pulled a paper from the drawer and passed it to me. It was a draft drawn on the Wells Fargo bank for four thousand dollars, made out to me.

"The academy I told you about, the one Reverend Durant started in Oakland, is now called the College of California. Myrtle has been talking to them about you, and you are enrolled to start next month.

"She explained that you have not had all the preliminary schooling most of their students have, but that you have been well taught by your folks. The Reverend says four thousand should take care of a five-year course, which he thinks you ought to have.

"That's what the draft is for. It's not to be spent for anything else, no matter what."

I tried to refuse, but Bob beat my arguments down.

"You found that mine for me. You got me started. Now I can help get you started. That's fair, isn't it?"

Three weeks later I was enrolled at the college. Things began to happen more swiftly than they ever had for me. There were something like two hundred students. They came and went so constantly that it was difficult ever to know the exact number, and for the first few weeks I was abysmally confused.

The school had three buildings and was struggling to keep afloat. Not until the state took it over and made it the University, several years later, did it have sufficient finances. But even then it had a dedicated faculty who awakened interests I hadn't known I had, and I became like a starving man at a banquet table.

In the beginning it was not at all easy. I saw Bob and the Stoops off for Europe. Sandy and I stood on the dock beside the lighter, clinging to each other, both crying and neither trying to hide it.

"I'll come back," she promised as the last warning whistle sounded. "I'll come back and marry you. Don't you dare marry anyone else."

I promised and she kissed me. "I'll write. I'll write every week."

She did not write every week. I had six letters from her in all. They were in France. She was in school. She was studying music and dancing. Paris was fairyland. And finally, about the end of my first college year, the letters ceased.

Part of it was my fault. I was so busy discovering my own new world that time flew by unnoticed between my letters to her.

I had loved San Francisco from the first day I saw it. Now it became a passion. It might not be larger than Columbia, its theaters might be no better nor its restaurants finer, but in the final analysis Columbia was an insular mining town. San Francisco was a port city, a gluttonous mouth into which the whole world poured customs and ideas and viewpoints strange and wonderful to me.

Columbia's glory began to dim as my year unfolded, kept alive mostly through Caroline's letters. She had developed into a surprising correspondent with an awareness I had not been conscious of. She and I had not had too much communication while I was at home. But though she was charged with interest in the progress of the miners' ditch

311

and their continuing fight against Mills, the urgency became more and more remote from my life.

Among my fellow students were several from prominent California families. Through them I was invited to the parties in the Mission district and to some of the fine homes in South Park and Rincon Hill, to the art exhibits at the Mechanics Fair and the new Cliff House which Sam Brannon had built with lumber and exotic fittings salvaged from a wrecked schooner.

There were now fifty thousand people in the bay city, and it grew daily, flexing its young muscles, brawling, posturing, flamboyant, gay, lusty. The newly rich grabbed at culture on the hilltops. Merchants from all the world melded in the hollows, and along the Embarcadero swarmed the dregs of the wharfs of all the seas.

When the school year ended I did not return to Columbia. On the advice of my uncle I secured a position from Mr. Buffam, then editor of the *Alta*, and continued with that paper each of the next five summers. I made only three trips home through those years.

The first was for the celebration of the completion of the Columbia and Stanislaus Water Company project. It was November and I took a week off from school, traveling as correspondent for the *Alta* to cover the ceremony.

That day was the pinnacle of the Mother Lode history. Nothing like it had been seen in any camp, although all the mining towns had a terrific penchant for celebrations.

They had reason to be proud. The company of miners had survived and persevered and overcome what at times had seemed insurmountable odds.

The tunnel, over three thousand feet long, had successfully been bored. The flume hung along the sheer wall above the north fork of the river, suspended by chains dropped from staples that were set in the rock face itself.

The water flowed more than sixty miles, from the heavy log dam that backed up the reservoir in the deep canyon to the sluice boxes of Columbia, Shaw's Flat, and Sonora.

Columbia had burned again in '57, with most of the business district laid waste, but it had been rebuilt again immediately. It was a strange sight to me, the new brick two-story buildings, with heavy iron fire doors and shutters and ornate balconies.

On this day the balconies were brightly filled with the leading ladies of the town. Caroline, my aunt, and three of her friends occupied the one above the print shop. The whole town was decorated with banners, flags, and green pine branches hauled down from the hills. There were arches of boughs spanning the parade route, from Main Gulch Bridge, along Main and Jackson streets and out the Gold Springs road. Tables were set up along the full length of Main Street, tables that groaned with food free for everyone. Liquor, everything was free that day, for twenty thousand people, and the provisions were the least of the show.

I stood in the crowd outside the shop. It lined the sidewalks six deep to watch the parade pass. James McLean, wearing his brass fire helmet and carrying his voice trumpet, led it off. Behind him marched Faxon's Sonora Band, then the Sawmill Flat Fusiliers as a guard of honor for the Honorable James Coffroth, whom the town had elected State Senator. He rode in a carriage with the officers and trustees of the Columbia and Stanislaus Water Company.

Then followed the Sonora Fire Department, Columbia Hook and Ladder Company, Columbia Hose Company. Every lodge, band, and organization was represented, but the wildest, howlingest demonstration of appreciation was reserved for the miners themselves, who had labored so long and faithfully on the ditch. The crowd swept in behind them as they marched with their shovels on their shoulders, all the way out to the new High Flume, where the water brought for sixty miles tumbled and sparkled in three lovely cascades.

There we milled in awe and admiration until we were drawn back, happy and hungry, to the food and Jim Coffroth's stirring speech.

That evening bonfires blazed on the hills and candles glowed along the streets. There were fireworks more spectacular than any Fourth of July, and a Grand Ball in Cardinell's Terpsichore Hall.

It was indeed Columbia's finest hour. Yet the day was climaxed by tragedy, a death, and possibly augury for the future.

I was dancing a quadrille in a set with Mary Leary and her father, the constable, when a messenger appeared and whispered urgently to John Leary. He left the dance and hunted up his deputy O'Bryan and Bob Mullen, the marshal, and the three went out.

Word spread around the hall that the two men suspected of murdering a saloon man named McDonald two days be-

313

fore had been spotted in town. The gay party instantly was transformed into a man hunt as we all pushed toward the door.

Celebrants a moment before, we all now spread out, searching through the open saloons and streets. I was near the Plaza when I heard Constable Leary's yell over by the lumber yard.

"Here they are. Come on out of there, you."

Even as I began to run a shot echoed, and the lone figure silhouetted by the flickering candlelight twisted and collapsed in the street.

Mullen and O'Bryan appeared from the shadows, ahead of me, and the crowd came baying behind. The officers were shooting down the mouth of a dark alley, and their fire was being returned. Then there was silence as we came up, bursting into angry confusion when we found that Leary was dead.

Men surged down the alley, but the killers were gone. The chase continued all night. Someone remembered having heard a yell from the alley, suggesting that a shot had found a mark there, and in the morning, going from one miner's claim to another, a miner was discovered with a bullet wound in his leg. He could not explain how it came there.

Leary had been popular, besides representing the law. The joyful exuberance of the day before was turned upside down by the shock of this civic insult, and an equally strong mood of ugliness swept over Columbia.

The wounded miner and his partner were spirited off to the Sonora jail and temporary safety. But then for some insane reason they were returned to Columbia for a preliminary hearing.

The result could have been predicted. Although the sheriff managed to escape the mob and return one prisoner to Sonora, the other was taken from him, hazed out the Gold Springs road that was still bedecked with the flags and arching boughs, and hanged from the new flume, below the dancing cascades.

One day a city had paraded its order and accomplishment. The next it lurched down the same road in the wanton abandon of lynch rule.

CHAPTER TWENTY-SEVEN

I STAYED OVER for John Leary's funeral. The following year I returned for another, much smaller service. Old Ike had taken a chill during one of his prospecting trips and crawled home only in time to die.

Ike's death was a shock to me, but Columbia was worse. She was like a beautiful woman overnight made old and ravaged. The streets, filled with people only months ago, now echoed with emptiness. Half the buildings had simply vanished and the ground on which they had stood gaped open, excavated down to the limestone bedrock. Some streets were torn up and dug out. The town was dead, and little groups of miners like coyotes picked at her exposed bones.

I stared at my uncle without comprehension. "In the name of heaven, what's happened?"

He had met me at the stage station and we were walking back toward the print shop. His mouth twisted bitterly.

"A logical but unforeseen irony. As the new ditch brought in plenty of cheap water the miners stepped up their production. They cleaned out all the gravel around the town, then they began tearing down the buildings and mining the town itself."

"If we had only got the capital . . ."

"It probably would not have made a great deal of difference." My uncle shrugged wearily. "A town needs more than state business to keep it running."

"But what are you going to do?"

"I don't know. The whole lode is finished . . . oh, there'll be a little pocket mining for a hundred years, but the bonanza days are gone. Certainly there's no place here for a newspaper. We sold less than a hundred copies of the *Clarion* last week."

I thought of the house on the hill that we had all worked so hard to build, of the garden my aunt had planted and nursed. In dismay I watched a group of men with a battering ram, doggedly butting at the two-story brick wall of Kilmer's Dry Goods Store.

We reached the print shop and pushed open the familiar door and the bell tinkled on its spring. There was a quick flurry at the rear and I saw Aunt Emeline catch up a shotgun and whirl, leveling it on us.

My jaw dropped. I thought she must have gone mad. Then she recognized us, dropped the gun and ran forward to throw her arms about me.

I glanced at my uncle in horror, and his twisted smile came again. "She's protecting the shop. They've been trying to buy it, to tear it down. Your aunt refused to sell and now she fears they may resort to force to compel us."

My breath stuck in my throat. "Someone must be crazy."

"All of them. They've gone insane." My aunt dragged me to a rear window and pointed across to where the Long Tom had stood. This had been the biggest gambling house in Columbia, and we had always been a gambling town, at the peak supporting a hundred and forty-three licensed faro banks with a combined capital of over a million dollars.

But the Long Tom was gone. Where it had stood were a few charred timbers, a few piles of broken bricks, and in the center of the rubble men were digging out gravel and throwing it into a sluice box. I recognized two of them, Teen Duchow and Jack White.

"They're the ones who want our shop."

I turned around. "From the looks of things you'd better sell."

"Austin," she gasped.

I took her shoulders and kissed her forehead gently. "Why not? You can't run a paper in a ghost town."

"That's what I try to tell her," my uncle said. "But she won't leave the house."

"Austin, it's my home."

My uncle's voice was tired. "It's all right, Mama, we understand. I've been talking to the boys at the Sonora *Herald*. Maybe they'll make a place for me and I can drive back and forth."

I didn't believe that would work either, but I saw no point in argument at the moment. We talked about other things, Ike and the coming funeral, and finally, when the undertaker's carriage arrived, I helped them in and took the seat beside the driver.

Ike had been one of the most popular men in Columbia and had he died the year before the procession would have rivaled that which followed Leary's coffin. As it was less than two hundred people escorted the printer to the cemetery beside St. Ann's Church on Kennebec Hill, and in a way the obituary we ran in the last issue of the *Clarion* was the obituary of the city.

Afterward, when the paper had been distributed and my uncle had ridden over to Sonora to see about the job there, I was surprised to see Aunt Emeline come bustling into the shop.

"When do you have to get back to school, Austin?"

I told her it did not matter if I stayed a couple of days or even a week.

"Then you can help us pack."

"Pack?"

She nodded briskly, an unusual tightness about her mouth. "You've heard about the silver strike over on Sun Mountain?"

I had heard of nothing else for weeks. Half the population of California had crossed back over the Sierras to a new town called Virginia City which was rising on the Comstock Lode.

"That's where Ben wants to go."

"But, your house?"

"I've been a fool, son. Can you vision Ben sitting here rotting, growing old in this wreckage?"

That I could not. My uncle Ben loved people and excitement, the bustle and hoopla of the mining camps, and he was too young a man to quit and deliberately bury himself.

"But you, Aunt Emeline . . . I hear Washoe is the most miserable place on earth . . ."

"Worse than Sacramento in 'fifty?"

I remembered back. I had seen the gold country through ten full years. I had seen it flower and now I was watching it fade, and there is a bitter sweetness in memory, recalling the happy moments and minimizing the harsh.

"I guess it couldn't be much worse, could it? It will be different anyway."

Her mouth quirked a little at its corners. "Maybe I'm getting worse than Ben. I got to thinking last night about your going away again . . . your visit brought it home to me, how lonely it's going to be sitting up on the ridge watching the lights get fewer and fewer in the valley . . . Can you stay and help pack the shop? Without Ike I don't know whether Ben could handle it by himself."

I helped them pack. I saw their goods loaded into two wagons, and watched them head north toward Placerville, where they would pick up the immigrant road back over the mountains to the new boom.

My uncle was a different person. When he had returned from Sonora and found me already packing the type he had put up an argument to my aunt that they were fools at their age to try to start all over. But his words held no conviction and we both laughed at him. The Mother Lode was dead but Uncle Ben and Aunt Emeline were not. With her laughter his eyes brightened and he began to talk excitedly about the new Nevada strikes.

They went on to see Virginia and Austin and the Reese River, and always the *Clarion* press was there to trumpet the praises of the newest diggings, to be part and parcel of the newest town.

I wanted to go with them but neither would hear of that. "You get your schooling," my uncle said as we shook hands before he climbed to the wagon seat, as eager as when he had climbed to the wagon in Wilmington, oh, so many years ago. "When you finish that I'll have a paper going and there'll be a place for you on it."

I went back to Oakland. During the long ride I felt lost, without an anchor, as alone as I had ever been. I had never really been homesick before but I was now, homesick for many things, for my uncle and Aunt Emeline and Caroline, for the people I had known who were scattered to the corners of the world, for Ike whom I would never see again.

And then I walked into my room and saw the letter lying on the table, and suddenly everything was all right. It was from Sandy, and she was coming home.